I STILL HAVE A SUITCASE IN BERLIN

STEPHENS
—
GERARD
—
MALONE

I Still have

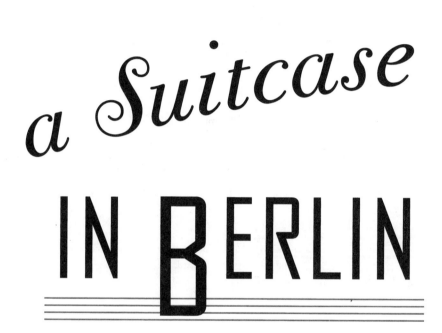

a Suitcase
IN BERLIN

A NOVEL

RANDOM
HOUSE
CANADA

Library and Archives Canada Cataloguing in Publication
Malone, Stephens Gerard, 1957–
I still have a suitcase in Berlin / Stephens Gerard Malone.

ISBN 978-0-679-31341-0

I. Title.
PS8626.A455112 2008   C813'.6   C2007-907351-4

Jacket Design: CS Richardson
Text Design: Andrew Roberts

Printed and bound in the United States of America

10 9 8 7 6 5 4 3 2 1

He who loves the more is the inferior and must suffer

—Thomas Mann

1932

Michael blew into his hands, then pulled tight the collar of his woollen coat. Being tucked in behind the old battery's crumbling concrete sure wasn't helping much in the way of keeping dry, not from snow so wet it was falling this side of rain, but there was no better spot around Halifax to watch the lights. Gene, plunking her arse down on a beached log beside her big brother, was more interested in seeing that shiner of his. And Jesus that looked like it was gonna hurt.

"He still mad?"

"Uh-huh."

They watched the back wheel of her bike spinning slowly to a stop.

"Some dark, eh?" Gene didn't care for Point Pleasant Park at night. Good thing her brother never ran off much farther than his own back yard. "Mrs. Herzfeld came by."

Michael threw a rock from the pebbly beach, but without moonlight there was no telling where it hit the water.

"Not right running away on her like that, Michael. She's old."

All that water gushing through the ceiling plaster and onto the piano, Mrs. Herzfeld flapping her arms, screaming for buckets? For sure, that whole upper floor was looking to come down. Well, Gene would've run too. Besides, the mess wasn't Michael's fault. Putting in a bathroom in that richie-rich house over on Oxford Street was too big a job for one man, not that his father had listened. When Michael got home—where his family still had to share a shitter out back with the neighbours—and told August what happened, the old man landed Michael with a single punch and only the second *goddamn* he'd ever said. And in German, *god* sounded less important than the *damned*.

Shit.

Michael wiped the wet snow away from his eyes.

"He's not sending you away 'cause of this." Gene wasn't sounding too reassuring. "Me? I'd go."

Not a chance, their father replied to that suggestion when Michael had made it. Send Eugenia by herself to Europe? What was he thinking? The girl was needed at home to take care of her mother. Michael had just proved he wasn't needed for anything.

"Dadda says our Nan lives in a big house by a canal. Some adventure you'll have."

Hissing through the nearby spruce made them glance behind, but neither expected to see anything. Only wind. Gene shivered. The thing was, their older brother Felix once shot a bird out of those trees, that last summer before the Spanish influenza. Michael always felt his father lost his favourite that year.

"That's not true." Gene slung her arm about his shoulders. "He says you'll be back before Christmas."

Then she smiled. Best expression for her and Michael. You didn't notice those dark rings under their grey eyes so much, something they got from their Renner side. Solid and boxy, Michael and Gene weren't likely to ever turn a head. Not like Felix. Athlete's build, a real looker. More like his mum, the happy Grahams.

"And who knows?" Gene said. "Maybe you'll even find someone over there you'll want waiting for you behind Saint Peter. Heaven can't be, well, Heaven if you're up there alone. When Dadda was your age, he was married."

Michael shoved Gene off the log. "Those copies of *Sweetheart Stories* in the shitter are for wiping your arse, not reading."

"Feel sorry for yourself then." And she tossed snow back up into his face.

Michael helped his sister to her feet as that light on the horizon, now a fully formed freighter, steamed into Halifax harbour.

"Where do you think it's from?"

"C'mon," Gene said. "Avon's mom invited us for supper."

Michael went for the bicycle. "We'll get home faster if I pedal."

As his sister climbed on behind, she held on to his waist and felt Michael trembling. Stay out of puddles, she warned.

In Michael's twenty-five years, he'd only once tried to spend a night away from home. He'd been shy of six and that was just to visit his uncles across the harbour in Dartmouth. Felix and Gene had been excited for days about the trip, but when their father got them all down to the waterfront, Michael kicked up such a fuss the ferry master crossed his arms and said that young fella wasn't going anywhere on this boat. No one tried again, even if that meant Michael missed out on Lake Banook skating parties or swimming off McNab's Island. Until now, and that damned letter from Aunt Beate.

Michael knew his father had been born overseas, not that August talked much about those days. By eighteen, he'd already worked his passage across to Canada. Claimed he wasn't putting up with his father's only two choices in life for him—scholar or soldier—when August really wanted to work with his hands. Sure, August taught his own kids the language, and he scoured the evening paper for any news about Germany, but the von Renners of Berlin meant nothing to him anymore. Besides, he had enough on his plate with Mum. Apart from her blindness, in the last few years her forgetfulness had gotten worse. No longer just names and faces of people she'd known forever, sometimes now even her own kids. And there was that poor neighbour of theirs, Mrs. Glyn, who lately Mum accused of stealing her false teeth, even when she had them in her mouth.

But Michael's grandmother had suffered a stroke and was being cared for by a doctor who just happened to be an old, dear friend of the family. Too dear, by Aunt Beate's account. The doctor's slippers were under the bed, according to her. With a sizable property at stake, someone had better keep a close eye on Nan. That someone wasn't going to be her. Aunt Beate's husband was an important something or other in Leipzig and needed her, so she couldn't be riding the trains back and forth to Berlin. Time for her older brother to see to matters. Enclosed please find one passage to Europe.

Except it wasn't August going, although right now, standing next to chains thick as a man's torso straining to keep the ship tied along-side the wharf, he sounded as if he almost regretted that.

"See it? It's like a floating city. Just look at it, will you."

August Renner was pacing back and forth, whistling over the grandeur of the *General von Steuben,* New York to Hamburg with stops in Halifax and Southampton, docked alongside Pier 22, its two stacks smoking in readiness. Boy oh boy. His son, he'd be sailing in grand style.

Michael and his family huddled against the wall of the low ware-house. Winter, not yet ready to concede, had surprised the city with an April dump of snow. Michael had had to shovel his way that morn-ing to the outhouse, where his last few hours at home were spent nursing a nervous stomach. Even Mrs. Glyn, rapping on the door, eye to the cracks, had asked if he was all right.

"It won't last," his father said, about the snow. "Lilacs'll be bloom-ing when you get to Berlin."

Mum, hooked on to Gene's arm and wearing her round blacked-in spectacles, wanted to know, were they going to her parents' house?

"They're dead, Mum," Gene said. "Don't you remember?"

"Oh? When did that happen?"

December 1917, after the Renners' house in Richmond, the one with the veranda, survived that munitions ship colliding with the *Imo* in Halifax harbour with only some broken windows. But the city inspectors came by, poked around the foundations, left with shaking heads. The whole block came down not long after. Church too, even Michael's school. They spent the winter under canvas in a park with other refugees while Mum got the glass fished out of her eyes over in the hospital.

Come spring, August found that row house on Waverley Terrace. Cockroaches had eaten away at the glue under the wallpaper, and what was left you could spit through, but it beat the hell out of living in a tent. Michael's father said they should all be thankful the old woman who'd died there hadn't yet gone cold or there'd have been a lineup to kingdom come for the place. And besides, they had real nice neighbours, the Glyns, with their son Avon who was just about Felix's age. So what if the trains grinding and rolling over tracks nearby made it hard to sleep.

Right after they'd moved in, before anyone could unpack, August carted his family off to nearby Point Pleasant Park where crumbling towers secured the harbour entrance from enemies that never came. Felix shot a blue jay out of those spruce trees with a pellet gun and Gene—she was Eugenia back then—cut her toe on a shell. Michael thought they were supposed to be having a picnic and got wet to his knees on the pebbly beach, but after his father told them Mum wasn't going to see again, no one was very hungry.

There was more. With a war on, lots of folks in Halifax were getting worked up, blaming the Kaiser for the city's thousands of dead after the explosion, one of those being the man August worked for, now somewhere in a mass grave. That meant Michael's father was going to have to make it on his own as a plumber and he was taking fifteen-year-old Felix out of school to apprentice. Renner & Sons. Felix went, yippee, but August said there was nothing to yippee about and it was as good a time as any to stop using the *von* before their last name, or speaking German outside of the house. Might not be safe and for sure the good folks of Halifax wouldn't want a Kraut and his boy cleaning out their pipes.

Thankfully, the war didn't last much longer. Mum came home, blind as a mole, and shops on Gottingen Street puttied glass back in their windows. Then people started getting fevers and aches. Felix caught the flu and everyone thought such a strong boy'd be up on his feet by week's end.

Gene yelped with the sudden horn raking the harbour waters, its echo bouncing off the Dartmouth shore. Time to board the ship and it didn't look like anyone else was coming. So much for hoping that someone other than family, who had to be there, might come round and say goodbye. Someone like Avon. Closest thing Michael ever had to a friend. On the night Mrs. Glyn had them over for supper, Michael had hoped to say, well, he wasn't quite sure what, but Avon hadn't shown.

August nodded towards the *General von Steuben* and Michael abandoned looking expectantly down the pier. His luggage, other than the small beige-and-tan suitcase his mother had used on her honeymoon trip to Niagara Falls, was already on board. His father's last-minute instructions were to write once a week, no telegrams—we're not made of money. Did Michael have his Aunt Beate's address in Leipzig? Good. If he needed anything, Michael was to get in touch with her. And practise your German. Most of all, try and be the man your grandmother needs right now.

August resolved the question of an embrace when he thrust out his hand for his son to shake.

Michael hugged his mother.

"You're cold, Mum. You go right home now."

She was having one of her spells and wasn't quite sure who he was, but she let him kiss her and told Gene she thought he was a nice young man.

He was afraid to embrace his sister, fearing that he wouldn't be able to let go. So he kissed her on the cheek. Gene threw her arms around him anyway.

"Don't worry. In a day or so, no one'll notice the eye. Now don't be scared," she added so that no one else could hear. "It'll be easier if you don't look back."

Passenger 912 turned away before his father saw tears, picked up his suitcase and stepped onto the gangway. Michael heard his mother ask where Felix was going.

Aunt Beate's generosity paid for a windowless third-class cabin barely larger than a closet with thick metal seams secured by fist-sized bolts, and a whitewashed plank floor. Kitty-corner to the bunk folded against the wall making room for the writing table and chair squatted a porcelain sink on rusting pipes. Still, the room was private, and Michael was sure he'd get used to the engine noises methodically exhaling directly underfoot.

Opening Mum's suitcase, he got the first inkling that something wasn't right. The floor was swaying, side-to-side, then up, then down. And the air, or rather the lack of it, why had it suddenly become so hot? Thank God the water closets were across the corridor. By evening, it appeared his bout with seasickness was here to stay. Luckily, with the bed open, he could vomit into the sink by just lifting his head.

Come morning, Michael was convinced he was going to be sewn into a shroud and dumped at sea, assuming that sort of thing still went on. Thank Christ he puked loud enough to be heard through a bulkhead. A passing steward rapped on the door, perhaps to offer assistance, but as the man didn't speak English or German—it might have been Polish—Michael, frustrated, closed the door on him and went back to his dry heaves. After that, twice a day, Michael found a tray of weak tea and toast outside his cabin.

He finally saw the sea, what was left of it, on a rain-soaked morning just outside of Bremerhaven. The *General von Steuben*'s upper deck was deserted. Passengers wrapped in fur or brushed wool were probably taking morning coffee out of the cold, perhaps in one of the covered lounges. Michael drank in the fresh air and took hold of the railing, letting his face take the wind. Jesus, but being up here felt good, except that after a few deep breaths, he noticed how the waves were rolling and he felt the sway of the ship. Cupping his mouth, Michael turned away as a small man, orange beret shading his eyes, strolled around the lifeboats. On his shoulder bobbed a similarly garbed monkey wearing its own miniature orange beret. The man nodded a greeting, sending Michael back over the railing to let loose the bilious remains of that morning's tea and toast.

"Dear boy, are you going to be all right?" The English was affected, the German accent thick.

Michael wiped his mouth with the back of his hand. "I'm dying."

The man in the orange beret laughed, and the monkey clapped. "Nonsense. How long have you been like this?"

Michael shook his head. "Halifax."

"God in Heaven."

That sent him over the railing once more.

"You'll want to face downwind."

The man, grimacing behind his hand, offered a handkerchief from his breast pocket. As he did so, he looked Michael over, one side, then the other.

"This is a blessing, really. That stupidly honest face of yours would look much better with some cheekbones."

The monkey reached under his beret and withdrew a slice of dried banana. After shoving it into his mouth, he gave off something between a cough and a choke.

"Zouzou, manners, my dear," said the man. Then to Michael: "This frightful monster is my dearest companion. Did you know he once danced the Charleston with Edna Ferber?"

No, but Michael was sure he and Gene had watched Joan Crawford do that dance in a movie. They used to spend Saturday afternoons sharing popcorn in the theatre on Barrington Street.

"Of course you did. Let's shake hands."

Michael allowed himself to be escorted to a row of deck chairs by Tristan, just Tristan, self-professed collector of lost causes and useless things like a taste for gin rickeys, a vice courtesy of Harlem's Happy Roane's on 141st and Lennox where he once picked up a dose of the clap from the cigarette girl.

Michael had no idea what that meant or if he was himself a lost cause or a useless thing.

Dear sweet country boy, smiled Tristan, glancing head to toe, adding that someone like Michael best avoid women wearing lipstick. Was he well enough now for a cigarette?

Michael didn't smoke.

"How peculiar. Well then, tell me. Where are you heading?"

"Berlin."

Now seated, Tristan lit himself a cigarette. "Surely? Why?"

Even truncated, the story of Michael's sick and troubled grandmother—living in a city, Tristan interjected, best seen at night—glassed over the man's eyes.

"But I don't want to go."

"Indeed. A boy like you could get eaten alive there. Seems to me just saying no would have saved you a great deal of inconvenience, my young friend."

Michael never said that to his father.

"Well, you are wearing long pants. Why not?"

They were interrupted by a bell.

"Right then," said Tristan, standing. "I've just the thing to set you up. Come, join me for lunch."

"I couldn't."

"Of course you can. Come! Come!"

Zouzou clapped.

"Trust me on this one, my dear Michael. What you need to settle your stomach is a strong dose of eggs sautéed in butter, fresh butter only or don't bother, perhaps some bacon brushed with a hint of maple. It's the fat of it. Does away with the queasiness. And fresh flowers."

"What are they for?"

"They're pretty. Now come along."

Right then, the *General von Steuben* took a deep roll on a rogue wave. Tristan, stumbling back only a step, clutched unsuccessfully for Zouzou sliding off his shoulder. Michael joined the man at the railing just in time to see the monkey splash into the white wake below, followed by the man's hat. The orange beret bobbed once, twice before being sucked under the ship.

"Oh, dear. He'll be hard to replace."

Before Michael had a chance to speak, Tristan turned his face away and held up a slender hand to silence him. It quivered briefly. Surely under the circumstances, Michael could understand that the pleasure of lunch would have to wait. The little man then fled the deck, leaving Michael to hear a sob unchecked by the wind.

The invitation arrived in the hands of the same steward who left the tea and toast. Main dining room, eight o'clock. Unsigned, but from Tristan, of course.

That'll be up in first class. And Michael with shiny patches on that made-over suit coat of his father's? He couldn't.

The steward, waiting outside in the hall, shrugged and left. Hadn't understood a word.

It crossed Michael's mind right then and there to just not show up, but he could hear Mum saying no son of hers was going to be that rude. Besides, Gene wouldn't be bellyaching over such an invite. She'd be jumping around the cabin, not giving a hoot about a jacket that didn't fit and so what if his boots needed polish. And she'd be goddamned right, too. So by half of seven Michael was sitting on the edge of his bunk fully dressed in a too-small shirt, tying his tie yet again, pondering phrases Clark Gable might use over dinner and convincing himself he was going to enjoy this. That was a mistake. Comparing himself with a mousy cowlick to Clark Gable? Maybe he should try to be more like Gene's current idol, John Gilbert. Delighted by your invitation to dine, Mr. Tristan, he'd say, tapping cigarette ash into a tray, if Michael smoked. Or should he call him Herr Tristan? Herr Tristan what? Did Tristan even offer a last name?

These practice runs almost didn't matter. A quarter before the appointed hour and one look through the glass door of the dining hall damn near sent Michael running. Inside, a sea of black jackets and white ties, women in gowns, diamonds almost as shiny as his elbows. And didn't the pale man opening the door with his white-gloved hands let him know. With an up and down glance, he didn't wait to hear

Michael say he had an invitation but hurried him across the polished wood floor, seating him opposite the grand piano, in an alcove by a large window. Michael tried to keep his elbows tucked in.

Would he care for something while he waited?

"No, thank you, nothing."

At least that's what Michael thought he replied. Now he wasn't so sure. He wasn't used to speaking German outside of the house and, being nervous, he'd stuttered. From the way that waiter choked back a smile, God knows what had come out.

Thankfully, seated behind the urns of greenery, Michael couldn't see all those eyes he was certain were staring in his direction. He might even begin to enjoy himself. Looking through the windows, beyond the outer railings of the deck, he imagined a nearby coast where lights would soon break through the void of a night at sea. Then he turned away. Even contemplating rolling waves out there and Michael knew he'd never keep down anything more substantial than toast.

After what felt like an hour, a young man in a buttoned-up smock arrived with a basket of rolls.

"I've been invited to dinner by Herr—Tristan. I think. Has he arrived yet? He might not see me back here."

The young man was just the busboy and couldn't say.

When his waiter did arrive with a menu, Michael was too embarrassed to ask again. So he continued to wait, expecting that Tristan would pop around the potted plants, blame his tardiness on being prostrate with grief over the monkey and apologize profusely. Until that happened, Michael could help himself to a roll, but he wasn't certain if they were included in the price of the meal and, well, no point in spoiling his dinner.

When he returned to his cabin, Michael found a tray of tea and toast waiting. The tea was cold. He set the tray on the sink, pulled his bunk from the wall and lay down, fully clothed.

After almost two hours and the waiter making plain that no one appeared to be coming, the table was wanted for another seating. Perhaps he'd be more comfortable below.

Michael reached for a slice of toast. It was cold too.

Come morning, he remained in his cabin until the ship docked and he was sure all those hoity-toity bigwigs who'd smirked at him being escorted out of the dining room were ashore.

⚭

Steaming wet coats swept past Michael and in through the arched and colonnaded doors of Berlin's sprawling Lehrte Bahnhof, while blurs of commuters criss-crossed bundles of freshly minted newspapers. Look! cried a girl hiding behind her Dutch hat and tugging at her mother's hand. She pointed at the sparrow trapped inside the cavernous glass sky beaded with rain. The platform shook with the latest train to arrive. Someone will let it out, reassured the mother, having to speak loudly, turning her child so she wouldn't notice the shivering pile of rags in the corner glistening with its own piss.

Michael hesitated. Surely something could be done for that fellow lying back there in the beat-up army coat. A taxi driver pulled him away, saying, First time to Berlin, eh? Well, leave the devil his due. Was that all the luggage Michael had?

Yes, well, the young man from Canada coming to take charge of the family had the rest stolen at the Hamburg Bahnhof when he'd left it and gone to change money. Suspecting that Shylock had fleeced him on the rate as his father said his kind no doubt would, Michael returned to the platform to find his luggage, other than Mum's overnighter, gone and no one in charge particularly interested. So:

Yes, one suitcase.

Outside the station, men in field coats with pulled-down hats listlessly gathered up remnants of torn placards painted with defiant fists and shredded posters of black angles, while ripped advertisements with hollow faces saying *Choose me!* blew through a windowless, charred truck and into the nearby waters of the Spree. The driver explained the truck was torched last evening. Something political. Did Michael want to be heading by way of the Lustgarten? The driver shook his head. Not recommended. Cost him more. Today was May

Day. Communists, Fascists, Social Democrats, National Socialists, left, right, up, down, who knows these days, but out in force. All foolishness, if you listened to the driver. He drove Michael along the river and said for a few extra marks he'd throw in a tour. Pointing to the horses atop the Brandenburg Gate, the driver asked if Michael knew the chariot had once been carted off by that filthy bastard Napoleon. No? Eh, no matter. Then he spit at an automobile that came too close.

Eventually the cursing of the driver faded away. Michael hadn't expected this: a city of trees, canopied boulevards of lindens and blooming chestnuts shading their route until the taxi swerved sharply down a curved lane alongside the Landwehr Canal and passed the undulating façade of an oil company's headquarters, Shell Haus. Just beyond, a white Italianate house with a water-side second-floor conservatory overlooked the canal, its portico and the marble fretwork along the roofline crumbling, its cladding soot stained. Sheets billowed out of the lower windows into a narrow grassed courtyard, gated and shaded with budding elms. A hand-painted sign, *Guthman's Laundry,* was tacked over the door.

Someone unseen shouted, He's a boy and boys don't disappear.

"You sure this is the place?"

That was the address given the driver. Anywhere else would cost Michael more.

A hard-ridden woman pushing her hair back came out onto the steps, demanding to know if they were trying to steal her laundry. Furthermore, she knew all about Berlin's Polish taxi drivers, insisting Michael had let himself be cheated and made no secret of wanting to sweep the driver into the canal, if she had her broom. The man who had navigated Michael's deliverance from Lehrte Bahnhof sped away without a thank you.

So. Had Michael seen her Valentin?

"Herr Doctor upstairs says my boy is an idiot and if I don't tie him up I'll be fishing him out of the waters. Tie a boy of eight up like a dog? What kind of a doctor would say that?"

"Frau von Renner?"

"Who wants to know?"

Her grandson.

The laundry woman looked as if she might cry. Then she did.

"Oh, she'll be so pleased. She's been waiting! Come, come inside!"

"She lives here?"

"Yes, yes!"

Frau Guthman pushed towels dripping soapsuds on pink-veined squares of marble out of Michael's way, ushering him under the cathedral ceilings of the monastic entranceway.

"Frau von Renner! Come out, Frau von Renner!"

She pointed to several doors on the second-floor landing. Across from where his grandmother lived was the doctor's flat; no need to tell the doctor what she'd said about him, if Michael pleased. Herr Leopold, that poor miserable soul, and Frau von Renner's other tenant, was confined to a chair with wheels and boarded in the attic.

Michael heard some scuffling. A latch unbolting. A door overhead opened and there she stood. Michael's grandmother was slender, her grey hair bobbed and waved, green eyes clearly expressive and her face remarkably unlined. Wearing a simple black skirt, sweater the shade of heather and single strand of pearls, there was no imperial frou-frou about Nan Carmel. Not quite the near-dead eighty-year-old Michael expected.

Frau Guthman was all grins and nods. Go on! Go on! Nan met him halfway on stairs long worn free of varnish, trembling, kissing both his cheeks, unwilling to let go as Michael pushed wet towels hanging from the chandelier out of his way.

"You look so much like your father." Tears moistened her eyes as she took him all in. "Oh, Doctor Linder, come, this is my grandson, Michael. Does he not look like his father?"

"I see the family resemblance."

Michael looked past the embrace to the man standing on the landing outside of her door. Shiny shoes, trimmed black-and-grey beard over a brushed coat, he fumbled with a gold timepiece.

No doubt, thought Michael, so he wouldn't have to look him in the eye and know that the von Renners were serious about protecting the old woman.

"All this fuss about my welfare. You can see for yourself, I am quite well."

"Is that all the luggage he's brought?" the doctor asked.

Thanking Frau Guthman for being so kind to show her grandson in, Nan escorted Michael into a lemon-scented flat stuffed with oversized chintz chairs, curio cabinets embellished with carved fruit and lined with blackened silver, off-centre paintings with chipped gilded frames and dusty shelves covered with sepia moments, all held in shadows to unsuccessfully conceal wallpaper stained from a leaking roof.

"This is my favourite place," Nan said of one particular room, the one of glass and potted palm trees overlooking the canal where Frau Guthman continued the search for her boy.

Va-len-tin! Va-len-tin, come for your sweets, my little asparagus.

Doctor Linder closed the windows, explaining the boy had been partially strangled at birth by his umbilical cord and why call him an asparagus when he was as round as a pear?

"But my Beate would not be convinced I am well and now you've been made to come all this way." Nan squeezed Michael's hand. "But thank God for this day! And your German is wonderful. My dear August did not forget that he was a von Renner. He did right by you in that."

Doctor Linder cleared his throat. "Perhaps we should allow the young man to rest now."

Michael nodded and, after another hug from his grandmother, wearily followed the doctor down the hall to a prepared room where he fell asleep before he could even remove his shoes.

Later, in his first letter home, he'd write *standing behind Nan with his hand on her shoulder* when describing his first encounter with the doctor.

⁂

The woman was clearing away breakfast. Glancing up, she nodded, smiled, and stuck a strand of thick black hair away from her flushed face.

15

"You the von Renner grandson from America?"

"Nova Scotia."

The clattering of dishes followed her down the hallway and into the kitchen.

"Never heard of it," she called back, her curt German sounding dismissive.

"It's in Canada."

The young woman shrugged.

"I'm Michael. Just Renner. We don't use the von in Canada."

"Is that something they make you do in America?"

Awkwardly, he explained that folks where he came from still blamed the Germans for breaking wind in Halifax, even though that happened fifteen years ago.

The woman raised her eyes, then fell over with laughter. "I think you mean to say *explosion*." She laughed some more and Michael felt prickly right up to his temples. "Well then. Does your grandmother know about your name?"

Michael shook his head.

"Don't tell her. She's not as strong as she looks."

She said his accent was quite funny as she tied on an apron and ate the bread crusts off the breakfast dishes. Had he travelled this way before?

No, but Michael thought he wanted to see Paris because Mum always talked about going. At least she used to.

"Wanting doesn't count. Besides, the French are filthy beggars, so you've missed nothing. Except maybe the Louvre. What did you do before coming here?"

"Not much really."

"Everyone in America that rich?"

"No."

"Then who gets to do nothing?"

"I worked for my father. He was a plumber."

"Yes?" She opened the door under the sink. "The pipe in here leaks. Make yourself useful."

"I'm afraid I'd make it worse."

"I thought so." She was staring at him now. "Too scholarly. And I bet you can't tell from me scrubbing pots that I'm the Baroness de Rothschild." She laughed at her remark. "So, you have friends back home?"

Michael didn't do so well with that, Avon probably being the last one. Something always seemed to mess things up.

"A girl waiting, then?"

Waiting for what?

"No girl?"

He avoided her gaze. No, nothing left behind.

Wiping her hand on her apron, she took hold of Michael's.

"I'm Hélène. Your grandmother's been a friend to me so I help here when I can. And when I'm not here, I work at a department store on the Ku'damm. So how are you making out with the old folks?"

"I look forward to getting to know my grandmother."

"But?"

Nothing. He just hoped to be home for Christmas, that's all.

"And the doctor?"

"I don't think he's happy that I'm here."

"Oh, don't let him put you off. He worries too much. Besides, with his teaching at the university and his private patients, you'll never see him. And what of Berlin?"

Easily, the population of Michael's home town might squeeze into a city block here.

The girl whistled. Almost as good as Gene.

"Don't know anyone then?"

There was that strange fellow on the ship who Michael never saw again. Frau Guthman of course, but Hélène said she didn't count.

"Well, your German's terrible, but not bad for an American."

"Canadian, and my father made us learn. Mum hated it. Always thought we were up to something. Maybe reading the newspapers here'll help."

Hélène waved that off. What was that old adage? The only way to learn a tongue was to take a mistress and immerse yourself in the culture.

Thank goodness there was Nan right then, coming down the hallway threading on an earring.

"Bravo, Michael, you've met our Hélène. I really don't know how I'd manage without her."

"He's coming to meet my friends tonight," said Hélène, back at the dishes.

"I am?"

"You won't get rid of that accent hiding up here."

"Yes, Hélène, it's a wonderful idea. You're right of course. Not if Berlin's to be his home."

"But—"

Nan outmanoeuvred Michael with a kiss on the cheek and banknotes to his pocket.

She was waiting on the corner of the Breitscheidplatz wearing a bulky overcoat and tying down a yellow-chequered kerchief. But what can you do, Hélène laughed about her unruly black hair. "You made it."

Yes, thanks to Frau Guthman's husband, who returning from his grocery store kindly offered to write down directions, otherwise Michael would have ended up on a train to Pankow.

"Ah, but I see on your face, our city's getting to you."

No denying Berlin was exhilarating, especially at night. Under the humming blinking glare of lights, you didn't notice threadbare coats and cracked pavement and gutters filled with grassy horseshit. Michael hadn't expected such a transformation.

Hélène secured his arm and stepped onto the street. This way, no! That way, through the buses, watch the wagons! In mid-crossing, Michael stopped to take in the four-storied Romanisches Café with its canopied bullhorn entrance towers. Hélène laughed—Do you want to get yourself killed?—and pulled him forward.

Past the grim-faced porter she ushered him into the realm of Berlin's coffee-drinking society, a den of mirrored archways under high vaulted ceilings, illuminated pendants, vast sheets of windows and tiers of balconies and terraces connected by a latticework of crowded stairs with polished banisters. Here gathered the intellectuals, the film stars, poets in the throes of creative angst, stratified by table, mincing and gawking and arguing through the upwardly circulating smoke of cheap French cigarettes. Distant tinny music struggled for an audience, coarse laughter erupted spontaneously as Michael and Hélène dodged waiters balancing trays around a woman who chewed on a cigar in the corner of her mouth, bared her breast and squealed, There! Now pay up!

Here, over here, Hélène shouted when Michael thought he'd lost her, only to have her pull him up the stairs. As they reached the inner terrace, a man waved.

"Ma petite choute, ton amour nouveau?" he said, looking at Michael, broadly embracing Hélène.

She pushed him off.

"Michael, I'm sad to say, these are my friends. Pia, there in the corner, is a cellist, possibly a great one if she practised more and stopped spreading her legs for married men."

Pia had large eyes, even larger glasses and blond hair and may very well have called Hélène a bitch, but Michael wasn't sure about the translation.

"How is this? She resists me," the Frenchman said.

"Ah, you're poor."

"Don't tell your new friend that. I have respectable employment in the publishing field."

To Michael, Hélène added, "Bodo translates the backs of naughty postcards and filthy novels. What did I tell you about the French?"

"You're forgetting the best part," a thin, translucent young man sitting beside Pia added, shivering. "Bodo's woman ran away to Berlin from Lyons and now he stalks her by day and plans her murder at night. A grisly one, so it will make all the papers."

"You lying horse-stuffed sausage of a Russian!" Bodo delivered with a clip aimed for the head.

The man ducked. A cigarette clung to the corner of his mouth. When he smiled, one side of his face squinted. He thrust his hand at

Michael, spilling a half-finished coffee that Pia had to fling her legs up to avoid, giving all a glimpse at the darkness between.

"That clumsy ox is Marius," Hélène said, grabbing the edge of the table to save the rest of the cups from being knocked over.

Gangway! Gangway! Now for the Brown battalions!/For Storm Troopers clear road o'er land!

A group of young rowdies by the front doors locked arms around each other's shoulders and swayed into another chorus of the "Horst-Wessel-Lied."

"Not again. Are we to listen to that shit all night?" Marius jumped up on his chair. His threatening fist only made their singing louder, though some of the young men stood apart and looked their way. "Bloody fascists—"

"Let me stand you another coffee before you set those dogs on us." Bodo waved; the waiter ignored.

Hélène pulled Marius down. To Michael she added, Brownshirts make Marius see red.

The convivial group gathered extra chairs and squeezed about the black-and-white tabletop. The crooners by the door were soon outnumbered by a throng of men with red arm bands. The song abruptly ended in a scuffle scooped up by the porters and shoved outside into the street. Marius cheered.

"Michael, you must help us raise Hasso's spirits." Bodo pointed to the final man in the group slouching at the table. Short, husky, with a boyish face and mop of mousy hair falling over his eyes, Hasso acknowledged nothing. "He's vowed to drown himself in the Spree."

Hélène sighed. "Once a week, at least."

"Yesterday he was going to hang himself," Pia said. She fumbled in her coat pocket. "I wish he would and get it over with." Did Michael have a cigarette?

"You'll all be sorry when I'm martyred on the altar of art, my name revered for all time."

"Yes, yes. To be sure. Those hen scratchings of yours will be worth something, don't you think?"

Everyone but the artist laughed.

"So, Hasso, what is the meaning of today's despair?" Bodo asked.

Marius coughed. "Neumann's Gallery has invited Hasso's rival for another exhibit."

"Otto Dix in Berlin? Hasso, what is it to be, pistols at dawn?"

"That man is a fraud, I tell you all."

Bodo laughed. "But one who can afford to eat."

"I'm true to my muse."

"And starving."

"Speaking of food, what have you brought us today?"

"See for yourself." Hélène handed her rucksack to Marius and from her coat made a pile of wrapped packages on the table. "Soap, canned sweetmeat, French perfume and six pairs of silk stockings."

Pia picked up one of the small packages and held it to her nose. Chanel!

"That's for paying customers." Marius snatched it from her hand.

"Give it to her," Hélène said. "It's all compliments of the KaDeWe department store anyhow."

A waiter with slicked-back hair slammed down a round of fresh coffee.

Bodo nodded towards Michael. "Looks like our new friend here disapproves of your thieving ways, Hélène."

"Eh, he's from America."

"Oh!" Now Pia was paying attention.

"Canada," Michael said.

Marius tossed him a package of cigarettes.

Someone thought you could ski through the streets year round, no? Pia was certain they were all rich over there. "Aren't they?"

"Not this one. He's a bad plumber."

Oh.

"So, just who is this new foreigner of yours?"

"Yes, Hélène, tell us more."

"He's Frau von Renner's grandson."

Pia was sure she could see the family resemblance. Too bad, but since she hadn't been paying attention before, she wondered to Hélène how tall he was.

Michael was coughing.

"We'll have you selling your soul for those in no time. Breathe in."

"Marius, don't," said Hélène. "You'll make him ill and it's his first night out."

Leave him be! They'll make a man out of him!

Hélène laughed and waved—All right all right!—but reached over to pull the cigarette from Michael's mouth.

"Welcome to our Berlin then." Marius toasted with his coffee. Out went his jaw. "Really, Hélène, we must have something stronger."

Hasso grunted. "You're all damned fools. Who'll order me another?"

Outside the café, Michael stopped laughing long enough to inhale an early-morning chill, his eyes watering from the stink of overripe cabbage billowing up through the grate. Low-lit streets groaned with wagons; the hour of homeless, hungry dogs sniffing the gutters, snarling viciously at anything coming between them and hard-won bones, plodding horses, automobiles and lumbering omnibuses raking the dawn with backfire.

"Is it always like that back there?"

No, it was a relatively quiet night.

He declined the offer of another smoke from Hélène's contraband. Enh. So she lit it for herself.

"I suppose you'll tell your grandmother, won't you, that I'm a common thief?"

"No, of course not."

"I don't take from her, if that's what you're worried about."

It had crossed his mind.

"I can tell from those sad eyes, you do think ill of me." Hélène chuckled. "Makes you look just like that painting of your grandfather in the front room."

"No, really. I had a swell time tonight."

Hélène slung her arm through his.

"Your grandmother's idea."

"It was?"

"Uh-huh. She wants you to stay. Made me promise to make you forget about home. Did I?"

"Yeah." Michael didn't know where to look.

"Hurry then. You can just make the last tram."

"What about you?"

The store wasn't far and would be open in a few hours. Until then she'd sleep in the cafeteria. "You should think about it."

"What?"

"Staying."

She leaned in and brushed him lightly with her lips on his cheek. Then she was running across the square, not looking back.

Michael needed air and chose to walk home. Hélène, her friends, drinking coffee at night in a noisy café that was more like a castle, so much to take in. His cheeks ached from laughter. He touched where she had kissed him. And Berlin?

Berlin!

A warren of shadowed corridors and mute alleys in that first anxious shift from night, where a light mist now fell on the canal by Potsdam Bridge. Nan's house was still dark until headlights reflecting along the still water brought a car to the door. A ribbon of light pooled into the street. Crossing over the bridge now, Michael watched a man, about fifty, perhaps sixty, peppery hair, taut gold chain across a thick waist, step from the back of the car. Doctor Linder appeared at the door with a young woman. The man took the fur-wrapped girl from the doctor and hurried her into the back seat. They were gone when Michael reached the gate.

The latch, the door hinges, the sound of night rushing in alongside him, then silence. Click-click, click-click. Michael tried quietly to take the stairs. He heard it again, above, and looked. Click-click, click-click.

"Who are you?"

The man asking was wrapped in a calico blanket and peeking over the banister, his butterscotch face looking pulled and glistening. Click-click, click-click, went the wheels of the chair to which he was confined.

"You want the doctor?"

"I'm Frau von Renner's grandson."

"Not for the doctor?"

"No."

"She doesn't know about him." Herr Leopold whispered this.

"Know what?"

"It's not for me to say. It's late. I don't sleep well. Tell your grand-mother about the roof. It leaks."

Michael promised he would.

"The rain comes in. You tell her! I'm not a charity case. I pay my rent."

Herr Guthman banged on the wall downstairs and shouted, Quiet, old man!

"Listen to that. And him with the retard—"

Michael slipped away. He'd hoped not to wake his grandmother, but she called from the darkness. He joined her in the palm room, but could barely make out where she was sitting by the window.

"Let me turn on a light, Nan."

"No, it'll be day soon. Come and sit beside me."

"I'm sorry I'm so late and if Herr Leopold out there woke you—"

"Yes, we've all had to make sacrifices. We used to have a girl you know, to answer the door. Your grandfather was very fond of her, a Negro serving girl, oh, with an unpronounceable name. He'd dress her up like a Hottentot princess. No one got past her. The climate killed her in the end."

July 17, 1932

Dear Gene,

Your second letter arrived this morning and I am just now finished read-ing it to Nan. We make an event of it. I take Nan down by the canal where she feeds the ducks while she listens and politely corrects my translation. You would not believe the pleasure it gives her to hear about you all, especially Dadda. She wants to know how bad was the burn Mum got from the stove and did you apply butter or some other salve right away? Nan says her younger brother went like our mother, so she knows how it is.

I am saddened to hear that Dadda is having a tough run of things. I suppose you're right. Times being what they are, folks'd be living with leaky pipes or making do with their outhouses. But if, as he says, I should remain here where I am needed most, I guess that's that.

Tell Dadda that Nan remains well. Apart from a little droopiness in her cheek, he wouldn't know she'd had a stroke. Doctor Linder remains overly sensitive as to her health, but I must say, I see very little else of concern. I have tried to speak with her about Dadda's and Aunt Beate's fears regarding the doctor, and, while Nan listens, she mostly just smiles. Once, when I was on the subject, she interrupted me to say did I know the doctor had fixed grandfather's watch when no one else could. Doctor Linder is much preoccupied with his practice and teaching at the university so we do not see much of him. He did chastise me once over Nan taking me sightseeing in a taxi, which I say to you was improper for him to do. Doctor Linder worries such trips are too much for her. I say, how bad can it be for Nan to have lunch on the Unter den Linden once in a while? I'm glad she does. You were right, Gene. There is much, so much to see here.

Mrs. Herzfeld replaced the entire staircase, you say? That's just like them, isn't it? Still, it was thoughtful of her to tell Dadda she bore me no grudge.

Now what's this you say about Avon? He asked you to the pictures? How odd. Of course you were right to tell him to go cook a radish. That was our special thing to do on Saturday afternoons and I can't imagine why Avon would want to take you.

It is hot here in my room so I will end my letter by saying that my German has improved. I only misunderstand every third or fourth word now. Ha ha. Miss you all. Kiss to you and Mum,

Michael

Michael put aside his pen and shelled a peanut, tossing it through the open window and down into the courtyard sun, where flies droned under the stifling heat of the afternoon. Then he flung another, this time trying to get it inside a wooden crate upturned on the pile of garbage below.

Something down there moved.

Probably a rat. Lord knows, there were enough of them around. Michael set aside the letter to Gene and tossed another peanut. Then another. More movement and this time Michael was sure he heard the mewling of a kitten.

On the stairs to the courtyard, he gave a passing hello to Frau Guthman, up to her elbows as usual, and where was her Valentin? With his father at their grocery. Then Michael was outside, running round back to the courtyard. Tossing aside the garbage, he dug through layers of mouldy fruit in a box and found a flour sack reeking of petrol. Inside, a litter of puppies, all but one dead.

Showing the sickly puppy to Nan, who was reading the newspaper surrounded by her palms, he asked who could have done this.

"I'm afraid there are many in the city who can barely afford to feed their children," Nan said. "Of course we must keep him, if that's what you want. There must be some milk in here for him. Will he drink that, do you think?"

Michael was sure he would and ran down the hall with the weak animal.

"I always wanted a dog. My brother Felix had one, but Father didn't want it after he . . ."

Nan joined him in the pantry with a drawer from the sideboard.

"I think a towel inside will make this a perfect bed for the little fellow."

The dog was hungrily taking to the milk.

"And Michael, we must bathe him."

"Thank you, Nan."

Michael's grandmother caressed his arm. "As long as you smile like that, my dear. But Michael, we best keep this to ourselves. The doctor won't approve. Yes, we must not tell him."

Sure, Michael was pleased Hélène continued to include him in her circle, really he was. They were, after all, charming and witty, over-flowing, sometimes bursting with ideas in between rounds of coffee or beer and vodka and stinky French cigarettes. There just wasn't a damn thing back home like these people. But they were all doing something, even Marius, who was making a career out of saying that what every-one else was doing, the government included, was wrong. All Michael did was contribute the few marks Nan slipped into his pockets to pay for the beer and coffee and dinners in smoky basement bistros. Maybe that's all they wanted him around for. Still, there were moments, like sitting in the dim illumination of the Kroll Opera House, an-honest-to-God-real-opera-house, the orchestra swelling, when Michael was thrilled to have been included and it didn't matter why.

"Pia adores playing Hindemith," Hélène said. "This cello concerto is one of her favourites. She does it very well."

From the crowd that night, you'd never know that the Kroll had fallen on hard times and had been closed the year before, its musical director let go. These days the opera house was rarely opened and only for special performances. The seats Pia had secured, although off to the side, put them close enough to the stage to see the cellist hard at work. Though when Pia played, she could be frightening, her head snapping back to keep her glasses from falling off, teeth grit in rap-ture. Marius and Hasso sat behind them, Bodo having excused him-self from the evening to nurse wounds inflicted upon him from his wife's latest muse.

"Stupid beggar, he'll live," said Marius.

Then he leaned forward and told Michael that in Hindemith's opera *News of Today* the soprano sang from a bathtub. "It was decadent."

"What?" said Hasso. "What do you say? How is that decadent?"

Someone said, Shhh.

"Well, it wouldn't have been if she were naked," Mario replied.

Something came out of Hasso halfway between a spit and a choke. "You ignorant Communist. Everything is decadent to you."

"A woman stands up in a bathtub to sing opera? Hasso! Are you an idiot? Context, put it in context. At least accept that in an opera house singing in the bath disregards the suffering of those outside the doors, lying in the street. People who don't even own tubs."

The person who shushed now told them to be quiet.

"Who are you telling to shut up?" Marius reached back and started raining his fists down on the man behind.

"Oh, dear," Hélène said.

She apologized to Michael, who didn't mind at all. Finding the Hindemith concerto dreadful, when he wasn't craning his neck to gaze at the crowd, he was rather amused at the show going on behind them.

Afterwards, Pia met them outside on the wide steps, inviting one and all to Gitta's, a restaurant in the Potsdamer Platz. She had it on good authority that Lotte Lenya might drop by and sing from *The Threepenny Opera*.

"No, no, it's all the same with Weill. Plays about black-eyed prostitutes banging their headboards over listless Lotharios," said Hasso. "Besides, I need my sleep. I have to work for a living."

Marius laughed.

"It's true," Hélène said. "Hasso's painting a section of the theatre by the Nollendorfplatz." But was troubled by inspiration, or rather, a lack of it.

"Did I say the Chianti was free?" Pia's latest conquest had offered to spring for dinner.

That was different. Would they walk or take a taxi? But who had money for that? Michael?

Yes, Michael would pay.

"You know, once she even managed a supper for us at the Adlon Hotel," Hasso said to Michael as they squeezed into the back seat. "Smoked salmon on biscuits as thin as paper. Mind you, those snotty waiters turned their noses up at us just because our cuffs were frayed."

"Their days are numbered," said Marius, staring out the window at the blurs of city traffic.

As it went, Lotte Lenya did not regale them, or even show up as they elbowed around sticky tabletops in booths with stained cushions and cloudy mirrors. A badly cooked supper of pork bits swimming in a fatty sauce, and a little too much wine to drink, left Michael quiet, and pale, in the corner. Pia was sitting in the lap of her much older patron, scratching him behind one ear on a bald head. Hasso rose and stretched and offered his good nights.

"Come with me to Wedding tomorrow, Michael. I know of a gallery showing some Grosz."

"You hate Grosz," said Marius.

"I'm not allowed to see what crap he's up to these days?"

Marius, insisting he'd be forgiven if Hasso give him a cigarette, followed the young artist outside. Pia, waving to Hélène and Michael, followed shortly after with her patron. Time for her to pay.

Returning to Nan's, Hélène more crutch to Michael than companion, they met the red tip of Doctor Linder's cigarette flaring in the dark outside the door to Nan's flat. Downstairs, the Guthmans were arguing over a certain Polish miss getting turnips cheap from their shop and too much attention from Herr Guthman. A door upstairs quietly opened. Click-click, click-click.

"There's nothing here to concern you, Herr Leopold," the doctor said.

The door closed quickly.

"Ah, look at him. And from you, Hélène, I expect better."

"It's not Michael's fault. Something he ate, I think. I couldn't leave him."

Downstairs, Herr Guthman was apologizing repeatedly.

"This cannot go on. Have you forgotten, your grandmother is a convalescent? Late hours can only be disturbing to her rest." Something of hearty soap masked with rosewater hovered around him. "Young man, do you plan on doing something other than spending your nights getting drunk? Surely you don't expect to continue to live off your grandmother?"

Michael covered his mouth against the dry heaves.

Doctor Linder stubbed out his cigarette in the ashtray he pulled from his pocket. "You'd best get him inside. And do it quietly."

As Hélène helped Michael into a chair at the kitchen table, he said that the doctor shouldn't talk to him like that.

Hélène put the kettle on the stove.

"Did you hear that?" she said.

Michael had his head down on his arms. "I'm too busy being drunk. I've never been drunk before."

"Listen. That scratching noise." Hélène looked up.

"I don't hear anything."

"There's definitely something in the attic."

"It's just Herr Leopold."

"Not right above us. Your grandmother uses that space for storage, she keeps her winter coats there. There's a stairwell from your room. Didn't you know?"

"Ah, let it go. It's nothing, Hélène. Hey, where're you going?"

"Michael, if this house has mice, or worse, we have to know. We can't leave them there." She went for the kitchen door. "Think of your grandmother."

"Wait." He reached for her arm and pulled her back. The effort almost cost him. "It's not a mouse. I found a puppy in the garbage. I've hidden it upstairs."

"A dog?"

"What else could I do?" His head was really spinning now.

"And what are you going to do when your grandmother finds it?"

"She's the one who told me to hide it up there so that old beggar wouldn't find out. Nan's happy about it. I always wanted my own dog, you know."

"Of course she's happy. She'll do anything to keep you here. And when you go, who's going to take care of a dog your grandmother can't even get out to walk?"

He hadn't worked that out.

"This is a mess, Michael."

"I know." Michael dropped his head back on his arms. "That's what they get for sending me to protect my grandmother."

"Protect her? From what?"

"From that doctor. My father and my Aunt Beate say he's cheating Nan out of her money."

Hélène laughed.

Michael managed to sit up. "It's not funny. You saw how he spoke to me."

"He's her friend. And he worries about her."

"That's what you think." Michael lowered his voice. "My father said he's a Jude, and you know what they're like."

Hélène went to get a towel and rinsed it with water from the sink.

"I bet if Gene were here, holy mackerel, but she wouldn't take any guff from him. No way. She's my sister. You'd like her. No messing with her."

She placed the wet towel across Michael's forehead.

"Oh, that feels grand. What was I saying?"

"You were feeling sorry for yourself."

"Oh, yeah. I can't do anything right. I can't even keep a job. What the hell am I doing here?"

"Apart from being a very boring drunk at the moment, you're giving your grandmother more joy than she's known in years."

"Doctor Linder's right. I *am* living off her."

"Enjoy your self-pity. Inform me when it's done."

As for the dog, Hélène insisted that under no circumstances was Michael to name it. If he did, he'd become attached. Herr Leopold would certainly make Nan's life hell with his complaining and what about Valentin? No knowing what that halfwit child would do around a dog. Get himself bit, then see how much trouble they'd be in. No, Hélène reiterated, the dog must go.

"Too late. His name is Pitou."

Men jumped from the back of a rushing trolley, tumbling onto the pavement just ahead of the human wave rolling after them into the Potsdamer Platz. Everyone was jostling for the best view from the promontory of the curb, sweeping Michael along, that leash dangling from his hand.

By Pschorr-Haus on one of the corners, the beer and wine hall's blunted façade flanked by a muffin-topped tower, a stout vendor of berliners had unfolded his cart. The hot doughnut-like pastries steamed in the cold wet air, their buttery perfume with lemon and apricot jam pushing back the ubiquitous odour of cabbage. But no one waiting for the marchers noticed. Yes! Come! Plenty for all, the doughnut seller grinned, wiping his large hands and black-haired forearms on his grimy apron. As more and more crowded around to catch a glimpse of the marchers, he had to steady his tipping cart. Watch out, you filthy louts! No one paid him any mind. The doughnuts rolled everywhere, under the feet of the crowd.

I want to see, get out of my way! growled half a veteran rolling himself on a board fitted with casters. Bumping against the teeming curb underneath the smiling poster girl for Persil soap, he had worked himself into a frenzy. Then tipping his board and lifting himself, the legless man shoved his way past Michael's feet and into the wall of trousers and long coats.

Piano music drifted down from an open window. Measured, delicate, out of step with the marchers on the street, a child practising maybe. A woman standing beside Michael said, They're so young, but Michael's German was still raw and she may have meant, young fools, or too young to know what they're doing. Then the music stopped. Everyone wanted to see.

Almost everyone. Michael caught sight of the young man, perhaps sixteen, as he moved through bits of black greatcoats and brown slickers, sagging stockings and worn-out shoes, bent umbrellas and crushed hats. His trousers were too long, his once-yellow shirt was buttoned to his neck and to his wrists, and over it was tightly stretched a shiny black vest. From under a worn hat fell strands of long, tallow-coloured hair almost covering his scowling face. He slouched against the windows of the beer hall and wiped his nose with the back of his hand. A tossed cigarette butt landed close by Michael's feet and the youth snapped it up hungrily with a victorious ah-ha! They appeared to be the only persons uninterested in the parade.

"Have you seen a dog? Brown marks over the eyes?" Michael held up the leash. "He slipped his collar. He's just a puppy."

The kid returned the look, said nothing.

At the sound of barking, Michael ran back to the curb and tried to push his way through the crowd. "Pitou!" Then he heard yelping. "Pitou!"

The younger man tore the leash from his hands. Michael swung around to see him bolt right into the marching brownshirts, pushing them out of his way, whistling, Here boy! Here boy! Those standing beside Michael on the curb began to laugh and point as those marching had to duck out of the way, and were none too happy about doing so. Pitou's champion took more than one cuff to the head for troubling the parade.

With the last of the marchers the crowd began to drift away, leaving only the blond youth limping up the street holding the dog. He poured the lifeless animal into Michael's arms and returned the leash. He had not needed to use it. Before Michael could speak, the boy stepped off the curb and ran between the streetcar tracks, past the colonnaded Potsdam Gate.

Later that evening distant curses cut into chopping hooves on cobbles. Then nothing but the weighted drops of October rain, ingested and excreted into the city's sewers until they could take no more.

Michael let the rain run over closed eyes, into his mouth. Overhead, Dutch tobacco wafted from the open windows of the palm room towards the canal waters and down the black-washed granite corridor as golden squares poked holes in the high curved avenue of doors and windows.

In his grandmother's flat upstairs, aspic cutlets sat congealing in fat, the table set with the last few bits of unsold china and silver, lit by low flames in widening puddles of wax. Hélène was clearing it away. Nan lay in her room at the end of the hall.

The party was to have been a surprise. His grandmother had wanted to celebrate the six months they'd been together. With Hélène's help and against her doctor's wishes, Nan had prepared a lavish dinner aided by the generosity of Herr Guthman. All of Hélène's friends had come; Pia was to perform. But because of Pitou, Michael had come home too late. Doctor Linder met him on the stairs and told him so, as Frau Guthman was consoling her boy, and said that it was quick, the old woman only feeling weak before it happened. Valentin wanted to pet Michael's dog.

But only that morning, Nan had been fussing with flowers over pastries and coffee, voicing her disdain towards the extremists battling for political supremacy down in the streets. And only last week on a visit to the Imperial Palace, she told him of her childhood, meeting his grandfather Wilhelm, the dashing figure he cut in uniform, life at court and the halcyon days at the house outside Leipzig where Michael's father and his Aunt Beate learned how to ride. Never mind that things now were not as they were. Always remember, Michael, Nan told him, you are a von Renner. Doors will open for you. There was so much strength in her embrace that day, surely she would live forever.

Now Doctor Linder was upstairs watching over her with a benign ruthlessness in a damp flat stinking of lye soap, crumbling plaster and rotting wallpaper.

Michael's hands trembled as he lit a cigarette. At least he didn't have to get it from the gutter. That boy who couldn't save his dog probably didn't know where his next smoke would come from, probably didn't care. There was nothing to do but stand in the rain and wish he could join its headlong rush to the sewers. By morning, dead cats would float in basement door wells, and putrid bits of rot, breakfast for crows and gulls.

Carmel von Renner was buried beside her husband on the third of November, 1932, in St. Matthäus churchyard. Over the door to the Familie von Renner crypt, soot-faced cherubs with dimpled cheeks grinned at the assemblage.

Back home in Nova Scotia it was the season of blood red and burnt gold, corn silk and fields of pumpkins. In Berlin, fall was just a darker shade of grey, rain, and knurled leaves swirling against the rust-stained marble of the mausoleum.

To get Nan inside, the boards nailed to the doors of the crypt had to come off. The groundskeeper had sealed the building in the spring after he'd discovered a cooking fire inside. Goddamned Gypsies, he complained. They crawled over the walls at night and slept anywhere that kept them out of the rain. Once inside, the pallbearers met part of the copper-sheathed cupola that had collapsed, clogging the interior of the mausoleum with debris that would have to be unceremoniously kicked out of the way before Nan could be lowered, vertically, into the cellar.

Outside on the narrow strip of pavement jostled sad-eyed Imperial remnants with drooping moustaches and medalled paunches, their women with blue-veined complexions and wrapped in furs reeking of rose-scented face powder and mothballs. Not once during Michael's stay had any of these people called on Nan, but they offered condolences and inquired, would there be a luncheon?

Through it all, Doctor Linder demonstrated a stoic reserve. Somewhat cold, thought Michael, but there was no denying, he was thankful the man had taken control. After the doctor telegrammed Aunt Beate, he saw to all the funeral arrangements, then made sure everything went according to schedule, even ensuring Frau Guthman met those returning from the service in a starched apron. One last time, Nan's home as gracious as she had once made it, save for the disinfecting odour of lye. Herr Guthman, having closed his grocery shop out of respect, took everyone's coats and hats while Hélène, having caught the early-morning tram from Charlottenburg where she shared a flat with four others, served the food she and Frau Guthman had spent all morning preparing. Only as Aunt Beate was overheard to say, none of this would be happening without her having arrived from Leipzig to manage the domestics.

"Well, I know you and the Guthmans have been a godsend, Hélène," Michael said as his friend washed Nan's remaining bits and pieces of china.

"I suppose it means something that you think so, but if that woman out there refers to me as *girl* one more time, she's going to find out what it's like to stick more than her hands in dishwater. The cow."

Aunt Beate and Uncle Torsten Eck had shown up with Cousin Catharina the day after Nan's death. Uncle Torsten was a municipal administrator in Leipzig and well on his way to being round, red, with lots of meticulously waxed facial hair. Aunt Beate had inherited none of Nan's self-control. She was fat. Cousin Catharina shared the same weak chin dimple as Michael, had pale blue eyes and a face perpetually pursed in the lips that only opened for her sharp tongue.

"And the way she is ordering Frau Guthman around, after what that woman and her husband have done—"

Michael agreed. Nice of the Guthmans to help out.

"Help out? Is that what you think? Michael, how much money did your aunt and uncle give you to pay for this food?"

"Perhaps they gave it to Doctor Linder."

Hélène stared, hard.

"I just assumed that my grandmother left something—"

"The Guthmans paid for all this food."

"No. She had money, surely?" Lots of it. Why else, then, was he there?

Hélène slammed down a handful of cutlery. "Michael, look at this place, cut up into flats, a laundry downstairs. Your grandmother had nothing. Nothing! She was only able to live out her days here because, well, never mind, but when that woman out there walks around ordering people about, itemizing the things she plans on taking when she never gave a pfennig to keep your grandmother . . ." Hélène, having gone back to washing dishes, was about to scrub the roses off the china. "We did what we did, because we cared for her."

"Did what?"

"You don't want to know."

"Hélène, she was *my* grandmother."

"All right then." Hélène met him face on. "What I take from the store, I took for her. Marius sells the stuff and gives me the money. And that barely puts food on her table. Doctor Linder, the man you thought was stealing from your grandmother, pays for everything else by helping out rich old counts."

Michael didn't follow.

"Oh! You are thick. When they get their young mistresses in trouble."

Shit.

"But your grandmother never knew," Hélène said. "And now you're going home."

"I guess so."

"Well, you must be happy with that."

"Yeah."

If she kept at it, Hélène was also going to rub the silver off the spoon.

"Maybe you'll write to me. About America."

"Canada."

She smiled.

He added, "I'm not very good at writing. Ask my sister."

Hélène stopped washing that spoon and looked at Michael, saw Aunt Beate standing in the doorway behind. Only the bottom half of her face was smiling.

"Michael, your uncle and I would like to speak with you."

Hélène, ignored, shrugged and turned back to the dishes.

Michael followed his aunt through the throng of guests enjoying Frau Guthman's food.

"Shall I get Doctor Linder?"

Not seen since leaving the churchyard.

His uncle closed the door to the palm room.

"This concerns only family. Please, sit."

Aunt Beate took her place beside Catharina on the sofa. Uncle Torsten's cigar smoke was being sucked outside, but open windows at this time of year would be harsh on Nan's palms. Someone should say something.

"It goes without saying that your aunt and I are grateful for your being here. Your grandmother in particular was very taken by your sacrifice."

Michael was glad that everyone was happy. He assumed he'd be leaving in the morning?

"Is that what you want?"

"Sure, yes."

"What would you say to staying?"

"In Berlin?"

His uncle nodded. "Your grandmother, apparently, unbeknownst to your aunt and I, took it upon herself to arrange a small annuity for you. Not much, but she wanted you to study at the university."

"You look surprised, Michael," Aunt Beate said.

"I . . . I am. She never said."

"You didn't know this?"

"No, of course not."

"Nevertheless, your grandmother felt you needed some purpose. She hoped you would consider medicine as a profession as it was once hoped for your father. Being a doctor would honour this family. Should you decline, the money reverts to Catharina's dowry."

The university? You just didn't think about going to such lofty places when you crapped in an outhouse.

"I don't know what to say."

"I do. Make him go home. I'm smart enough for the university."

"But Catya, you're an engaged woman. You'll have no time for such things and Braum would never allow it."

"Of course this house is ours," Michael's uncle said. "But with the political unrest in Berlin these days, we'd never get a good price if we sold now. If you stay, we'd like you to live here, manage the property. It would help us greatly."

Generous. Very generous. But what about Hélène and the doctor? The Guthmans? Shouldn't any money go back to them?

"Supporting my mother? Wherever did you get that ridiculous idea? I know. It's just the sort of thing I'd expect his kind to say." Meaning Doctor Linder. "Not one pfennig of this family's money will that man see. Now what is it to be?"

Michael thought he should at least write his father. Things were tough at home. He might be needed.

A frond fell from one of the palms. Outside, Valentin was singing loo-lee-tra-lee-loo to a duck on the canal.

If Michael had ignored his father's prohibition regarding telegrams, he'd have his answer already. Something like, *Duty done stop miss you dreadfully stop come home stop.* Well, maybe not quite like that. Far too emotional for August and, at the cost per word, expensive. But, as Hélène suggested, waiting for a reply by return post meant it could be after Christmas before Michael had to unhappily give up riding streetcars to occupy his days.

This morning found him at the white-dusted Alexanderplatz, where hardy early risers dodged streetcars gliding past the Tietz department store. Automobiles sliding on the icy streets honked and passed quickly underneath the raised rails entering and leaving the bahnhof, through which trains filled with shopgirls and accountants and clerks rattled on their way to government ministries. Hélène, who was busy pouring overstuffed matrons into Christmas dresses back at KaDeWe, said to stay away from that conflation of streets. Political parties liked to play Red Rover there and it wouldn't do to get caught between ideologies.

So he ducked into a below-street-level café, ordered coffee, very hot and milk-white, and apart from the noisy trio tucked in back, he quietly watched slush-covered boots and shoes hurrying past in the square of greasy window.

" . . . not as long as Hindenburg . . . no no no I tell you it's to be von Papen, von Papen's the man . . . have you heard what that Austrian said . . ."

Michael lit a cigarette, finished his coffee and turned back through streets of light snow, finding himself eventually, as he often did, in the Potsdamer Platz. The man selling doughnuts from his cart was gone, but there, against the grimy window, that's where the blond youth had stood. That's where he'd picked up the cigarette. And Michael, sometimes catching the streetcar gliding past the columns of the Potsdam Gate, wondered, now that it was so cold, how was that kid making do?

For Christmas, he bought cream tea for Mum and chocolate in gold foil for Gene. The bookseller had recommended *Mein Kampf* to

Michael for his father, but flipping through it, he found it wordy. August would no doubt savour it because it was impossible to find German books at home. Michael then bundled up the packages and posted them, knowing they most likely wouldn't reach Nova Scotia until April, when, sure, he'd be home.

No, young man, he was told, no mail for you in return.

The smell of bread welcomed him back to his grandmother's. Frau Guthman must have spent the day by her oven. Mum used to do that. Michael could almost hear in the kitchen the clunking of her crockery and tinkling silver used only for special occasions like Sundays and Christmas, nutmeg and cinnamon and roasting apple filling the air, Gene in the front room intently decorating the tree, because it just had to be right. Mum'd be singing. She liked those old carols, belting them out in that horrid voice of hers in a yeast-scented kitchen as Michael iced shortbread cookies and Mum made date squares. Then he got to lick syrupy dates off a spoon while she danced in front of the stove and made him laugh. Outside, snow fell thick as peony petals and no one could make a snowman quite like Avon—

The knock on the door startled him. On the landing, tossing off one of Frau Guthman's wet sheets he'd picked up on his way, grinned a tall, husky fellow, a few years younger than Michael, but already balding. He carried a suitcase.

"Michael von Renner, I am your new best friend," Braum Kunstler said.

One hour before midnight and the streets were crowded with frayed and top-hatted merrymakers alike, falling yet again for the promise of a new year. Michael and Braum stood outside the Eldorado, a club a few blocks from the Nollendorfplatz.

Had Braum been here before?

The big man grinned and slapped Michael manfully on the shoulder. "Every time I come to Berlin. And I'm not married to your cousin yet, so not a word from you, eh?"

Catharina's fiancé, after settling in with the explanation he needed a good job in Berlin to keep his woman happy, had decided they should celebrate, and, more importantly, Braum needed a night on the town.

"Hear that? Nigger music. Best club in Berlin for jazz."

Painted leather curtained off the inside door. Michael hesitated. Braum took his arm and pulled him into the blue-smoke glare of the cabaret. Everywhere he turned, rectangular mirrors reflected bits of men in evening dress, hour girls in sweat-stained silk gowns, swarthy labourers tightly buttoned, Egyptian-eyed women, shopgirls laughing loudly and drunken boys under big hats slouching over the bar.

"Braum, honey! You big Prussian bull! Where've you been hiding?"

A blowsy woman with fiery unkempt hair leapt from behind the bar and squeezed Braum, crushing her mouth to his, cleaning it out with her tongue.

"This is—" Braum gulped for air and the woman kissed him again. "What name are you going by tonight, you boy-cunt?"

"Tonight I am Tonia. Come in, find a seat and I'll bring you a drink. You save a dance for me?"

Braum sent the creature away, slapping his hand off her arse. Pushing his way across the room, he laughed at Michael and found them a table by the stage.

"I know what you're thinking. Harmless. It means nothing." He pushed Michael down into a chair. "How can it? That whore pisses through a dick."

When Tonia returned, she put down two glasses and caught Michael staring.

"Oh, he's a sweet one, honey."

Braum roared with delight over Michael's discomfort. "Bet you've not seen the like, eh?"

Girls with whirligig tassels on their nipples tiptoed onto the stage, gyrating.

"Don't you just get that music? You know what, tonight I think I'm going to get me some black pussy. Tight as all hell." Braum winked. "Oh, relax! You, my friend, need to get drunk."

A drum roll shattered with a cymbal crash. Bits of coloured paper rained across the table. A woman behind Michael pulled him backwards and covered his mouth with a coating of waxy lipstick tasting of licorice. Braum was on his feet, glass in the air, flinging his brown beer everywhere.

When the woman grappling with Michael set him free, he sat up and through the stifling, crowded, sickly sweet-scented room, recognised a face at the bar. The boy who'd tried to save Pitou was with an older man and laughing. As he leaned over to kiss his companion on the cheek, he saw Michael and, pausing, appeared to recognize him as well.

"You look like you've seen a ghost, my man." Braum had to shout close to Michael's ear to be heard. Then he looked to see what had Michael's attention. "Oh, the fucking perverts, eh? Best show in town though, and it's all free."

Midnight had come.

1933

Herr Leopold was invited to the Guthmans' New Year's dinner, but he'd rather starve to death in his garret than be around that mongrel of theirs. No one should be alone on the holiday, fretted his hostess, so Michael and Braum cheerfully picked up the wheelchair-bound man and carried him screaming and flailing with nails of cat-like sharpness down two flights of stairs. It took Braum threatening to drop him in the canal if he didn't behave for the young men to bring him to the table. A glass or two of wine to dull his outrage and Herr Leopold admitted that he'd not been down those stairs in over three years. Another glass and the old man joined in toasting the future well into the night, feasting on peppercorn chicken and stuffed pork, washed down with warm beer.

Now, plates and covered bowls cleared away and the table linen brushed of crumbs, Valentin was permitted to drive the mechanical train Michael had given him across the floor, bringing tears to his mother's eyes.

"Ah, my wife. She barks at me, but that boy is her life, so there must be good in her." Herr Guthman refilled Michael's glass. He set the bottle down in front of him, then leaned back at the table and folded his arms. "We don't mean to pry, but if you could tell us about the flat? It's just that, well, we were wondering what you had decided to do. If your father requests that you return home, your aunt and uncle may be forced to sell and we might have to leave."

Michael, feeling the ill effect of too much to drink, the eve not yet worn off, was effusive with concern. Winter would be a helluva time to be searching for a new flat, one where Frau Guthman could carry on washing and hanging her laundry.

Maybe he should post another letter home in case the first one had gone astray.

Valentin heard the soft rapping first. He stopped playing with his train and pointed.

"Now who could that be?" Frau Guthman said on her way to the door.

Doctor Linder greeted her from the hall, then handed an envelope past the woman, to Michael. "This telegram was delivered to me by mistake." With a curt bow, he apologized for disturbing his neighbours' evening before climbing the stairs back to his flat.

"Should we ask him to join us?"

"Maybe it's from your father," said Braum, closing the door. "You've been waiting for that."

"No—"

But it was. Michael tore open the envelope and realized how his father had been able to afford it. It didn't cost much to say: *Stay stop.*

Braum slapped him on the back.

"Let's drink to your old man, my friend."

Hélène, bundled against the late-January cold and a biting chill blown off the Landwehr Canal, waved to them as she hurried past Shell Haus, a large paper bag in her arms.

"Now there's a warming sight," said Braum.

"You're drunk," she said by way of greeting. "Could hear you three blocks away. Must be why I haven't seen you, Michael, for the last few weeks."

"We haven't met, I'd remember. Braum Kunstler."

Catharina's fiancé, Michael added stupidly.

"You must be the Hélène he talks so much about."

She smiled. "Good thing I brought more than enough. The café at the store was going to throw these buns out. I've even got coffee beans."

"A beauty and an angel!" Braum said. "Let's get you out of this cold."

Michael was back to singing: *The Swastika gives hope to our entranced millions,/ The day for freedom and for bread's at hand.*

He and Braum then raced up the narrow path in front of Nan's house. Braum jumped over the metal gate; Michael left it clanging behind him. Frau Guthman, making an early start on the day's laundry, fell out of their way.

"I sing too!" Valentin was choo-chooing his Christmas train along the edge of the step.

Braum thrust his face into the boy's and growled savagely, laughing as he took the stairs two at a time. Not like Frau Guthman to not say anything. Valentin began to shake until Hélène handed him a bun.

"That little mongoloid gets on my nerves," Braum said as they entered the flat. "Time for new tenants, my dear Michael."

"No, I couldn't ask them to leave."

Braum yawned. "It's not really your decision to make, is it? But probably too much trouble to do anything about it right now."

Hélène went quietly into the kitchen, where Michael found her heating up the stove to make the coffee.

"You should've been there, Hélène. People everywhere, marching through the Brandenburg Gate, we had to stand in the Adlon's window boxes—"

"Tell her about the concierge." Braum yelled this from the palm room.

"Yes, and the concierge tried to chase us away until Braum said no one is telling us what to do anymore and threw him into the garden fountain and people were up in the trees, Hélène, actually sitting in the trees all along the Unter den Linden. I've never seen anything like it! Not even on Dominion Day from Citadel Hill."

Hélène had no idea what that was.

"Oh, never mind, and there were torches and singing and drums and everyone was cheering, oh, Hélène! I could feel the pulse of the marching go right through me! And then we ran after them down the Wilhelmstrasse and guess what, the Chancellor came out and waved to the crowd. We actually saw him!"

Stumbling home drunk at dawn had become a regular thing in the month since Braum had introduced Michael to cabaret life. Like 'a horse out of the gate, the big man had laughed. But this morning was different. As had been the night before.

Witness something wonderful, something magnificent, Braum had shouted, carried away by emotion, bathed in torchlight. History will recall this night! Be a part of history, as you must be. You belong here, Michael, this is your destiny, our Fatherland!

Now the morning sun was low and silvery. Early-morning steam rose off the canal, hinting of spring. And there were stale buns and fresh coffee. What else did a body need?

Soon Hitler's banners will wave unchecked at last, / The end of German slav'ry in our land.

Horst Wessel's lyrics were still ringing in Michael's ears from the night before, still vivid in the cold of day. At last, something he wanted to be part of. More than a prayer, a promise.

"Maybe Braum's right, Hélène, maybe God has brought me here to be part of this."

"Yes, yes, all this, just for you. You keep this place filthy. What would your grandmother say?"

Michael shrugged. Braum appeared in the doorway. He practically filled it.

"She's too pretty to be your mother even if she sounds like it." He reached over to the table and lifted a bun off the plate, tearing into it hungrily.

Hélène went back to grinding the coffee beans.

"The day for freedom and for bread's at hand . . ." Braum lumbered down the hall to the palm room, where he threw himself across the sofa. It squeaked under his weight.

"How long is he staying?"

That didn't matter. "You really should have been with us last night."

"The new Chancellor won't last two months. They never do."

"You'd think differently if you'd been there. You know, Braum's right. It was every good German's duty to be out last night."

"Are you saying I'm not a good German?"

As Hélène then pointed out, it was a bunch of thugs marching down the Unter den Linden, that's all. If it's not the National Socialists, it's the Communists, and if it's not them, it's the anarchists, or if you want real excitement, starving mothers baring their breasts to show they're so poor and hungry they've no milk left. Michael had been in Berlin for all of five minutes as far as Hélène was concerned, so what could he possibly know about being a good German?

All wasted on Michael, who was by then vomiting in the sink. From the palm room came the sound of snoring.

At first, Michael declined the invitation to the evening benefit at the Kroll Opera House orchestrated by Pia. She had invited officials of the new government on behalf of the friends of Otto Klemperer, former musical director and *enfant terrible*, in the hopes of securing funding to permanently reopen the neglected venue. For Michael, it meant having to dress up. Of course there'd been a change of Sunday best in his stolen luggage, but he wasn't saying.

So Hélène, assuming they didn't wear suits in Canada and that Michael was being too proud to say he couldn't afford a new one, suggested his grandfather's would do nicely. But when she insisted that Herr Leopold was the only one who could finish the necessary tailoring in time, Pia balked. He pisses into a bucket and it stinks up there, she'd protested. But he was cheap, refusing to take any money because Michael brought him his paper every morning and didn't mind running the occasional shop errand. Reluctantly, Pia followed her friends upstairs to the angular attic loft bisected with brick chimneys and cobwebs.

With Michael standing on the footstool, arms outstretched, Herr Leopold wheeled about, directing Hélène where to pin in the places he couldn't reach.

"I have a new dress on, you know," Pia said, pushing open a window and fanning the air in front of her with her hands. "It can't get soiled. Where am I supposed to sit?"

Herr Leopold would not have his art minimized by her distracting presence and he instructed her to go into his tiny galley kitchen to make tea. "There's some biscuits in that red and blue tobacco tin, the one with an Indian head on it." He wouldn't say so, but the old man was clearly delighted to be playing host. "And by Christ, girl, close that window. Do you want me to die in this chair of pneumonia?"

"I can't find any tin in here." There was some rattling of crockery, then she squealed. "I saw something move!"

"For God's sake, Pia," said Hélène, "can't you just make tea?"

"I mean it. There's something crawling in here."

Michael turned to look and cracked his head on the low rafter as Herr Leopold made a gesture with his hand to suggest Pia was full of shit. Hélène looked away so he couldn't see her smile.

Pia rejoined them in the nook by the dormer and after a passing inspection, sat on a wooden clothes chest.

"Forget it. I've got too much on my mind."

"To make tea?" asked Michael.

"Yes! I have things on my mind. I'm torn, if you must know."

"Pia's met a set designer from UFA who wants to get her into the movies," Hélène said through a mouthful of pins. "But it means giving up the cello."

"As an actress?" said Michael.

Hélène laughed and just had to spit those pins out.

"Well? I could be an actress."

"Too true. I've seen your performances off screen."

"You could try to be more helpful, Hélène," said Pia. "The opera or the movies?"

Downstairs, Valentin was calling, Here kitty. His mother chided him, That's what happens when you leave the door open.

"Foolish women. As if you had any choices." Click-click went Herr Leopold's wheels.

"Don't we?" Pia said.

"No, no, not there, girl, pin it here. Hold still."

Michael flinched.

"Of course you don't have any choices. Take it from me, everything is ordained."

"Hélène, I did not come up here to be spoken to like this—"

Herr Leopold wheeled his chair about. "I know what choice you will make, young lady, because I know you have none."

"And why is that?"

The old tailor shrugged. "Ah, well, years ago I did costumes for the Kroll. I know Klemperer. I know his kind."

Hélène kept pinning Michael's jacket.

"And?"

"He's a Jude," said Herr Leopold.

Michael cracked his head again and stepped down off the stool to rub it out.

Pia couldn't see how that mattered, not when they were talking about a *prominent* Jude.

Herr Leopold shrugged again.

"Michael, is your cousin coming to the benefit? I did leave an invitation with you for him."

Michael couldn't say. Braum only had time for political meetings these days. Pia sighed. He stood back on the stool and eyed the ceiling. This time he saw the hornet's nest, but Herr Leopold said it was ancient and not to worry.

Hélène gestured for Michael to turn around.

"I still can't believe you're going to make him wear that old thing," said Pia, going over to the window, bending low to miss the slope of the roof, and rubbing a circle into the dirty glass. Then she noticed where a swallow had gotten inside and started to build a nest. She poked at it.

From where he stood, Michael could see out to the whitecaps on the canal. The wind had picked up.

"I'll have you know, young lady, I made this old thing," Herr Leopold said. "And Wilhelm von Renner was not the only minister at court I dressed."

But hard times had reduced the once-proud tailor to a boarder for a once-proud client. And that woman was a saint, he'd cross himself, when he wasn't bitching about the leaky roof.

"That must have made you one of the best tailors around," Hélène said.

"Still the best in Berlin, not that it matters much these days. And I was the only one who would dress that poor soul for Judgment after the way he died."

"What poor soul?" Michael asked.

"The young man does not know about his grandfather?"

Hélène looked trapped. Pia, intrigued.

Herr Leopold persisted. Why keep such a thing from the young man?

Yes, echoed Pia. Why?

"It's no secret," said Hélène. "I'm certain if Michael's family wants him to know, they will tell him."

Herr Leopold wasn't waiting for that. "Wilhelm von Renner never got over being marked as a November Bandit." That's what they called those who sold out the Fatherland after the war, he explained, signing that hateful Versailles Treaty on behalf of the Kaiser, carving up the map, reducing honest, hard-working people like him to penury. "Then Herr Minister lost everything. Oh yes, during the panic, the estate in Leipzig, and when the investments went, he took his life savings and bought a one-way tram ticket to the Alexanderplatz. I heard it cost him over a million marks for that ticket. Shot himself at the end of the line. They had to replace the glass and charged his dear wife for it."

Hélène told Michael she was finished and that he could step down from the stool.

"Mind you, I never believed all that other business."

Did he mean the gossip? Hélène asked.

"That his grandfather did what he did because there was someone else in his bed." The tailor was giving a final adjustment to the lapels.

"Another woman?" Pia's eyes lit up.

"Like I said, I never believed that."

"You're just an old storyteller, Herr Leopold," Hélène said. "I'm sorry, Michael. I guess your Nan didn't want you to think poorly of your grandfather."

"Yes, some might say cowardly to leave such a fine woman on her own," Herr Leopold said. "Now, let me see to that tea."

The reception room overlooking the Königsplatz, across from the dark silhouette of the Reichstag, was decorated awkwardly with the red and white and black flags of the new regime. A long linen-covered table in the centre of the hall overflowed with glasses, bottles of wine, silver bowls of fruit and cheeses and towers of creamed pastries from the kitchens of the Kaiserhof Hotel. No expense from the pockets of the wealthy private patrons had been spared to compel the officials from the Ministry of Culture into opening the public purse.

"I don't know about you," Hasso said to Michael, who was feeling stared at in his grandfather's coat, "but I'm eating a week's worth. When are we going to see a table like this again?"

"Pia invited you," Hélène said, "hoping you might meet someone from the ministry to help you get a new commission. Try not to look like you've been starving."

"And what, Hélène, would our jackboot thug of a Chancellor know about art?" Marius said, helping himself to a dainty off Hasso's plate.

Pia swooped down and, taking Hélène's arm, said to Marius, "I see you're not averse to eating the food of the bourgeois."

"That would be rude."

"Hélène, guess who's here? That director I told you about, Angerbauer. Remember we saw his movie at the Admiralspalast?" It's just that Pia couldn't remember what it was called.

No point in Hélène's reminding the awestruck Pia that at the time she thought the film dreadful.

Michael wanted to know if anyone else could smell something burning, but no one was listening.

"Sounds as if you're giving up the cello."

"My dear Hélène, that stinky old tailor was right after all." She whispered: "You know, about Klemperer being Juden. I heard he's on a train to Paris."

Michael looked for, but could not make out, the famous director. While searching the room, he brushed against the arm of a tall dark-haired man.

"Excuse me. Not paying attention."

No harm done. The man said something else, but it was lost when a woman standing by the window screamed. Everyone turned, then joined the crush out of the hall to the front door. Shouting, bells and sirens, racing trucks and people running from everywhere met the guests pushing out of the Kroll to see flames engulf the darkened government building out front.

"The fire will make quick work of it," said the man Michael had bumped into.

Hélène and Pia joined them on the stairs of the opera house just as plates of glass splashed onto the pavement of the square. There were screams. Maybe someone was shooting, no one knew for certain. Everyone ducked. Over the trees of the Tiergarten, flames leapt into the night. The glass dome of the columned building shone brilliantly, before collapsing into the tearing of ceiling and wall.

Fire trucks eventually ringed the building. Heavy black smoke spewed out of the windows. The crisp February air was rancid with it. Police disgorged out of the back of vans, shoving through the crowd and barking orders. An ant-like line formed, crawling in and out of the main doors, saving what they could, struggling with boxes, heavy gilt frames, books and carpets. Water hissed and dripped from hoses, quickly crystalline under the night cold.

Later, at home, when Michael opened the windows, purifying the room with the icy morning blast, the palms shivered. He was still numbed from standing in the long night, watching the flames die. His grandfather's suit coat on the chair stank of smoke. But she didn't. Hélène always smelled of Persil.

"Thank you for letting me come home with you," she said, by him.

"Are you still cold?"

"A little."

"I'll make coffee."

And Michael left her to close the windows.

Over the skyline, a thin bluish pink was cut by smoke from thousands of roof stacks etched over city canyons. Downstairs, Frau Guthman's laundry was already drying, and outside, the milk wagon passed by walls of flats, inside which news of the terrorist torching of the Reichstag was most certainly circulating.

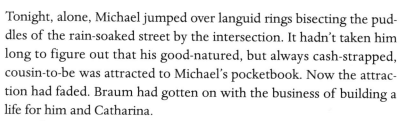

Tonight, alone, Michael jumped over languid rings bisecting the puddles of the rain-soaked street by the intersection. It hadn't taken him long to figure out that his good-natured, but always cash-strapped, cousin-to-be was attracted to Michael's pocketbook. Now the attraction had faded. Braum had gotten on with the business of building a life for him and Catharina.

And tomorrow, for sure, Michael would ask Doctor Linder for help getting into the university. Oh. But probably best to say Uncle Torsten was paying for it.

The rain had stopped as Michael skipped down the steps of the Nollendorfplatz bahnhof. Scritch-scratch against brick raked his echoing footsteps; three men under watch by brownshirts in arm bands mutely scrubbed off *Lenin shows the way!*

Outside, ah, spring. There was a warmth to the air. Looking up, Michael saw one, then another, then another. Tiny red glows spreading from balcony to balcony. Cigarettes lit after the evening meal.

For a Saturday night, the streets should have been alive with young men loitering outside, flicking butts under the trees. But rounding a corner expecting to see the lights and sounds of the now familiar Eldorado, Michael found a van blocking the front entrance, the building mute. Notices were being pasted to the door by, of all people, Braum.

Michael, crossing into the street, raised his arm to hail, when the doors to the club swung open. Policemen began escorting the patrons, shoving them into the back of the truck. A woman, trumpeting foulness, had to be carried.

That's Tonia, Braum must see that. Why doesn't he help?

"Hey—"

A man with a smoke hanging out of his lopsided face dragged Michael into the alleyway and shoved him against the wall. He pressed his hand against his mouth.

"You idiot. Do you want to get arrested too?"

The pounding in Michael's chest slowly numbed the underside of his arms and spread down to his fingers.

"They're being closed down," said Marius. "Kleist-Kasino, the Monokel-Bar, Mali und Igel. All of them."

"But why? What's happening?"

The doors to the van were shutting, opening a view of the cobbled tree-lined street behind. Braum climbed into the passenger's side. Signs blackening the windows of the Eldorado were by Order of the Prussian Minister of the Interior. Closure by reason of moral degeneracy, with reference to Paragraph 175 of the Penal Code.

"Things are different now. Go home, Michael. You were lucky tonight it was me."

And disappointed.

⚮

Doctor Linder peered past Michael's open door.

"That's very kind but no, I won't come in. Yes, I am well, a little trouble sleeping, that's all. It's just that, there's some difficulty with packages of medical supplies and other implements I use for my practice. They are normally delivered. Now they are not. I've even found packages outside on the road. Ruined. Why would someone do that? I must have these medicines for my patients, you understand." Doctor Linder glanced over Michael's shoulder. "I have already spoken to Herr Leopold and Frau Guthman."

"Are you certain you won't come in and sit? You look—" Tired wasn't quite right, but Michael had noted that expression before. "I'm sure they wouldn't have anything to do with that. Perhaps I should have another lock put on the entrance door?"

The doctor put up his hands and shook his head. "With all due respect, the boy downstairs says he saw a man tell the delivery truck not to bring any more packages." Doctor Linder paused awkwardly. "He believes it's the young man staying with you."

Michael laughed. "You can't take Valentin's word. Braum would never do such a thing."

Doctor Linder nodded. "Then I'm sorry to have troubled you."

"It's no trouble. In fact, I've been meaning to talk to you. The chat we had about the university?"

"Of course. I'll make the inquiries."

Doctor Linder bowed slightly in that polite way lost to Michael's generation and crossed the landing to his flat, taking the banister for support. That's when Michael remembered when he'd seen that emotionless gaze before.

A few weeks back, Braum was throwing papers, photographs and books into a fire blazing in a metal drum. Around him in the courtyard sat boxes of bric-a-brac, picture frames and odds and ends from inside the flat.

Are you burning us out? Michael had called from his bedroom window.

Braum had waved. That Hélène's right. The place was a mess. Feels like a goddamned museum. Who needs it? Braum tossed another handful of brown-and-cream photographs onto the fire. As Catharina's fiancé, maybe he did have a right to this stuff. They were after all, Michael told himself, just old pictures of Nan curling and peeling away in the flames.

Turning, Michael had caught the doctor watching the flames from across the courtyard, with that same vacant look, until he noticed Michael watching him. Doctor Linder dropped the curtain.

Frau Guthman secured a curl back from her face with a pin. "I'm in a hurry to get over to the shop this morning."

Saturday before Easter was a busy trading day. With chapped hands she hung another pillowcase in the entranceway.

Michael was heading out in search of a new necktie he convinced himself he needed because of the summons. It had been delivered by a formal-suited burly man pounding on the door with a smile hovering between smirk and grin.

Your presence is requested. A car will be at your disposal at 10 p.m. Signed, *An old friend.*

Michael hadn't been in Berlin long enough to have old friends. Just Braum and Hélène and, well, more her friends than his, and none of them could afford a car.

Braum was of no help. He, like the papers, was lauding the recent government cleanup of degenerates and those elements bent on dragging Germany into further chaos even if it meant curtailing a liberty here or there for the greater good. This was to be expected. Braum had been strutting a new sense of self-importance since becoming a member of the governing party. It's not that I'm political, he claimed, but you'll have to be a member now of the National Socialist Party to go anywhere, so why not, eh? And he expected to go somewhere.

That being the case, Michael saw no need to ask about the night at the Eldorado. Those places were now out of fashion, and happily so, trumpeted the Church over the closures and the ban on naughty books. After all, the Eldorado was a diversion, a diversion best grown out of. Certainly couldn't feel sorry for those people, acting like that, bringing the law down on themselves. Braum was right. Time to get on with it. Still, Michael would have welcomed his big friend tagging along for this new adventure, but he had been summoned himself, back to Leipzig by Catharina for wedding preparations. He nonetheless instructed Michael before leaving, Don't be an ass, of course you'll go, then tell me all about it.

"You'll be busy at the grocery then?" Michael said to Frau Guthman.

"And about time the government saw right to support German grocers over those foreigners." Frau Guthman smiled with anticipation, her taut clothesline pinging with each added pin. "Even Valentin is going to help out today."

"Yes, me too," the boy said, thrusting his hands into the air.

Berlin, it seemed to Michael, was completely infected with Frau Guthman's optimism, if gauged only by the U-bahn to the Alexanderplatz jostling with morning shoppers. Although the KaDeWe department store would be closer, Hélène would no doubt slip a tie into that coat of hers if she found out why he was there. But after all she had done for Nan, that would be just too embarrassing.

So he decided upon the Tietz's department store. Under a cloudy sky breaking apart with sun, the square in front of that architectural confection was already crowded, women weighted down with gutted chickens secured in brown paper or pulling prams loaded with asparagus. Giant canvas signs announcing the Easter sale were snapping in the wind over yellow daffodils that were practically scrambling out of overcrowded tubs.

Ten, maybe fifteen people had gathered in front of the doors as Michael approached. Two men in arm bands flanked them, one of whom was arguing with a woman stuffed into a tightly buttoned wool coat.

"I'll shop here like I do every Saturday."

"Germans do not shop here today."

The other brown-shirted youth stroked *JUDE* broadly on the glass window with yellow paint. A streetcar rumbled past, bells dully clanking, and someone in back of the line wondered if they were to be let inside.

"Get out of my way."

The woman in the wool coat pushed the young man aside. She was not stopped, but no one followed.

Lamplights marked the kilometres. Grey government ministries, foreign offices, the cafés and shops of the Wilhelmstrasse and the Unter den Linden receded into Prenzlauer Berg tenements, warehouses and a patchwork maze of overgrown windy lanes, soot-blackened factories littered with rusting machinery. Maybe it hadn't been such a good idea to accept such a cryptic invitation. Then even the street lights began to fade until Michael and his driver reached a place blacker than Toby's arse, as Michael's father was fond of saying, thickened with the oily stench of dead factories made noticeable in the dark only by the occasional blink from a window. No rumble of trucks or clodding horses, no hum of life. The silver car slowed to a crawl on a heavily treed street and stopped effortlessly.

Where were they?

Here.

Where's here?

No answer.

The door snapped open and the driver, not a word the entire trip, but still grinning in that annoying I-know-something-you-don't way, pointed. Michael stepped into a cobbled courtyard clogged with rusting axles, barrels and engine bits and bobs, all yellowing underneath a single electric torch against the far wall. To the right, a cloister lit by candles in iron fixtures bleeding ochre onto stone.

This way, came from the shadows. An elderly man with a benign smile and wearing evening attire two sizes too large stepped forward. The well-tuned hum of the car signalled its departure. The doorman insisted, congenially so, and escorted Michael down the cloistered passageway to its end, sealed with a shiny panelled wooden door. With the gentlest of taps, it swung open. Cool air and distant music surged forward.

Descending a staircase, Michael emerged on his own into a vast colonnaded hall, lit by hundreds of candles in floor stands. The towering columns were thick and plain and fanned out underneath the ceiling. Running water gurgled nearby, the air damp, and although the music was even louder here than upstairs it was somehow muted in its resonance.

The hall was ringed with arches opening into an even larger room, cavernous as an amphitheatre and reached by crossing one of two bridges over a canal. On this side of the bridge: a couple quietly conversing, a man enjoying a languid smoke, a woman leaning against a wall wiping her eyes and smearing her makeup. They shifted around a column as Michael passed, escaping view.

Moving beyond, flickering gas lamps lit stone walls bearing only faint traces of red paint. High overhead, the street-level windows had been bricked shut. And the stink: violets and lavender, rancid cooking oil and the trace of an abattoir's effluent. An iron catwalk, leading from a door in the wall, spiralled downwards, snatching the cobbled square island it connected from being washed away under an arch by the dark and moving waters of the canal. From overhanging concrete balconies, patrons chatted and called one another from tabletop telephones, waved and whistled, served by hobbling and snarling midgets tossing plates down as if the tables were bottles in a ring toss.

Michael covered his ears. The din, and its echo, was almost deafening: American music, young men tossing nearly naked girls around, the squawking from the cages overhead confining parrot-like birds, bawling to be set free.

"Michael?"

"Hasso? Thank God, a friendly face. But how?" Michael's pulse finally relaxed to a steady beat.

"You won't believe it. I was touching up the mural at the theatre and this man comes over to me with his card. Did I want a commission? Can you believe he wants me to paint this ceiling?"

The early outlines of Hasso's fresco emerged vaguely, almost two and a half storeys overheard.

"But it's so dark up there. Who'll see it?"

"Spotlights. Say, how do you know *him*?"

"Who?"

"Tristan de Mallon. Isn't that why you're here?"

"I met a Tristan coming over on the ship."

"Ah! So you've seen him?"

Not under the most flattering of circumstances.

"Unusual fellow, wouldn't you say?"

Michael thought so. He did have a monkey, but not anymore.

"Well that's just it. He's not like any man I ever met. I shouldn't wonder though, he'd have to be, I don't know, *odd* to pull this off." Hasso gestured to all around them. "Everyone here is dying to know anything about him. These little people think he's the bastard son of the Kaiser. Or one of them. And as rich as King Tut."

Michael couldn't say. "How'd he find me?"

"Being able to run this place, these days, he must be well connected," Hasso said.

"Any of the others here? Pia?"

"No . . . say, Michael, you haven't seen Marius, have you?"

"What?"

Not since that night in the Nollendorfplatz, but Michael kept that to himself.

"Neither has Hélène or Pia. Well, he must be somewhere. Can't have just vanished."

Then Hasso pointed to the squawking birds dangling from the ceiling. One of the dwarfs was running around tying to catch the green-and-red feathers as they floated down.

"Pretty wild, huh?"

Michael was no longer listening.

On the other side of the canal by the circular staircase, wearing a tailored suit, hair slicked and with a velveteen moustache closely trimmed, stood the teen-aged youth from the Potsdamer Platz. He was smoking, trying terribly hard to appear nonchalant. After catching Michael's eye for a moment longer than necessary, he slowly turned his head. At the same time he lifted his cigarette, bumping it against his chin and knocking it into the water. He straightened up and flicked the ash off his arm, glancing once again at Michael. His moment of indifference failed when Michael started to laugh.

The young man laughed too.

Sweaty, crotch-hugging dancing to riotous music, blurs of turquoise and saffron silk whirled over tables as a little man dashed past, chased by the lion who'd sent dinner plates crashing. Here kitty, a very drunken woman sheathed in sequins squealed as the lion sheepishly padded around in front of her. Tossing her arms about it, she hugged the beast. For a moment the lion relented, then it gored her face, tearing away her nose and cheek. Several men in tuxedos jumped to the screaming woman's aid as the lion continued after the midget.

A little man in biblical garb with a pitted face and long beard had pushed his way out of the dancers and stood tugging at Michael's coat.

"You. Follow me."

Opening a path, he led Michael on a merry roundabout up to the dais and empty table where a wine goblet waited. Below, those in pursuit of the lion caused an uproar amongst the diners. The dancers shouted obscenities for having to dive out of the way.

The telephone on the table rang.

Cigarette clinging to the side of his mouth, Michael's mystery youth climbed over the railing and straddled the other chair. A lock of creamed hair had fallen over his eyes.

"It's for me. Don't answer it," he said.

It rang for a long while, the younger man looking at Michael, Michael looking at the phone. When it stopped:

"You know Tristan?" was all Michael could think of to say.

"Doesn't everyone? I've seen you before." Then: "I want champagne." He waved over one of the Old Testament midgets, who sullenly looked to Michael for approval before pouring. "I wouldn't touch that stuff," the young man said of the proffered wine. "And not the cheap bottles, either!" he yelled after the waiter. "You talk funny," he said, turning back to Michael. "American?"

Without waiting for an answer, he tucked a glass vial into his nostril and threw his head back before offering it to Michael. Michael hesitated, not knowing what it was or what to do, then, surprising himself, he took a snort. Fire shot into his head. The rampaging lion seemed funny. The young fellow lit another cigarette.

"Will Tristan be here?"

"Later. He never socializes when he's *in theatre.*"

"You've been here before?"

"Of course. My friend Kai, he's a very important officer in the Reichswehr, he brings me and spends lots of money. But he's in Cologne tonight, so I'll drink with you."

The champagne arrived.

"Pour it, you idiot."

Glasses were angrily plunked down and hastily filled, spilling most of the fizzing drink on the tablecloth. The blond youth shrugged. "What can you do about his kind?" And then waved the little one away. After that it was all about Kai, his family was old German, he'd been noticed by his commander and was going places, Kai, Kai, Kai, until the champagne bottle was drained. "Why are you staring at me?"

Michael apologized.

The music stopped in mid-cadence. A drumbeat began, joined by reedy watery music evoking pharaohs and languid Nile barges.

"Behold, water into blood!"

Cheers greeted their host, who appeared on the catwalk as Moses dressed in a black and burgundy robe, false beard and staff in hand. Then screams as the murky water from the fountain in the wall darkened to blood red.

Beaujolais!

A girl in white satin was pushed off the bridge into the canal by the crush to see the transformation. Surfacing, gasping for air, her now pink sheer gown clinging to nipples and curves and crevices, she clutched one of her shoes and poured the blood-red drink over her head and down her breasts. Everyone shoved to the canal's edge and dipped glasses and cupped their hands into the gushing torrent.

Tristan's changed water into wine! Hail Tristan.

Booming drums thundered as the kitchen doors spewed forth little men weighted under trays steaming with roasted meats and split fruit.

The younger man forced his way through the miasma of pressed grapes, filled a glass from the fountain and brought it back to the table, soiling the white cloth with slopping red stains.

"Moses went through a lot of trouble for this. He won't like it if you don't drink."

Tristan, amused by his own spectacle, appeared at Michael's elbow, his taffeta dinner jacket rustling crisply as he peeled off his costume and tossed it over an empty chair. Behind them, out on a stretcher went the woman gored by the lion, her face wrapped in a gallant young fellow's dinner jacket.

"My dear Michael, you find me more the man than you knew on the *Steuben*. Am I forgiven for abandoning you at sea?"

"Yes! How did you know where I was? How did you find me?"

Tristan blithely waved that off and extracted a case from his inside pocket. "Still working on those cheekbones, I see." Opening the case, he scooped fine powder onto his small finger and snorted it. He offered the same to Michael, who declined, still reeling from the narcotic the young man had given him.

"Will she be all right?"

"Who?"

"The woman they took out."

"Hard to say. You know, that ball-less beast is usually afraid of its own shadow. I used to have peacocks until he ate them. Have you any idea what a peacock set me back?" Tristan then shoved his hand into the air and snapped his fingers.

A surly dwarf with a stocking cap brought over a glass of cool fruity punch.

"House specialty. You look as if you need this."

Instructions were given to keep Michael's glass full and for him to keep it empty.

"Do I detect my little friends intriguing you?"

"I've never seen one before."

"Indeed." Tristan gestured to the crowd. "Don't you think having them around makes you feel superior? Well, even more superior than the government says we are."

"How do you manage? All the other bars—"

Tristan now lit his cigar. "The greater the oppression, the greater its excesses. And someone gets to provide them. That someone is me. Look around you, my boy. There are only two rules here: no rules, no uniforms. That is why this place thrives. So what's it to be, Michael? Even you must have a secret desire?"

Tristan glanced at the younger man listening, then lavishly bestowed his favour on Michael with a kiss to each cheek.

"I see you've met our Jan. And you, you overpriced whore, have been drinking my champagne. Don't think I won't dock you for that."

Jan stuck out his tongue.

Tonia, in full regalia, sashayed by, looking happier than when Michael last saw her. She squealed and waved, mouthing with her big red lips: Tristan saved my life, isn't he a dear?

Below them on the dais one of three corpulent, overly dressed middle-aged men was protesting as miniature men in brown shirts brandishing truncheons surrounded him. The girls sitting at the trio's table, too young and beauty-shop finished to be their wives, stopped looking pretty.

"Tell me, Michael, what are you up to now that your grandmother is dead?"

"You know that?"

"Of course. The death of a von Renner is news. And I make it a point to know everything new."

"You're rich?" asked Jan.

Michael smiled. "Hardly. There's a bit of money left me to go to university, but my sponsor, my grandmother's doctor, doesn't seem to be helping sort things out."

"We can't have you packing up and going home, back to that dreadful snow and cold. We won't hear of it, will we, Jan? Besides, Michael here doesn't do well at sea."

"My cousin Braum, he's not really my cousin but he's marrying my cousin, says I should join the party. They'd help with the university."

"Then you must."

The miniature brownshirts were poking at the fat bearded man with clubs. His genuine outrage only egged on the laughter from surrounding tables.

Tristan snapped his finger, and a knobbly man, or maybe it was a woman, with one hip riding higher than the other limped over to the table.

"A bottle of the '26 Moët et Chandon. The best." Turning to Jan: "Go."

The tinny music picked up the tempo of "Deutschland über Alles" with a swing beat while the fat man was herded onto the stage. Protesting, calling out to his smiling and clapping friends, the man was shoved into a chair and secured with rope.

"My dear boy, much can happen these days," Tristan said. "You mustn't give up hope for the university, or leave us too soon. Promise?"

Full-size brownshirts silently assumed positions by every exit. Chairs scuffed across the stones, glasses were hastily emptied. The phones stopped ringing.

"No uniforms, you said?"

Tristan leaned close, his hot tobacco breath upon Michael's cheek. "Enjoy the show."

A gunshot sliced into the canal waters. In that cavernous room it stung loud and long. Even the birds dangling in cages fell silent.

The SA guard who had fired his revolver strode towards the stage, focusing attention on the man in the chair. He said something, but no one could hear what because the band, oblivious to it all, began pounding out the anthem. Sit or stand, no one knew what to do, no one dared move. Tristan clapped with delight until the song ended.

But I am not Juden, the man in the chair insisted. His girlfriend said to her girlfriend, I told him to shave off that beard.

The first blow caught him unawares and his head snapped back with a crunch as bits of his skin and a tooth pelted his companion, the young woman, or perhaps it was a girl heavily made up to look older, who had been sitting with him by the stage. She dabbed her coat with her napkin and said to anyone who'd listen that what he'd said was God's truth because she wasn't getting paid to sleep with one of those. Good for you, the other woman at their table replied.

The second blow rendered the man in the chair unconscious. That'll teach you to look foreign! The anthem gaily carried into a second verse. One of the miniature brownshirts tossed a bucket of water onto the seated man, also dousing those sitting nearby. It brought him back to shouting and applause.

Tristan leaned over. "Do you hear that?"

Michael heard nothing except the indignant cries of, Shame!

"Precisely."

The misshapen waiter refilled their glasses, but Michael could not drink. The hall was hot and he was getting drunk.

"Never waste good champagne, my boy. You never know when it will be your last glass."

The anthem came to a thundering conclusion. The little brownshirts gathered at the edge of the stage and curtsied. Tristan's fooled us all again! The audience charged into laughter, wildly clapping. The unconscious man in the chair was kicked over and dragged off the stage.

A few days later, Michael and Hélène agreed to meet at a café midway between the Opernplatz and the old Imperial Palace straddling the Spree. She'd been given tickets to a Mendelssohn concert by a customer who couldn't bear the idea of attending, now that the composer was officially out of favour. While Michael waited, he ordered coffee and spread the pages of the *Berliner Tageblatt* over the round table.

He'd been perusing the newspaper, not really paying attention, when something caught his eye. A photo of a large house on the In den Zelten, near the Tiergarten. Beyond the open door, the hallway appeared awash with books and papers. The article explained that students had forced the closure of Magnus Hirschfeld's Institute for Sexual Science, notorious for its controversial theories about inversion being quite natural in some people. In the photo, two staff members from the institute looked terror stricken.

Of course, no makeup, but that one, that's Tonia.

"Sorry I'm late," Hélène said, kissing him on the cheek. "Happy anniversary."

"Huh?"

"Where's your head at these days? Yours, silly. One year in Berlin."

Michael told her the mayflowers would be in bloom right now in Nova Scotia.

"Oh, that," Hélène said, peering over his shoulder at the paper. "Another casualty."

She meant since the Reichstag fire.

"What do you think about it?"

"God knows. Social perversion? Biology?" Hélène slipped into the chair beside him and undid the top buttons of her sweater.

"I think I met someone . . . who's like that." Christ, on second thought, that terrifying, disturbing, incredible Tristan's had been full of them.

Hélène looked to be served. "Some people think it's a sickness."

"Can it be cured?"

"At least contained. That's what the government plans on doing to them."

"Oh."

"Would you want someone spreading cholera? Typhus?"

"No, of course not."

"Look, a woman has her role, a man has his. These people, they're not normal, Michael, for whatever reason. Round them up. At least I agree with the new government on that."

The waitress known as Marliese to all who chose to eat at her café brusquely interrupted them with a pitcher of coffee. A patchwork of red dots covered her face.

"Just so you know, the smell of coffee makes me sick," she said. "Reminds me of my poor husband. Only thing he could drink while the cancer ate him."

A woman in a double-breasted coat hurried by on the sidewalk, absent-mindedly shoving a loose strand of hair under her hat.

"And now my daughter will only eat stewed meat and vegetables grown above the ground," the waitress continued. "Have you seen those prices? And what is the government doing about that?"

Two men with ashen looks, carrying briefcases, passed in the opposite direction. One of them furtively looked at Hélène. A younger man paused to glance at his watch.

Marliese was still talking. "What's a mother to do? You'll know yourself soon enough, I'm sure."

Hélène didn't know where to look. Michael fought the urge to giggle.

"And my sister, she lives with me now. Imagine, her husband took off the rotting back stairs without telling her. Fell down two flights, she did. The lid of a jar imbedded in her face. I say she has to divorce him."

Out of consideration, Michael and Hélène did not order more coffee, but rather bread and cheese. Marliese returned with their food, adding that her daughter Adelheid could not eat cheese, it gave her gas.

Across the road two brownshirts in arm bands strode down the empty pavement sharing a jest. This side of the sidewalk seemed unusually busy.

"Is anyone else joining us?"

Pia was on her back in Babelberg becoming a UFA actress. Hasso was on some mysterious project he wouldn't discuss, and Marius, well, who had seen Marius?

Michael kept his mouth shut.

"And now they've changed the program for tonight to some dreadfully ponderous Wagner thing. I hate Wagner. Everything these days seems undependable."

"That reminds me. You hear Doctor Linder's been let go from the university?"

Hélène wasn't surprised. "Yes, well, the Juden have been dismissed, haven't they."

"Why?"

"Would you want one of them teaching you?"

"I guess not, but I got the feeling teaching was his life. Now he says he's going back to Vienna. What'll he do there?"

"Nothing, but spend all day in cafés, eat chocolate and thank the government for retiring him. Besides, aren't you glad he and his thieving ways'll be out of your family's hair?"

Yeah, about that. "My aunt and uncle will want that flat rented. Be hard to find as good a tenant."

Hélène agreed, it was all very inconvenient.

"You know, Nan was right. It's an opportunity I don't want to give up even if Doctor Linder can't help me. Maybe I'll do what Braum says."

"That being?"

"Join the party."

"Oh, well, if it means staying."

"I am getting used to Berlin. And the people."

Hélène lightly touched his arm, but Michael was looking behind her.

"What is it?"

People around them had noticed as well and were standing up to see the reddish glow over the surrounding rooftops.

"That'll be the students," said Marliese, bringing out bowls of coffee to a nearby table. Other patrons had not been deterred by her queasy stomach. "Bonfire tonight on the Opernplatz. Herr Goebbels will be there to speak if you hurry."

"Why?"

"They're burning the books, I hear."

"Drink up, Michael," Hélène said, standing.

Cheers carried from the distance.

"Do you want to watch?"

No, she did not.

Michael returned home to find Frau Guthman bouncing excitedly from foot to foot, her head butting against sheets hanging in the entrance hall.

"For you. And look, very important."

With a black crest. The man from the telegraph office explained she was to give it to Michael personally.

"I don't believe it. I'm to report to the administrator at Humboldt University."

The woman was all joy and kisses, leaving him to his good fortune. "Valentin, come and hear!"

The happy boy came skipping and clapping, even though he didn't know what for.

But I haven't even applied.

1934

January 21, 1934

My Dear Brother,

Please promise me that you will find some quiet place to be alone before you read any further. I am so sorry to have to write and tell you this. Mum is gone. Of course Dadda cannot be the one to tell you, but he is doing much better with each day.

It happened just after Christmas. Mum had been doing well, although she got tired easy and more confused by the end of the day. She was looking forward to the holidays as best as she could. She even wanted to make date squares, thinking you'd be eating them. It was a blessing the stroke came during the night. Dadda found her in the morning. She could not talk and could barely move. You would've hated to see her like that. Dr. Elliot said there was nothing he could do, but he'd heard of an eminent doctor in Montreal having some success in treating patients like Mum.

I've never seen our father like he was, hearing that. Dadda insisted we take Mum right away. He made all the arrangements for the train and I went along to help. Dr. Elliot telephoned this eminent doctor, Dr. Wilder Penfield, who *met us in Montreal at the train station. He took Mum to the hospital right away but there was nothing even so eminent a doctor as he could do. I like to think she knew where she was, and was happy about that. We found a place to bury her on the mountain. I know it is in a foreign city, almost to say, a different country, and all her life, Mum never left Nova Scotia, but the cemetery has a wonderful view and I think you'd say we did right by her.*

Michael, all this cost a great deal of money, the train, the hotel, the doctors' bills, and you know how Dadda is about owing people. I have to tell you, he sold his business. I tried to talk him out of it, but you know how he is when his mind is fixed and he's never listened to me anyhow. He sold it to Avon. Avon came over and made the offer when he heard of our situation. Who knew he had that kind of money, but you know how thrifty Mrs. Glyn has always been and it seems she had some sort of annuity or something. Anyhow, Dadda was thankful for the money but when Avon asked him to stay on, Dadda said he'd given away the handkerchief to some snotty kid, he wasn't going to wipe the nose too. Times being what they are, I hope he'll change his mind about that.

But you mustn't worry about us, we'll manage, and you mustn't take this too much to heart. Mum did not suffer much for it was quick and it was no life for her at the end. You must remember her as she used to be. She'd want you to be happy in your new life, as do I. But always know this, Michael, there are dates in the larder to make you squares when you come home.

Yours,
Gene

Gene used the word *eminent* three times in her letter. Maybe it was her way of making sure Michael knew they'd done all they could, that Mum really hadn't suffered.

"That letter was opened when it came," Catharina said. "Sorry about your mother."

"You know, when I was eight, I fell through the ice on Tibby's Pond with Daphne McKendricks. It wasn't a pond at all, not really. Just part of the harbour in Africville where the darkies live and we weren't ever supposed to go down there. But Daphne got a new pair of skates and a white coat trimmed with rabbit and she just had to try them out.

That pond was attached to the harbour and the ice didn't get very thick. Some boys playing nearby tossed me a rope, but Daphne, she floated around out in the harbour for weeks before they got hold of her. Even after she thawed, they had to tie her arms and legs together so she'd fit in that white coffin. My father was so mad, he'd have put me in there with her. Would've, if hadn't been for Mum. Now she's alone in a cemetery in Montreal."

"I'm sure that's all too bad, but could you step away from the door, the dining room furniture is coming up."

The stairs outside the landing were choked with movers. Catharina had ordered the van to wait outside on the street even as Doctor Linder, clutching his valise, had made his goodbyes on the stairs before leaving for Vienna. Now Michael's cousin's ornately carved sideboard was taking six men to shift.

It's not gonna go in, lady.

You'd better not get a single scratch there, you hear me?

The contraption got tangled in Frau Guthman's sheets, yanking down her morning's effort.

"Oh and Michael, I'm not completely insensitive, but I do need to talk to you about that shopgirl."

"Hélène?"

"Yes, that one. That sort of liaison may have been all right in the past, but better things are expected of you. If you are to be a doctor one day, that sort of girl won't do. You mustn't be keeping her here."

Michael realized he'd been holding his breath. "She's just my friend."

"I don't want to hear what you call it. You're part of this family and Braum and I have our reputations to think about. Please, show us some consideration."

Damn those movers and that ridiculously large piece of furniture lodged on the stairs. Michael swallowed until he almost choked, determined not to show that hateful woman any emotion until finally, the sideboard shifted into his cousin's flat leaving the way down blessedly free.

Now to get away, run if need be, find some place that felt close to home, close to Mum, like under the glass sky of Lehrte Bahnhof, among a tide of hats and coats and carrying cases and rolled-up newspapers and bags of gumdrops. In all of Berlin, that would be as near to Nova Scotia as Michael could get, somewhere no one would notice one more empty face missing his mum.

But when he wiped his eyes and looked up, there was a half-empty glass in front of him, and beyond the grease-streaked window of the beer hall a tram crossed the square. Michael had only gotten as far as the Potsdamer Platz, half hoping to see Jan.

The bad news from Gene was partly to blame for the half-chewed pencils and scribbled notes, heavily annotated with curlicues, fanciful castles floating on clouds and hearts dripping quarts of red, spilling off the sofa and covering the floor in front of Michael. The arrival of spring sure didn't help. This school business was slow going. Felix, he'd have breezed through these make-up classes at the university. For sure he'd have justified whatever Nan had done before she died to get her grandson into the university. Michael always needed Mum to prod him. She even threatened once to paint over his bedroom window if that'd stop him from mooning over freighters steaming into Halifax harbour, where they came from, where they were headed, at the expense of his homework. I just want you to amount to something, she'd said. Make her proud. He smiled at the memory of her words meant to goad him into the priesthood after her attempts with Felix failed miserably. Michael got as far as a short-lived career as an altar boy. Fainting every time Father Fergusson waved around the incense put the kibosh on that. But the church was an honourable calling, Mum insisted. Couldn't he just tough out the smell? And, well, it didn't look like Michael was ever going to . . . Wouldn't he want to make his mother happy? Perhaps one day he'd become a bishop.

"No!" Valentin was saying, down below.

Michael sat up and looked through the open windows of the palm room.

Because it's time to come in. Frau Guthman, outside on this early evening, was cajoling Valentin.

Nearby, on the green waters of the canal floated a gull mindful of nothing. Soon it would fold itself for the night on its bridge perch. Not yet. Two girls, one with a stick, were hanging over the railings hitting the water and watching the rings circle outward. Their muddy stockings had fallen down around their ankles. A man on a unicycle, in a coat that might have once been red, hurried past with an abrupt jingle of bells. On his back he wore a sign advertising tooth powder. The girls stared, then went back to tapping.

No fair and it's still light out and Valentin was not to be convinced. He ran to the weeping willow bending into the canal at the corner of the back yard and dived under its canopy.

He did not stay long.

There's a monster in there!

Frau Guthman was having none of Valentin's stories. Monsters indeed. She took her son by the arm and dragged him in for the night.

Michael smiled and leaned over the sill. Ah, to still believe in things that go boo in the night and to hell with body parts and blood flows and German words three inches long. Valentin's monster had stuck his head out from under the branches and, seeing Michael in the window above, signaled: come here.

Jan wasn't so haughty now shivering by the trunk under the cascade of willow boughs, knees tightly clutched against him. Gone was the thin moustache, and his much-worn clothing had been torn. Mud patches and dried blood were smeared across his face and encrusted under his nose.

"What happened to you?"

Jan glanced about. "You'll help me?"

"There's no one here," Michael said.

But what about that woman?

Frau Guthman lives in the house and does laundry.

"Not her. The other one. Face screwed up tight."

"My cousin? How long have you been watching?"

"Are you going to help me or what?"

"Come inside."

"I can't let her see me."

"Why?"

"Because I can't!" He grabbed Michael's hand. "Tristan threw me out of that hole he runs."

"Why?"

"My friend got drunk."

Ah, so that was it. "And your friend did this to you?"

Jan nodded. "Tristan said he couldn't have that happening in his place and I had to go."

"So you came here."

"Aren't you going to help me?"

Think. Think. Michael ran his hand through his hair. First things first. Get Jan into the house.

"Don't you get it? There's too many people out there. No one can see me."

So they waited under the willow.

The bell over the door chimed inside the empty grocery, announcing Michael's entrance. Hélène, kneeling on a pile of crates against the window, smiled as she held up a sign while the Guthmans, vacillating near a black crepe–draped portrait of President Hindenburg enshrined on the counter, shook their heads.

"Higher?" Herr Guthman said.

"It's no good. It won't do."

Valentin was stacking turnips in a wooden box, adding each one meticulously to the pile. As it grew higher he asked if it would get in the way of birds.

One look at Hélène and Michael guessed she'd been holding that sign for quite some time and would be glad that this day was almost over.

"But why can't it say No Juden, *Please?*" Frau Guthman wanted to know.

Her husband silently threw up his hands.

"I don't want to offend anyone. I just don't want them shopping here." She turned and saw Michael. "Ah, it's you! This letter I get from the doctors, they want to see Valentin. I don't understand why. You're studying to be a doctor. You can tell us what it means."

Her husband asked his opinion about the sign.

Michael wished there'd been one at the university pointing out that the benches against the back wall were for the students with yellow stripes on their books. It would have saved him the embarrassment of having his professor say he was not permitted to sit with the Juden.

"I think I have the letter here," Frau Guthman was saying as she went out back, fingers making her point to the air.

Hélène crawled down from the pile of crates and straightened out her back, her thick black hair falling loose. She pulled Michael aside and quietly thanked him for rescuing her.

Working in the grocery was a far cry from being a clerk at a department store. You're one of the best girls we have, Herr Hanfstaegl, manager of women's fashions, had insisted, but there are men with families and the government says women belong at home now. Hélène found herself let go from KaDeWe. Thank God for the Guthmans. They needed help, couldn't pay much, but it allowed Hélène to pay her share of the rent in her Charlottenburg flat.

"But the two of them drive me crazy."

Frau Guthman returned with an official-looking envelope and along the way told her son, "If you put a flag on the top, Valentin, the birds will know not to fly there."

Michael offered to take the letter and make some inquiries.

"You go with him," Herr Guthman said. "It's almost time."

"What are you saying? Look at the clock? Are we now paying the girl for holidays?"

The man shook his head and shooed Michael and Hélène out of the store.

"Nice of you to settle Frau Guthman's mind," Hélène said, slipping her arm through Michael's. "She's been in a state since that letter came. Won't shut up about it."

Michael felt the envelope in his pocket and wished he hadn't offered. He had a pretty good idea what it was about. There'd been a lecture about the right of the mentally feeble to procreate and Michael sure didn't want to tell Frau Guthman that her son might be a candidate for forced sterilization. He couldn't deal with her kicking up a fuss right now.

"It's such a beautiful evening, why the rush? Let's walk along the canal."

"Not tonight," Michael said, hurrying them past shops closing up for the day.

"That silly grin on your face must be good news. You passed your exam, didn't you? See, I told you you would."

How could he even think about school when there was that young man, a friend of someone he'd met on the ship over and who needed help, a place to hide for a few days.

"Michael, you didn't, did you?"

"Well, yes."

"You idiot. Where is he?"

"I gave him something to eat. He's in the attic."

"In your flat? Did your cousin see him?"

"No. Why? Hélène, you're scaring me."

"You should be scared. You read the papers."

They were walking quickly along the canal as Hélène tied a kerchief about her hair.

"You don't seem to care that people might be watching what you do. And this Jan? How well do you really know him, or what he's gotten mixed up with?"

Truthfully? Not well at all.

"I thought not."

They found Jan quite at home luxuriating in a hot bath, the room filled with candles.

"I'll wait in the hall," Hélène said.

"Who was that?" Jan stood in the tub and waited for Michael to hand him a towel.

"She's a friend."

"Acts like she's got an itch up her twat."

"I thought she could help you."

"Can she cook? I'm hungry." Jan slowly towelled himself dry.

"I'll wait outside."

When Jan joined them in the palm room Hélène was saying, "He's got to go. Now."

"Why?"

"Yes, why? I like it here," Jan said, throwing himself into an armchair. He was wearing Michael's bathrobe. "You said you weren't rich. Looks to me like someone was holding back. I could stay here. There's lots of room."

"I'm not rich."

"Why are you here?" Hélène said.

"Like I told him, my friend got drunk and beat me. I had no place else to go."

"You're lying."

"Hélène, I don't understand why you're being so—"

"If you want us to help you, tell us the truth."

"Don't let her talk to me like that."

"The papers are saying Storm Troopers wanted to overthrow the very men they put in power and the Chancellor has ordered a purge to contain it."

"Hélène, what's this got to do with Jan?"

"He shows up now?"

"But he's not one of them," Michael said, looking uncertainly at Jan.

"Then he can go somewhere else."

Jan sat back quietly. "I can't."

"Why?"

Because he'd been at Tristan's waiting for his soldier, Kai, the night they'd come looking for Ernst Röhm, leader of the Storm Troopers.

"Michael . . . Michael," said Hélène, slapping her balled fists against her lap.

"Tristan told me to come here. He said you'd know what to do."

"About what? Has something happened to Tristan?"

Jan nodded, then said, "No. Maybe, I dunno. That fat pig Röhm is his business partner." He looked away from Michael as a smile broke over his face, then laughter. "You should've seen Tristan with that pistol, oh, and the first time he ever held one for sure. Voice getting all girly, hands shaking." Jan mimicked a terrified Tristan saying, "I'll shoot whatever comes through that door."

"Shoot what? What are you talking about?"

"When they came!"

"Who?"

"I don't know, do I? Those men that came to Tristan's."

"Did they do this to you?" Meaning the cuts and bruises.

Jan tinkered with the cord on his robe, then glanced at Hélène.

"Your friend didn't do this, did he?"

He nodded, chewing the inside of his cheek.

Michael needed a chair. "Was Tristan still there when you left?"

"He'll be all right. He had the gun, didn't he?"

"Well, Röhm is dead. Executed," Hélène said. There was no need to add what she thought Tristan's chances were.

Michael glanced at Jan. "I have to help him."

"There are plenty in this city who really need help, and through no fault of their own. Besides, your cousin watches everything."

"He could stay upstairs in our part of the attic."

"What about Herr Leopold?"

"Jan'll be very quiet."

Hélène shook her head. "I don't understand you in this, Michael."

"Just until we get him out of Berlin. Look, he's practically a kid. What would anyone want with him?"

"He knows more, and he's already lied to you."

"Please, Hélène, just for a few days."

Jan's eyes welled with tears.

"You're a fool if you fall for that, Michael."

They came swarming unexpectedly, tearing laundry off lines, banging up the stairs, pushing aside Frau Guthman, who had been standing at Michael's door with another letter from the Hereditary Health Court.

My darlings, it's been like a fairy tale, Pia explained after she, her driver, her maid and two other men—Michael and Hélène never figured out what they did—settled in with gifts and chocolate for the visit.

"I was having coffee at the Schön Café, you know the one, chère Hélène, on the Unter den Linden, when Egon introduced himself to me—"

"Egon?"

"Egon Angerbauer."

Pia had finally connected with her famous director.

"He was next in line to do *Der Blaue Engel* if von Sternberg took one more tantrum. Between you, me and the bedstand, he's the real prima donna on set."

Michael wanted to know if this posh accent of Pia's was for a role, but was ignored.

"And he said I was made to be in the movies. Just like that. Can you believe our meeting got written up in the *Lustige Blätter*?"

Indeed. The magazine detailed what Pia wore (black hat, tan gloves, knitted teal suit) and what she ate (crème brûlée, side dish, pears) when she was discovered.

"Pia, did you really meet him on the Unter den Linden?"

"Of course. Why would you ask?"

"I know you."

Hélène was right. Pia had run into the director, literally, at a hotel on the Meinekestrasse, well known as a trysting place for second- and third-rate film luminaries. Angerbauer was apparently smitten by Pia during the encounter, which angered his female companion. During an argument the woman fell or was pushed down a flight of stairs and broke her neck. Her name was Rachel Schellenberg and so nothing more came of the incident other than a police report.

"And shortly after, darling, I was in front of the UFA cameras in Neubabelsberg. But do let's go by the *official* version. Now tell me, how can every shop in Berlin be closed?"

Hélène poured coffee. "Yes, Pia, very inconvenient for President Hindenburg to have his funeral today. More chocolate?"

"What's the point of having money if you can't spend it?"

Through the open window, they heard Frau Guthman telling Valentin to keep his hands off the big black car because he didn't want to get the lady upstairs mad at him, now did he?

"It's dreadfully hot up here."

Hélène suggested her friend take off the fur.

Pia slammed her cup down and pulled her coat in front of her.

"Hélène, is it just me, or do I sense some resentment?"

"Oh, my God!" Jan, down from the attic where he was under orders to remain, covered a silent squeal with his hands. "You're Pia Tornsgaard!"

Michael looked hastily to Hélène. Jan helped himself to a chocolate.

"Tornsgaard?" she asked. "When did that happen?"

Jan brushed past Michael and knelt at Pia's feet.

"And who is this?" she asked.

"He's a friend of mine staying here for a few days, who is *supposed* to be upstairs."

"I saw you in that divine movie *Quarantäne*." Jan turned to the others and gushed. "She was a nurse who gets infected with typhoid and she has to leave her family and go into the mountains and care for other typhoid victims and no one helps them because they're afraid they'll get sick and they all die. Oh, my God, you were magnificent!"

"Tornsgaard? What happened to Mueller?"

"Shut up, Hélène. Anything Swedish is nouveau these days." And there went the accent. "Haven't you seen at least one of my films?"

Hélène didn't think she had.

"Michael never mentioned anything about a charming young man." Pia cast a wondering eye his way. "Why's he been keeping you under wraps?"

Hélène laughed. "I hardly think what goes on here would interest a really big movie star."

To a woman who adored being adored by men, Hélène let slip that this young, attentive and attractive boy was in need of a job. Anything really and couldn't Pia find something for him to do?

Of course Pia could manage something.

Jan added, it would be divine to have an autograph.

Pia glanced at her watch. The entourage plus one, laughing, listening to nothing and leaving just as wildly as it had arrived, left behind gifts and laundry trodden in the hall downstairs. As thousands flooded into Berlin for the president's funeral, Pia's chrome-trimmed Daimler, with Jan inside, sped unnoticed the other way.

In the aftermath, Michael and Hélène sat dazed on the palm room's sofa, a silk scarf in an open box in Hélène's lap, and undoubtedly the world's largest sausage in the kitchen.

∽

Herr Ehrlich's summons came near the end of the lecture. Thank Christ. Michael couldn't get out of that darkened hall or away from those flickering black-and-white images fast enough. Doctor Jennings had been speaking on the advancements and viability of castration as a suitable form of birth control for the mentally feeble. His lecture, accompanied by a film, packed the large university amphitheatre.

For the first incision, a small cut is made underneath the scrotum. Care has to be taken, for although this is a relatively minor procedure, the area contains many blood vessels. The testicles are then extracted and sliced free. Into the white enamelled dish they went. Two jelly blobs. *Eight stitches close the wound.*

Someone asked about anaesthesia.

Certainly there was some discomfort during the procedure, but the retarded, and inferior races, don't feel pain like others.

That's when the student sitting next to Michael leaned over and passed along the note requesting Michael's attention in the administrator's office.

Thank Jesus.

"Are you unwell?" asked Herr Ehrlich, offering the chair across from his desk.

He'd be fine, if Michael could just open the windows in the office and stick his face into the leaves blowing around in the courtyard. Gurgling water through the heating pipes brought Michael back, but he avoided Herr Ehrlich's gaze and looked to the severe black angles on the flag behind the desk, the only decoration in a room without books.

"Now, unless you begin to apply yourself, I will have no choice but to discharge you from the program."

Michael apologized. It wasn't the first time he'd fidgeted on a hardwood chair across from a teacher being told he daydreamed too much. Herr Ehrlich clearly felt he, at twenty-six, should be beyond such distraction.

"You don't seem to appreciate the gravity of your situation, young man. Much effort was made to provide you entrance here. It will be looked upon unfavourably should you fail. Do you understand me?"

I understand tutors are always goddamn busy with youth groups, marching or listening to silly speeches and classes get cancelled because of mindless rallies and parades and the smell of formaldehyde makes me faint. And the only students who study are the Juden, but I'm not allowed to ask them for help.

Maybe he was coming down with something. Michael promised to try harder.

"See that you do."

He left the interview only to discover afternoon classes were cancelled. The notice on the bulletin board directed everyone instead to a lecture on eugenics.

Attendance be damned, Michael wasn't going to get through that one. And even though a fall chill was in the air, the day was too nice to waste a coin on a streetcar. What he needed was to clear his head. Walking down the crowded mid-afternoon Unter den Linden would do it. As Michael passed under the Brandenburg Gate, he entered the quiet, still-green Tiergarten and lit a cigarette. He'd cross through to the Bellevuestrasse this way. The old men lining the park's benches were lucky bastards. Sitting all day in the sun, having a smoke. Now there's a life. One asked him for spare change.

Shit. Frau Guthman would be waiting for him at the house. That damned letter. She'd been after Michael for weeks now to look into it for her. Why did Valentin have to go back to the doctors? He was perfectly healthy. After this morning's lecture, Michael knew beyond any doubt why, but he hoped he didn't have to put off telling the boy's mother yet again. After all, it wasn't his place to say anything.

Looked like it wasn't going to be necessary. There was no laundry hanging when he arrived home.

No sheets, no undershirts, nothing. Not a single piece of linen hanging over the stairs, dripping onto the marble floor. Only once before had this happened, the day Nan was buried. Not even President Hindenburg was accorded that honour.

Michael put his ear against her door. Something inside, like the mewling of a kitten.

"What are you doing there?"

Catharina startled him. She descended the staircase tugging on a pair of gloves.

"Where's all the laundry? There's always laundry."

It made no difference to his cousin what that woman was up to. Catharina'd made it clear, the sooner the Guthmans were out on the street, the better. Boarders in the von Renner house were no longer fitting.

Frau Guthman's latch fumbled from inside. But she never locked her door, and in spite of her long hours and helping her husband at their grocery, she always maintained a tidy appearance. This wasn't the woman in front of Michael now.

"Oh, I thought you were someone else," she said, rubbing her swollen eyes, wiping her nose with a handkerchief.

"Has something happened?"

She nodded. "They took Valentin this morning."

"Who? Why?"

"We made a visit to the doctor. They said my boy had to have a procedure."

"What kind?" Catharina asked.

The tears welled up anew. "My Valentin will never be a man."

"I'm so sorry," said Michael. "What can I do?"

Nothing. She closed and locked her door.

"For Heaven's sake, stop looking like this is your fault. I dare say, that boy won't carry on half as much as she is." Catharina continued down the stairs. "Oh and Cousin, Braum and I still expect you for dinner tonight."

"Because of what happened to Valentin?" Braum said, relaxing after dinner. "So, you're not cut out to be a doctor. There are better things you can do with your time."

Michael could not believe the transformation in the place. Fresh paint, mouldings, a new wall here, an old one gone and the most exquisite furnishings, polished wood and bevelled glass, completely obliterating any trace of Doctor Linder. Braum was doing well.

"This may be the last meal served by her hand. She's after me to get her a cook. The next thing she'll want is for me to throw you out and restore this old place to the way it was before your grandmother cut it up."

He was smiling when he said that, but not laughing.

"Smoke?"

Braum then refilled Michael's glass. Catharina had cleared the table and vanished into the back of the flat. Contact with her cousin was as politely necessary.

"Look, I'm no university man and I get by, well indeed. Just say the word and I'll get you on at Tschelock's. The way things are heading, Germany'll be the centre of the new order. Everyone knows that. And Berlin, the centre of Germany. Always on the lookout for a good man." Yes sir. Braum inhaled deeply. "And see for yourself. There's a lot of perks to the job."

Michael stared at the wine glass in front of him. This time he refilled it himself.

"We're family, Michael, so I speak freely. If you don't mind me saying, man, this being out of sorts is because you're alone too much. You need a woman."

Herr Ehrlich would disagree. More time with a book, maybe.

"What's happening with that Hélène?"

"Nothing."

"Catharina doesn't think so."

"I know, but she needn't worry."

Braum nodded through his cigarette smoke.

"Maybe you should toss a fuck into her."

"Can we not talk about this? She's like my sister."

"All right, all right, but you know, sometimes I look at you and I could swear there's someone. If it's not that Hélène, then who?" Braum leaned back into his chair. "The old days, eh? You know, sometimes I miss those places, the Nollendorfplatz."

"Me too."

Suddenly Braum wasn't so congenial. "Yes, well, the police know all about them. Lists, my boy. They'll get them all." Then he grinned. "No one says you have to get married."

"What?"

"I'm saying, Michael, a man's got certain needs a wife can't always meet."

"Are you—"

"No, no, keep it down! You want your cousin to hear? Mistresses are complicated, expensive. What you want is a cunt, and no matter what your cousin thinks, that Hélène's a fine-looking one. Oh, come now. Don't look at me like your stomach's draining out the bottom of that chair. What Catharina doesn't know won't hurt her. Besides, think about it. Young unmarried fellow such as yourself, you don't want anyone thinking there's something wrong now, do you?"

Noonday always found the Victoria Café on the Friedrichstrasse crowded. Outside, the awning-covered sidewalks were jostling with office workers wrapped against the cold looking for a place to lunch.

A thin line of brown milk from Michael's *milchkaffee* discreetly highlighted his upper lip. Hélène had not touched hers.

"You're surprised?" he asked.

Two women, permanents held down by bell-shaped hats, scooted in through the door with a blast of cold air and slipped into the chairs around the last available table by the window. Removing their coats, they laughingly waved for the waiter.

"I didn't know you'd been thinking about going back home."

She might have said more if not for Jan.

"My two favourite people." He squeezed in beside Hélène and kissed her cheek. "I've forgiven you for all those nasty things you said about me." Then, "Are you just going to stare at me, Michael?"

He helped himself to a piece of Michael's cake.

"What are you doing here?" said Hélène.

"That poxy slut actually accused me of stealing from her."

"Pia?"

"Can you believe it?"

"Well?"

Jan laughed. "Not as much as she's wailing about. What did she expect? I was to be a decoration for nothing?"

Hélène was amused. "You were supposed to be working."

"By the way, she's a terrible actress. If you can even call her that." He mimicked Pia with contorted faces and wild hand movements. Hélène laughed. "She spends all her money on cocaine, you know. Takes a crew of makeup artists and a tub of pancake to prep her for the camera. Aren't you going to say hello, Michael?"

"Is it safe for you to be back?"

"The only dying happening here is me, for a coffee. And maybe some more cake if someone, Michael, cared to spot me."

The young couple sitting at the table beside them had called the waiter over, and, with a nod towards the recently arrived women sitting by the window, were fussing about the smell. It's garlic, isn't it? This used to be a respectable café and that tribe shouldn't be allowed.

"What are you going to do now?" Hélène asked quickly.

"Staying with friends in Wedding. I'll find something." Jan met Michael's eyes. "It's great to see you again."

The three of them found themselves in between words.

"Oh, dear. Did I interrupt a rendezvous?"

"Michael's having troubles at school and thinks he should quit and go back home."

Jan put his elbows on the table. "Really?"

The colour crept back into Michael's face.

"It's just exam jitters." Loose talk, Mum would have said.

Coffee and cake were ordered and promptly set down by the waiter. Jan clapped. Michael paid.

Hélène watched the two women by the window, after a brief word with the waiter, hastily pull on their coats and leave the café in tears.

1935

Jan, a shock of straw hair having fallen across his face, slouched against the stone wall by the steps of the university. Spring rain blowing sideways down the boulevard was making it tough to light a cigarette. His clothes, gifts from Pia, had begun to show their wear. It wasn't the first time Michael found Jan waiting for him after class.

"You shouldn't make fun."

"Oh, come on, look at them," said Jan. "Those boots and their flags and those stupid little hats. They're ridiculous."

Jan had been pulling faces at a group of students. They were assembling for a march to the Brandenburg Gate to celebrate Germany's repudiation of the Treaty of Versailles. The very reason for Catharina's upcoming social event.

Michael hoisted his rucksack over his shoulder and pulled Jan away.

"Just be careful."

They headed into the rain.

"Does that mean be careful of you?" Jan was grinning.

"Me?"

"You're one of them."

"I am not."

"Why lower your voice?"

Jan began to skip around him while an approaching elderly woman in a midway black coat was struggling up the sidewalk ahead. Her ankles were swollen, and from the shortness of her breath and the redness of her puffy face, she was having a helluva time carrying her groceries. A young woman clutching her coat against the biting rain tried to balance her hat on her head as she darted past Michael from across the road. Had he not been watching, Michael would have missed her very quickly turn and spit. The elderly woman staggered, her hand going to her face, spilling several brown paper packages onto the sidewalk.

"Did you see that?"

Michael went to help until Jan grabbed him by the elbow.

"Say, you couldn't lend me five Reichsmarks?"

"Is that why you're here?"

"Screw you, then."

Michael reached into his coat pocket and pulled out a handful of coins.

"Thanks, Sweets." Money in hand, Jan was all smiles and joy.

The woman stooped to pick up her parcels.

"Jan, look, my cousin is having a party. There'll be lots of people there. The man Braum works for, too. He might be able to put work your way. Real work. A job."

"You mean, so I won't ask you for money? Well, don't need one. I'm meeting a new friend. He's a clerk at the Reichsbank and he's got a house in Potsdam for a few weeks. So, we're off."

Michael knew what a *friend* was to Jan.

"Don't look at me like that. If someone wants to be nice to me, so what? Besides, you give me money."

"It's not the same thing. And it's money I don't have to give."

"But you will, because I like the look on your face when you do."

They walked on.

"I've been reading in the papers," Michael said, "the police are cracking down on, well, you know. Hundreds, they're saying in the last raids. Aren't you concerned?"

The group of students coming up behind were singing now.

"I don't go to those other dumps anymore and no one bothers Tristan's."

"Tristan? He's back? He's okay?"

Jan spotted a half-smoked cigarette on the pavement and picked it up.

"Sure, awhile now."

"I thought he was shut down."

"Not for long. Knows the right people. Eh, maybe I had it wrong about him and Röhm."

"Say hello—"

"Can't. Like I said, off to Potsdam. Thanks, Sweets."

"Hey! When'll you be back?"

But Jan had run into the busy boulevard. He turned once and waved, then was gone.

The early-morning argument brought Michael out to referee.

But there were paying customers who needed their clothes and just when would her highness propose the laundry get done? In the middle of the night? Frau Guthman folded her arms, her hands curled into fists.

This never would have happened if Nan were alive! Catharina was so angry she even stamped her foot. Imagine, that laundress forcing respectable guests and party officials to traipse through wet underwear and bedsheets on the event of Catharina's first big social occasion.

Michael himself dreaded the thought of this evening. This wasn't going to be a kitchen party like when Mum's brothers came by with fiddles, his dad reading his paper in the shitter out back until all that Scottish warbling and foot stomping was over. And God help the day if Uncle Patrick brought that fucking bagpipe of his. Renners without the von never sent invitations saying *evening dress required*.

"Look, as crazy as this sounds, Braum had said, "your cousin's got it in her head to be the wife of the Gauleiter of Berlin. She says we've got to meet the right sort of people if I'm to advance that high up the party ranks. So, I'm sorry, my boy, there's no out for you. Besides, you're the entertainment. With those Juden in America trying to get a boycott against us, she figures she'll be a star after you say how wrong they are."

Michael didn't even know what the American boycott was about, or why.

"Maybe they think a country should treat its citizens with dignity," Hélène said later, when Michael complained to her about the evening.

"None of the other tenants are invited. I won't know a soul."

"Apart from Braum and Catharina."

"They don't count. If only—"

This sounded like an invitation to Hélène.

"Pia and I once showed up at a party at the Danish embassy. You would not have believed the food. And champagne. Your cousin will have food, yes?"

Michael was sure she would. He didn't think there'd be champagne.

"Oh, come on, it'll be fun. What do you think she's going to do? Throw me out?"

"You're late."

"Michael had trouble with his tie," Hélène said. "Nice of you to invite me."

Catharina thought she'd come to help serve.

Michael could feel the heat blanketing his face. Thank God for Braum.

"Hello! Michael. And Hélène. What a surprise. Come in, come in."

He wrapped his arm around Michael's shoulder and ushered him into the crowded suite of rooms that made up the parlour. There was a new set of upholstered chairs, and dramatic full-length burgundy drapes swept back from the windows. A platter of cheeses, expensive to come by these days, was spread over a table. Braum was indeed doing well.

"Everyone, this is our American von Renner, Michael."

There was a polite round of applause as Braum shoved a large glass of vodka into his hand.

It went down too quickly.

"Steady, my boy." And Braum refilled it while boasting to those guests nearby, "You know, our Michael is a brilliant medical student at Humboldt University."

"You look as if you needed that," said a man in a black uniform.

"Lieutenant Luft—"

"Please, Frau Kunstler, it's Peter." He took Michael's hand and smiled. "We bumped into each other before. At the Kroll, the night of the Reichstag fire."

"Yes, well." Catharina then had to almost choke out an introduction for Hélène. Thankfully, demands from the other guests pulled the Kunstlers away.

The handshake ended.

Hélène offered to refresh everyone's drink.

"That's very kind of you," said Peter, handing over his glass. When she was gone: "You were with her that night. Your wife?"

Michael glanced over at Hélène. "No."

"Your date, then?"

"Friend."

Peter gestured to the seats in the window alcove. "Do you hate these things as much as I do? Smoke?"

Michael was grateful to have something to do with his hands other than bury them in his pockets.

"A student, I think your cousin said. Medicine?"

Michael nodded. "You?"

"Military intelligence." The Abwehr.

Peter leaned back in the window seat and grinned at Michael's discomfort. "I get that reaction a lot."

More guests were arriving. There was laughter from across the room. The Comedian Harmonists were singing on the radio. Turn it up, turn it up, someone was saying.

"But here, sit, join me. Exactly, where are you from?"

Michael explained, after nervously making a jest, was this an interrogation?

Peter chuckled. "Canada? Yes, I've heard of Nova Scotia. During the war there was an explosion, destroyed most of your Halifax."

"Not many people here know that."

Peter offered another cigarette. "So tell me, what do you think of Germany?"

"You have a lot of parades."

That sounded ridiculous and Michael instantly regretted saying it.

Peter laughed. "That we do."

"Sometimes it's better than home."

"And other times?"

"Alright, the other day I watched a girl walk by an elderly woman and spit at her. For no reason at all. Just spit at her."

"She probably looked Juden."

"My cousin doesn't understand the Juden problem," Braum said, passing by with a bottle of wine on his way to find a corkscrew.

"Is that so? Perhaps it's that British sensibility of yours that clouds your judgment. Are we here in Germany to forget the indignity of Versailles?"

"Well, no."

"Surely, Michael, even you must acknowledge the war they brought down upon this country?"

Of course he did, after all, hadn't Dadda always said so? "It's just that—"

"Do explain."

"Must they be made to suffer?"

Peter flicked ash into a nearby tray.

"If you found a cockroach in your flat, you'd spend all afternoon trying to catch it and set it free in the park? I think not, my friend. You'd step on it."

Catharina, escorting another late-arriving couple, an older man and a young woman, gave Michael a glare. He guessed what it meant: how dare Michael monopolize one of her prize guests.

"So tell me, how is the life of a student?"

"Harder than I expected." In spite of the uniform, Michael found Peter easy to talk to, probably on account of the vodka. "I'm not so sure I'm cut out to be a doctor. My grandmother thought it would be a good profession for me."

"And you?"

"I wasn't any good as a plumber."

Peter laughed. "You don't have the look of a tradesman about you. And there are other ways to serve Germany. You know, I've heard about your grandfather. Wilhelm von Renner would be delighted to see what is happening here. He was very much against the treaty, you know. He resigned over it."

Michael wondered if Peter knew about the brain matter on the S-bahn window.

"Don't you think you owe it to the von Renner name to find some way to help rebuild the Germany your family believes in?"

"To tell you the truth, I'm not very political. Besides, my grandfather served the Kaiser. I don't know what he'd say about the new leader."

"What do you say?"

"Well, the woman who lives downstairs, Frau Guthman, her son was taken away by the government and castrated because he's mentally retarded. Can that be right?"

"I'm sure there's more to it than that, but as a medical student, you more than anyone should understand the need to keep a people healthy. But if you like, I can voice your displeasure over at headquarters."

Christ! How could Michael have been so reckless? The man was with the fucking Abwehr. This is what he didn't need right now. Where was Hélène with that drink?

Peter laughed again and tapped Michael on the shoulder. "I wish you could see the look on your face, but forgive me. I was just having some enjoyment at your expense. Now I suggest you get over there and rescue that attractive *friend* of yours."

Hélène was being held hostage in conversation over by the cheese.

With a curiously inviting handshake, the lieutenant excused himself and crossed the room.

"New friend?" Braum said, handing Michael a crystal glass, then filling it. "A good man to know. He's with the Abwehr."

Yes, didn't he know. Bottoms up. Michael's head was really spinning now.

"I hear he's rooting out the inverts in the military. They're sending them to work camps in Oranienburg. That'll turn those bloody sodomites around. Oh, here, someone I want you to meet. Tschelock and his daughter."

Near the blue-tiled stove a white-haired, broad-faced man was chatting with a young woman, naturally flushed in the cheeks.

"Bruno Tschelock, my cousin Michael von Renner. And this is his daughter, Lonä."

Unlike the lieutenant's hand, Lonä's was cold and damp. Still, blond, robust, high soft facial features, the woman was easily the room's beauty.

"The famous Michael we hear so much about? My man, when are you going to come and work for me?" Bruno Tschelock shouted when he spoke. "I've done well by Braum here. Go on, man, tell him."

"The moving business is very lucrative, Michael. We could use you."

Michael said he'd think about it.

"Not good enough. Come on board part-time. I've a notion to expand in the next few months."

Lonä glanced at Michael, then she stared. Maybe she noticed too that the room was spinning. Something vague followed about Braum asking everyone to raise a glass for a toast. Did Michael tell Lonä about living in Canada or was that somebody else and had Hélène returned, lightly touching his elbow as she spoke, her breath hissing in his ear? His cousin was glaring again. She'd really overdone it with her perfume. Chanel No. 5 was it? Hélène didn't think many people could afford it. Like incense. Michael felt sick. Really sick. Catharina was furious, but she'd be mortified if he vomited on her new carpets.

Michael made it to the door, relieved when it closed, shutting him on the dimly lit landing. Catching his breath, he tried to keep his stomach from full flight.

"Accept it. You just can't drink."

Hélène helped him down the hallway to his room.

Oh, Christ. He heaved again.

As she helped him onto the bed he thought he caught a whiff of apples, green apples, the ones in Guthman's shop. Like the ones in Mum's pies.

"You smell good."

"Get into bed, fool. You'll feel worse in the morning. Serves you right."

"You shouldn't be here."

But Hélène slipped onto the bed beside him and, leaning over, brushed her hair away from his face.

"Herr Leopold sees everything. He'll tell Catharina."

"So, let him." And she lightly kissed his lips.

Gene had written. Their father was full of praise for all he was hearing. The rest of the world might be weary of the Depression, but in Germany, it sounded from Michael like it wasn't even happening. August was even thinking about seeing things for himself.

"I wonder what he'd say if he heard the Guthmans complaining about food shortages and having to turn away paying customers," Hélène said.

"Oh. And hear this, I think my sister is being courted by our neighbour's son."

"You don't approve?"

"No! He's not right for her." Then, "You're not listening."

Hélène and Michael were walking to Jan's, who had unexpectedly invited them to a thank-you dinner for getting him out of Berlin. Although the interlude as Pia's errand boy was over a year ago, Jan was only now in a position to play host. And as Michael suspected, to show off his latest trophy.

Michael for one was glad for the diversion and eagerly looked forward to the evening. Since Hélène had been out of sorts lately, he thought she'd appreciate the dinner as well, but with her unusual moodiness, Michael wasn't so sure. Whatever was bothering her, she kept it close. Not that he was asking.

Jan's flat was on the second floor of a brick building taking up the corner lot on the In den Zelten, with a splendid view alternating between the Kroll Opera House and the Spree. He met them at the door swimming in an oversized silk kimono embroidered with florid gold, blue and crimson orchids. His hair was longer and blonder and he wore it back with brilliantine.

"What, no flowers?" Jan kissed Hélène, both cheeks.

The flat was a modest size, but stuffed with rich brocaded fabrics of gypsy colours, camel-back sofas, gilded lanterns hanging from the ceiling, floor urns filled with fresh blooms. Billie Holiday, a silky but scratchy recording, wafted out of a back room. Jan revelled as master of the manor. The flat's owner, a tall, fortyish man, thin with a clipped Vandyke, did not. Introduced as David Arend and, effusively, the Swiss ambassador.

"Trade attaché," he said, shaking first Hélène's hand then Michael's. "Jan thinks anyone in foreign service is an ambassador."

David led Hélène down the hallway to a table set for the four of them by the window, past a wall of another life, its many framed photographs all of the same smiling woman and two look-alike girls.

"I sleep on the sofa," Jan said matter-of-factly to Michael as they passed by the open door of the bedroom.

He offered nothing more about the relationship.

"You have a beautiful place, Herr Arend."

"Please, it's David. You'll find it's much pleasanter now that the government closed down that Hirschfeld sex clinic. Bad sorts, you know, went there."

David insisted on wine, and he and Jan fell into a duet of easy domesticity. Michael felt a twitch of something he attributed to hunger. As a foreigner, David had access to food hard to find in Berlin as well as a housekeeper, so Michael and Hélène were supped with kingly courses of lamb, feta cheese and omelettes, followed by sorbet and raisin-spiked cakes. Jan gushed about the trip he and David had taken to Rome last month and the older man's expectations for promotion. When Jan laughed at something David said in reply, he lightly touched Michael's hand. The hairs shivering on his arm became an unexpected rash of anger.

Michael barely noticed the napkin thrown down beside his plate.

"She's been out of sorts lately. I'm not sure why," Michael said after Hélène excused herself to the lavatory.

"Yes, it was nice of me to invite her. She's not my biggest fan."

David returned from the kitchen with coffee on a silver tray.

"You and Hélène together?"

Jan's question slapped Michael in the face.

"She is living with you, isn't she?"

"I have the room."

"You've embarrassed him."

David spoke with the gentle chiding inherent and allowed in domestic bliss. It was disgusting. Sure, Michael knew what Jan was, but he didn't want to think about it. There was much he didn't want to think about. And yet the frailty of this arrangement betrayed in David's eyes, Michael understood: this thing he had with Jan couldn't last, and fear of the day when that happened.

Hélène returned and suggested an early departure. Now it was Michael's turn for silence as they walked home. He'd made the offer of a tram, but Hélène admitted to feeling somewhat ill and hoped the evening air would help.

"Not used to that kind of food," she said. "Jan's landed on both feet, I'd say."

"Always does."

More silence.

"I don't care to go back there."

"But Jan is my friend."

"No. He is not."

He could see that she was crying and trying not to. So Michael watched the officers on horseback clip-clop past.

The bench offered a good place from which to watch the birds on the water and the flower ladies at their colourful stalls on the other side of the canal. Today had not been a good day and they were packing up early. Drizzle persisted, and most people were too concerned with holding newspapers over their heads and getting to somewhere warm to buy bouquets. The ducks swimming by Michael headed mid-canal. He hadn't thought to bring bread.

Hélène was the reason.

Michael stood and leaned over the railing. He should have listened to Mum, become a priest. He wouldn't be in this fix now. Michael hadn't seen the inside of a church since he'd come to Germany, well, except to bury his grandmother, but enough religion had stuck to know he was doing wrong by Hélène.

Living together? That wasn't right. And she wanted more.

If there were other people in all of Berlin that evening, Michael was unaware of them. The city around him felt deserted, without light, without warmth, strangled by this canal of green water, its bridges, the iron gate closed behind him, the willow that wept and laundry dripping on the marble floor.

Five more minutes. He was already soaked from sitting so long out front in the rain, what was a few more? Grey was heading into night and even the ducks had disappeared. His legs felt leaden and unequal to the task. Maybe, if he was lucky, when he willed it, they wouldn't move. Or, better yet, he'd turn to water, round and round, chugging down the drain, sucked out of his own body and into a sewer, back to the sea.

Instead, five minutes later, he found Hélène unpacking her suitcase on his bed.

You'll be the smart one in the organization, Tschelock told Michael, on account of his time at university. He'd finally accepted Tschelock's offer of work and had started clerking in the office for a couple of afternoons a week, sorting through invoices, inventorying warehouse stock, arranging for the shipments of household goods

Tschelock's moved across Germany. Then almost overnight, business exploded.

"When you look at all this," Braum said loudly, "it's pretty hard to believe the Juden are hard done by. See anything you like, my boy?"

Braum was inspecting the apartment with Michael. With a growing waistline and a new moustache Braum did look older, but *my boy?* Who did he think he was?

The flat was off the Kurfürstendamm near the zoo. September brightness filtering through windows imbued the woodwork with a honey glow. The owners, a young architect and his wife, waited in the kitchen with their two children.

"Five thousand Reichsmarks?" the sun-bronzed man said, sweater tied around his shoulders. "For everything?"

"Not bad, eh?"

"That's not possible. The Cassatt paintings alone are worth four times that amount."

True. The flat was a showplace.

"Eh, the furnishing won't fetch much at auction."

Bauhaus was officially decadent, Braum reminded the architect.

The man didn't have to ask his wife growing pale in the autumn sunlight what she thought. The boy and his sister were standing dutifully beside her, staring at Michael. He wished Braum would just get it over with.

"Good. When do you leave?"

"Two weeks."

Braum was taking a tally. "Where?"

"New York." Barely audible.

"That's a piece aways." He tore out a receipt. "We'll have a van here Thursday."

Michael made note to suggest to Tschelock that owners not be present when tallying up their assets. Paying these kinds of prices was embarrassing enough.

Braum warmly shook the man's hand and thanked him again for the business. If anything, he was respectful. Down the stairs and out from under the children's stare, Michael was relieved to be on the sidewalk where late-summer begonias were drooping from the flower boxes.

"I've a mind to pick up that dining-room table for Catharina before the auction. Think she'd go for that?"

The clogged boulevard was busy with afternoon shoppers. Two policemen were giving directions to a woman and her daughter. Across the street, the clerk in the window of the hat store was rearranging old stock.

"Hey, Michael, what do you think?"

He mumbled an apology.

"Just what's with you?" Braum closed his file folder and fixed his attention. "You haven't been yourself in weeks, and I'm not the most intuitive fellow. Don't you like this work?"

"It's not that."

"Then what is it? For Christ's sake man, from the look of you, you'd think we just robbed a grave."

"I asked Hélène to marry me."

Actually, it was the other way around.

Much to Michael's surprise, Braum was delighted. Too fucking bad if Catharina thought it was a disgrace to the family that her cousin'd been consorting with a shopgirl in a house that once entertained ministers of the state.

"She's a fine-looking woman, Michael," Braum said with a brotherly punch to his shoulder. "Don't mind my saying, I was getting concerned about you. You know how things can look."

"Braum, wait."

"Don't worry about your cousin. She can be high and mighty at times. She'll come around." He laughed. "Now when's the big day going to be?"

"Soon. Before we go back to Canada."

Huh?

"Hélène doesn't want to live here. She says if there are children, it would be hard for them."

"Of course there'll be children, man, but what is she going on about?"

Michael closed his eyes. "She's Juden."

Braum looked as if he hadn't understood, he gazed into the busy street, then taking hold of Michael, he dragged him into a doorway.

"What?"

"Hélène is Doctor Linder's niece."

Yes, and that had come as much of a punch-gut surprise to Michael as it now did to Braum.

"He brought her to Berlin from Vienna to help out when Nan got sick."

"How come we didn't know?"

Michael himself hadn't known until she told him. "She said her uncle knew how everyone in the family felt about him, mostly my aunt."

"So they lied?"

"I guess Doctor Linder thought it best if no one knew."

"Of course he did."

"I'll have to marry her now, Braum. I've agreed."

"Yeah, and I'll bet that's what that bitch's planned all along. Did you know about her before you slept with her?"

"No."

"Michael, listen to me. You won't marry that woman. You can't even see her again."

"Why?"

"Because you're German."

"So is she."

"Not anymore. What you've done is against the law."

Michael laughed unsurely.

Braum slipped his hand easily around Michael's throat. "I'm serious. Think of what this could do to my position in the party. You've got to get rid of her before anyone else finds out. Christ, Catharina will be furious." Then he let go.

"Braum, I have to do what's . . . honourable." The word sort of got stuck.

"Grow up, Michael. She's tricked you into this for an exit visa. Treacherous. That's what you don't understand about them. You've never understood, Michael. It's over, Cousin. It's the only way."

Michael couldn't go home after talking with Braum. Hélène was to have spent the day looking into arrangements to sail to Canada. She'd be waiting with dinner and a table full of brochures. How could he face her? And Catharina? After Braum finished telling her what Michael had done, there'd be feathers on the floor. Well, not now. He couldn't deal with any of it.

Instead, Michael unburdened himself at Jan's door. Then he noticed the arm band. "What's this?"

"This?" Jan was pulling it off. "People are always arguing on the tram because they don't look German and shouldn't be taking up seats. Or, worse. Why am I not in the Hitler Youth? This saves me a lot of grief." Jan checked the clock. "Sounds like what you need is a boys' night out."

Michael, put off by Jan's apparent lack of concern, balked at the idea.

"But Tristan's having one of his theme parties tonight. Costume. Everyone'll be there. And David can't go."

He was detained at the Swiss embassy deciphering the new laws, or so Jan said. Not that Jan knew or cared.

"We'll get very drunk at Tristan's expense and in the morning, you can kiss your Jewess farewell. It'll all work out. You'll see. Besides, you can't let me go alone."

It didn't seem right to go off leaving Hélène. God knows what Catharina was saying to her right now.

"All the more reason to be out of there," Jan called from the bedroom. "And we've got a car and driver." The embassy was sending it around. "Fuck. Where's that invitation? Keep an eye out the window for the car. It'll be the big one."

But Michael didn't have a costume.

"My dear, you've proven one of my unshakable truths. Everyone who leaves here drunk, vowing never to return, does."

Draped in ivory muslin loungewear trimmed with fur, a long ebony cigarette holder waved about like a sceptre, Tristan looked ready for bed.

The invitation stated *Intimate Party—appropriate dress required.* No one quite knew what that meant until they arrived to find the cavernous hall at the bottom of the stairs fitted out as a change room where everyone was obliged to shimmy down to their under-garments. Party officials, however, were permitted their insignia.

"Michael thought you were dead," said Jan.

Tristan rolled his eyes. "Inexplicably still fabulous. Besides, there are so many who depend on me to be, well, to be here."

That was his only explanation for surviving the Röhm purge.

"Have a word with that bulldog you have at the door," Jan said. "He didn't recognize me and wasn't going to let us in."

"Hard to believe there's someone in Berlin who hasn't known you, my dear, in some fashion."

Jan pulled a face.

"But there's tighter security than usual," Tristan continued. "Confidentially, Herr Goebbels is rumoured to be coming. He likes his film stars. Especially near naked ones. Hope the poor man doesn't trip. Cripple, you know."

In his shorts and undershirt Michael was painfully uncomfort-able, so too most everyone else. That's why it was hard to believe the line waiting to get inside. All those people wanting to take off their clothes. Jan, on the contrary, revelled in being so lightly attired, and with his slim figure, looked wonderful, or so he trumpeted.

"Michael, tell me if that witch shows."

"Who?"

"Pia. She hasn't forgiven me for leaving the way I did."

"Or taking what you did when you left?" Tristan smiled. "How much was it?"

"Why do you always think the worst of me?"

"Because I care so much for your welfare."

"You care for the rich clients I bring you."

"And where is your latest conquest? Stole him, I hear. Herr Arend, is it?"

"Working. Always working."

"Ah, yes. Too bad. That would be on account of those pesky Nuremberg laws."

The club was filling quickly with a bizarre medley of guests shorn of their outer garments, rushing to the bar to dull their embarrassment.

Tristan snapped his fingers and a boy of about sixteen, tall for his age and well muscled, wearing only a pair of leather hiking shorts and sandals, appeared by his side. Drinks were offered and ordered.

Michael insisted upon keeping a clear head tonight, but that was ignored.

"Where are the little people?"

"Who wants to see *them* half naked? Don't you prefer him?" Tristan fondled the shoulder of the boy waiter, who looked ready to bite.

"Michael's not interested. He's got himself engaged."

"Really, Michael? From you, that is a surprise. What next, soldiers for the Fatherland?"

"The Fatherland won't want them," said Jan, stretching his head above the crush of people, waving to a familiar face. "She's Juden."

Jan clapped, See you, and disappeared into the crowd. On the tiny stage a line of black dancers began two-stepping to brassy jazz, breasts flopping like empty banana skins. Naked except for their yellow satin shoes with oversized bows, they were wildly applauded. Coloured skin was a novelty.

"Oh my. How did this happen?"

Michael explained he thought it was the right thing to do. You know, being honourable.

"The surest way for a young man to find trouble," said Tristan.

"But I had no idea she was, well, what she is."

"And so understandable. I mean, those people will do anything to get out of the country, especially since we've made it so obvious we don't want them. Really, my dear boy, someone should help." Tristan took a long pull on his cigarette. "I take it she wanted an exit visa for a wedding gift?"

Michael nodded.

"And you can't marry her now, can you?"

Before he could reply, a trumpet blast sent the chorus line scurrying and the lights dimmed, letting Tristan slip away unnoticed. A man wrapped in a bathrobe appeared on stage. Tristan's commission had been lucrative for Hasso; there was a second chin now.

"Ladies, gentlemen, esteemed guests from the Ministry of Culture, I give you . . . my masterpiece. Capital Germania!"

Any more of a speech would have been shouted down.

Grandly, Hasso signalled the floodlights to illuminate the ceiling. The crowd gasped, then hushed, as blond and square-jawed men and steely-eyed women beating anvils and brandishing wrenches marched in step before a smoking arsenal of factories, sleek, racing trains and acrobatic aeroplanes, all appearing to leap off the concave brick canvas.

The applause was thunderous and genuine. Hasso, after gesturing upwards in homage to the mural's central motif—the black claws of the swastika—bowed.

"I thought I saw you," Hasso said to Michael. "Come, join me in a drink to celebrate."

At the bar, that drink pushed Hélène further and further away. "Congratulations, Hasso. But I was sure after the trouble last year—" Michael dropped his voice. "You know, with Röhm, you'd be finished here."

The artist nodded. "Michael, my friend, all I can say is that I know of no man who could pull off the comeback Tristan did. He's more successful than ever. Can you believe even the mayor of Berlin is here tonight?"

"But you? Your work really is magnificent."

"Yes, I always knew one day I'd come into my own. You read in the papers about Dix? Degenerate bastard, serves him right. They've taken away his teaching post at the Dresden Academy. Can't even show now."

"You must be happy."

"Thrilled. What news do you have of the others?"

Michael confided that Hélène was well, which didn't really feel like a lie. Pia hadn't been seen except onscreen since that day she scooped

Jan out of Berlin.

"Have you heard about Marius?" Hasso said. "They arrested him."

No. Was anything to be done?

"What did he expect? He's a Communist."

"What?"

"Oh, Michael, everyone knew that."

Each man looked into the crowd. Jan was nowhere to be seen.

"So what's next for you?"

"The Olympiad. Thanks to Tristan, the government has been very good for me, although I had to join the party. No matter. It's just a card in your billfold, right? Hélène did not come with you tonight?" A half-naked boy waiter pushed his way between them. "I suppose this wouldn't be her thing," he added as an afterthought.

Michael wondered if Hasso knew about her, then figured he didn't. Perhaps he should reveal her deceit, and was about to when a cluster of women in blood-red lipstick and snoods, their silk stockings attached with clips to the ends of their girdles, swarmed the artist, clattering and cooing praise for what, one gushed, was the new Sistine Chapel. Everyone agreed, Hasso's ceiling would be as famous as Michelangelo's. Under such a siege, what could Hasso do? He raised his arms in meek protest and waved adieu to Michael as he was pushed away to meet more well-wishers.

Back on the stage, the dancers returned with different shoes. One of them began to sing. Her voice was throaty and velvety and warm. As the music's tempo increased, young men climbed up on the stage and began to dance with each other. Tristan, watching from his cat-walk, blew him a kiss. Michael wanted to be shocked by it all but wasn't, so he drank more and tried to feel nothing at all.

Michael drifted awake to find himself wet, lying on a sofa in the steamed air of Tristan's. Beside him, a redheaded woman whose breasts had fallen out of her chemise lay as a dead weight across her man, himself in oversized shorts and a stained undershirt. Above, the ever-watchful eyes of Hasso's marchers appeared to blink. Michael wasn't sure if they laughed or mocked. Did anyone else notice, or feel the room spin as roundly as he could?

The dancing had been frenetic for most of the night, couples falling into the water, pulling themselves out, exchanging partners. The band surrendered the stage to another, then another. Revellers too satiated to move littered the cushioned chairs and sofas around Michael. The man under the redhead pushed his burden aside and staggered to the edge of the canal, where he pissed unsteadily into the water.

Michael barely cared, until he saw Jan. Behind him stood a man who looked strangely familiar to Michael, a soldier perhaps, but without his uniform. He was embracing Jan, running his hands underneath the young man's thin cotton shirt, pulling hard on his nipples. Jan was holding on to an iron railing, his eyes closed, his mouth grasping for air. The man bit his ear as he pulled down his shorts and shoved himself into Jan from behind, forcing him against the railing.

It'll all be forgotten in the morning, the voice in Michael's ear whispered. It sounded like Tristan's, as comforting as a mother's. But marriage, ah, well, now that is forever, at least it feels that way with the wrong one.

The man behind him panting, and finished, Jan grinned foolishly as he stumbled across the bodies groaning on the floor and splashed across the sofa beside Michael, reeking of tobacco and something like ashes and cinnamon. His skin shimmered with sweat; Michael shivered when he felt it against him. Jan said nothing. His breathing became measured as he drifted off to sleep.

Michael let his fingers lightly graze the smooth skin, the small nose, the hollows of Jan's cheeks. If only they could brush away the arrogance on those lips now soft, and moist on his own.

Jan moaned lightly, rolled out of Michael's arms and said, "Christ, you must really be drunk."

Late next morning, Michael stood beside Hélène on one of the platforms at Lehrte Bahnhof. He'd remember her this way: a black hat perched on the back of her head, grey coat buttoned up to her neck.

Gloves. Pinned into her hat securing a red feather was a five-ringed medal for the upcoming winter Olympics. Odd she'd wear that. Her kind'd likely not even be allowed to attend.

Catharina stood apart, watching.

"I'm sorry," Michael said.

It was the first chance they'd had to speak. When Michael returned from Tristan's, Catharina had met him on the stairs and put him to sleep on her sofa. Certain that Hélène'd try mischief and talk Michael out of her plan, she hadn't even allowed Michael to see Hélène until the ticket to Vienna was in her hand. Catharina thought that was too generous, but Michael insisted. She accused him of being soft and easily manipulated. No damn wonder he found himself in this mess, her having to clean it up, and need he be reminded that without her family's continuing support he'd find himself on a ship to Canada? Goodbye Berlin. This pollution, as his cousin put it, was not going to get in the way of hers, and Braum's, ambitions. The von Renner name was not going to be stained.

"Catharina means well. I know it doesn't seem that way to you."

Whether it did or not, Hélène didn't say.

"If things could be different, you know I—"

Her look told him to not even bother.

"It's best. You'll be happier back with your uncle, huh?"

The train was nearly boarded. Last-minute passengers were running down the stairs and along the platform.

Hélène glanced towards Catharina. "Best for whom?"

"Hélène, what else can we do?"

Even Catharina was surprised at how quietly and quickly Hélène agreed to go. That was the law for you.

The whistle sounded the train's departure. Michael reached to help Hélène with her suitcase, but she raised her hand to him.

"I am sorry, Hélène. If things could be different."

"No, Michael. I'm the one who's sorry. I knew even before I asked you, you could not be the man to marry me. But I wanted so much for things to be different." No condemnation, no blame. Matter-of-fact. "Not going to ask why?"

He did not reply.

"That night at dinner, the way you looked at him."

The whistle blew again.

"You're wrong."

"There are worse things than being a Jude." Hélène stepped onto the train without looking back.

"You're wrong, Hélène."

You're wrong.

On time, the train pulled out of the station for Austria.

"Now this, this I did not expect," Catharina said from behind.

He turned. She smiled.

"You, my cousin, looked positively relieved."

1936

April 19, 1936

My Dear Brother,

Can it be that you've forgotten us in your new life? Perhaps you've run away with the Gypsies, or joined a circus? Maybe it is because my brother, who will one day be a famous doctor, is too wrapped up in studies? I only ask because while your letters were few and far between, now they've become so rare little Jake Swain, you remember him—he's not so little anymore, he delivers our post—he actually runs down the road waving it overhead, as excited to deliver it as we are to receive it.

Dadda says I am not to worry and is certain you are preoccupied with all that is going on over there this year. He doesn't miss a single newspaper and thank goodness he had something else to go on about instead of the death of the King. You can imagine Dadda's reaction—he never had a kind word to say about George V or any of the royals, but you know that's the German in him. I don't suppose you folks in Berlin care too much about dead English kings.

Dadda was particularly glad to follow the winter games in Garmisch and Partenkirchen. *Did you know he and Aunt Beate used to ski there as children? I did see a picture of Sonja Henie in the* Chronicle. *How thimble-like she is. The article quoted her saying how charming Mr. Hitler was when she met him after winning the gold medal. She sounds very nice. If you happen to run into Miss Henie, do ask her for an autograph, as you have a sister in Canada who's only excitement comes through you! If, as Dadda says, this is but a warm-up for summer, then no doubt Berlin with its lights and flags, and streets filled with the famous and beautiful will concern you more than news from us.*

And, brother, news I have.

By the time you read this letter, I will be Mrs. Avon Glyn. While I don't think this will come as much of a surprise to you, I mean, we've known Avon for years, he seems to think it will. Hopefully, you will take the news better than Dadda. When Avon came round and asked for my hand in a very sweet, old-fashioned way, our father threw him out of the house and has refused to speak anything about it, except to say Avon is not man enough for me. Whatever can that mean? You know Avon spent those few years in the Navy. But our Dadda, when he closes his mind, that's that. I don't know what to think about our wedding day. Perhaps no one will give me away, so I wish you were here more than ever. Dadda's behaviour is so unreasonable, and all this after Avon so kindly took over the business when we needed that money for Mum. He has been such a good friend to all of us. He even asks about you and when you will be coming home. While I am sure that he is as disappointed as I that you will not be here on our special day, he said to me just last night how nice that you'd found a reason to stay in Berlin.

Now I must know, have you received your baptismal records and birth certificate I sent you? Father Fergusson was asking. He was so helpful in getting them for me, especially when I told him you needed the documents for your race identity card. He had heard the Catholic Church in Germany was being very helpful in proving just who is Jewish, so you must not hesitate to contact a priest should you need more assistance. It is times like these I am glad that Mum made Dadda convert. I can't imagine those Lutherans being of much use to you in this.

That being said, Michael, there is growing talk here of a boycott against the games in August, led by the Americans. I don't understand it all. Dadda says it is partly because of the fuss the Jews are making, partly because Germany is just trying to defend itself by building her army, but after the last war that makes everyone nervous. What do you say? Is it really as bad for the Jews as some papers make it out to be? What about this talk of mobilization?

If so, maybe you should consider coming home, although you will find much changed. Renner & Sons continues to grow under my husband-to-be even though folks are still watching pennies. Avon says it's best to remain cautious during these hard times, so he wouldn't be able to offer you a job if you returned. But I know things will pick up. Sounds as if Canada is not like Germany, as so many men are still looking for work. Is it, as you said in your last long-ago letter, hard to get a lot of things in Berlin, even certain foods, because demand is so high?

And just last week I took Avon back to Richmond to show him where we were all born. I have many fond memories of there. But with its new streets of houses made out of hydrostone, I recognized nothing. I guess it is good the city is moving on and that day in 1917 is now long past, but I was saddened. Do you remember our porch? Father painted it white. Mum hated anything white. Said it showed the dirt. Dadda says I was too young to remember any of that, but it's not true. Didn't we used to sit there in summer and drink iced tea? Dadda says iced tea taste like cold, well, you know, and only the Scots would drink something nasty like that. Now Mum is all by herself on the hillside in Montreal. Do you think any of us will ever get there to visit her? Jeepers, Michael, I miss her.

By the way, you remember Mrs. Herzfeld? She died before the holidays and that big house of hers is to be carved up to take in boarders. Avon used to drop by her place every now and then to check on the plumbing. She always asked to be remembered to you. Avon hopes to do the conversion.

I'm enclosing a taste of Nova Scotia for you, your favourite, some maple butter. And Avon says we shall drive to the Annapolis Valley for our honeymoon where I'll be sure to bring back a bag of apples to make compote for you. Then you'll be able to share in our joy. I'm also enclosing some McCall's magazines, and that old favourite we used to keep in the outhouse, Sweetheart Stories, just to make you laugh and in the hopes you find one.

So I must finish and get this package together. Jake has offered to save me a trip and take it to the post office when next he calls. Avon joins me in wishing you well as I'm sure you will do for us. Study hard. Write soonest.

With much affection,
Gene

"Can you believe the hypocrisy of those Americans?" Catharina said as Michael folded away his sister's letter, "complaining about things here when I heard they have white-only park benches in their South?"

That was in the United States, Michael pointed out.

"Watch it, my dear, you're getting red in the face," Braum said, mixing celebratory drinks over in the corner of their ever more stylish flat. "Let's leave it to the Führer. You know what he says. Only God will judge us and Germany."

Michael and Lonä were settling in on the horsehair sofa after their afternoon flight on the Hindenburg. Pia had arranged the tickets as thanks for Tschelock's helping to furnish her opulent new townhouse. And because of satisfied customers like Pia, Lonä's father had needed to purchase another two moving vans to keep pace with demand.

The Zeppelin flight promised a unique viewing of the Olympic grounds, but no sooner were they off the ground than Michael, looking blue-green, mumbled something hastily about it being the *Steuben* all over again and dashed to the lavatory. Braum checked on him once. They were right over the stadium, did he want to see? Michael doubled over, leaving Braum to laugh: Jesus, what a stink. Freeing himself near the flight's end from needing the lavatory, Michael slipped into the back of the smoking lounge, where the captain was holding a reception. You, you there! Everyone turned to look at Michael. Where'd he come from, the captain demanded of the steward. Had anyone seen him before? Was Michael a stowaway?

He closed his eyes to the embarrassment of it all.

"Are you feeling better now?" Lonä asked as Michael shook his head at the offer of a drink.

He nodded, feeling awful that being airsick had left Lonä on her own to make their announcement to his family on the Hindenburg.

"Well, just let them," Catharina said, still going on about the American boycott.

"They won't do anything that stupid," her husband said. "They'll make noise about it in their press to make themselves feel righteous. Come August, they'll be here with the rest of the world. Hope they're practising their German."

"That reminds me, Braum. Are we to get tickets? You know I have to see the opening ceremonies."

"Hard to come by, dear. Impossible, I'd say."

"You must know somebody."

"I think I can help," said Lonä quietly. "Poppa said he will get tickets for us. As an engagement gift."

Michael thought he might throw up again.

The engagement came about so quietly that Michael wasn't even aware it had happened until everyone started talking about where and when for the wedding. Sure, he liked Lonä, liked being with her. Sometimes, she even reminded him of Gene. No-nonsense. He figured they were even dressing alike, Lonä in that frumpy farm smock-type dress she was fond of wearing, hair buttoned behind her head. Quiet and thoughtful, Lonä was a great admirer of Hitler. She told Michael once, thanks to the Chancellor, she could hold her head high as a German. Too bad about her one passion, though. Lonä had been training to be a teacher, but men got those positions these days. Good thing for her the Winter Relief Fund and the German Women's League could always use another pair of hands.

At first, Lonä'd invite Michael over to spend evenings together, listening to the radio with her father, discussing issues of the day. Although Tschelock discouraged women talking politics, Lonä helped Michael understand the controversy surrounding the Rhineland. He had mixed feelings about the reoccupation, all that hoopla about the last war being the war to end all wars. Wouldn't this, Michael reasoned, provoke another? Lonä explained it simply: how can something that thinks German, feels German, speaks German, not be German?

Can a line on a map determine otherwise? Michael's grandfather, she pointed out, probably would have agreed.

Catharina and Braum noticed the rapport taking root when Michael was working part-time for Lonä's father and began inviting the two of them out for dinner, sometimes over for drinks. No evening could pass without listening to the Führer on the radio, and if Lieutenant Luft dropped by, a bottle of wine in each hand, there'd be heated politics argued late into the night. What of the war in Spain? And the German/Italian alliance? Braum waved that off with a snort. Bad for Germany. He'd been to Rome as a boy on a school trip. There'd been a misunderstanding over the daughter of the family who billeted him. After so much wine, his details were sketchy, but Braum did remember a cow getting shot. For that reason, the Axis wouldn't be good for Germany. The countries were too mismatched.

Peter opened the second bottle with a *pop!* Italy would serve Germany in the short term, but longer? Japan was a better fit.

Braum laughed until he cried: the Japanese as honorary Aryans? All you had to do was look at their yellow skin and slanty eyes to see that Germans were superior.

Who was stupid enough to align us with that? Michael wanted to know.

Lonä, the only sober one in the room, whispered that it had been the Führer. Everyone went silent. Then Peter laughed. Good thing most of them were drunk, he toasted.

And somehow, after enough of these late-night drinking sessions, Braum posing to Michael the next morning the what-if scenarios, followed by the better-off-if-you-were talks, the engagement just happened. So when Lonä shyly explained about the tickets to the Olympiad's opening, no one was surprised.

"Oh, Lonä! That would be delightful. I hope your father'll get us good seats. Are you sure I can't get you something to drink? But damn those Americans, if they ruin this for us now—"

"Jesus Christ, Catharina, you're not back harping on that?"

"Yes I am. All this poor, poor Juden—Americans don't understand."

Lonä, her hands tucked under her thighs, agreed with the foreign outcry.

"How so . . . dear?" Michael said.

Catharina and Braum stared at her, waiting to hear.

"You don't mistreat a puppy because he chews a slipper or digs a hole in the garden or makes a mess indoors."

"You're not comparing those people to puppies?" Catharina had to down the rest of her drink.

"Well, yes, in that they're animals and it's only their nature to be the way they are."

"You mean avaricious and deceitful, dragging us into that hateful war—"

Lonä nodded. "But we have to accept some of the blame for that. We've allowed the Juden to infest our banks, our shops, even our government, and it's right that we take back Germany for Germans."

Braum, standing behind his wife's settee, half drained the tumbler in his hand. "I'm certain our guest doesn't want to spend all evening talking about the Juden."

"Not at all," said Peter. "I'm curious to hear the young lady's solution to the problem."

Simple. Send them all to Palestine.

"To be shot at by Arabs?" Michael asked.

Catharina joked that if they were God's chosen people, He could sort it out for them. Then, "And how do you propose we do this? Offer them a first-class ticket to Jerusalem and say, please go?"

"Of course not," said Lonä.

"Maybe some way other than first class," said Braum. "What do you think, Michael?"

"I think I agree with Lonä."

She slipped her hand over his.

"Of course you would, wouldn't you? My cousin has never had an original opinion. I say it again, the Olympiad better not be ruined for us." Catharina looked at Michael as if to say he'd be personally to blame if they were.

Braum laughed and said the marriage was doomed to failure, as

Lonä was to take Michael's opinions in these matters, not the other way around.

"Yes, and you must write your sister directly and tell her our news. Tell her that I hope she and I will meet soon and be great friends, and that she and Avon will be as happy as we will be."

He doubted that.

"And take that foul-looking matter with you when you go," Catharina said, the idea of butter from something drained out of a maple tree being unsavoury to her.

Lutter & Wegner's on the Charlottenstrasse had been a young man's haunt for Herr Leopold, so he was not surprised to hear from Peter that the wine house was now a favourite with youthful officers of the Abwehr.

"Do they still have the finest cellar in Berlin?"

"A while since you've been there, eh, old man?"

Not since he'd been confined to his wheelchair. Years ago now. Imagine, got through the war only to have a set from an Ibsen play come crashing down at the Volksbühne.

Peter, in a uniform jacket with as yet no sleeves, was flexing his shoulders in front of the mirror. Michael was right. Although his cousin found their tenant odious, Herr Leopold was by far the best tailor in Berlin. And Peter had insisted Michael accompany him to the attic to help pass the time during the fitting.

"Michael, we must go have a glass of *Sekt* there. Let me repay you for sitting up here with me."

Of course, and it was arranged for the next day, but when the hour came, Peter didn't.

"Ah, well, that's to be expected," said Herr Leopold from the landing. He'd been watching Michael sitting on the bottom stair. "It's the military. Always something at the last moment."

Michael stood, feeling foolish that he'd let himself wait for over an hour. But why waste the day?

"Would you like to go, Herr Leopold?"

"What? Me?"

"Why not?"

"No no no."

"But you want to."

There was no denying that, but he was an old man in a wheelchair. These things did not happen for him anymore.

"But, you know, if you carried me down, and I don't weigh much, we could take a taxi."

"Now that's the spirit!"

Sadly, Herr Leopold was little more than bones, and after Michael helped him into his finest coat he carried him easily down the two flights of stairs.

"Now I am to pay for everything, and I won't hear no from you. I've been doing very well by those officers the lieutenant sends round, all wanting to show off in their uniforms, so today we celebrate on me. Is that understood?"

Michael smiled as the old man clapped his hands and made him wait so that Herr Leopold could drink in the air from the canal.

When they arrived at the Charlottenstrasse establishment, Herr Leopold had Michael carry him down to the cellar, where they ordered sparkling wine and a light supper. The old man approved of so very little changing over the years, although he was disappointed that none of the waiters remembered him.

"How long has it been, being outside I mean?"

"Ah, well, your grandmother was still alive. She used to take me out once in a while. She wanted I should have air. Then that Jude moved in. Claimed it was too much for her. Drink up, drink up!"

More wine was ordered.

"Now, my young friend, we have to make sure your cousin does not know about this. I told her I'm too weak to move out. If she sees that I've been with you, she'll have my mattress by the curb."

"Oh, you're wrong, Herr Leopold. Catharina wouldn't do that."

He shook his head. "She's hard, that woman. Not like Herr Tschelock's daughter. Now there's a kind soul. Very much like your grandmother, she is. She'll be a good match for you, if you don't mind my saying."

No, he didn't mind.

The old man nodded. "Eh, if your cousin has her way, she'll have you married to that woman very soon. No long engagements." The next part he whispered. "I think she worries about the way Kunstler looks at her."

"That's ridiculous. And, no, I'm not ready to marry. Why rush?"

Herr Leopold smacked the tabletop. "You should have been married years ago, young man! You need a family. Keep you out of trouble." He sighed. "Too bad about Hélène. I liked that girl."

Michael drained his glass.

"If we'd only known what she was up to. But damn it, your cousin is right about you." Herr Leopold finished by looking through the bottom of his glass. "Yes, I know all this. I listen, don't I? You can hear everything from up in that attic." He waved to the waiter. "And you know what else I know? That woman would like nothing better than to see you leave Germany. There! That's what I know. So, what's wrong with that nice boss's daughter anyhow?"

Michael didn't think anything was wrong with her, especially after that awkward evening when he'd found himself alone with a very determined Lonä, but he'd rather wave over the waiter to refill their glasses than say so.

"If you're going to marry her, then you must spend more time with her."

"I guess."

"You'd be better off spending your time with her than, well, him."

Michael's hands clasped the base of his glass.

"What are you talking about?"

"Eh, I've see him. That young one who waits for you by the bridge." He added slowly, "The one you hid."

Michael began circling his glass around the tabletop as if the need to make some comment could be ground away. Herr Leopold tossed back more wine as if he felt it necessary to wash out his mouth.

"I know his kind."

"You've had too much to drink, my friend."

The old man tapped Michael on the chest. "Yes, yes, I have and I thank you for that. I can't tell you how wonderful it is to be back here. So my young friend, don't you worry. Your secrets are safe with me."

"But Herr Leopold, I have no secrets."

"Ah, everyone does, and a tailor knows how to keep them. Why, the things I could say about those soldiers, coming to me, begging me to make them look more of a man than they are. Except that Lieutenant Luft, now there's one to please the ladies."

The waiter reappeared, wiping his hands on a towel. Would the gentlemen be wanting anything else?

"Herr Leopold?"

The old man slumped back against his seat.

Out cold. Then Michael heard the trickle of urine from under his chair.

Michael had fully intended to write Gene with news of his engagement, but somehow, everything just got away on him. Anything he wrote now was bound to appear unexpected, even hasty. After all, he was twenty-eight, and what's a man to do by that age but marry and start a family? Catharina said it was not only the right thing for him to do but it would improve his prospects when he'd come so close to ruining everything. As difficult as his relationship was with his cousin, he still owed her for getting him out of that mess with Hélène. And Catharina made it known that it was time for Michael to help restore the von Renner name to prominence. Hasso and Tristan echoed her sentiments, saying that marriage would serve him better than remaining single. Even Frau Guthman claimed he could do no better in a wife, and having been married as long as she had been she should know.

Lonä wanted no extravagance. They were married in Tschelock's garden, followed by a supper. Lonä hoped that someday they would make a honeymoon to Munich, as that's where she believed new Germany had risen, but with the business of moving and auctions being brisk, they had to make do with an excursion to the Olympic park. During a walk around the stadium she told him about the baby. That fumbling night, a month before the ceremony, would always be for Lonä her true wedding day, she added blushingly.

Of course they'd live in Nan's house, although Catharina wanted to restore the place. Michael could work full-time for Tschelock, as Lonä proudly would not accept handouts from her father. She couldn't even bring herself to accept the incentives from the government for a child, as that money should go to someone who really needed it. And in honour of Grandfather von Renner, they'd have to name the child Wilhelm. She was already imagining how fellow officers would address him and under no circumstances was Michael to call the child Billy because she'd gotten it into her head from someone that everyone in Canada had a nickname. Everything for Lonä was perfect, or would be, if the child was a boy.

Lonä sounded very far away to Michael, who suddenly longed to feel Halifax harbour winds through Mum's wizened lilacs, apple blossoms and mayflowers, all saluted with fog horns. When Lonä said she expected to be ready next year for another child and that there'd be a five-child Mother's Cross for her if she had her way, Michael wanted to run down to the Spree, find a rowboat and row all the way back to dear, dear Nova Scotia where he could magically turn back time and lie shirtless in the grass by the beach in Africville where children kicked around a ball, fog rolling in so quickly as to send him and Avon shivering . . .

In June, the apple compote arrived from Gene as the sound of saws and hammers sang over the rain of plaster dust. Her package reminded Michael that he still hadn't told his family about his marriage and the coming baby. Now he'd have to tell them he'd left the university too. He hoped Nan in Heaven wouldn't think poorly of him. Leave that to Catharina, furious that part of Nan's legacy had gone to waste. No doubt the folks at home'd be disappointed when they found out, but so what. Studies hadn't gone easily and Michael thanked Jesus to be done with dissection. The dream of practising medicine must belong to another generation of von Renners. And besides, as Lonä had pointed out, a growing family required that he work full-time.

Business at Tschelock's was better than ever, and Michael's father-in-law put him in charge of accounting. Many clients not wanting to sell before were suddenly desperate to leave the city, glutting the market with fine furniture. Herr Tschelock, the ever-doting father, made sure that if his daughter refused money from him not duly earned, her family would at least be surrounded in luxury earned by her husband's labours.

Good news then that Catharina was renovating again. Michael and Lonä moved to the ground-floor apartment, the Guthmans gone. Herr Leopold remained in the attic, which suited the old man just fine. The only way they'll get rid of him is to bring the house down over his head, he was fond of saying.

With the end of the laundry business, so too the arguments between Frau Guthman and Catharina. For a while it sounded like there'd be no end to them. Catharina dictating terms, Frau Guthman defiantly hanging underclothing in the middle of the day. Finally, Catharina announced it was no longer fitting for the Guthmans to be there, with Braum now midway up the party ladder. Frau Guthman waved her lease in front of her, pointing to the signature. But that was with Catharina's grandmother and had lye-in-the-brain made the washerwoman forget that Nan was dead? The Guthmans relented after Catharina threatened to have Lieutenant Luft report the couple, and what then, huh, if they were carted off to the Kolumbia Haus jail for running an illegal business.

Michael felt bad for the woman. Trying to find another apartment in Berlin was difficult with visitors arriving for the Olympiad and the government confiscating properties for their rebuilding program, which would see whole neighbourhoods torn down. And complicating the Guthmans' troubles, Valentin was taken to an institution. The doctors felt he'd be taken care of better there, but sadly, the little fellow died of pneumonia shortly after. His mother became hysterical. Then she got it into her head that the doctors were euthanizing children like Valentin and begged Michael to find out if it were true. He could only wonder where she caught wind of that nonsense, as he wasn't about to go asking such questions. He did want to slip the couple some Reichsmarks to help them along, but Lonä reminded him that they had their own to take care of now.

Jan was watching Americans in the Askanischer Platz coming and going from Anhalter Bahnhof when a man approached him. Not like the Americans this one. Short, swarthy in a dark suit, wearing a hat too big, he handed Jan a small packet, which he promptly slipped into his pocket. Michael, watching, waited for a break in the traffic, then called to him as he darted through the passing streetcars and ran across the boulevard. The transaction was complete, the man gone when Michael, breathless, caught up with Jan by the newsstand.

"What was that all about?"

Jan sniffed. Something David wanted him to pick up. "I don't know why I have to meet you here."

"I told you. And I work just around the corner."

"It's that cow you're married to. You don't want her to see me."

"No, this is supposed to be a surprise, remember?"

"Right. So how is the little mother?"

"Awful. Mornings are rough." Having shared quarters with Hélène and now with his pregnant wife, women sure had a lot of female complaints. "Did you find it?"

In a shop in the Alexanderplatz, which was not close by, and Jan let Michael know that he'd been all over the city looking for it so he'd bloody well better be thankful.

"But I heard that Mann's books were for sale again."

"They are, when they can keep them on the shelves. But don't worry. I asked the clerk to set it aside."

"You did that?"

"I wasn't giving up my whole day going back for nothing."

"Lonä will be pleased. Maybe she won't feel so bad if she has something to read while she's—"

"Baby! Baby! Baby! You're not going to start on about that again, are you? It's all you talk about these days. Why don't you ask about me?"

"Stop it."

"Baby! Baby! Baby!" Jan added in a jig, tossing his hands in the air as he swanned around on the sidewalk. "Somebody's having a baby."

Michael said everyone was watching him flit about like a blue-arse fly, an expression Jan had never heard before. At least his laughter stopped his dancing.

"I get it. You don't want a baby."

Of course Michael did, or would, maybe, if everything slowed down. Engagement, wedding, pregnancy in what felt like a heartbeat with never a chance to catch his breath. If he tried, there was Catharina and her pinched hateful look. And Braum? Some help he was. You'll be fine, my boy, it's all part of being a man. Christ, Michael didn't know which end was up.

"I'm not ready to be a father."

"You can always run back to the North Pole."

"No. No, I couldn't do that."

Jan rolled his eyes and sighed and spit out a rapid little grunt of air as only Berliners could do. It meant I'm bored, you're crazy or don't be so stupid. Take your pick.

"I'm sorry. We could have lunch at the Excelsior. You'd like that?"

Jan said no. He and David were leaving in the morning for Frankfurt. Vacation at some spa or other, Jan couldn't be sure except that he had to get back and pack.

"Besides, I looked in. We'd never get a table. Never seen the place so busy."

By July's end, Berlin, dressed to dazzle, burst with the first raucous sounds of the party. Lonä, not wanting to miss a moment, insisted they see the Unter den Linden with its golden eagles on gleaming pillars lining the broad avenue and flags taller than one-storey buildings snapping in the breezes of the Wilhelmstrasse. You couldn't help but think that something magical and memorable was about to unfold. And the English. Tears came to Michael's eyes hearing it everywhere as he and Lonä walked down the avenue looking for a coffee shop that had room to squeeze them in amongst all the foreigners.

More than once, Michael offered to help translate when they happened upon a pair of hapless tourists, maps in hand, trying to make sense of U-bahns and S-bahns, which way to the Brandenburg Gate and where might be the best place to catch a glimpse of their famous Führer. After Michael had steered the visitors in the right direction, they'd often insist upon a drink in one of the geranium-ringed sidewalk cafés or lunch in a restaurant, its windows open to the crowded boulevards. Lonä glowed with her city's transformation. She whispered to Michael how surprised she was to find the English and the North Americans so friendly and that she wouldn't be afraid to make a trip to Canada now to meet Gene and Avon and Michael's father.

Braum surprised Michael one night by carting him off to old haunts near the Nollendorfplatz, reopened for the pleasure of the city's guests. Along the way they noticed leather-bound editions back in shop windows, books once consigned to the flames in the Opernplatz for being too progressive, too avant-garde, too un-German. Surely, then, there was no reason why Lonä couldn't accept Michael's gift of a copy of *Tonio Kröger*, by her favourite writer, Thomas Mann. Although Lonä said Michael should not have paid for the extravagance, as she called it, she sternly rationed her reading each night to make the book last.

To Catharina's great joy, Herr Tschelock had parted the heavens and secured tickets to the opening ceremonies of Berlin's Summer Olympiad. Michael could only wonder at the strings pulled to get those, and anticipation mounted for all as the big day neared. So no face was longer than Michael's cousin's when on the morning of the ceremonies Lonä awoke to the most virulent sickness she had yet experienced.

Herr Tschelock was already on his way with the car to drive everyone to the stadium. Catharina, bathing Lonä's forehead with cold water, insisted she'd feel better if she got down the weakest tea and plainest biscuit. Braum and Michael were in the palm room smoking, Michael hating the sound of his wife vomiting and getting up to close the door, Braum sighing, fearing all was lost. Then just like that, Lonä got out of bed and, pale and somewhat shaky, announced that missing the ceremony was unpatriotic. Within the hour they joined a convoy of buses, trams and automobiles on the Kurfürstendamm, stopping along the way when Lonä needed to hang out the back of the convertible.

Crowds overflowed the stadium, flags and flags and flags, walls of light, music, marching, warm August sun, trumpets, oh, it was all so grand! They were surprised in an atrium by the stadium to find a huge fresco celebrating German athletes and painted by Hasso. Michael kept saying excitedly, I know him! I know him! So Lonä insisted a photo be taken for Gene, and Catharina wondered if Michael could get them some of Hasso's work for free. When the runner, Fritz Schilgen, relayed the Olympic flame into the stadium, Catharina gushed that it had been lit in Greece and carried on foot all the way to Berlin. Michael felt his skin tingle as the roar of the crowd surely was heard in Heaven.

And then the Führer arrived. As Herr Tschelock's tickets had them sitting on the other side of the stadium, lower than the official box, no one could really make out any of the dignitaries. But it was worthwhile just the same, sighed Catharina. Michael, meanwhile, was quietly bathing in pride, seeing the Canadian flag under the shadow cast by the Hindenburg floating overhead.

Standing for a better view, he felt Lonä's hand upon his arm. Could he get her something cool to drink? The heat in the stadium was dreadful. Damn. This was no time to be looking for water, and hastily rounding a column cursing that he was missing all the good stuff, Michael, not seeing the beast of a camera swinging down on a crane, stepped right in front of a crew from one of the ministries filming the Games.

Regaining consciousness at the medical station, the only injury appeared to be a crushing headache and a bruise to his dignity. That face, that uniform hovering over him, he recognized. Peter Luft had seen the collision and carried Michael down to the nurses' tent, where he refused to leave his side until he was certain Michael was steady enough to return to his seat, having missed most of the opening ceremonies.

"It's the least they can do after what that Riefenstahl woman did," Catharina said on the drive home. By way of an apology the horrified officials had given Michael tickets to some other events and a set of silver souvenir pins. "Will there be enough for all of us?"

Lonä thought it would be nice if Michael sent his sister the pins as a souvenir.

"Your wife is well?"

"Happy in Dresden."

Peter followed Lonä down the hall and into the shadowy front room where Michael lay on the sofa looking out over the canal, rather, would have been, had the drapes been opened.

"Your good woman told me and I couldn't believe it. Here she is the perfection of health."

"And as big as a tram," said Lonä.

"And you, Michael, still sick. I insisted I see for myself. Now, my friend, what is this all about?"

If only he knew. "Dizzy spells mostly, but I can't risk doubling over at Tschelock's."

"You know Poppa said to take as much time as you need." To Peter she speculated that Michael must have some kind of concussion left over from his accident.

"Ah, so that's it."

"It's nothing. My mother just would have given me a spoonful of cod-liver oil."

Lonä thought that sounded barbaric and would Peter care to stay awhile. She was late for her Women's League meeting and she'd feel better if Michael wasn't alone.

"Of course. And do what I can to put some cheer into your husband while you're away."

After the door closed behind Lonä, Peter dropped the books he'd brought on the table beside Michael's unfinished letter.

"I see she cares for you a great deal. Lucky man." Then, first things first. Open the windows. "It's a splendid October day out there. Fresh air will do you wonders."

Michael insisted he couldn't. The sun hurt his eyes. So Peter took a seat.

"Now then, what are you doing?"

Michael explained that he'd owed his sister a dozen letters at least, the latest one to thank her for the copy of *Gone With the Wind*. He'd been reading it aloud to Lonä, doing his best to translate into German on the fly. He figured they were at least getting the gist of the Old South.

Peter glanced at the letter. "And what have you got to say to that Gene of yours?"

"So far not much. I'm a terrible writer. She thinks my letters are so brief, she's got to read between the lines to find out what I'm really saying. I was going to tell her what we'd heard from Braum about the plans to rebuild Berlin. Hard to say how true this is, but if so, we could be in the path of a grand boulevard south to Tempelhof. You know how bad the housing situation is and none of us, except my wife, wants to face the possibility of having to look for a new home. Lonä thinks being down here is too small with the baby coming. She says that with another child next year, we'll be falling over ourselves." Michael leaned back against the sofa cushion. "Another baby. Can you believe it?"

"And that doesn't please you?"

"Why would you say that?"

"You're wearing it."

"Well, sure it does, I guess. But sometimes I think Lonä's commitment to duty, oh, excessive."

"SS officers are expected to have four children with or without their wives."

Michael thought his friend was joking. "I just thank God we're not Juden. With their rental agreements out the window, they can find themselves on the street."

Peter hadn't heard that turn of phrase before and he chuckled over people getting tossed out of windows.

"Imagine that happening to us with hungry mouths to feed."

"You'd tell this to your sister?"

"You don't know my sister. Can't sugar-coat anything for her. She's political, you know. Reads in the papers of the arrests, the Jehovah's Witnesses, the Catholic priests and the talk of war. She's worried. Me, I don't know why anyone would care about those things."

"You know as well as I, Michael, these priests are guilty of corruption—and worse, with young boys if you can believe it. It has nothing to do with a crackdown on religious freedom. Jesus Christ, Michael, if it's moral degeneracy she wants to find, ask her about her king running off with that American divorcée." He wagged his finger at his friend. "Now there's a disgrace. But I can tell your sister is a thinking woman. That'll be a curse to her husband."

Yes, Avon.

"I know some of the things she writes upset Lonä." Like being concerned about Germany's military manoeuvres. Braum had explained they had been the largest since before the last war. "The Chancellor says it was just an exercise. I have to echo Lonä, the government must know what it is doing."

"Then tell your sister that."

"But what really bothers Lonä is why Gene keeps asking about the Juden. As she doesn't believe half the things she reads in the papers here, she wonders why my sister would. But I have to tell you, Peter, it is strange. You know, sometimes, days, even weeks go by and I'm not aware Germany has Juden. Sure, you hear the stories of them trying to look like us and how they smell like garlic when they come into a room. And *Der Stürmer* printing those things about sacrificing babies and raping virgins—"

"No one takes everything in that party rag seriously," said Peter.

"Then something happens and it's usually the simplest of things.

That's when I find myself questioning. Like last week, I had an appointment with my doctor and took the tram. An elderly woman with her arms full of packages got on. It was crowded. She had trouble standing and no one offered her a seat. Then a man sitting nearby, obviously a Jude, you could tell by his nose, tipped his hat and offered his seat to her. What did she do? She turned away from him and said she'd never sit where a Jude's arse had been."

Peter stretched and yawned.

"Now come, Michael, in all fairness, the government has brought many positive changes to Germany in a very few years. Tell your sister this, there's no Depression. Besides, it's not just the Juden who suffer, and what is coming their way is rightly deserved. Who do you think profited from that insane inflation after the war? You, my friend, must stop thinking of them as people." Peter reached over for the travel books he'd placed on the table. "Now look here. Ever been to England or France?"

Travel. Michael sighed. Such things were behind him now.

December 27, 1936

My Dearest Sister,

First, forgive me. I write this long-overdue letter, including thanks for all of yours, from the Victoria Café on the Friedrichstrasse. The place is not particularly close to home but it is a favourite of mine. I was to meet a young friend I have not seen for some time in the hopes that I might offer him a Christmas greeting. Not much mind you, but a trinket that I thought he might take pleasure in. It's just that he's been a friend to me and I do enjoy his company, all too rare these days. The café here also serves a nice cake that he likes very much.

As I have not had the opportunity to send off a holiday package to you this year, my news will have to be my gift. I join you and your husband in the ranks of newlyweds. You will remember me having mentioned my employer's daughter, Lonä? We were married this past summer and now expect our first child. Father will no doubt be surprised. I am. Wish us well.

But it appears from the waiter asking me yet again what I shall order that I am to remain alone. I hope nothing has happened to my friend. Perhaps I'll order some cake just in case.

My apologies for such a short note, but you know me. I'll post it on the way home. Best wishes for the coming year to you and all.

Michael

P.S. I was able to secure workmen with the money you and your husband sent to make the much-needed repairs to the family mausoleum. Aunt Beate is grateful and says she will write you directly. Very generous of your husband to do so.

The pins are from the Olympics.

1937

Michael began each day at Tschelock's in the water closet, the four panes of painted-over glass open to the grind and rumble of Anhalter Bahnhof. No one could hear him vomiting in there. Then he closed his eyes while he splashed water on his face to avoid seeing the once white porcelain so long in need of a scrub, its black streaks taking on an orange tinge. And whatever you do, don't think about why your shoes stick to the floor.

As he pulled a handkerchief out of his pocket to wipe his face, his identify card fell to the floor. The one Braum had marched him down to the party office and insisted he register for. Make life easier. Open more doors. Enjoy a better life for his pretty wife. So Braum claimed.

Michael picked it up, caught himself in the mirror and stared back at the face. Plenty of cheekbone now, along with puffy eyes and shaggy brown hair in need of a trim. Sleepless nights were responsible for that, and the dark circles. Faithful Gene and her letters from home had helped overcome the sleeplessness when it first began. Now they made it worse. All anyone ever wanted to ask about was the baby the baby the fucking baby until all Michael wanted to do was walk out the front door and headlong into the canal.

For Christ's sake, it's perfectly normal to be out of sorts, Braum explained after being snarled at once too often. Even he could guess what the problem was. Being prevented from enjoying the charms of a woman like Lonä must be one helluva hardship, but in a month or two after delivery when Lonä was able to, well you know, Michael would be right as rain. And until then, if Michael needed relief, then Braum could fix him up with a lady he knew. No, no, it's not cheating if the fuck was for medicinal purposes.

Christ Almighty! That was the last thing Michael wanted, but the more he tried to explain to himself what he did need by explaining it to Braum, the more muddled it became until Braum asked, Hey, do you even want this baby?

Better to spend time with Jan. Michael happily disappeared into those precious few hours because Jan only ever wanted to talk about himself, then drag Michael off to Tristan's. But their last night out had been months ago. Where was he when Michael needed him?

One more splash with the cold water, then Michael was at his desk. From the second floor of a warehouse near the Excelsior Hotel, he stared out a wall of paned glass overlooking the street. The window made the office bright and airy. Downstairs, wall-sized mirrors, dining tables, chairs and armoires purchased at auction by agents for wealthy clients awaited shipment. The small shed behind the building concealed crystal chandeliers packed in crates stuffed with straw. They'd been sold to customers as far away as New York and Buenos Aires.

Michael shared the floor with his boss's windowed enclosure and sundry rows of dented cabinets, files and ledgers piled on crates, and a mummified potted ivy. The only garbage bin was an oil drum in the corner. As the moving men gathered here at midday and used the drum for their lunch remains, the air grew misty with fruit flies.

Most of his day was spent working here alone. Michael would take the initial inventories, cross them against the auction lists, then sort out the money. He'd a real knack for bookkeeping, his father-in-law often said. Michael was going to go far, maybe even take over one of the branch offices. Until then, by way of appreciation, why not take his pick from the furniture stored below. Make Lonä happy. Only rarely did he have to help out at the auctions. For that Michael was grateful. In recent months, the auctions had become unpleasant.

With Braum in charge of new business, he doggedly sought out new clients, mostly Juden in urgent need of liquidating their assets. Taxes somehow always the reason. How Braum knew where these people were Michael couldn't figure, but Braum always seemed to have lists, knowing where to find them. When Michael mentioned to Lonä that he thought this peculiar, she agreed it was odd that anyone would not want to pay their fair share of tax to the Reich, not when they themselves worked hard keeping food on their new polished oak dining table.

Michael often escaped to the perfumed and airy peace of the coffee shop in the Excelsior Hotel, sitting by the caged canaries in the windows. The Games over, the Americans gone, he had no trouble finding a seat. With a London paper and pot of hot coffee by his side, for a few blissful moments, Lonä, that baby, Tschelock's, Braum, the card in his wallet were all someone else's life.

"You could say something." Shaking, clutching his coat about him although it was warm in the café, Jan looked painfully thin. "Aren't you glad to see me?"

Yes! But Michael just pushed the plate of rolls towards him.

The boy reached into his coat for a cigarette, but had trouble lighting it. Michael took the matches while Jan steadied himself. His hands were raw.

"Thanks, Sweets."

"When did you get back?"

"Weeks ago."

"And?" Michael could not bring himself to say the name.

"Gone back to Geneva. Nice while it lasted."

"Couldn't you go?"

"The Swiss aren't that open minded. And why are you staring at me?"

Michael looked away.

"I've told you before to get out of here." The brass-buttoned waiter with the white apron took hold of Jan's collar, rather what was left of it. "We don't allow his kind in here, sir." Directed rather loudly, as if to reassure Michael. "This is a respectable establishment."

The murmuring in the café stopped.

"Herr Berenson is a decorated war hero and a friend of mine."

"Then he's not . . . bothering you?"

"Please, bring more coffee and another cup."

After the waiter left, Jan indignantly pointed out that he was too young to be a war hero. They both laughed.

"Thanks."

Jan took a roll.

"So, no job?"

"David set me up, a bit of cash. It won't last much longer. That's why I came to you. Just until I land on my feet."

Michael had to pull his gaze away from Jan's face, to the caged birds, to the automobiles outside on the street, to anything.

"Well?"

"It's not that I don't want to."

"Oh, I knew you'd be pissy about it."

"Jan, wait."

"Don't worry about me. I won't starve."

Michael pulled his coat from the back of his chair and took Jan's arm.

"Let go of me!"

That upset the birds.

"Everyone's looking." Michael threw down money on the table and pushed the young man through the door onto the street. "I didn't say I wouldn't help you."

That brought the old Jan back.

"Lonä handles our money. She'll know if I take some."

"C'mon, I know you can help me. I'll pay you back, every Reichsmark."

Michael knew better.

"Seventy-two Barutherstrasse. It's in the Kreuzberg behind the graveyard. Come soon."

Michael said he would.

Jan remembered something else. "Oh, I didn't tell you. I saw Hélène."

"In Berlin?"

"Someone who looks like her is."

"Did she ask about me?"

"The platz was crowded. And I only saw her for an instant."

"Did she—?"

Didn't Jan say she hadn't seen him? "Too bad about her."

"You didn't think so at the time. You agreed she probably tricked me."

"I did? No. Hélène wouldn't have done that. What's it like anyhow? With a woman?"

Michael thought about Hasso's overwhelming ceiling canvas at Tristan's. And Hélène in that coloured floral robe opened to her velvet mound as she daubed liner around her eyes. The way she twirled her earring while she read the morning paper, not knowing why she bothered anymore as they were full of shit. Beads of sweat on her upper lip and the tiny chip in her front tooth. Like Hasso's realm. Vast. Flat. Unreal.

"Did you care for her?"

It wasn't allowed, Michael would only say. And he was drunk, that first time.

"I always liked Hélène," Jan said as if she were dead and to be spoken of in kind tones.

Michael was right about Lonä and money. Not a single Reichsmark went astray.

As the afternoon traffic rumbled by Anhalter Bahnhof outside, a sharp, blaring horn startled him. The ledger Michael was staring at had given him an idea. The lists of inventories. The lists from the sales. Then there was the money. He knew it all, and only he because Tschelock trusted him. Cross off a chair here a table there, deduct the sale money from the proceeds, no one would know. Keep it simple, small items, and he could help Jan indefinitely without drawing attention to himself.

But it's stealing.

Michael paced. Old man Tschelock had been good to him. He was his father-in-law, for Christ's sake.

But it's only temporary.

Jan'll pay it back.

No one need know.

It's just borrowing.

That's all. Just a loan.

A sparrow landed on the sill.

If I don't—

Michael didn't want to go there. There were whispers, and not so quiet ones if you listened to Braum, about what happened to those like Jan, particularly a recidivist. Cut their fucking balls off, Braum put it more plainly, and hooray for that if they aren't going to use them like a man should. The rehabilitation camps would straighten out what was left.

Jan had to be kept off the streets.

Michael could hardly wait to get back to him, and that wouldn't be until the end of the week, when he could skim enough funds for Jan to live on for at least a month. After that?

First, Michael figured, he'd deal with the next five minutes.

The narrow building at the end of the street was shaded outside, softly lit inside. Its pupils were never seen, only heard, like gurgles in hidden water pipes.

"Ah, Herr Renner, always a pleasure."

Frau Merten reminded Michael of his grandmother, even appended an apology for the lack of a doorman he doubted ever really existed.

"I hope I'm not disturbing classes."

"No, no. My doves don't flutter. You know the way."

Jan had said the students of Frau Merten's school were really whores and they dressed like young girls because the men who used them wanted it that way. But the place was safe enough, Jan had said with a laugh. The good mayor of Berlin was a patron and Frau Merten had a nebulous association with Tristan. According to Jan, it could very well be the safest place in Germany, well, next to Tristan's dance hall in the slaughterhouse.

As Michael made his way down the hall, a door opened, throwing light onto the yellow-and-red linoleum. The girl peeking out giggled: Oh, excuse me! She closed the door. At the end of the passage, stairs rose past lead-lined windows overlooking the cemetery wall and its quiet green beds, up to the eaves and Jan's room.

He opened his door wearing only a towel. The walls were the brick fireplace flues and the room's single window was no larger than a man's face. A camp cot doubled as a chair for the worm-eaten table. A humming, bare light bulb dangled from a cord twisted through the beams. Michael hated this place. Although he hated even more to think about Jan living in comfort with another David.

"It helps me look younger," Jan was saying about his application of powder.

"Why?"

"Old men pay more for boys. Quick. Light me a cigarette. I'm late."

Jan turned back to the piece of mirror propped against a teacup on the table. "Now why the long face, Sweets?"

"I thought you were going to get a job."

"I have one.

"You know what I mean."

"Oh, like waiting on tables, or how about selling bedbug powder? Big trade in that, I hear."

"It would be better."

Jan stopped with his face. "Better than what?"

"Than what you do."

"I sell my arse, Sweets. That's what I do. That's all I know how to do."

"But that's not—"

"What?"

"I was going to say, it's dangerous now. Have you ever thought about getting out of the city? Maybe even Germany?"

"Let me guess, to your precious Canada where it's right as rain to sell your arse there?"

"I'm trying to help."

"So fuck off."

"Look, Jan, I know someone in the Abwehr—"

"Never trust the military."

"But . . . I trust Peter."

"You've been warned."

"He says they have names. Lists."

"Of what? Boys like me who suck cock for money? Don't look so shocked, Michael. Everyone'll be on a list for something or other, eventually."

"Those men go to prison."

"Only if we get caught."

Michael was staring at the small packet of white sugary crystals sitting in the china saucer.

"That? Just something David and I used to do. Course, he could afford it."

Michael had seen it before. Even tried it. Snow at Tristan's was as certain as winter in Halifax.

"Lying to my wife, stealing from my boss, and that's what you're spending the money on?"

"Don't be ridiculous. What you give me only covers my room here. By the way, I'm into the warden downstairs for the rouge. Could you spot me, Sweets, on the way out? Frau Merten's a hellcat if you owe her money."

"Do you know what I've done? What I've been going through for you?"

"You're hardly doing this for me."

"No?"

Jan shook his head and grinned lazily. "You do it for this." He took hold of Michael's crotch and squeezed. "Surprise! I figured you'd be hard. 'Have you ever thought about leaving Germany?' With you, huh?"

Michael shoved Jan and the boy fell across the cot.

"If it's just a fuck you want, Michael, you should have said. Be cheaper for you and I wouldn't have to listen to you moan."

"I'm not that."

"No? It's so bad, I can smell it on you, all over you. You're desperate for it. Sweets, I've seen more married men with that look than you'll ever know."

You're wrong. "You're wrong! I'm not like that."

Michael was out of the room and down the stairs.

"Why are you running then?" Jan ran into the hall and leaned far over the banister. "Wait! Don't go. You said you'd help me. Do you want me to go to jail? Is that what you want? Do you know what they'll do to me?"

The doves were all aflutter with the commotion. *What's going on? Why are they yelling, Frau Merten? Frau Merten!*

"Please don't leave me."

Damn him.

Michael left behind a handful of bills thrown onto the stairs. Jan, in his towel, followed and picked up each one.

Sitting outside on the steps, Michael buried his face in his arms, a light February snow falling. Somewhere in Berlin, his son was being born.

The three fashionable Bellevuestrasse townhouses were a coup for Tschelock's. Not only would it be their largest auction, the commissions would be enormous. In the moving trade, this was the stuff of legend.

"We've done moving for the family over at their gasworks, you understand," Braum explained, "office furniture, industrial equipment. So it was natural they'd come to us. Old Joachim Berthold, a war hero, even decorated by the Kaiser, started the company. Used to race cars in his spare time, till he gave it up a couple of years ago.

A true gentleman. He'd talk to you like you were regular people. His son Kaspar runs the gasworks now, or did. That's a different piece of work. When it comes to holding onto pfennigs, there isn't a bastard alive that'd hold tighter. I heard he cut back salaries and shut off the gas for war widows who couldn't pay just so he could build himself a lodge near Luckenwalde. But that's typical of them. You know, the kind that gives them all a bad name."

The second floor was stifling. Spreading Vs darkened Braum's shirt under his arms. Oblivious to the summer heat, he perched on the edge of the unused desk next to Michael's, speaking through a wide, self-satisfied grin.

"Old Joachim built the house, and when his son and daughter got married, he added onto each side for them. Three prime pieces of real estate filled to the roof with only the best."

Where could he be?

Michael hadn't seen Jan since the day they'd argued. Months now. Sometimes it was like he couldn't breathe for the worry. Frau Merten had even let out his room.

"You know, Michael, you could be a little more interested. This is big news for us." Braum stood and stretched.

"Sorry. So why are they selling?"

"The government's taking over the gasworks. My guess is because it's considered war essential."

"War?"

Braum laughed. "Where are you these days, Michael? Of course there'll be a war. Doesn't the Führer say so almost every day? Anyhow, Berthold and the son and his family are immigrating to Palestine. Ruth, the daughter, she's already in New York. By the way, Michael, you should be thinking about putting something aside. Times may get tough for a while."

Tschelock called from inside his glass-enclosed office. The Berthold auction was confirmed for the eleventh.

"And make sure the newspaper advertisements say that it's a sale of Juden assets. That always gets the crowds."

Michael rubbed his forehead.

Who's he with? "I need air."

Braum chuckled. "It's the baby, huh? Taking some getting used to? Don't worry, if Lonä has her way you'll be an old hand at this before you know it. We'll try not to let this auction keep you away from the arms of your good woman too long. "

The Berthold auction was set for mid-morning. By eight, the Bellevuestrasse in front of the gated townhouses was so congested the police rode in on horseback to keep the street open to traffic. The chance to cart off a valuable heirloom for a handful of Reichsmarks had drawn bargain hunters and the curious from all across Berlin. Tschelock's had never seen anything like it.

Michael, having finished tagging the lots of plates and stemware down in the kitchen, hurried upstairs with a handful of labels. Once the auction began, it would be his job to run back and forth, ensuring the lots were brought to the auctioneer by Tschelock's men in the order printed in the brochures. On the second floor he found Kaspar Berthold at a window, hands clasped behind his back, surveying the crowded street below. Middle-aged, portly, groomed bushy moustache counter-balancing a thinning dome, the former president of Berthold/Berlin Gasworks appeared completely unmoved by the pending sale.

"Look at them. So many."

Michael looked down on the people below struggling to get in, like a mass of rats.

"This room used to be the nursery when I was a boy. I'd sit right here and watch the officers riding their horses in the park."

"Herr Berthold, it might be best if you and your family left. You don't want to see this."

"How thoughtful. But leave? Certainly not. I intend to look every man and woman in the eye who buys something here today."

A policeman was trying to back the crowd away from the gates with his horse. There were angry shouts from women demanding to be let in before all the good stuff was gone.

"Michael, there you are," Tschelock said. "I've been looking everywhere for you."

They left Berthold at the window and descended the marble staircase. In the hall, windows had been thrown open to the green lawns out back bordering a garden walled by a high brick enclosure, softened by rows of bronze cannas, gladioli bursting with gold and red. A dog barked playfully and a child was giggling in that carefree way her throat could hardly contain.

"All the rooms are full," Tschelock was saying.

Michael paused to watch the girl in her pink dress and patent-leather shoes playing with her dog, a red chow chow.

"We'll lay out the fine china and linens out back."

That fell to Michael to organize, so he ventured into the garden. Frau Berthold was reading in the arbour, surrounded by custard-yellow dahlias with edges trimmed in burgundy. Water was trickling out of the mouth of a stone face on the wall, splashing into the pond near Frau Berthold's feet. The crowd on the Bellevuestrasse could be heard even here. Judging from her porcelain countenance and the page never turning, Michael wondered how many times she'd read the same sentence.

The dog let out a low growl. The girl stopped laughing and looked towards her mother to see if she should run into her arms. Frau Berthold put down her book, carefully, on the bench beside her and stood. Michael didn't expect the woman to be gracious.

"Mishka's just protective, she won't hurt you," she said about the dog.

Neither of them could have known that the gate at the front of the house buckled then, under the press of anxious bodies. The crowd rushed the stairs to the townhouse, those who could not keep up tripping under the weight of shoving from behind. Tschelock, seeing the panic, flung open the front doors, but too many tried at once to enter and those who could not squeeze through were pushed to the side, falling or jumping over the balustrade and into the laneway. As more people saw this as another way into the house, they followed, forcing the policeman on horseback to gallop ahead of them. The clopping hooves on the cobbles, the onrushing wall of people, frightened the girl in the pink dress. Spinning around, flinching backwards at the horse, she screamed. Her dog barked. The horse reared and the policeman struggled to remain seated, drawing his gun as he was thrown. Frau Berthold cried, No! The dog lunged and the gun went off.

It felt to Michael that a very long time passed as he turned from the frightened man falling off the horse to the dog recoiling from the shot. The bullet shattered her muzzle, spraying her eyes outwards, coating the child in the pink dress with red. Those at the front of the crowd stopped, but were briefly inched ahead by others in behind who could not see. The policeman scrambled to his feet and got his horse under control as the girl choked on pockets of air.

Then the garden was still.

The fountain gurgled behind the arbour. Michael stared at the blood splattered down his front. He dragged his hand through it, as if to make himself believe, yes, this is real.

"What could these people be thinking of? They're not even allowed to *own* dogs," said a woman in a blue print dress, her hair wrapped in coils of a kerchief, tears welling in her eyes. "That poor, suffering creature."

⌾⌾

"Naturally, I understand how you feel," Michael's father-in-law said. His office chair let off one helluva creak as he leaned back. "Regrettable, yes, but these things do happen. Still, our most successful disposal ever."

Michael had struggled with the decision, not even discussing it with Lonä. No need to guess how unsupportive she'd be. But this business sickened him. He was careful to point out to Tschelock that it wasn't in sympathy for the Juden, he just couldn't stand to see anyone suffer. Never could.

"Of course," said his boss.

Tschelock relaxed in his chair and looked at Michael awkwardly at attention before him, quietly and for so long that Michael nervously began to tap his thumbs together. The older man's desk was covered with invoices pertaining to the Berthold sale.

"I know you have concerns about Lonä, but I assure you that—"

"Leaving is quite out of the question, my son."

Something about *son* didn't sound right.

"But, I've told you how I feel. I simply cannot do this sort of work anymore."

His father-in-law nodded. "Sit the fuck down. Let me tell you how things are going to be." Not so jovial and fatherly now. "You will go back to your desk and process the receipts from the sale. At the end of the day you will go home to my daughter and be a loving husband. Tomorrow morning, you will be back at your desk ready to work. Why do I continue to be so generous? You see, Michael, I know you've been stealing from me." He thrust up his hand. "Please, spare me the denials or explanations. I've known for how long and how much. If you weren't my daughter's husband, I'd turn you over to the authorities, and gladly. As it is, I won't have my good reputation blackened nor my daughter's life ruined. And I certainly don't want anyone in the business thinking I'm a fool. You make a good wage here and I've been fair to you. In return, you've cheated me. Consider yourself lucky that continuing to work here is your only penalty. As long as my daughter wishes it."

Michael rose and dragged himself to his desk and the dead ivy and the fruit flies.

From behind his glass walls, Tschelock shouted, "And from now on, I'll do the bookkeeping. The Juden auctions are your responsibility."

Although Michael hadn't been in a church since his grandmother died and the Berlin Cathedral was not of his baptized faith, he still believed in the inherent holiness of such places. The girls who had followed him in to get out of the downpour were laughing and chatting, their shrill voices carrying under the vast domed ceiling.

It's the Hitler Youth that does that to them, Frau Guthman had once claimed after her son had been tormented by some local toughs.

She'd been glad they wouldn't have Valentin, when there was a Valentin. All this talk about the future belonging to the youth makes them think the present does too.

Like mongrels that haven't been house trained, thought Michael, and I don't care if they are looking at me. He leaned back in the pew and closed his eyes. Although the rain had only caught him across the street he was drenched in the short run inside. Drops, beading off the edges of his coat, fell with a plop into the widening puddle on the marble.

Michael walked a lot these days. The fresh air offered some relief against the crushing migraines. Sometimes he'd walk along the canal, or in the other direction up through the Tiergarten then lose himself among the lunch crowds on the Unter den Linden. When the pain shrunk his eyesight, he'd find a bench or café chair on which to sit it out and wait for the nausea to subside.

Just being on hallowed ground, remembering childhood promises of forgiveness and redemption, drew the tension from his knotted neck and shoulders. Somewhere off in a nave or gallery, a man was singing in a faraway voice. How beautiful, Michael murmured, and the girls watching him giggled. He guessed they were pointing at him. So what? He was hearing the voice of an angel, strong and controlled and compelling, it intoxicated and soothed. Something old and Austrian, but he couldn't place the song. Maybe there was something to those old tales of Mum's, you know, archangels and blowing horns. Heaven. And Hell. Michael lay down on the pew. Just five minutes and he'd be able to get back to Tschelock's.

Five more . . .

"Michael."

The girls were snickering.

"Michael."

He sat up with a lurch and faced the uniform and insignia of the Abwehr.

"Are you all right?" Peter looked worried, his hat under his arm.

Michael glanced around quickly, confused.

"Do you know where you are?"

He nodded.

Peter turned towards the girls, who prudently thought it best to take their chances with the rain. Their footsteps resounded off the stone floor until the swoosh of the great wooden doors swept them out of the cathedral.

"Headache." Michael rubbed his eyes. "Sometimes if I can sleep for a few minutes, it helps. What are *you* doing here?"

"Practising."

"That—that was you?"

Peter smiled.

It brightens his whole face.

"You find that odd?"

"Well, yes."

"I trained as a boy and I sing with the choir here. We're doing Haydn's *The Last Seven Words of Christ* on Sunday. You should come."

The gaze was long and Michael broke it.

"I better get back to work."

Peter followed him to the door.

"How's the baby?"

He thought it would be like getting a puppy that he'd immediately take to, but the baby was always loud or attached to Lonä's breast and only made Michael wonder what he was supposed to feel.

Peter laughed and put on his hat. "Wilhelm, is it?"

"Maybe when he's grown up. He's Billy to me, but Lonä hates when I say that."

"That'll be the Canadian in you. Tell me, how are things at Tschelock's these days?"

"Can't complain."

"Sounds like you are."

"No, really. Everything's fine."

"That's why you're lying in a pew in the middle of the day."

Peter opened the door and although overcast the glare still caused Michael to flinch. At least the rain was little more than drizzle now.

Taking a small notebook and pencil out of his breast pocket, Peter scribbled down an address. "Here. Take this. Five o'clock."

Without giving Michael any chance to comment, Peter bowed slightly and left Michael on the steps of the cathedral.

Although Michael had grown comfortable around Peter over time, even Braum with his lackadaisical attitude towards authority never made light of the secret police. So when the address on the paper brought Michael to an apartment complex by the Reichsbank with a leaf-filled fountain in front, and not a ministry building on the Wilhelmstrasse, he breathed easier, then chided himself for doing so.

"Good for you," Peter said, opening the door to number six.

Gone was the black uniform. Peter had changed into a shirt and hiking shorts, bare feet. He led Michael into an apartment of hardwood floors, arches, soft green paint and a large window opened to the summer afternoon in a treed courtyard.

"Like the country, don't you think?"

On a table, an open bottle of an Italian white and two glasses.

"My wife hates Berlin and I have to spend so much time here. This place suits me. It's close to my work, furnished and quiet. Not much room, but I'm lucky to have it with space the way it is in the city these days."

He poured for Michael. "To friends?"

Why not?

"Now then, tell me what's wrong."

Almond-cane furniture with flower-printed cushions. African violets on the radiators. Faded prints on the walls Michael wouldn't remember five seconds after looking at them. Nothing that belonged to Peter. No personal insights betrayed. It should have been disorienting, but as Peter stretched out his long legs, Michael slipped into comfort and drank easily of the wine.

"Please, I got rid of the uniform. I figured you'd talk to me more easily, as your friend, without it."

"Oh, no. That didn't bother me."

Peter laughed, reached over to top up Michael's glass.

Easy man to like considering his occupation. Jan's warning be damned, what did he really know? With another glass of wine, warm breeze through the window, the conversation trailed delicately through Michael's hatred of his current situation, leaving out the unflattering parts, like stealing from his employer, and why his head pounded and what the hell had happened to Jan.

"That's unfortunate about your auction, but those sales bring out the worst in people." It wasn't an apology. "So, why do you stay?"

"He's my father-in-law."

"Nonsense, and since you've confided in me, I don't mind telling you, you're wasted working in a moving company. A man with your abilities could go far. I could put in a few words on your behalf."

"I couldn't ask that."

"You didn't. And don't worry about Tschelock."

This time, Michael refilled the glasses.

1938

The visitor from IBM New York was explaining, in English, the latest changes requested by Michael's employer.

"You'll see that we've redesigned the punch cards here and here, items for nationality, race, religion, community, employment, gender and so forth. These will be cross-checked with the cards from the various church registries and local census results for verification. You will be able to identify any segment of the population, by any category, in this way."

Ina interrupted brusquely to say that Michael's wife was here. Michael was Ina's supervisor, and he was certain the woman hated him for his sudden appearance as a manager at Deutsche Hollerith Maschinen Gesellschaft, or Dehomag, IBM's German subsidiary. Even though he'd immediately explained to her that he was a married family man, thus more deserving of the management job, and she only a single woman, the effort did little to dispel the animosity. The woman's tightly bound hair, which drained all expression and colour away from her face and left her narrow eyes creased in a perpetual icy state of loathing, sure didn't help matters. Just the sound of her heels in the outside hallway was enough to put him on edge.

"Please go, I can wait," said Michael's guest, in German.

"That won't be necessary. Ina, Herr Mercer leaves for America today so we must conclude now. Please tell my wife I'll be along shortly."

"But your wife has never visited you at work. Perhaps it is important."

"We won't be much longer."

"I had no idea you were married," Mark said, switching back to English once they were alone. "Any photographs?"

Michael shook his head. Just a wooden desk covered with reports and lists and punch cards facing a window overlooking the Friedrichstrasse.

"Long?"

"Almost two years."

Mark Mercer had made the trip from New York twice during these early months of Michael's employment. Michael liked the IBM man and they had progressed to a first-name basis.

"Any children?"

"Billy."

Who'd reach out his arms to him and smile whenever Michael looked into his crib, even though Lonä insisted the baby was too young to show affection. No one was making Michael believe that, though he kept it to himself, alongside wondering if maybe Jan's father, or lack of one, had made his own son the way he was. Michael was going to be different.

"Aren't you the dark horse."

Michael smiled.

The whir of the keypunch machines downstairs was constant.

"A kid changes everything, don't you think?"

"I guess."

"Ever think about going home?"

"This is my home."

"No, I mean back to, Nova Scotia is it?"

"Why?"

"It's just that, Germany's—"

"Germany's what?"

Mark hesitated. "Is this the best place to raise a boy?"

"I know some things may appear strange."

"You call your Jew laws *strange?*"

"They're laws to protect this country." Nicely echoed.

Mark had caught Michael off guard. Then it occurred to him:

"Are you?"

"Does that matter?" said Mark.

Silence.

"No, I'm not, but I don't think I'd tell you if I were. So, do you agree with them?"

"Of course not, but I live here. Has anything happened to you? I could—"

"No." Mark sounded disappointed. "It's not the sort of thing a visitor readily gets to see, do they?"

Now, perhaps, it was best to see what Lonä wanted.

She appeared dwarfed, sitting in the middle of the empty row of chairs underneath the red, black and white flag. Her feet were placed neatly in front, her handbag tucked in her lap. The hall was large and bare, purely functional without betraying what went on in the clicking, sorting recesses of the building. Ina ruled here from a desk at the far end where she nodded curtly to Michael and showed Herr Mercer to his waiting car.

"Lonä? Is it Billy? Is something wrong with Billy?"

Michael had yet to see his wife cry. When she was upset, a quiet, stern resolve clung to her, as it did now.

"He's fine. Catharina's with him."

He sat alongside his wife in the row of empty chairs.

"I just realized, I've never been here before."

"I know."

"I'm sorry."

"No, no. It's fine."

"Nice of Braum to drive me."

Very.

"You sure it's not about Billy?"

Lonä lightly rested her hand on his. "Can we go somewhere?"

"Of course."

As it was almost lunchtime, they hastened out from under the disapproving glare of Ina. Michael suggested the Victoria Café, close by. Lonä had no objection. The café had not yet filled and they easily found a table. There were no dishes with meat that day, the waiter tossed off in passing.

Lonä removed her coat and draped it on the back of her chair. Michael wished she'd kept it on. Beautiful as she was, those homemade dresses made her look dowdy. They may be officially approved attire, but the party bureaucrats' wives and girlfriends Michael had seen dressed like stylish movie stars in English fashions and no one said boo about that.

"This came this morning."

She took an envelope out of her handbag and handed it to Michael. It bore an official stamp.

The door to the café swung open then and Peter strode in, all smiles and snug in full regalia. Passing a couple by the door, he pulled a cigarette out of the woman's mouth and wagged his finger: a proper German woman does not smoke, he reminded. And a proper German man sees to that.

Of course, the woman's consort replied.

Lonä caught Peter's attention while Michael read. "How nice to see you again."

Peter managed to conceal the awkwardness of surprise and bowed slightly.

"I forgot," Michael said. "Peter usually joins me for lunch."

The lieutenant waved that off. "Another day?"

Michael glanced from his wife to look at Peter. "No, join us."

Lonä reached across the table but her fingertips barely touched Michael's elbow. "I was hoping we could be alone. We haven't been since—"

"I understand completely, madam."

But Michael pleaded the letter. "Perhaps he can give us some advice," he said to Lonä.

She smiled, and Peter swung over a chair from a nearby table. The waiter reminded them there was no meat.

"Now, what has put lines on this beautiful woman's face?"

Michael handed over the letter. "Are we to be evicted?"

"It just can't be right."

Peter undid the top button of his coat as he read. "I'm afraid so, madam. I'd heard about the Führer's plan for the city. A grand north–south boulevard. Heard he hates Berlin. Thinks it's ugly. I had no idea this would affect you."

"Can you help?"

"Peter has done enough for us," Michael said.

Like arranging for the job at Dehomag's subterranean facility close to the Alexanderplatz, punching cards with a tabulating technology that had barely existed a few years ago. And after a few months Michael was supervising his own crew at the Friedrichstrasse office preparing for the yet again delayed census that would count, sort and plan the lives of every German. Furthermore, thanks to Peter, Tschelock was never given a chance to voice his dissent. In uniform, Peter had presented himself at the man's place of business and suggested the Reich had a need for someone like Michael. Tschelock wouldn't want to stand in his way, would he? Naturally, Michael's father-in-law did not. Perhaps he was even glad to be rid of Michael and his thieving ways, but he said nothing about that to Peter. The new job paid more and the prestige that came with it would be vested upon his daughter. On the surface, Michael was forgiven and sent on his way with Tschelock's blessing, the books between them wiped clean.

"I'll be happy to make inquiries, Frau von Renner, but judging from this signature, you should prepare yourself for the worst."

Michael couldn't believe it. The von Renner home to be torn down for a House of Tourism.

"Everyone says it's impossible to find apartments in Berlin," Lonä said. "What'll we do?"

"Difficult. Not impossible. But if I can't help you with this," Peter handed back the letter, "I can find you a new home."

The waiter returned. For the officer and his guests, he had found some meat. With the owner's compliments. The couple by the door had left, their coffee unfinished.

⁂

Michael wasn't certain when exactly Lonä took to disliking Peter, surprising after all he'd done, but no doubt, she had become less animated in his presence. There was no denying the cold front after he told his wife his plans for their son's party.

Michael's feelings for Billy had overwhelmed him quite unexpectedly. Those early months, he felt nothing for his son, the baby defined only as an insatiable mouth, howling when not feeding. Then as Billy neared his second birthday, something of a personality emerged. Who is this little man? His boy, his son—this being making him feel not connected to the whole, but whole, Michael had to know.

"I thought it would just be family," Lonä said.

"But why not invite him? You know he adores Billy and, besides, he's alone here."

"If he is, then he should insist his wife join him."

"What? After all he's done for us?"

But not even Peter could help Michael save his grandmother's house. A line on a piece of paper signalled Berlin's renaissance, and nothing, not Peter's intercession nor the von Renner name was going to stand in the way of the city's transformation into Germania.

Peter did manage to find them a flat on the Kronenstrasse, close enough for Michael to walk to work. In a city grappling with a housing crisis, this was nothing short of miraculous. According to Peter, the place had unexpectedly become available in a large block recently declared *Judenrein*. Even so, Michael hated the thought of moving there. Four storeys of stairwells choking of cat piss, screaming babies, drunken neighbours and the flushing toilets of dozens of families. They'd also have to share a kitchen with the house warden, Frau

Albrecht, who'd made it quite clear she was not above turning in even members of her own family for the slightest infraction. The privacy, fresh air blowing in from the canal, gone.

In the morning, Tschelock's trucks would be around to take them to their new apartment. The Kunstlers, having found a flat by the Savignyplatz, would move several days later. So amid the chaos of boxes and straw, Michael arranged the small gathering for Billy's birthday. The evening did not pass without tears.

Catharina's maternal instincts had surprised everyone, even herself. With no children of her own, she had doted on Wilhelm like a second mother. She'd offered Michael to prepare the birthday supper to go along with the set of wooden soldiers she and Braum were giving the boy. She and Lonä had become like real sisters. Catharina sniffled as if she would never see her darling Wilhelm again, though she'd already planned his first adventure to the zoo near her new home, even certain as she was that the smell of wild animals was going to make her sick.

Nonsense, dismissed Lonä's father as he made funny faces at the boy. He had it on good authority that the hippos were washed down daily, and they smelled the worst. The boy clapped for his grandfather.

Tschelock asked, cordially, how his son-in-law was getting on in his new position. Michael wanted to spit in his face, good riddance to being your clerk, now that he was highly regarded. *Helping the government solve problems by identifying, isolating and eliminating through key-punching,* just like his department's motto claimed. Michael even had uniformed officers open doors for him when he attended meetings at the police agencies in that formidable building on Prinz-Albrecht-Strasse. But all he said was, fine. Tschelock ignored him for the rest of the evening. No one appeared to notice the rift.

Herr Leopold had insisted upon being carried down the stairs to join the party. The elderly man brought with him a boy's wool trousers and matching military coat, although the young fellow would have to grow into them. The elderly man, as yet, had not made any arrangements to leave. Don't worry about me, he insisted, I've got my affairs in order.

Peter appeared, all smiles, as Lonä was applying the last of the frosting to the cake. Such a shame, she greeted dryly, that your work keeps you and your wife apart.

"Made all the more bearable by spending time with you and your family, gracious lady," he replied. He had with him a present of a boat with a canvas sail. Would Catharina pass the birthday boy over for him to hold awhile?

Lonä brought in the cake and gifts she'd held off opening until the party. There were birthday greetings from Gene, and from, of all people, Pia, who'd sent a foppish studio shot of herself in an oversized hat, framed in silver with a note saying she was to star in Veit Harlan's new film, *Jud Süss,* a pet project of Doctor Goebbels.

Name-dropper, sniffed Catharina.

Michael ruefully wondered what Hélène would have said about the shameless self-promotion, then quickly tried not to think of Hélène at all. Lonä thought the gift a kind, albeit perplexing, gesture.

But it was the equally unexpected birthday note from Hasso that shook Michael up. Brief, congratulatory, Hasso added that he was back at work adding to a long-standing commission.

"What is it?" Lonä asked, Braum helping her to hand round cake.

"Nothing. Nothing at all."

Michael convinced himself his visit to Tristan's was entirely a matter of trying to save the house. From what he gathered about the odd little man, if anyone could help, it'd be him. No need to share his intentions with Peter. Michael wasn't sure how Peter would take to hearing that he knew someone like Tristan. Peter would certainly dissuade him from going. Or worse. Want to come along.

"My darling boy, how have you been?" Tristan said with a flurry of kisses, none hitting their mark.

The loud, noxious, overflowing nightly circus stumbled on but with ever more military uniforms making telephone calls to pretty girls whose curls went limp in the damp subterranean air. Hasso had indeed been at task. His legions of Aryans and smokestacks bled out and downwards from the domed ceiling.

"Yes, yes, of course I am open for pleasure. It's all a matter of supply and demand and, of course, a great deal of Reichsmarks. But as you can see, there is a need for some to step away from all that cussing and brimstone we get poured over us, and as long as there is, I'll be here to provide an escape." Tristan took Michael's arm and led him to a table by the canal. "Now I hear you have a new job with some ministry or other. Do tell."

One of Tristan's little waiters brought a bottle of wine.

"Where are all the others?"

"Dying on me faster than hothouse roses, if you please. Shame about that. And just try and get anything that deformed in Germany these days."

Michael told him about the eviction notice. Tristan lit another cigarette and smiled wanly, eyes glassing over.

"My dear, I'm flattered you think I can somehow hold back the will of our Leader, but I assure you, there is nothing I can do. My only advice is to move, and quickly. The government will not stop their plans even for you von Renners."

Michael was disappointed, but not surprised.

"Jan, is he here? I haven't seen him in ages."

Tristan's expression never flinched. "He was arrested months ago." He drew on his cigarette languidly. "Oh, my dear. I see you really didn't know. Well, come now, our Jan never was the most discreet of young men. Surely that was obvious even to you."

Tristan waved his hand and insisted his waiter bring something stronger than wine for his guest. He looked to need it.

"There must be something we can do?"

"I wouldn't advise it. Boys like him are usually sent to Neuwied for a few months, and, if they straighten up, then released."

"I have a friend in the Abwehr. He could make inquiries."

"Don't draw attention to yourself, Michael. Doing nothing would be the best thing you could do for him. And for yourself."

Michael had been too agitated to notice the subtle change in Tristan's voice: calm replacing indifference.

"But I haven't done anything."

"Silly boy. Nowadays, just thinking wrong is forbidden."

"I have to help him."

"Help him by doing nothing. It's a nasty offence, but he could be released shortly. If you come forward, you will only jeopardize yourself. People will ask why. Think of your position, your work."

Billy.

"That's better."

According to von Renner family legend, Nan had propagated her African violets, the purple ones, from a cutting given her by the Empress Augusta Viktoria over forty years before. Certainly the palms that had survived Braum's neglect had the wizened look of time about them. The miniature pink-and-white roses, however, had been nicked from KaDeWe the Christmas before Nan died. All lovingly nurtured by Lonä, but even she could not prevent their determined decline in the shadowy corridor running the length of their new home. Within a month, undoubtedly, everything would be dead.

Although it was bright outside and the open windows embraced the distant sounds of yet another marching band on the Friedrichstrasse, sun never made any inroads into Michael and Lonä's apartment. It didn't help that the ever-lawful Frau Albrecht had hung a flag from the roof and the damned thing blocked the view when it wasn't wrapping itself around the pole, requiring someone to get out on the ledge and untangle it.

She opened the door in place of Lonä.

"Herr von Renner, you're home early."

Lonä was circumventing the large oak table to place the sleeping boy in his crib. None of the pieces of furniture they had bought through Tschelock's fit in these rooms and most of it would have to go.

"Michael, this is a surprise."

Not, This is a surprise, darling, or, This is a surprise, my dear.

"Isn't it wonderful, the news? Frau Albrecht and I were downstairs listening to the speeches on the radio."

Michael turned his gaze out the window for an uncomfortably long time. Then he asked, "What news?"

"The Anschluss," Frau Albrecht said. "Have you not heard?" Like it was his duty to know.

The open window allowed the flat to fill with the excitement rising from the street.

Michael dragged his hands across his face and, taking off his jacket, sat. "What's wonderful about that?"

"Austria had always been rightfully part of Germany," Lonä said. "Now it is again."

"I wonder what the Austrians think about that." *And Hélène and Doctor Linder.*

Lonä quickly thanked her neighbour for her help with Wilhem and ushered her away.

"Why do you say things like that?" she said when they were alone. "And what's wrong? You look pale."

"My grandmother's house came down today."

Lonä joined him on the ottoman, placing her hands into his. The gesture felt foreign and forced for two who had not shared a bed since the birth of their child.

"I'm sorry. You do know I was happy there."

"I didn't know it would happen today. I was out for lunch and went down to the canal. You know, just to have a look. I walked on the bridge so I could see it from the other side. A crew was already there. They'd knocked down the conservatory and the porch. I didn't think it would bother me that much to see it go, but the house meant everything to my grandmother. I think it kept my grandfather alive for her." He looked at his wife. "They must have meant so much to each other."

There went that damned flag again.

"And now her home's made way for a greater Berlin. She'd be honoured by the sacrifice."

"Honoured? She'd be sickened by what I saw today."

"Michael, please. You shouldn't talk like that."

"Oh, yes. I'd forgotten your new friend. Does she listen at keyholes?"

Lonä let go of his hands. "Stop it."

"Let me tell you about honour. When I was on that bridge, watching the crane ready to knock down what was left of the house, I saw him. Herr Leopold. Sitting in his chair by the window on the top floor."

"Michael, no . . ."

"Even from where I stood I could see that he looked resigned, peaceful."

"Surely someone checked?"

"For what? A cripple in a chair? He must have had no place to go."

"Why didn't he tell us? Why didn't *you* stop them?"

"I tried! Christ, I tried. I was too far away, the noise and the ball was swinging. I screamed from the bridge that someone was still inside, but no one could hear me. When I got to the site there was nothing, bricks, just nothing."

Lonä put her arms around him and dutifully kissed his cheek.

"Why?" Michael said. "He was just an old man. How could this happen?"

"If Herr Leopold didn't want to leave and hid from the authorities, you can't blame yourself."

Maybe the time had come.

"For what?"

"To go home, back to Canada."

Lonä pulled away. "You're talking nonsense. Listen to those crowds out there. We can't leave now. It's happening. Everything the Führer has promised is happening. Braum says—"

"I'm stifling here. We're like ants in this hole. Sometimes, I . . . I can't breathe."

"It's only this apartment. I know you don't like it, we'll find another, Michael. We can work this out. You can't give up."

But that felt so much easier.

"What about our son? You'd deprive him of his birthright? And me? Don't you know how much I care for you?"

Sadly, he suspected as much. "Of course you'll come with me."

"You'd make us leave all this, those that care for us, behind."

Yes.

"I was hoping, especially after what happened today in Austria, that we would celebrate our own new beginning."

Lonä probably blushed, but Michael couldn't tell in the dim afternoon light.

"Wilhelm's old enough for a brother or sister. I know I'm ready. And another child will be good for us. Bring us closer."

"Another child? Are you mad?" *Oh, Christ.* "I'm sorry. I didn't mean that."

She rose in front of him, stood very quietly.

Wading at the beach in Wannsee, afternoons too hot for strolls in the Tiergarten, flower boxes weighted down with red and white petunias and lindens canopied in green: summer had arrived without Michael's noticing. His work was all-engrossing. It had to be. After the Austrian Anschluss, a series of new laws compelling Juden to register their assets, then their businesses, resulted in piles of requests on Michael's desk. The steady, round-the-clock clatter, hum and shake of Dehomag's sorters, punchers and tabulators struggled efficiently to keep pace. Lists of Kreuzberg's and Schöneberg's and Wedding's Juden. Juden in the military. Lists of Juden with police records. Lists of Juden with no police records. Lists of Juden businesses. Lists of half Juden and quarter Juden and maybe even Juden with green ears and fish tails. Michael didn't care. Didn't question. At least the work carried him over the worst of his estrangement from Lonä.

There aren't enough hours in the day, not enough staff, not enough of anything, he complained to Peter over their regular luncheons. Trained men being taken for the Wehrmacht, factories competing for his skilled women and the requests for information from this ministry and that ministry, the military, the city, accelerated daily. And what did the big shots at Dehomag do to help? Lots of hot coffee. Okay, real coffee and not the ersatz pulp-tasting stuff made from acorns that was now being sold in shops. And stretching breaks every hour. Can you believe that?

Peter would quietly stifle a grin behind his fist during these rants then suggest Michael should get away. A Strength Through Joy trip to Madeira might be what he needed, but the government-subsidized vacation would have to be taken with his wife. Michael chose not to pursue it.

The census, delayed again by millions of Austrians having been annexed, brought Mark Mercer on another visit from New York. Michael invited him home this time, where the Yankee charmed Lonä over dinner, and after, had rolled up his sleeves to help Billy float his boat in the bathtub, but Peter's birthday gift had gone missing and Lonä couldn't say where. Later, he shared news privately with Michael: America knew Germany was mobilizing. Even though Roosevelt had recognized the Anschluss, Germany couldn't expect to keep expanding without provoking a war. And the flood of fleeing Juden was headlining the world's newspapers, underscored with horror stories of persecution. Gene had been writing too, urging Michael to bring his family back to Nova Scotia.

I'll wait a month and see how things are. If need be, we can make a quick dash to France and from there, England and home.

He'd get their papers in order. Put money aside. It didn't matter that Lonä refused to go. That would sort itself out, somehow.

But what about Jan?

∽

Ina tossed a disapproving nod towards the schoolgirl sitting along the row of empty chairs.

Up close, she was no schoolgirl.

"Herr von Renner? Frau Merten sent me." She smiled a practised smile.

Ina was watching intently from the corner.

"Yes, of course. How is my old friend?"

"She said to tell you that the one-pot dinner for the Winter Relief Fund is tonight. She knew you didn't want to miss it and that if you don't come tonight, there might not be another."

"How kind of her to let me know."

"She also said she needs five Reichsmarks. To hold your ticket. Otherwise she'll have to let it go."

Michael reached into his jacket pocket. "I understand."

He escorted the girl to the door.

"Tell Frau Merten that I'll be along."

The girl giggled and was gone.

"Good of you to help out the poor," Ina said as Michael returned to his office.

The secretary was writing and did not look up.

Michael had to walk, in no particular direction, just to control the shaking in his limbs. At the leafy edges of the Tiergarten he turned back to the Bellevuestrasse and the Berthold house, rather, the former Berthold house, its lawn gated to all unpleasant associations. Michael knew from Braum that the place had been sold, well below market value, to a high-ranking official in the Luftwaffe. A flag hung from the roof over the entranceway. No way of seeing if the custard-yellow dahlias, their edges trimmed in burgundy, still grew out back were Frau Berthold had liked to read.

The Guthmans' greengrocery was not far, and as Michael had not seen his former neighbours since their eviction, he thought he might visit. It would give him an opportunity to buy some sweets for Jan, who undoubtedly would expect it. He wondered if they knew about Herr Leopold.

From the street the tiny shop appeared unchanged, except that the sign inside had been moved over the door and changed to *Juden Forbidden*, with a small sign attached underneath: *Room for Let*. The canary canvas awning, the wood tables weighted under tubs of peonies and day lillies, yellow, red, pink and orange and all shades in between, missed only one thing, Frau Guthman, hearty and fussing, tending to her customers.

"Gone," the short woman in the starched apron behind the counter replied, the bell over the door still ringing. "Are you a friend of theirs?"

"Old neighbour."

The shopkeeper shook her head with a long, deep sigh. "Terrible business for them, their son dying. Never got over it. Herr Guthman joined the army and his wife went back to her family, somewhere in Bavaria I think. My husband and I run this place for them now. We're thinking of buying it."

Michael thanked the woman, Frau Proessel, and gathered some apples, a piece of cheese and an orange.

"From Vienna. Expensive," she said, noticing his eye taken with the chocolate. "You like for the wife, yes?"

He nodded.

Laughter and the clinking of glasses and cutlery spilled out of the open windows and doors of the Barutherstrasse cafés in the Kreuzberg suburb. The flower sellers were crowding out sidewalks filled with soldiers and young women who had to skirt around baskets of mums and lilies. Flags hung limp in the breathless summer twilight. Long black cars and canvas-sided trucks jostled on the streets with bicycles. Two Hitler Youth in uniform were poring over a map. A boy jingling coins in a can was selling the evening *Tageblatt*.

Frau Merten was in her sitting room by the front door and stopped Michael from going upstairs. He would find his friend much altered, she warned. The money he'd sent had secured Jan's old room, but she'd have to have more by the end of the month because she was a businesswoman and not running a hospital.

That sent Michael hurriedly up the stairs, where he found Jan, asleep, under a dirty wool blanket in the same cramped, airless room he'd occupied months ago. The tiny window, its sill littered with dying flies, would only open a crack. Under the humming naked light, the young man was all yellow skin stretched over bones, his breath rattling. Michael sat by the bed. However long, he'd wait.

"Ah, it's you."

One of Jan's front teeth was broken.

"What happened? Where've you been?"

"Go away."

"Look, I brought you something." Michael laid out the fruit, cheese and candy on the rough table.

"I said go away."

"But chocolate is your favourite. See—"

Jan's eyes closed. He was barely able to move.

"I've been so worried about you."

"Leave me alone."

So Michael did, getting as far as the other side of the door where, son of a bitch, he'd had enough, enough of worrying and lying and tying himself up in knots. No more. Ungrateful little bastard. Michael should be with Lonä, playing with Billy, not here, not like this.

Damn it. He could hear Jan crying.

So what? All Michael had to do was go down the stairs and be done with the selfish little whore forever. Friendship over. Christ, it cost him too much. Isn't that what Avon once said? And until now, Michael had never understood what that meant. How could being a friend cost you? Well, goddamn it, now he knew, only too well. He gripped the banister. Down the stairs, out the door was all it would take. Back home to where he should be.

But Michael leaned against the wall and slowly sank to his knees. Hard to say who he loathed more right then, Jan or himself.

Come morning, Frau Merten, bringing water and fresh linen because, she sighed, always a sucker for an invalid, found Michael sleeping on the landing outside Jan's door. So that's the way of it, she offered. Well, she'd seen that before. Once had a set of twins in the school. If one had troubles, the other suffered. It would end badly. But after checking in on the sick young man, she thought Jan might like to see him now.

Frau Proessel was only too glad to let out the flat above the grocery store to Michael. She even helped him get Jan up the narrow outside stairs and into the bed.

"My cousin's been in an automobile accident," Michael said. The lie explained Jan, so thin, shaved head, his unsteadiness, his shaking as he let Michael cover him with a blanket. "I fear he will have a long convalescence and needs to be someplace quiet."

The grocer's wife shrugged and took the month's rent.

"Why?" Jan said, when he and Michael were alone.

"You couldn't stay at Frau Merten's."

"No. You're right." Jan closed his eyes. "Why are you so good to me?"

Michael spread another blanket across the bed, made sure it was tucked in securely.

"That's no answer," said Jan. He was so weak, Michael barely heard him. "Maybe you could get me out of the city for a bit." He knew of a place where the grass was waist high and there were grapes for the taking.

"Not for a while, Jan. You're not well enough."

"When I am?"

Michael nodded.

Now, did he need any help cleaning himself up?

Jan shook his head quickly and said he just wanted to sleep.

When Michael returned home, he'd been away for almost two days. Thank goodness Lonä was very understanding about the irregular nature of his work. *In the service of the Reich,* he explained.

Of course.

⌒⌒

When Michael reached his desk he put the photograph of Billy, the one of him laughing, reaching for the flag outside the apartment window, into the wooden frame. The only picture in his office. He'd been admiring the frame for several days before he bought it, the handiwork of a one-eyed carver who'd set up around the corner on the Friedrichstrasse. A barefoot boy was playing with a dog in the lower corner, gulls flew up top. It reminded him of Nova Scotia, but to his horror the artisan had pulled out his knife and quickly sliced in several swastikas to complete the sale.

Ruined.

But he'd paid for the frame and thanked the man.

"Is this how an employee of the Reich's information bureau spends his time?"

Peter towered over him in full uniform, Ina looking around his shoulder. His friend had never visited Michael in this office before.

"This is a surprise."

"It will be. I've come on official business."

Peter then sat on the edge of the desk. Thank you, go away, to Ina standing in the doorway. No arrest today, fräulein.

"Official?"

"I'm off to London for a few days. You and me."

"London?"

"I need someone I can trust, who speaks the language. My English is terrible."

"Lonä—"

Peter waved it off. "Reich business comes first. Your dear wife will agree."

"I don't know—"

"What?"

"Where I put my suitcase."

Lonä, alongside Frau Albrecht, saw them off. The house warden watched, arms folded, not quite sure what to make of Michael's association with the officer. Not until they were in the car driving south to Tempelhof did Peter announce, We're flying.

"Air travel is nothing. We'll be in London in a few hours."

Maybe so, but it would still be longer than that horrible Zeppelin flight.

Peter parked the car, where, from across the tarmac, they could see cranes and heavy tractors clawing and digging around the limestone-clad office buildings, turning Tempelhof into an unrivalled world air terminal. Then they were escorted past a row of Messerschmidts to the swastika-emblazoned Junkers waiting with its props spinning for takeoff. There were only twelve other passengers on this flight, and like Peter, dressed in civilian clothing. Shortly after Michael squeezed into his narrow seat, the engines loudly spun and the plane taxied.

Peter had to shout: "Not many people get to see Berlin from the sky."

Neither did Michael.

"I was going to tell you as soon as we were airborne," Peter said as the car cut its way through the crowded London streets.

Michael's first clue Peter had been less than honest appeared upon landing, when his annoyance with an emigrating German family had become loudly evident. Their wading through the myriad forms and official papers had slowed the line down and wasn't that just like them, Peter said in perfect English, glancing at their J-stamped passports. Get them out of Germany and they cause trouble here. Prior to that, Michael had been too doubled over to notice anything other than disapproving glares. Being airsick was apparently unmanly. Violently airsick was just plain rude.

Why the subterfuge, he wanted to know.

"Would you have come if I said, let's get away for the weekend and fly to London?"

The foul-mouthed cabby, who was fucking-this and fucking-that, turned off the Chelsea Embankment onto the Royal Hospital Road.

"You'd have made some excuse about not leaving Lonä or Billy. Or work. Or you couldn't afford it."

"Then you don't have any business here?"

"Not really. Just wanted to visit some friends for a few days. And I know how miserable you've been lately. So enjoy it. And try not to think about the flight back."

The taxi stopped in front of a narrow ash-streaked townhouse on Ebury Street. The thin, elfish boy who opened the door struggled with their bags. Wet climate, bad food and poor exercise, Peter whispered, gave the English their pasty look.

Peter! greeted a large, rolling man with black shiny hair and rheumy eyes as he came groaning down the stairs. Some exotic ailment was eating away at their host beginning at the extremities; his fingernails had fallen off, leaving festering open sores.

"Our prime minister heads to Munich and you arrive here. Fair exchange. Who's this?"

Peter introduced Michael to Robert Deslauriers, an old friend from Paris claiming an association with the Bourbons but, alas, circumstances had reduced him to running a guesthouse.

"You'll find everything to your satisfaction."

Robert escorted them to rooms separated by the hall. Not large, but elegant with puddling purple and green velvet drapes, cherry-wood and marble-topped tables garnished with epergnes of choco-lates and candied fruit. Robert helped himself.

"I'm having a small, intimate gathering of friends tonight for dinner. Of course you'll both come."

Two men, twentyish, impeccably dressed with identically groomed moustaches, were sorting through a pile of records by the gramo-phone while listening to Benny Goodman. Summoned by the music, another man, wearing saddle shoes and a jacket tapering at the waist, flung open the doors and threw himself into the middle of the room, Hotcha! his only greeting. As if possessed by the beat, he writhed and contorted, swing-dancing with fingers fanned out and trembling. One of the men by the gramophone laughed at the spec-tacle, tossing back his head, while the other, ever so lightly, smiled, resting his hand upon his companion's arm.

"Do you know all these people?"

"Friends of Robert's," Peter said, before excusing himself.

Peter's English took Michael some getting used to.

"Gentlemen, if you please."

Robert opened the doors on the opposite side of his sitting room and waved his guests into a long, high room, Doric columns midway, a fireplace at each end. Waiting, a line of boys in black coats and white ties holding silver trays of hors d'oeuvres. The chatter briefly gave way to appreciation.

"Hanley, some gin for my young friend." Robert then offered Michael his choice from one of the trays, insisting he must be hungry. He'd heard about his troubled flight.

No thanks. Michael couldn't get beyond the man's disintegrating fingers and wondered how he'd manage the weekend without food.

"Are you a fan of Benny's?"

Somewhat older, with flecks of grey in his hair, the man asking was doing the same thing as Michael, standing alone, staring into a drink.

"The recording?" Michael said he hadn't heard of him.

"Don't get swinging in the Fatherland, eh? Been to Berlin once myself. Now there was a town. A Yankee buck was worth its weight in gold. But that was before your Mr. Hitler started mopping things up."

Where's Peter?

"Say, you don't sound German. I mean, German German."

"I'm from Nova Scotia."

"Don't say? From Boston myself. Came here for the war and haven't been able to leave. Guess I'll be around for another one at the rate those Jerries are going. So, what's your business here?"

"A couple days' holiday."

"Quite the looker, he is."

The man nodded towards Peter, who, upon returning to the room, had retreated to a corner and was quietly conversing with two men.

Michael excused himself on the pretext of getting another drink.

"No need to run off. Look, I've got something upstairs better than what Robert serves."

In pulling away, Michael spilt gin across his shirt. Christ, but it was an excuse to extricate himself from the American and flee to the safety of his room.

Peter rapped softly at his door a few minutes later.

"What happened?"

"Spilt drink, no harm."

Peter closed the door behind him. "You sound different in English."

"Peter, this is an odd place."

"Sorry. My contacts wanted to meet here."

"I thought you were off duty."

"I am. Just a few words with party members from Denmark. They've been working towards securing the North Slesvig for Germany. But enough of that. You're right, we're here to relax."

From the window, London, Berlin were pretty much the same. Racing cabs. Clanging trams. Dogs sniffing, pissing on stoops, mindful of no one. Housewives hurrying home laden with brown-wrapped bundles to cook the evening meal.

Peter was very close, smelling of sweat, of tobacco, of a soap-laundered shirt. Brown soap like Mum had used to get the grease out of his father's work pants. Nothing got them cleaner, she used to say.

The fluttering of a finger; the brushing against his arm. London's lights shimmering in the thickening coal fog, the omnibuses rumbling and screeching along the boulevard, the hurried faces that never paused to look up crowded between them through the open window. Then Michael stepped away and Peter's hand fell to his side.

"It's been a long day."

"Yes. I suppose it has."

As Michael got into bed, he could hear the radio across the hall in Peter's room, news about Chamberlain and peace in our time and Britain and France carving up Czechoslovakia sounding like a jingle for Yorkshire Gold Tea.

Dreams about Mr. Glyn, Avon's father, came not long after. Mr. Glyn drank a lot after he couldn't work on the docks. He'd sit out back and in that melodic voice he had, almost sing his yarns about the S.S. *Atlantic* going aground on Marr's Head in the eighteen-somethings. In Michael's dream, hundreds died. Women and children, thinking they were safe in the hands of the captain, were shouting, You're wrong, you're wrong. Those who weren't trapped inside froze in the water or drowned in the surf. In the morning, apart from hair washing up like kelp, there was nothing on the beach except a young man in a shiny vest looking for cigarette butts. When he smiled, Michael saw he had a chipped tooth.

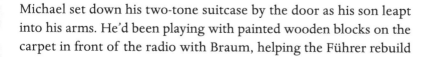

Michael set down his two-tone suitcase by the door as his son leapt into his arms. He'd been playing with painted wooden blocks on the carpet in front of the radio with Braum, helping the Führer rebuild

Berlin all day, smiled his mother. Berlin was forgotten when Michael gave Billy the model airplane Peter had insisted upon buying.

How was your trip?

Fine, fine.

He was back sooner than expected.

Too bad about Peter being called back to Berlin after only a day, agreed Braum as he took his leave. Did he say why? Michael didn't know.

They sat down to boiled potatoes and sausage tasting like grain, bread and turnip soup.

Had Michael heard? Braum had been promoted to party *Zellenleiter*. That's only a cell leader, Lonä explained, but Catharina was excited about his joining the elite. Michael pretended to care. What about London? Foggy and Michael coughed a lot. Oh. Did he want more bread? Michael shook his head. Lonä held her head in her hands, looking interested and quite beautiful. Billy crawled into Michael's lap. How was work with Peter? Michael shrugged and said he needed some air after that godawful flight. There was no question of her joining him. Lonä took Billy for his bath.

Frau Albrecht, head out the door as Michael went down the stairs, observed, Going about so soon after arriving home?

A little queasy from the air travel, maybe some fresh air will help, good evening, Frau Albrecht.

He hated that woman.

Early October now, days noticeably shorter, hedges and vines browning in anticipation of winter, but red geraniums in their window boxes were still round in bloom.

It must have come from the Spree, that coolness, a sea-like moistness washing pleasantly over him. There'll be fog tonight, Mum'd say from her chair on the porch, needles clicking on one of her afghans, seashell pattern. Michael's father'd be running his forefinger over the words in the *Chronicle* on the hunt for any tidbit about European politics, glasses perched on top of his thinning head. Felix and some fellas would have a game of ball going in the empty lot at the corner.

The moment scattered in the fluttering of flags, strewn like poppies across Berlin's city block canyons, the bonhomie of the

Czechoslovakian appeasement. Everywhere, everyone, echoing Prime Minister Chamberlain.

"You must have a word with that young man," Frau Proessel said when Michael stopped into the grocery to pay the rent.

The prices were higher, the shelves leaner, but she insisted business was good.

"He plays that radio very loud. It won't do. You must talk to him. You know, if you ask me, he should be in the army instead of listening to that radio all day."

The young man had dispensation due to poor health, Michael reminded the shopkeeper, but assured her he'd talk to Jan about the noise. He slipped a few extra marks in with the rent before he went around the back, off the street to the stairs.

Jan was flipping through the dog-eared *McCall's* magazines Gene had sent. He adored *McCall's* and its views of America, where everyone lived in fashionable Cape Cods and strolled along beaches with their trousers rolled up, walking well-groomed retrievers.

"Where've you been?"

No hello. Michael removed his coat and sat down.

"I'll go mad if I don't get out."

"You're still too weak."

Jan was flipping angrily through the pages. Rest and proper food had been a tonic.

"You can't lock me up forever."

"You're hardly a prisoner."

"Why can't you be nice to me?"

When he first brought Jan here, he was all gratitude. Not a large room, it had one big window overlooking the street above Guthman's entrance, a tiled stove and hot plate, a mattress bed and several upholstered chairs around a table. Now that Jan was mending, the room had become too small, too hot, smelled of rotting vegetables, and there was nothing to do. No good would ever come of Jan being idle.

"I'm sorry."

"So, where were you?"

"London."

Jan stopped flipping and sat up. "London? And me here, bored? You bastard."

"You're supposed to be resting."

"Resting? And miss all the excitement you've arranged for me?"

"What do you mean? Nothing happens around here."

"That's what you think. Come here and see for yourself. You see that flower shop on the corner with the umbrellas in the window? There's an old woman who comes out every morning and washes her stoop and the pavement. And down there, see, at the other end. The building with the blue door? There was an old man who'd walk his dog around the block every day at the same hour. He's got a wooden leg. His dog always took a piss on the woman's stoop. She'd come out with an umbrella flapping to chase the two of them away. Boy, he'd curse and rattle his fist. 'That's no way to treat a man who fought for Germany.' And she'd scream back that she was going to report him and his filthy mutt. She knew he was one of those Social Democrats and wouldn't the authorities like to know that! She wasn't fooling. When they came for him and carried him out the door, he wasn't wearing his leg. They said he wouldn't need it where he was going. Next day, after all that, I see that crazy woman walking that old man's dog.

"And across the way, there, is a boy who lives with his mother. He's very beautiful. She's ugly and lies in a bed all day. He's in the Hitler Youth and the walls of his room are covered with posters."

Michael pulled the drape farther aside and cranked his neck to see clearly. "How can you know all this?"

"I've got eyes, haven't I? Every day after school the boy plays marching songs on a gramophone and does calisthenics. Then he warms soup on the stove and feeds it to his mother with a spoon.

"And there, those three windows across from the grocery? The woman in there is fucking Frau Proessel's husband. Her own husband is in the navy and comes home on leave once a month, but his pay isn't enough for her so after the grocer fucks her, he leaves fruit or potatoes, sometimes real coffee and sugar. His own wife doesn't know because she's too tired at the end of the day, but his mistress waves and whistles to her from her window." Jan chuckled. "Frau Proessel thinks she's touched in the head.

"So there. How could anyone rest with all that excitement? And I adore London. Or I know I would, if I could just get there."

Michael was laughing. "Believe it or not, you had a better time looking out this window than I had in London."

"Why didn't you take me? Did you bring me something?"

"It was business." The Abwehr part was best left unsaid.

"David always took me on his business trips." Jan flounced on the bed, tossed *McCall's* on the floor. "I'm going crazy cooped up here. Hey! Let's go to Tristan's."

"Promise me you won't go back there."

No way.

"Besides, Tristan's is probably closed now."

Jan shrugged. "Nothing'll close down Tristan. I could stay with him. At least I wouldn't be bored."

Michael gave up watching the street light up under the flashing flares of passing trams and truck lights. He sat on the edge of the bed. Shyly he touched Jan's arm.

Jan rolled himself across the bed and languidly picked up another magazine from off the table.

"I've read this a hundred times already. When are you going to bring me some new ones?"

The hall at Dehomag crackled with the gnawing clatter of hundreds of keypunching machines. Between the rows of operators, clerks pushed trolleys stacked with cards and file folders. Tables weighted with sandwiches and urns of steaming java lined the wall underneath the windows darkening in the November twilight. A woman with very short hair and wearing a gym romper was leading a small group of operators in a quick shoulder, hand and finger stretch to help keep them from cramping.

Michael looked around the file room at the end of the corridor usually patrolled by Ina. On duty elsewhere, she'd left her empty desk in the care of a twisted philodendron curling towards the floor. The door was not locked; Ina's wary glance was enough of a deterrent against unauthorized entry. In metal cabinets stacked to the ceiling sat copies of the reports requested by various government ministries, assembled, cross-referenced and verified by Michael's operators. He liked the quiet here. He'd imagine hearing the dust hit the floor and if the telephone outside did ring, you'd never know. He found the cabinet he'd been looking for. Thick manila files kept from light and damp contained Reichsbahn passenger capacities, import quotas for oil seed and Gypsy populations, amongst thousands of other requisite topics. And here in this cabinet for prison camps, drawer S, he filed a folder of new arrivals for Sachsenhausen.

"Telephone, Herr von Renner. Abwehr headquarters."

Jesus. Michael was convinced Ina took grim pleasure in keeping him on edge, sneaking up on him. This evening, she was especially delighted in saying the call was from the Wilhelmstrasse.

I hoped you'd still be there, the voice on the telephone began without introduction. Peter. Not seen since their return from London.

Oh.

Dinner?

Sure.

The nearly empty restaurant, a landmark for its Alsatian dishes, was panelled in oak wainscoting, a series of candlelit private booths walled off like medieval chambers. Peter was waiting for Michael in uniform.

"Finishing or starting?"

"I have to report later." Peter signalled for their server.

The man returned with beer and, The beef dish is very good tonight, but it is made with rabbit.

"Where have you been?" Michael asked after they had ordered.

Peter lit a cigarette and tossed off a casual reply about too much work. He dropped the match into the ashtray. "You?"

"With the census coming in the spring, you can imagine."

"Lonä and your son?"

"They're well."

Peter sat back into the booth and languidly freed his neck from the buttons of his uniform. The table's votive candle sputtered and hissed. He tap-tapped his cigarette against the tray, returned it to his lips. Michael looked away, and toyed with the folded napkin by his silverware. When he glanced back, Peter was staring.

"Is something wrong?"

Peter drew on his cigarette. "Why do you ask?"

"You seem distracted."

"Perhaps I am." Peter smiled.

Two men in suits and two blond women in deeply cut dresses laughed in a nearby booth as one of the men pounded the table with his fist. " . . . can't see from back there? Then here, darling, put your head between my legs . . ."

The waiter brought bread.

"And your work? It goes well?"

Michael said it did.

"Do you ever wonder what it's all for, what you do?"

"What do you mean?"

"The information your department compiles. What do you think is done with it?"

Michael didn't know how to respond.

Peter drained his glass. Michael followed suit.

Steaming dishes, bowls of potatoes and squash were set down among the bread. Michael hesitated, gesturing for Peter to serve himself first. But Peter stamped out his cigarette and looked at the dinner before him as if confused by its arrival. His plate remained empty. Their waiter wanted to know if something was wrong. More beer was ordered and Peter dismissed him with a curt flick of his hand.

The other diners were laughing again, heartier than before, as their table was cleared.

"Not hungry?" Michael asked.

Peter relaxed back into the booth and lit another cigarette. He gazed intently at Michael through the smoke. "Do you ever think about going home?"

"Berlin is my home now."

"Maybe you should consider going. Think of it as a visit."

"Lonä will never leave."

Their glasses were filled. But not for long.

"You must care for her a great deal, your wife," Peter said.

"And Billy."

"Yes, your boy."

"And you?"

"My wife and I, enough to say, we both acknowledge the way things are between us."

Peter rapped his empty glass on the table, then held it aloft. The waiter hurried over with a pitcher. Michael groaned to himself and glanced at his watch. He'd drunk too much already.

"My apologies," Peter said, insisting he take care of the bill. He glanced at the barely eaten meal between them. "The food is usually much better here."

Michael, getting up and putting on his coat, glad this awkward evening was ending, said it was fine. He was really feeling the drink now.

"Be careful," Peter said as they stepped out onto the sidewalk, noting the bitterness of charred wood in the air. "There was an assassination at the German embassy in Paris. There'll be trouble in the streets tonight."

They departed, each glancing back as if something was not finished. Or in fact, just had.

A dimly lit street here, a square bedecked in flags.

Yes, boy. You boy! Price of admission, demanded the white-faced clown with whale-blue tears. One Reichsmark. Two Reichsmark. Three Reichsmark, four! Hand them over hand them over. Yes! You my boy are tonight's lucky winner!

Michael could offer the policeman just his papers.

When had the circus arrived?

The street behind the clown exploded under fizzing rockets as the show began, dancing monkeys and feathers falling like snow. To the right, the Midway of Excess, left, the Lane of No Return. Hurry! The fireworks will begin as soon as the snow stops.

But it's not snow, they're feathers.

They're from their beds.

What will they sleep on?

The clown shrugged, but pointed to the orange in the sky.

You don't want to miss the show. It's the last night. Tomorrow we go to work.

Under the big top painted like night danced ribbons of square lights, little monkeys clutching the balcony railings, gulping, unable to breathe because of the feathers.

Try your luck, sir?

Michael, dizzy from the drink, didn't think so.

But three tosses of the brick per try. It's the night of breaking glass. Down they go, windows dissolving into rivers of tears spilling into the road washing the yellow stars away with them. Everyone's a winner. Take what you see. Grab what you can. No one goes home empty handed.

The centre-ring show began with the clanging of bells and wee fire trucks chugging up and down the streets. Floppy ears and big noses came with their clubs to shoo shoo shoo. Away from the fires! Don't put them out! Let them burn. Clang! Clang! Clang!

The monkeys were made to dance on the street corners, standing on crates for everyone to see.

Pull their beards, cried the children. Hard! Harder!

But monkeys don't have beards, said Michael. Juden do.

Clap! Clap! Oh, yes, Poppa, make them cut their beards! It makes them squeal so! Clap! Clap! Now kiss pigs! Make them kiss pigs! Look how that makes them wrinkle up their great big noses!

Down the midway thundered clowns with truncheons and hand-painted smiles.

Catch them!

Catch them!

Black bird for the pie!

Don't let them get away.

Don't let them run and fly.

But they're not blackbirds, said Michael. They're children in bed-clothes and bare feet.

Don't you believe that, sir. Black little beggars. Mystical little crows. Why do they have apples if they're not destined for the pie?

I gave them those, said Frau Proessel, pulling a disoriented Michael out of the crowded street and into her doorway. They came and asked to perch, those poor dears, so I gave them apples and sent them on their way. It's cold and their poor bare feet. But remember, I gave them apples.

Feathery flakes were white and warm. The crowds were circling round the flames. Everyone was dancing. Husha. Husha. We all fall down.

"Jesus," said Michael, closing the door behind him. "It's a nightmare out there, all over the city."

He staggered over to Jan at the window, his head pounding. The synagogue was on fire. It started hours ago. The police had done nothing except keep the firemen away, only letting them douse nearby structures so the flames would not spread. Not to worry though. The gas and electricity had been shut off before the troubles began. Frau Proessel and her husband were standing outside on the curb to get a better look.

Michael tried to pull the curtains.

Jan stopped him. "Don't you want to see?"

"I've seen enough tonight." *Peter's right.* "It's time for me to go."

"Then go."

"No. Home, to Nova Scotia."

"Because of this? This'll be old news by morning." Jan glanced at him sideways. "You got too close to the fires. Looks like you got a sunburn."

Michael reached for the tenderness on the side of his face.

A siren wailed, the crowd outside began to cheer. Come with me, was drowned out by the cupola on the synagogue crashing through the roof, filling the heavens with new stars.

Jan was applauding.

1939

In the weeks leading up to the new year, Dehomag's little punch cards multiplied into a gushing torrent, processing and cataloguing the latest round of restrictions. After the smoke and broken glass of that November night, the government levied a billion-Reichsmark fine against the victims to pay for damages. Michael couldn't believe it. Then came the Aryanization of Juden businesses and the mountains of paperwork that entailed. Followed by a last-minute dash for all Juden to comply with the order to change their first names to Sarah or Israel by year's end.

It's so obvious they're not wanted here, why don't they just go?

In January, a tour of officials from IG Farben came through his department, and after Michael explained what he and his staff did, the visitors took him aside and made an offer. IG Farben need a top-notch man to manage a project identifying European chemical assets. He'd work at their office, not far from the charred remains of the Reichstag and the new Reich Chancellery on the Wilhelmstrasse. Interested?

Michael gave Dehomag short notice.

His first assignment was to oversee cataloguing deposits of prussic acid, traded by IG Farben as Zyklon B, a gas used to exterminate roaches and rats. Meant nothing to him if the company wanted to know about deposits belonging to other European companies. The job paid well, which would help support Jan, the hours were reasonable and, best of all, it had nothing to do with Juden.

Lonä was waiting for him on the couch, the late-afternoon sun behind her, shadowing her face. She was not alone.

"This is unexpected," Michael said.

Coming home, he'd gone out of his way, near to the Potsdamer Platz. There were no crowds. No bands. The doughnut seller was gone. Columbus Haus across the Königgrätzerstrasse was draped in giant flags, one of which had come loose and was listlessly flapping in a May breeze. There was where he'd first seen Jan, seven years now.

Billy struggled in his mother's arms, calling for Dadda. Frau Albrecht blamed the outburst on Michael. Too much coddling. The boy would never make a good soldier. Catharina, jaw and shoulders set, completed the unhappy female triumvirate. Most surprisingly of all, Braum was there, at this time of day, standing by the window, quickly downing a drink and looking for another.

Michael set his briefcase on the hallway table and noticed his two-tone valise by the door.

"Lonä, is something wrong?"

"What's wrong, indeed."

Lonä put up her hand to silence Catharina. "You'd better come in and sit down."

He entered the room, but remained standing.

"I'm pregnant," she said quickly.

What! How? Michael couldn't even remember the last time they had sex.

"Certainly not by you," his cousin said.

An awkward silence fell. Frau Albrecht sat back and folded her arms.

"It's Braum's," Lonä said.

Billy wriggled free of his mother's arms and once on the floor hurried to his father. Frau Albrecht intercepted the boy and carted him screaming down the hall. A door slammed after them.

"Sit down, Michael," his wife said.

Braum?

"What did you expect?" His cousin's harsh tone struck him like cold water.

"You knew about this? About them?"

"I suggested it. It seems I'm unable to have children. You, you are unwilling to do your duty."

Lonä had faltered, but apparently she was determined to show no tears. "You go to work every day and do your part. I can do nothing but have babies. I want a Mother's Cross."

Braum continued to look away. The boy caught with his hand in the cookie jar. How many times had it been in there?

"Have you nothing to say?" Catharina said.

Relieved. He actually felt . . . relieved.

"No matter. Anything you say now is irrelevant. What you're going to do is go."

So the suitcase was for him.

"Lonä? Bill—?"

"He'll be better off without the likes of you."

"Catharina—"

"No, Lonä, it must be said. Yes, we know about you. We all do." Catharina was shaking. "But it is only for the von Renner name that we'll say nothing. Thank God dear Nan Carmel is not alive. This would break her heart. And to think we brought you here to protect the family. You are a disgrace. And you're a thief."

Michael reeled.

"If it were up to me, I'd report you."

"No," Lonä said.

"Didn't think we knew about him, did you? You stupid, stupid fool," Catharina said. "Go back to him, that boy of yours."

Oh, Christ.

For the first time Braum spoke.

"I warned you, Michael."

Frau Proessel?

"Things haven't been right between us for a long time," Lonä said quietly. "I knew something was wrong. I thought it was another woman so I started following you. Sometimes to work, sometimes after."

He must have looked hurt.

"Is it so hard to believe that I might have been jealous?"

"There is your suitcase," Catharina said. "Leave Germany, Cousin. The sooner, the better for you."

Lonä waited, maybe still clinging to the hope that he'd deny everything. But all Michael could do was go.

Frau Proessel pointed to the empty flat across the street once belonging to the boy who did calisthenics and his mother, thinking Michael would enjoy the latest gossip. Turns out, the old woman had been a Jehovah's Witness. Her son rightly denounced her, but they shouldn't have taken her like that from her sickbed. Frau Proessel shook her head and went back to stacking the spring produce. She didn't notice the suitcase.

In the flat over the grocery, Michael found Jan stretching his legs in front of the window. His hair was longer now and he was growing unfashionable sideburns. Jan had returned to a healthy weight and there was a glow to his colour, even if being flightless resulted in usually less than happy moods. As to his time in the work camp, he refused to speak. He didn't care to look up when Michael entered.

Jeanette MacDonald was demanding San Francisco open her gold gates from a second-hand gramophone Michael had found in a nearby shop to ease Jan's boredom. The younger man didn't understand a word of the song. He hadn't noticed Michael's luggage either.

"Do you see, everyone walks head down, like walking through rain," Jan said.

Or an unexpected wall of water, sweeping everything asunder, and all you can do is hold on until this nameless thing you feel and can't control is torn away. Maybe that's why Michael had been caught off guard, hadn't seen the confrontation with Lonä coming.

Jan had not looked at him as Michael told him this.

Did he expect to stay there?

"I have nowhere else to go."

Jan shrugged. "You can sleep on the floor."

Michael's route to the IG Farben offices in the Pariser Platz brought him up the Wilhelmstrasse, past the Chancellery to the eagle-lined Unter den Linden. It used to be an enjoyable walk. But these days foreign dignitaries and attachés, uniformed officers, motorcades with sharply snapping flags and the order they represented served to remind Michael how precarious his situation had become. Remaining in the city undoubtedly was straining Catharina's good will. How long could she be counted on to not denounce him? Jesus Christ! What would his employers say if they discovered he was no longer living with his wife. And Billy? Surely, there was some way to see his son.

Often he came home with an armload of work, hopeful that this arrangement with Jan would begin to evolve into something more satisfying. Into exactly what, he couldn't say.

The bed with the cast-iron frame and the oversized stuffed chair were Jan's domain. From the chair, feet on the sill, he'd do nothing all day but watch the street. The worn velvet sofa by the door and the nearby table that rocked formed Michael's half. A few sundry other sticks of furniture—plant stand, stool and some shelving—remained as common territory. Draughty, noisy, creaky, drippy, and redolent with the sweet vapours of downstairs' overripe fruit, the room afforded scant privacy. Jan hid in the water closet whenever he wanted to change.

Although vocal to the contrary, Jan had been reluctant to venture outside. Michael supposed the lingering effects of his arrest still troubled him, something he still refused to discuss. But frustrated by this kind of imprisonment, Jan was ever poised to row over imaginary slights the minute Michael walked through the door.

Ensuring domestic peace, then, became Michael's end-of-day ritual. Find anything that might put a glint of distraction into the young man's eyes: bananas from the Kurfürstendamm and sold by a Negro, a colourful necktie, *Life* magazine when it could be found. Sometimes the gesture worked. Often the gifts failed miserably.

"What's that?"

"I found some fresh asparagus. I thought you'd like—"

"You know I hate that shit. It makes your piss stink."

Jan could not continue in this isolation, and Michael, he couldn't give him up.

"Then tell me, what else is there but to go?" Jan said during one of those rare occasions when he'd even discuss a future outside of a smelly walk-up flat over a grocery.

"Leave Berlin?"

"Why not? From what you told me, it'd be better for you. Hey! We could go to London. You've been there, right?"

"But I couldn't leave Billy."

"Jesus. He's got a mother, a couple of them. What about me?"

"Maybe we could—"

"We? There is no *we*."

The cut zinnias still lay wrapped in newsprint on the table. Jan's clothes hung on the pegs by the water closet and his slippers, the ones Michael had bought, sat by the bed. Jan liked those. He'd have taken them if he'd left.

Thank God. He was only out. Not gone.

Jan came through the door half an hour later.

"You're home early," he said.

Michael was still in his coat, unmoved at the table.

"My regular time."

"Really? What are we eating?"

Michael was relieved enough to allow himself to be annoyed. "Where have you been?"

"The zoo." Jan hung his coat on a peg. He was humming.

"I thought we might go out for dinner tonight," Michael said.

"No. I'm too tired. You get me something. That bakery on the Seydelstrasse has those buns with the raisins I like. I'd have got them when I was out, but I didn't have any money."

Michael pointed out that the Seydelstrasse was nowhere near the zoo and there wasn't a raisin to be had in all of Berlin.

"So?"

"Just be honest."

"What for? You won't believe anything I say."

"Please, Jan, don't be like this."

"No! Let's do. I'm sick of this, sick of being with you, sick of hearing that please please please voice of yours. Sick of you watching over every move I make."

"I'm worried for you."

"Fuck you are! You want something from me. Everyone does."

"That's not true."

"Always with the please-let-me-fuck-you look in your eyes. You're pathetic."

"Stop it."

Jan grabbed the flowers off the table. Michael thought for sure they'd hit the floor, but Jan, taking the jug off the shelf over the hot plate, filled it with water.

"It's never going to happen, Michael. You couldn't pay me to fuck you. Look at me. I can have any man in this city, certainly one with a lot more money than you."

"You're not—" Michael felt his stomach flip.

"So what if I am? I have to live somehow."

"It's dangerous. The newspapers—"

"I don't read them."

"You don't need money. We can go away. London, like you wanted."

"Fuck, Michael! If you want to go, go!" Jan pulled his coat off the wall peg.

"Where are you going?"

"Out."

"Wait, I'll come."

"Don't you fucking get it? It's time for you to go home."

The front window rattled when Jan slammed the door behind him. His thumping footsteps down the back stairs faded into the alley below.

Michael lay curled on the sofa, prevented by its width from stretching out, listening to the voices and the stacking of crates downstairs as the Proessels locked up. Trucks lumbered along the street taking God knows what God knows where. When the shopkeepers were gone, the pipes filled the void with creaking and dripping. It rained for a bit. Jan still did not come home. Michael still did not sleep.

Somewhere near dawn, Jan stumbled in, reeking of stale tobacco.

Michael watched as Jan dropped his clothes on the floor and slipped into bed. He did not stir as Michael rose shortly after for work.

<hr>

Billy flapped his arms, whooped and circled around the Gendarmenmarkt, chasing away the pigeons trying to cool off in the August sun. No way was he sharing the plaza!

"Let them be," Lonä said, but the boy ignored her. She was showing heavily.

They sat underneath one of the soot-mottled cherubs playing the lute astride a lion, guarding the steps of the classically columned Schauspielhaus. It occurred to Michael that he'd never brought Lonä to see a play here. She would have liked that. Wide, blue skies sailed over the soaring verdigris cupolas of the square's flanking French and German cathedrals.

"Bad news?"

Michael stared at the letter from Gene in his hands and nodded. "My father. He's gone. My sister says it was a stroke. Same way Mum went."

"I'm sorry, Michael." Lonä put her hand on his, then held it gently. "Will you be all right?"

Relieved actually. The old man's death meant he'd never know about their estrangement. And maybe, if there was indeed something to the afterlife, Mum wouldn't be alone anymore.

"My sister said it was quick. He fell asleep listening to the radio after dinner. Never woke up."

"Will you go?"

What for?

Billy had decided he was now an airplane and why was Dadda sad. He was sent to be nice to the pigeons after being told it was just the sun in Michael's eyes.

"You could have just sent this to me," he said.

"I wanted to talk to you."

Michael was looking at his son. "I miss him."

"He misses you."

An open-air Daimler, a small flag snapping from its hood, motored down the Markgrafenstrasse in front of them.

"Michael, maybe it's best you didn't see Wilhelm anymore."

"Jesus Christ, Lonä, I'm still his father."

"But your living arrangements—"

"Can't you get it through your head that we share a flat because I don't have anywhere else to go? That's all."

"He's a child, you can't expect him to understand." She turned away. "I don't."

Billy waved frantically, Watch me Mumma watch me Dadda. Then he tore into the flock of pigeons he'd allowed to settle, sending them flapping aloft.

"Don't be mean to them, Wilhelm, or the Juden will come and nibble on your toes while you're sleeping." That got the birds a reprieve. "Did you ever care about me?"

Michael closed his eyes and tried to find some way to hold this image of Billy, giggling, his arms circling overhead as he twirled around through the flock.

"Catharina's right, you should go back to Canada. It will be easier for Wilhelm as he gets older."

"You're tearing me in two."

"Think of him, Michael."

Michael returned to his flat, where Jan, flustered, bustled around the hot plate. He'd tied one of Michael's shirts around his waist as an apron.

"It's only a mash my mother used to make. At least I think so. Who knows what that evil fairy put in it. Frau Proessel was kind enough to give me some vegetables. You can pay her later."

The table was set with all of their dishes and cutlery. Flowers were already dripping petals, pooling around an uncorked bottle of red wine.

Michael picked it up and read the label. "French. Wow."

"Isn't this nice, Michshu, what I'm doing for you?"

"How? Why?"

"Oh, shut up and sit. Have some wine. Weren't you off to see that old cow of yours?"

Yes.

"And?"

Michael couldn't bring himself to say.

"Look, I know you've been bothered by that kid, not getting to see him—"

"His name is Billy."

"I know. I mean, I know it's Billy. I just wanted to say thanks for all you've done. But I'm okay now."

So that was it. There weren't enough chairs for all the nameless back-alley fucks that might as well be joining them for dinner, the dinner they'd paid for. Michael tried to conceal his disgust. And worse, his anger. After all he'd done, after all he continued to do, Jan could only thank him with a gesture full of ridicule.

Michael picked at his food and claimed it was wonderful.

Returning from work late, Michael found Jan in front of the mirror, fixing a tie.

Where was he going?

None of his business.

It's not safe.

Cluck. Cluck. Mother hen.

"What's the matter with you? After what you've been through? Aren't you worried?"

"I'll be fine. I know how to take of myself."

Oh, no. Michael was going along then.

"No!"

"Jan, I can't go through it again, if something happens to you."

"That'll only happen if you don't leave me alone."

"Is he so important to you?"

"Who?"

"Whoever the hell it is you're so desperate to be with tonight. Let me guess, that Kai?"

Jan smirked. "It's not going to be you."

Christ.

Banging on the floor from below with a broom, Frau Proessel had heard enough.

"Then stay here—"

"Why?"

"Because you owe me that. I've given up everything to help you."

Jan took one last side-to-side look in the mirror. "That reminds me, I'm tired of those records of yours. Heard them a million times. Get some new ones, Sweets."

Michael moved in front of the door. "Don't come back then."

Jan shrugged.

"I mean it. I can't go on wondering whether you've been arrested or worse. I can't find you like I did at Frau Merten's again."

"Get out of my way."

"You can't stop me, Jan. I'll follow you. I'll see where you go."

Jan shoved Michael out of his way. "You stay away from me, you pathetic, fat old man. I mean it!"

He slammed the door after him, the sound of his footsteps on the stairs outside trailing off to silence.

Michael slumped onto Jan's bed. This is what jumping off a roof and smashing into the pavement feels like. Face first. Numb, unable to move, but feeling every wound that cuts to the bone.

Slowly, it passed, making room for the next wave to roll over.

What is this? Why can't I let go?

Then he was out the door.

Michael didn't have to look far. Jan was sitting on the bottom of the stairs, smoking. He did not turn around as Michael slowly came down the steps.

"I'm begging you. Don't come with me tonight, Michael."

"Why is it so important?"

"It just is. Do it for me."

"I've done enough for you."

Jan looked at him. "I know. But don't follow me tonight." He crushed his smoke out on the wooden step. "I didn't mean it. About you being fat."

Then he ran into the evening.

They waited under a canopy of lindens dwarfing the red-brick terrace of an apartment on the Zimmerstrasse.

"You bastard," Jan said.

A shadow appeared behind the frosted glass of the door.

"Jan, is that you? Everything all right out there?"

"No. And he's not staying," Jan said.

Michael insisted he wasn't leaving.

"Well then, it looks as if your companion must come in before someone sees. Gentlemen, please, let's bring it off the street." Victor Wulff, authorial in white shirt, trousers and muslin sash, spoke to Jan as if they were well acquainted. "All are welcome. Enter, kittens."

Jan left Michael to his own introduction.

"Ah, I'm just a friend."

"Yes. My Jan has lots of those, although we must be careful nonetheless."

My Jan?

They passed through a brilliantly lit orangery to the stairs opposite.

"Delicious that scent, don't you agree? I haven't seen you at one of my parties before, friend of Jan's. And do call me Vic, kitten.

Michael was escorted into a flat handsome with earthy browns and greens, urns of reeds, sparsely decorated with black-and-white photographs, which, Michael was to learn, had all been taken by his host. Clusters of men and women, their conversations subdued, drifted in and out of the apartment, its large windows open to a back terrace that overlooked a manicured court. A man slouching against the piano played with the keys. Jan was nowhere to be seen.

"Tonight's a bit of a send-off for me," said Vic. "Once upon a time I was a journalist. Back in the days when folks wanted to know what was really happening. Tomorrow I bid adieu to Berlin for London. Getting out with what I know, before the war."

"You think there'll be one?"

"Kitten, not if, when. And sooner than you think." Vic led Michael over to a sideboard and mixed up a Manhattan. "Try this." He then steered him over to the piano. "Now my advice to anyone who'll listen: get out while you can."

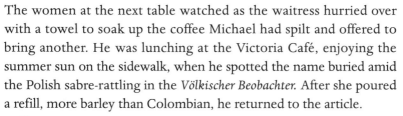

The women at the next table watched as the waitress hurried over with a towel to soak up the coffee Michael had spilt and offered to bring another. He was lunching at the Victoria Café, enjoying the summer sun on the sidewalk, when he spotted the name buried amid the Polish sabre-rattling in the *Völkischer Beobachter*. After she poured a refill, more barley than Colombian, he returned to the article.

Damn.

Michael sat back from his paper.

The Unter den Linden in late August was clogged with cars and trucks, air oily with exhaust, its sidewalks thronged with shoppers, women in summer hats, soldiers laughing, home on leave. Clay pots adorning the sidewalk cafés and shops had small flags planted in amongst the shrubbery. Eagles straddling the columns sparkled in the sun.

"Excuse me, do you have the time?"

The man asking had blocked the sun, but he was very polite and even smiled as he bowed. Before Michael could respond, the man nodded to the polished Mercedes-Benz idling by the curb. Beside the automobile waited another man. Michael had missed their arrival.

He folded his paper and left it on the table. Rising, he placed his coat over his arm and put on his hat. His departure was executed with such dignity that the women sitting beside him did not interrupt their conversation and had no idea Michael von Renner had just been arrested.

Michael was taken to the four storey building on the corner block on the Prinz-Albrecht-Strasse, a place he knew well. Upstairs in the third-floor boardroom, senior police officials used to shake his hand and smile when he'd arrive with an armful of manila folders, each one bursting with results from his team of keypunch operators' research on their behalf. But he never knew about this rear entrance the police were guiding him through now, nor these cellar corridors painted a torpid pea-soup green, lined with windowless doors, behind one of which a faint bluish tinge coloured his skin under the humming light.

"But I am a von Renner and my grandfather was a minister to the Kaiser and I know Lieutenant Peter Luft. Could I see Lieutenant Luft? If he could be contacted at Abwehr headquarters, I'm sure we could sort out this misunderstanding."

The metal door shut, locking Michael into a narrow cell with only a cot and chair. No word came from Peter. What time was it? They'd taken his watch. No one spoke to him, not even when he was escorted to the lavatory and regularly brought food that was, if plain, at least nourishing. Doors opened and slammed shut. Were they coming for him? A child in the cell across the hall made frightened noises, sometimes whimpering, sometimes crying. What could he be here for? If only the gentle tones of a woman's voice too tremulous to be of any comfort would shut the child up. A roach got under his chair. How? Lucky beggar. Michael wanted to trade places. In you go. Out you go. No one cares about you. No one notices. If only that crying kid would shut the fuck up. Thank God Billy was safe. Who's that? Oh yes, the footsteps in the hallway were the worst. Are they coming for him? Not this time. Someone else, thank Christ. But they must come eventually for him. They couldn't leave him there. This is gotta be at least three days' growth of beard. Why not just get it over with. But what would *it* mean? Jesus! All the warnings, all the signs, Gene's letters begging him to leave. Coffee at the Victoria Café—the article in the *Völkischer Beobachter*—Victor Wulff, a former journalist, arrested. One chance, Lord, just one more chance. If he got out of this, Michael was on the first train out of the country. Enough. Any more of this and he'd start to blame the one person he couldn't bear to.

When he placed his hand against the wall Michael could feel the vibrating rumbling of lorries. The street must be close by, people sitting in cafés and reading newspapers, not knowing, not caring about those going mad in cellars beneath their feet.

A kind of stupor followed, a numbness blurring the soupy walls into fog. In that cold mist, stands of spruce nodded in sea winds and there were blue jays in their branches. Mum was saying, Hurry up, you're to go with him, just you.

No, it was that woman across the hall trying to soothe the child. He'd been quiet until the boots had returned. A door opened. Now the boy was screaming.

Michael dragged his chair to the door and stood on it to peer out the narrow slit. The cell door across the hall was thrown wide open. Beyond it, the child kicked and wailed as the woman was pulled away by two men. Like Michael, she appeared to have spent several days in the cellar. Dishevelled black hair, her dress and coat rumpled. The boy, in short pants with a dirty striped jumper, had the scuffed brown knees of a playground champion.

"Hélène!"

She didn't hear Michael. The boy had bitten down on the hand restraining him. The child was grabbed by the waist and swung, his head coming down against the metal frame of the cot.

It took Felix all summer to grow those pumpkins. He was going to sell them at the fair. They made such a funny sound when I dropped them. Ker-ack!

Even Mum had to smile. She said she couldn't be angry with me when I smiled.

Like that other one. He smiles like you.

He made such a funny sound when they dropped him.

Ker-ack!

Who, Mum?

That other little boy.

The one with the pumpkin head.

"Are you all right?"

Michael felt himself gently lifted and struggled to open his eyes against their determination to remain closed. Peter.

"That woman across the hall—"

"Terrible business. Unfortunate that you had to see it."

Why's Hélène here?

"Calm down, Michael. Everything's going to be all right."

"Where've you been?"

"In Prague. On assignment."

He wore new insignia on his black jacket. Captain Luft, now.

"And you've got yourself into trouble in the meantime."

Seeing Peter made all the difference. Michael'd be out of this nightmare soon enough.

"It's a misunderstanding."

"Of course. Why do you think you're here?"

"It's that party on the Zimmerstrasse. The one in the paper. The journalist who was arrested there."

"Did you know him?"

"No. I'd never met him before. I was only there to keep a friend out of trouble."

"Did you succeed?"

"I didn't see his name among those arrested."

"And who was that?"

"I can't. I don't want to get him into trouble."

"Michael, now is the time for you to trust me."

But Jan said not to . . .

"Jan Berenson."

"Ah yes, young Herr Berenson."

"You know him?"

"A very resourceful young man. He's been our guest before."

Peter offered him a cigarette. It had been days.

"You say he is your friend."

"Yes."

"That's all he is?"

Michael nodded.

"I think you're lying. And I think that young man came between us in London."

"Peter—"

"My dear Michael, this is a sad suit of clothing we find ourselves in. You haven't turned out as expected."

"Me?"

"Grandson of a von Renner. The doors we opened for you. The university. Your work at Dehomag and IG Farben. You could have made a name for yourself. Instead you desert your wife and child for—"

"A friend."

"A misplaced friendship."

Peter deliberately paced, doubled back, looked about the cell.

"Jan's not like that."

"Ah, let me tell you about that young man. He's been helping us to ferret out these national pests like himself."

No.

"Look at you. Crushed. You think he sent you here."

"Did he?"

Peter dropped his cigarette to the floor and scraped it out with his boot.

"Didn't need to. But your *friend* was at that apartment on the Zimmerstrasse as part of our arrangement. Did he tell you about it?"

Michael shook his head.

"As long as Herr Berenson turned over names, he, and you, would remain free. Surprised?"

"Jan did that?"

"That was our agreement."

"Then why am I here?"

"My dear Michael, you've been denounced. Are you not curious?"

"It could only be my cousin."

"Her husband. Braum denounced you to the party. Turning in someone like you would reflect well on him, I'm sure. And from what I understand about your current domestic circumstances, very convenient."

"What happens now?"

Peter pulled an envelope out of his pocket and spread its contents on the table: passport, racial documents, tickets, Reichsmarks, American dollars.

"Now you go home."

"Peter, I . . . thank you."

But the captain was already closing the door behind him.

Through the window, Michael watched a young soldier across the platform, slouched against the wall, waiting for his own departure. Someone had carelessly dropped an unfinished cigarette by the soldier's boot and he stooped to pick it up.

Jan tried to save me. Me. He did that for me.

The Paris train lurched.

On the rack over Michael's head was tucked his two-tone suitcase, which Peter had thoughtfully packed with a shaving kit and change of clothing.

No way to leave word for Jan. No chance to see Billy. No goodbyes. No way to help Hélène. Nothing left to do for that boy—

That boy with her, so familiar, who—

His mind stopped. *Save only what you can.*

You go on the Paris train, Peter had reiterated. He allowed himself few other words.

Lehrte Bahnhof was thronged with travellers, most in uniform.

The homeless had long since been swept away. Red, black and white hung everywhere. Peter watched from the platform.

Michael had gone with him through busy streets, each looking out their own window, their official flag-bearing Mercedes honking its way through intersections, dodging trucks filled with soldiers. Michael would never know Peter's thoughts. His own surely could be heard above the din of city traffic. Is everyone in this city crazy? their driver snarled as they locked bumpers with a speeding car from the Russian embassy, only to veer off swearing over a dented fender.

The Paris train lurched again. It would not be late. Time for one last glimpse of a city darkening under summer sun. Leaning against his arm on the window ledge, Michael listened to the steady ticking of the watch on his wrist. Peter had given him his own to replace the one taken in the Prinz-Albrecht-Strasse cellar. Then he'd held Michael's hand. Safe journey, he said.

The train moved. Peter nodded briefly and hastily turned towards the stairs.

Now, the sound of time running out roared.

I can't do this.

Jan had betrayed his friends before he'd betray him. All those horrible things he said meant something. But what did they mean? What do you call this? Enough for Michael to not let it end this way. Not without knowing. Not without goodbye.

I can't. I just can't.

Michael glanced at his watch, then to the clock over the platform, the minute hand. One chance, one only.

No!

Do it.

No.

Do it.

Damn.

Go!

Snatching the suitcase off the overhead rack he hurried to the door as the train began to move more quickly out of the station. Glancing up and down the platform, no police in view, Michael let go a string of self-recrimination and stepped off the train at the same moment the Luftwaffe crossed into Poland.

⁓

Frau Proessel was too preoccupied with rumours of invasion to notice anything unusual about Michael.

"They say the Poles will bomb us tonight."

They being the block wardens who had come around to bark black-out regulations, telling the Proessels it was forbidden now to listen to foreign radio. One of them yelled and pointed at Michael watching from his window over the shop, Turn off your fucking lights!

The plan had been simple. Go back to the flat, get Jan, say goodbye to Billy, be on the afternoon train to Paris.

But no Jan.

When the sirens had wailed over the darkened city, Michael had thought about taking shelter. But he couldn't risk being seen or missing Jan when he came back. So he sat in the water closet until he heard the crowd on the blacked-out street below singing and cheering. The alarm had been false. Now the packed hall across from the charred synagogue was handing out beer to its overflow of patrons, dancing in the street.

Sleep, Michael. He hadn't done much of that in the last few days, but every hour in Berlin was dangerous. Besides, who could sleep with all that he had to worry about? What should he bring? They'd have to travel light, but what to prepare for? If Jan didn't show, where would he even begin to look? How long before someone found out Michael was not on that train?

Another full day passed, Michael painfully aware of what that meant to their chances of escape, before Jan returned, not at all surprised to see him.

"Jesus Christ! Where've you been?"

"What's with you?"

"I've been worried, you don't—"

"If you must know, mother, I've been at Tristan's. Farewell to the boys bound for Poland. My dear old friend Kai was there. Well, not as old as you. And here's me thinking he was dead. What have you been up to?"

"I've been in the basement of Gestapo headquarters."

Jan did not move in the afternoon shadows. "It wasn't me."

"No, I have my cousin Braum to thank. But they arrested Victor because of you."

"They made me. You don't know what they did to me in that camp."

"Believe me, after what I've seen, I have a pretty good idea."

"Then you know I had no choice."

"I know you did it for me. Why?"

Jan sat down. "You're not like those men."

"Is that it? Christ Almighty, I don't know what I am. One minute I'm on a train to Paris wishing I could never see you again, next thing I know—"

"You idiot! Why didn't you go?"

Michael couldn't bring himself to say.

"You were on a train out of here and you didn't go? Damn you!"

"Why, Jan?"

"What does that matter?"

"I need to understand."

Jan looked out the window. A few hours yet until black.

"It's okay. No one followed me."

"Maybe not you, but what about me? If they see you're not on that train they'll come and arrest us both. I can't get arrested again, Michael."

"Then come with me to Paris where you won't have to."

"I can't."

"Why not?"

"I don't have papers."

"Things are confused now. We'll say we had to get out in a hurry. We could even pretend we're Juden."

"Damn you, Michael! I fucking hate you for this."

"You can't stay here. Not now."

"I could live like a rat for however long it takes. I can vanish, but not with you dogging me. Every time you open your mouth, we'd be in trouble."

"Please, Jan. Come with me to Paris."

"No."

"Then I stay too."

Jan sat on the edge of the bed, his hands resigned into his lap. When he spoke, it was in a way Michael had never heard. He spoke with the voice of a man.

"When we get to Paris, we part ways. I mean it, Michael. I'm not your fucking Lili Marleen."

His trembling came upon him quickly, without warning, while watching Jan pack what few belongings he had. All he could do was sit and wrap his arms about himself.

"Hélène was there."

"You never said."

"She had a boy with her."

He had a head that cracked open like a pumpkin.

"Well, she had no business being in Berlin."

Michael started to sob. Jan took over folding his shirts.

They left before dawn, carrying only a suitcase and a rucksack. Skirting the overtaxed public transit to avoid authority as much as possible, by mid-morning they'd reached the sprawling glass-ceiling station, crowds already seething by its high arched doorway. Thankfully, nearby along the Spree they found an almost deserted café underneath a loudspeaker dully playing German folk music. The proprietor, like most of Berlin, was distracted by news from Poland.

Michael, his appetite returning for the first time since his arrest, overlooked the dead flies and oily stains on the table as he tore into several slices of bread. There was no butter and the brown liquid sold as coffee was undrinkable. Jan had left him, darting along the embankment and moored barges, across to the station to check on the trains. Of course, with Jan out of his sight, Michael panicked, fearing Jan would desert him or be arrested. His fears were unfounded. No one followed, Jan explained breathlessly upon his return.

"I told you, I know how to be invisible."

Michael hated to admit it, but the thing he loathed the most about the young man might actually get them out of the city.

"No more trains. Everything is for the military."

This could not be happening.

"Did you hear me?"

"How can there be no trains?"

The café began to fill with soldiers stocking up on whatever food-stuffs they could purchase before joining their units.

"Later. We'd better go."

Michael paid, calculating how much money he had and how long it would last, then added some rolls to take with them. The sweet ones. But Jan would still turn his nose up at them for having no raisins.

"Trains are still leaving Stettiner Bahnhof for the south," Jan said quietly.

"But what about Paris?"

Jan shook his head. "It looks like Switzerland. Besides, if we have trouble at the border, David can help."

"Why do we need him?"

"Not now."

"But why?"

"Because I told you, I don't have any papers."

Damn. Michael sank to the curb and rubbed his face with his hands. "I wasn't thinking. Hey, the Kronenstrasse's not far out of our way."

"Don't be ridiculous, it's nowhere near the station and if you want to get out of Berlin, we go."

"If I could just see Billy to say goodbye. Make certain he has my sister's address."

"There's no time."

Jan started running.

Damn him.

Michael followed. Jan quickly got them off the streets, staying to back lanes and cutting through courtyards. Luckily the city was mobilizing. Two men with baggage were just part of the patriotic rush to war.

When they reached Stettiner Bahnhof several hours later, they found it a crowded, sweaty mass of desperation and thinly veiled panic. The station was the last door open to foreigners, determined to leave with all they could carry.

Michael and Jan were halfway across the busy street, the station entrance in sight, when England and France declared war on Germany.

The trouble with collecting things, Tristan was explaining, is that you're never sure if your faith in their future value is misplaced or not.

Coffee out of barley and acorns, now that was a crime this regime was truly guilty of: Tristan's only direct condemnation of the government. But every morning, as they had done for the almost four months since they'd arrived, Michael drank real coffee with real cream. Not, as Tristan called it, the roasted nigger sweat he had to serve in the club. Where the real stuff came from, Tristan would only say, Somewhere in Bolivia, I believe.

Jan was the one who'd realized they'd have to go to Tristan's. No way could they return to the flat over the grocery, and they had to get off the streets. It sure didn't bother Jan that Britain, and by extension Canada, was at war with Germany. Like Jan said, who else but Tristan had the money and network to get them out of Berlin? They had no travel papers, no ration cards; Jan didn't even have a racial identity card. Michael, when the shock of war had subsided, knew he was right. On foot and by night, they made their way northeast, to the Prenzlauer Berg suburb.

In grand fashion, Tristan had met them with open arms and silk pyjamas, his uniform until evening, nonplussed by their dilemma, almost as if expecting them. His only caveat, Do as I say, my dears, should I ask. Michael was grateful, but there were times, such as over morning coffee and swimming through the smoke from Tristan's

Brazilian tobacco, that he'd find himself almost afraid of the slender little man. Something in his bearing had changed.

It's only because you don't know him, Jan had said.

He was right at home in Tristan's baronial domain, a complex web of abandoned factories. From the outside, derelict. Inside, his personal quarters over the labyrinth of damask-concealed brick walls was filled with purple lounging chairs trimmed in gold braid, galleries of Paul Klee, Kandinsky, Max Ernst and Otto Dix fanned by potted trees blooming under skylights. There was even a cosy movie theatre and next to it, a round room sheathed in stone with the markings of heavy machinery still on the floor, now home to a grand piano whose only function was to serve as a tray for Tristan's silver cigarette case.

The club below either ran itself or was run by someone else, for their host hardly ever appeared occupied by its maintenance. Most of the time he was languid, sporting a white top hat with his pyjamas, occasionally coming to life when he recounted some anecdote about one of his guest's proclivities, like who knew that Reichsführer Himmler liked to suck between the toes of his prostitutes. Politics were of no interest to Tristan. Even the myriad of conflicting regulations he had to navigate to remain open elicited no complaint other than a yawn.

Who else then but Tristan could plan with Jan for his friend in Switzerland, David Arend, to help them. Suddenly it was all arranged, as if escape were no more complicated than a trip to market. David arrived early in December on official embassy business. He would secure the appropriate documents and on Christmas Day, when authorities could be expected to be less vigilant, he would escort Jan and Michael out of Germany.

"You're jealous of Herr Arend?" Tristan asked Michael, sipping his coffee before another slice of cake. "Yes?"

As always, they breakfasted on the window-shuttered balcony. Generations of ill-conceived factory improvements had relegated remnants of an overhang walkway to the side of the building, several storeys up, with a clear view of David and Jan returning home on the street below.

"No. Of course not."

"Then why not join them on their outing?"

Because Michael had wanted to see his son before leaving for Switzerland and Jan claimed it was too far, too dangerous to attempt. But it was apparently all right to go out shopping with David.

"So you're jealous, is what you're saying," said Tristan.

Jan and David were walking closely together down an alley more than a street, sided by bricked, windowless walls, narrow winding sidewalks and cobbles here and there broken by errant grass. Snowy wind was rattling the panes in the balcony enclosure, and in the street corners below, angry thick columns of white flakes exhausted themselves until whipped up by the next gust of wind. Even from where Michael perched, he could see they were laughing, Jan holding on to a brown-wrapped box.

"You know, he will never care for you the way you want."

"I . . . I don't know what you mean."

"He is incapable of it. I suspect coming from a life of nothing, our Jan takes great pleasure in being adored. But if it's any consolation, Herr Arend is just a means to an end." He placed a small piece of cake into his mouth. "As are you."

David had slung his arm around Jan while from the other end of the alley a group of youths on bicycles rode single file. Michael could see both sides, Jan and David could not. The boys had erected a ramp of old planks and one by one took their bikes aloft. At the pinnacle of the jump each boy let go of the handlebars and raised his arms with a whoop. The couple had to press themselves against the building's wall to avoid the boys as they passed.

"Is it wrong to want him to be safe?"

"And where will it be safe for those of us who are different?"

The boys made it to the end of the alley. David and Jan continued walking in the opposite direction.

"Tell me, is your country any more accepting? You're mistaken if you think so."

"Maybe I am, but it's not right to be treated so harshly because of—"

"Something he cannot control?"

"Exactly."

"Hmmm. Like being Juden."

"That's different."

"How so?"

"I don't know. They just say it is. The Juden brought this on themselves. Everyone says so."

"Well, *everyone* can't be wrong."

Michael turned back to watching David and Jan. The boys, having stopped at the end of the street, were watching the couple as well, pointing, laughing.

There were five of them, closely cropped hair, strong-looking boys in their mid-teens, no doubt built up from their athletics with the Hitler Youth. The boys began to slowly pedal their bikes towards the two men. David's arm dropped from around Jan's shoulders. The tallest of the group circled with his bicycle, cutting them off. He was talking. David shook his head. The boy got off his bike. It fell and bounced on the cobbles.

Michael slowly stood.

David instinctively tried to shield his friend. Thrown back against the wall he was the first to go down. The boys gnawed about his face with their boots. Jan was dragged along the stones, held by two others, hit in the stomach repeatedly by a third. One. Two. His head fell over. One of the boys pulled it back by the hair. Again to the face. Then the stomach. Three. Four. When they pulled his head up again, his mouth was red with blood.

David had rolled against the side of the building trying to avoid the blows. That only infuriated the boys, who grabbed hold of his shoulders and pounded his head against the pavement until it wobbled loosely.

Michael was frantically clawing at the window latch. He couldn't get to the street in time, but if he yelled, he might scare the boys off. He felt the press of cold metal against the back of his neck, heard the click.

"I asked only one thing of you when you came here. Now get away from the window."

"Tristan, what are you doing?"

"I am doing the one thing that might save them, and you. Trust me, Michael. Back away or I'll shoot."

Michael turned. The weapon pointed at him was steady, as was the clear intent in Tristan's eyes. Jesus. The man sure wasn't afraid to hold a gun now.

Below, David's body jerked at the impact as the others ran and jumped into each kick. The man's face was unrecognizable, surrounded by blood-matted hair. His arms shook. His hands, no longer defending himself, trembled. A broad pool of piss spread out between his legs.

Jan was on his knees. His attacker kicked him in the chest with his boot, then his side, his other side, then, with Jan's hands held aloft, the groin. Jan spilled over and vomited on his attacker's foot. Enraged, the boy kicked him again as one of the others pulled his head back and slammed it against the brick wall, leaving a smear of dark red. The young man bounced and slid to the sidewalk, then incredibly began to crawl.

"For Christ's sake, Tristan, let me help them!"

The boys jumped back on their bicycles and pedalled around the corner as Jan struggled into the middle of the street. Reaching the brown package he had dropped, he pulled it to his chest.

They lay in the street until nightfall and a dusting of snow covered them. Michael, shaking, stood starting at Jan. Tristan was on his knees, brushing the blood-matted hair from the young man's eyes. David Arend was dead.

"Pry off that cover. We'll have to dump him in the sewer," said Tristan.

"No, not like that."

"You want questions about a dead diplomat, the Swiss demanding an investigation?"

Michael did as he was told. Oh God oh God oh God, as the body scuffed against the sides of the culvert into the stink and splash of Berlin's shit.

Jan they carried inside and up the fiendishly convoluted staircases. The occasional whimper told them he was alive, but Tristan said, He'll probably wish he wasn't.

"At least you must be happy," Tristan said, catching his breath after he and Michael got Jan into bed.

Jesus Christ, happy?

Tristan darted into the next room for a bowl of water, returned to wash away the blood from Jan's face.

"Maybe you'd be in the sewer now, with Herr Arend. Who says jealousy is a bad thing?"

Bubbles of red foam frothed at Jan's mouth.

"Here. Take this." Tristan handed the basin of water and cloth to Michael. "If he doesn't get a doctor he'll die."

"Here? But how?"

"I'm owed many favours. But first, I'll have to dress for downstairs."

Be still, Tristan reassured Michael when he returned with company several hours later.

The army doctor wearing the insignia of a major glanced at Michael without expression and went to his patient.

"What have you done?"

"Hopefully saved his life."

"By turning us in?"

"Nothing of the sort, my dear."

The doctor, hooked nose with large, clumsy-looking hands, removed his coat and set his bag on the nearby table. He was in dress uniform, having been snatched from a seasonal event. No indication on his face whether he was relieved or annoyed by the summons.

"Both of his legs are broken, at least two fractured ribs." He moved to the other side of the bed. "Could be internal bleeding, possibly a ruptured spleen. He'll die if I don't operate. He'll probably still die."

Tristan looked to Michael for permission.

"But to operate here without equipment?"

"I've done more in the field. I'll need light. A large table. And American whiskey. Luckily, he won't feel a thing."

Michael waited in the hall for hours, clutching the blood-stained brown-wrapped package as the doctor and Tristan worked on Jan using the piano for an operating table. Every time he closed his eyes, there it was, Jan crawling on the cobbles for this. What could have meant so much?

You fucking little whore.

Michael tore off the string, opened it.

A toy motorcycle. When the wheels spun, a red light glowed on the front.

1940

Christmas had passed. Jan neither improved nor worsened. Michael kept vigil.

"You're not eating, you don't leave this room. You'll get sick, you know. And Jan is partly to blame for what happened."

Tristan could be a heartless bastard at times.

"Every night I see them come in, flaunting that hungry look in their eyes. Rather like you, Michael. You all open yourselves to this kind of thing."

"I'm not like him."

"Of course you're not. Neither are you with your wife making more babies. It really has nothing to do with what that Ministry for Combating Abortion and Deviancy, or whatever it's called, says about Aryan morality. It's all about fodder for the Führer. Marching boys become marching soldiers, and if you boys are licking each other's rear ends, you're not making babies. And since they believe it's, at worst, your choice, at best, a disease that spreads, there can be no solution other than eradication. So you see, your real crime, my dear boy, is that you stayed away from your sweet wife's bed instead of keeping her heavy with child and never learning the lessons of discretion."

Michael wished Tristan would just shut the fuck up.

"Good thing you're not Gestapo or SS or even the police. They shoot their own for looking too long at a beautiful face, like you watch him, without troubling the Special Courts for a mock trial. And we Germans have so many beautiful faces, don't we? No, if they catch Jan again, it'll be the camps. I hear they make bricks out of their ashes at Sachsenhausen."

In the factory courtyard, an elm had punched through a crack in the concrete. By staring at its budding leaves, Michael watched winter turn to summer. He'd stopped wondering when Jan would be strong enough to travel. In addition to the life-threatening injuries, he'd lost several teeth and his jaw had been broken. Solid food was out of the question. Jan did, however, manage to request that a certain curly-haired waiter from Tristan's act as his nurse. If he couldn't bathe himself and empty his own bedpan, he might as well have someone worth looking at do the honours.

The army doctor continued to see his patient regularly while only rarely speaking to Michael, not looking at him if he did. The major wasn't much of a talker, except when bringing the latest score. Germany: six. Denmark, Norway, Holland, Belgium, Luxembourg and by June, France: zero. Arriving surreptitiously after dark, he'd inject Jan with morphine, eventually turning the task over to Michael when he discovered the latter's brief medical training.

"My dear, you have absolutely nothing to worry about," Tristan said, trying to allay Michael's concerns that the man would one day denounce them. "I'm too valuable to the good doctor."

And to prove it, several nights later, Tristan invited Michael to tour.

"In my main hall, as you know, propriety, or some semblance of it, prevails," said Tristan. "But should my guests require entertainment of a more exciting nature, it can be provided for the right price."

The corridor they walked had embrasures cut into the concrete wall, through which one could look down over Tristan's abattoir. Brassy music soured as if slowing to a pour from the hot white-lit musicians on the stage. Cackling women's laughter, their feathered hats frozen as if in tableau, droned underneath the distorted faces of Hasso's masterpiece. The clatter of glasses. Twinkling chinks of an iron chain. Running water. Then a series of dark passages. A groan, a low rumbling cry, almost a wail.

"They used to slaughter pigs here."

The groan sounded human.

"It's just the pipes, pipes everywhere. Who knows what any of them are for."

The warm, damp hallway opened to a chamber of doors, each with a sliding eyepiece.

"Now you must be very quiet, for our good doctor likes something special for himself."

Tristan took Michael to the middle door and slid open the metal plate.

"Nothing like it, he says . . . pays me handsomely, in gold."

The heat from the nearby boiler room was becoming unbearable. Sweat beaded down Michael's face. He peered through the square, then pulled away.

Tristan forced him back.

"You wanted to know why I trust the man. Go on. Watch."

She was tied, not pretty, skinny. No tits even.

"They're just German whores, who'd miss them? He likes to cut off their breath."

With piano wire.

"Watch. He goes slowly, she'll pass out and come to."

The doctor, naked, toyed with her.

"A featherless stewing cock without that uniform, don't you think?"

Surely to God what makes us human isn't so easily stripped bare. The woman whimpered. Michael tried to turn away, but Tristan persisted.

"No, look, he's in her. They never cry out. Probably never realize.

Oh. No more struggling. It's almost over. It's all for that one moment when her pussy twitches before she dies."

Drink this, Tristan counselled.

Michael forced it down, hoping the burning alcohol would blot out the memory of the doctor's mottled skin sagging over thin limbs.

"Tell me it's not real."

"Everything's real, my dear. If you think it is."

"How, how can you do it? How can you indulge a man like that?"

"Would you prefer I did not?"

"Of course."

"Then Jan would be dead."

"How can I ever be near that man again?"

"You will and you'll say nothing. You will treat our doctor with courtesy and respect and be thankful he keeps your friend alive and blessedly stupid with morphine."

Tristan needed a change of white silk pyjamas before heading below. That was always done in his private quarters.

"Now Michael," he said, emerging moments later, "as a flatmate you're becoming dull. You can't spend all of your time sitting by our young friend."

"I don't mind."

"But I do, dear boy. As it so happens, I need you to help me. Come along. What do you know about elephants?"

The only black woman left in Berlin had been lured by Tristan from the Golden Horseshoe to host his soirées. Sophia was no beauty, her face being somewhat broad and flat, her figure ample, but she could work a room like no other and did so from atop her baby elephant, Ada.

Sophia's entrances, heralded by fanfare, were the talk of Berlin, at least among those not preoccupied with rationing, blackouts, shortages and the increasing fear that a Juden underground was terrorizing the city. Sophia, wearing only coloured glass stones pasted to her body with sugar, would exhort her patrons with a whip made from ostrich feathers. A stage show followed, the woman dancing far more nimbly than her girth might suggest. At every performance she'd single out a lucky man to buy her drinks, get her tipsy and, if he was particularly beguiling, bed her behind an opaque screen for the voyeurs in the crowd. The boys from the Russian embassy were a particular favourite of hers. She claimed they were well hung and vodka gave them stamina.

Reality was somewhat less rosy. Ada, billed to have arrived in Europe via the same route as Hannibal, was not well. Lately, as she carried Sophia into the nightclub, she splashed a foamy trail of shit down her backside, which inevitably slopped its way onto nearby patrons. Hence, Michael standing now in her pen.

"Can you help my poor Ada?"

Sophia's German accent, when she was off duty, slipped into something much more American. The faux rubies, emeralds and diamonds were replaced with a tattered baby blue terry-cloth robe and kerchief reeking of cold cream.

"Do you know anything about elephants?"

"Ah, they're from Africa?"

"This one's from India, apparently," Tristan said from a few feet away, handkerchief over his nose.

Sophia went into unnecessary detail as to the nature of Ada's complaint. Her spattered pen in the hall behind the abattoir and its stench provided ample evidence of her affliction, if no clue to its exact cause.

"I don't know the first thing about elephants. Until today I've never even seen one." Ada shyly caressed Michael with her trunk. "But when I was growing up, if a dog got this way, feeding them rice helped to bind them."

With nothing else to suggest, Michael took it upon himself to cook the rice in bucket-sized quantities down in the club's kitchen, feeding it to Ada as often as she'd take it. He also washed her backside and cleaned her pen. In a couple of days the trail of droppings ceased. Sophia was singing his praises.

"Yes, an honest to God elephant," he said to Jan.

Now able to eat solid foods, Jan was sitting up, but having to retrain himself with the spoon and fork. Speech was slow and he had to struggle for words.

"That woman hasn't the time of day for the poor thing, so I get her ready to go on stage, bed her down and take her into the walled courtyard for exercise every morning. She really is just a big puppy. You'll like her, Jan."

Could he see?

Yes, but only when he could walk down by himself.

Michael was getting Ada ready for her entrance when the floor swayed and dust rained upon them. There, there, he soothed the elephant's wailing.

Snug in their gothic factory, Michael had almost forgotten the war. Blackout regulations meant nothing in a complex with bricked-over windows. No one ventured outside during the day and for the most part the wailing air-raid sirens at night could not penetrate the thick walls.

The Royal Air Force bombing had come, then, without warning. The next explosion was farther away, the floor only trembled. The round, wire-covered lights running along the wall of the concrete pen flickered. Michael held on to the elephant's trunk, calming Ada, and himself, as the raid moved to another part of the city.

He hurried back up to their rooms and found Jan struggling to get out of bed. It's over, Michael calmed, pushing him back against the sheets. Jan wouldn't let Michael leave, so together they waited out the night with oil lamps in case Tristan's generators failed.

Several nights later the RAF returned. Closer this time, depositing chunks of concrete ceiling in the corridor into Ada's pen.

"It's to be expected," Tristan said matter-of-factly at midday, his breakfast time. "The Luftwaffe has been bombing London for days."

"Because the British are bombing us?"

"That's what Herr Goebbels is saying. But the fact is, we started it."

"How do you know?"

"I don't quite recall who told me that, but the American chargé d'affaires did join my table for drinks last night. You don't suppose he said it? Do pass me the butter and enjoy it while you can. It's getting hard to come by, even for me."

Tristan elegantly swiped a thickly coated knife across his croissant.

"Now then. We might consider moving our quarters down a level or two."

Jan hadn't felt the sun in over a year. Inside a walled concrete courtyard, he turned his face to feel the little warmth in the December light.

Thanks, God.

"What's the matter with you, crybaby?" he said to Michael.

Ada bellowed, impatient to be noticed.

Jan was like a child that first visit. He walked around Ada, giggling boyishly, delighted and completely unafraid. A few days later he rode atop her for the first time, and the walls, much less a prison than a sanctuary, resounded with his laughter and baby talk as Ada claimed yet another devotee.

"But he never talks about David," Michael said to Tristan, that anniversary fast approaching.

"Not a word?"

"Once, he said he was sorry, but—"

"Yes?"

"I don't think he remembers."

"Shouldn't that make you happy?"

Eventually, Jan adopted the task of feeding Ada her bushel of carrots after each night's performance. No matter how poorly he felt, for his improvement continued amid setbacks, he insisted he be with Michael in the pen to greet Ada when she was done, vegetables and kind words waiting.

1941

I believe Tristan," Jan said, scrubbing Ada's hide. "He saw the one at the zoo. They'll keep them away."

Even though there had been no air raids since last October, Michael didn't share Jan's belief that the flak towers designed to be the vanguard in Berlin's air defence would end the RAF bombing runs. In fact, Michael suffered from the effects of those attacks more acutely than ever. Just waiting for the air-raid sirens guaranteed him long, sleepless nights. There had to be some way out of Berlin.

Have patience, Tristan insisted, for something was happening. What? He couldn't say. While the newspapers, the radio, posters on park columns pointed to German preparations to swallow England into the Reich, rumour had it that soldiers, tanks, munitions and Juden were all being shipped east on trains. Lay low for a while longer, he cautioned. Besides, two young men out of uniform, no war injuries? They might as well just present themselves for arrest.

How about Switzerland? Surely there is still some way? Michael wasn't a German national.

Jan and Tristan laughed.

Too much Germany to pass through and anyhow, according to Tristan, the Swiss wouldn't jeopardize their neutrality. But he was working nonetheless on getting them out. He couldn't have them underfoot forever. Perhaps even in the next few weeks.

But the weeks only brought the end of winter and the return of air-raid sirens. For six weeks the RAF showed Berlin, regardless of her defences, that she was not immune to further attacks. The only thing in the city untouched by blackouts, reduced rationing, sirens and crowded bomb shelters was the nightly revelry of the German elite, Russian officers and the dwindling diplomatic corps at Tristan's, safe under hundreds of tons of concrete.

Occasionally, before heading down to greet his guests, Tristan would join Jan and Michael for supper, cooked in the kitchen below and sent up on a dumb waiter.

"Berlin took quite a beating last night, my dears. The Linden down to the Spree, the opera house, the library—poof. Up in flames. At least it saves our Führer from having to tear it all down."

Michael pushed away his plate.

"Not hungry?"

"Billy," Jan said, not unkindly.

"Michael, surely your good wife will have sent the boy out of the city? The mayor has ordered it."

"Lonä would think it un-German."

"That patriotic, huh? My dear Michael, your woman was worth keeping. Shall I make enquiries?"

Could he?

Next day Tristan was able to report to Michael that so far the Kronenstrasse was untouched by British bombing. Couldn't say the same for the Wilhelmstrasse. Used to be the avenue to the Chancellery was forbidden only to the Juden. Now it looked as if nothing was able to pass.

Jan placed an apple on his head.

"Look, Michael."

Ada sniffed it with her trunk and shoved it into her mouth.

Giggling, Jan did it again. He then had to swat her trunk away from the basket of apples in the corner.

"No more for you, missy, until the show's over."

Listen.

But Ada and Jan were having a good laugh.

"Shut up."

Jan made a face. "You're such a worrier. We're safe in here."

The rumble overhead was faintly discernible. Ada's headdress was vibrating on the wooden table. The abattoir was full that night and noisy, so Michael guessed that by the time they heard the planes, the aircraft must be directly overhead.

Then explosions, and the floor swayed. Lights blinked, sputtered, went out. Blasts sliced through layers of concrete, bringing darkness and choking dust.

Michael found himself curled in a corner, something hard boxing him in. He thought he heard Jan call out his name, but he couldn't see, couldn't get to him. He pulled his shirt over his head to filter out the dust. Dust thick as fog. The floor stopped moving. Silence.

Incredibly, tucked away in the bowels of his complex, Tristan's generator kicked in. The lights blinked on with a hum.

Michael forced himself from underneath the pile of broken concrete, his left side badly bruised.

Jan was covering the only part of Ada not buried, her head. She had wrapped her trunk around Jan's leg, and held on. The rest of her was crushed underneath tons of wall that had collapsed from above.

"We have to help her!" Jan, unhurt, tried to pry loose some of the large chunks of stone.

"I'll get help."

"Don't leave me!"

"Jan, we can't do this alone."

A piece of ceiling collapsed in the far corner.

"Do you understand?"

Jan let him go.

The complex had taken several direct hits and groaned under its wounds, raining bricks and arm-length splinters of wood. Smoke billowed along the corridor's ceiling, either from fires inside or blowing in from the surrounding rooftops. The lights flickered and plunged Michael into darkness.

The building gave up a series of guttural shifting laments as Michael pushed his way through hallways knee deep in overturned chairs, broken glass and brick. The ceiling in the piano room had collapsed onto the instrument. Tall glass cases filled with books in what must have been Tristan's library had tumbled, rare folios sluicing into the hall where burst pipes bled away ancient ink. On the floor, flushed out from an upended desk, a gun.

He returned with it to Jan alone.

"They must all be trapped downstairs."

Ada was silent. Her ear flapped, her trunk still clutching Jan.

"Listen to her. I didn't know elephants cried. What are we going to do?"

Michael hesitated.

"I found this." He pulled the Luger from where he'd tucked it behind his back. "It must be Tristan's."

"No, Michael."

"We have to."

He expected Jan to react violently. Ada looked on with one impassive eye.

"Yes, but you do it. I can't."

Michael had never held a gun before.

"My brother shot a bird once."

Ada let out a sound that was either a cry or a sigh, he never knew for sure.

"I made him promise never to do it again."

Trembling, he put the gun to the elephant's head. Forgive me, he said. The shot startled them. The elephant's trunk unwrapped itself from Jan's leg and Michael threw the gun into the rubble.

⌇⌇

After an inspection, Tristan shrugged. Business as usual. The damage had been localized and those pesky incendiaries, dropped in the hopes of igniting a city block, had burned themselves out on the concrete roof. In fact, the attack had hardly been noticed down in the former abattoir, where the party had continued. Knowing that the once impregnable nightclub was no longer immune to attack only increased its popularity.

"Especially popular with the Russians," said Tristan. "I'm the only place in town that doesn't water down the beer."

Michael and Jan occupied themselves with putting to order the damage to Tristan's apartments, his collections and their own personal quarters. Neither spoke much of Ada, nor could they bring themselves to go where she was now entombed. Her size making it impossible for her removal, Michael and Jan sealed the pen room, while down below, a toast to her memory was offered by the Russians. Sophia bemoaned her loss. Without Ada she was just another novelty chorine whose time had passed.

"Do they have elephants in Nova Scotia?"

A chautauqua came to Halifax when Michael was a boy and some folks said there was an elephant in the tent show. Michael thought it had come from New York.

"New York!"

"Yes, it's not that far from where I lived. You could get to it easily—"

Jan objected. Not that again. Why not ride out the war here in luxury?

Sure, Tristan watches out for them, feeds them, does everything, but how long could it last? The bombings were getting worse.

Jan was more afraid of being gutted by a roving gang of Juden.

"Who told you that?"

"Sophia. Someone told her. She's so afraid of the Saujuden, she's going back to Paris." Prefixing them with *swine* was her way of blaming the Juden for the death of poor Ada.

If even Sophia was leaving, Jan be damned, Michael was adamant. He'd see Tristan, determined to make their host understand the urgency of their situation. There must be some way.

Michael found him in his chamber, the only room with a door that locked. Jesus, when it came to modesty, Tristan seemed to have a lot more to hide than even Jan. But after a light knock, Tristan showed Michael where he'd been packing a steamer trunk large enough to sit inside.

"A vacation, my dear. Italy, I think. The Mediterranean is as smooth as glass this time of year. I never know what to take, morning, luncheon on the deck, après dîner. I'll be sure to send you boys a postcard of something delicious."

Michael ran his fingers over a faded diamond-shaped trunk label from the *General von Steuben.*

"Oh, I'll not be gone long and I'm sure you boys can manage for yourselves. I know you may not think so, but all this bombing has me rattled. A week or two under June sun surrounded by Italian beauty, I'll be my old self. Now, be a good fellow and come along while I pick out some wine for dinner. There's got to be one or two bottles of something French that survived."

Battery-powered torch in hand, he and Michael descended several levels into the factory complex. In places, they crawled over the rubble left piled after the raid.

But this wasn't the way to the wine cellar.

"We're not going there," said Tristan. "What I'm about to show you is to remain between us. Perfectly clear?"

Michael nodded, feeling the chill of the deepest levels.

The ceiling height decreased as they walked farther, the floors and walls grew rough, almost as if hewn from rock. He felt dampness, heard distant trickling and thought they must be at the level of the sewer, perhaps even underneath the club itself. Passing through several heavy metal doors, they emerged into a long corridor. At one end, a sawhorse with empty bottles lined across it. On the floor underneath, piles of broken coloured glass.

Tristan noted Michael's interest. "Well I wasn't born a brilliant shot, was I?" he said. "Now come through here."

Another door led them into the heart of Tristan's complex: a bewildering jumble of rusting, dripping metal arms and legs, hissing steam and puffing dials, the power works, much of it decayed and unusable.

Against the blackened brick wall stood a large iron chamber, one of several. The room sounded to be itching from a giant scratch. A wave of the torch revealed the source.

"Steady, my boy. They're only rats."

Always a problem in Tristan's realm, now worse thanks to bombings disturbing decades' worth of burrows and nests.

"This furnace is unused, but still connects to much of the piping. From inside, the sound travels. You can hear many things."

"Inside?"

Tristan opened the small metal door. Small, but large enough for a man to crawl through.

"What is this?"

"Less luxurious accommodations than what you and Jan enjoy, but essentially, the same thing."

Michael could see that the old furnace had been fitted out with several cots, bottles of water, even a hot plate surrounded by canned food.

"You're hiding someone down here?"

"Me? Oh, no. I merely provide the space and some capital."

"For who?"

"Anyone who needs to get out of Berlin. I've always been a pushover for the meek and the feeble."

"Why? The danger—If anyone found out."

Tristan smiled. "Ah, for the thrill of it! It makes me feel alive, like a man should, don't you think?"

Michael looked back into the furnace.

"Now my dear boy, I want you to listen to me. If there is one piece of advice I can give you to help you survive, it is this. Be here, in the moment. Not somewhere off in dreams of a world that doesn't exist. If you remain one of the walking wounded, you'll never see them come for you."

There was no liking the sound of this.

"I'm telling you this because I have to leave you for a while."

"Italian vacation?" Michael tried to sound less frightened.

"Something like that. But you'll be on your own until I return and can arrange for you and Jan to leave. The day may come when you'll need this place. No one will ever look for you here. Prepare yourself for it. And there is no need to mention any of this to Jan. He's always been terrible with secrets, and the thought of getting dirty."

The ringing slam of the furnace door hung in the damp air.

"Now come along. We still have a bottle of wine to fetch."

Jan put into words Michael's fear: Tristan was not coming back.

By then he'd only been gone for a week, so Michael readily dismissed that conclusion, as much for his own peace of mind as for Jan's. There was plenty of diversion, books and outdated British newspapers and periodicals, as well as a mountain of film canisters Jan was determined to watch. But by mid-June, worry trumped distraction. Food still arrived at the appointed hours, but as dishes piled up Jan pointed out, No one is coming to clean.

"Perhaps he thought it best no one come up here without him," Michael said.

Yes, but where was the postcard saying, See you boys soon? Jan asked.

A few days later, Michael had to tell him the dumb waiter came up empty.

He'd found Jan in his room, standing very still by his bed, his bare feet in the light pooling around the side table.

"Listen."

"I don't hear anything," Michael said.

"That's just it."

"So? We're the only ones around."

"At this time of night? There should be hundreds of people below."

"What do you think it means?"

Jan nibbled his thumbnail.

"If Tristan's not back in a day or so, we leave," said Michael, remembering the furnace. "But in the morning, we get ready."

"Where will we go?"

Unable to answer that other than to curse Tristan for clearly having deserted them, Michael lay awake for most of the night. Somewhere near dawn he drifted off to see Billy ride a motorcycle, then lurched awake to the aroma of fresh coffee.

He found Jan at a table piled with rolls, cut meat, fruit, even pastries. A silver pot of coffee steaming nearby. And real butter.

"All this?"

"From downstairs."

"You know what Tristan said about going there. No one is to see us."

Jan was eating like he'd not seen food for days. "Doesn't matter. I was right. The place is deserted. This is what was left in the kitchen."

That did in Michael's appetite.

"That's it then. We've got to get out of here."

"Why? There's still plenty of food. Who needs Tristan?"

Michael began to rummage through desk drawers, tossing out papers, mentally calculating what to pack.

"You think what Sophia said is true?"

"Shut up about that. Aren't you going to help me?"

Jan was still at the table, watching. "I don't think I can do this."

"Don't be ridiculous. It's not like Tristan's going to know."

"I mean, go with you."

"What?"

"I can't go out there."

"You've got to. You can do it. You're the one that got us here in the first place, remember? I had to hand it to you, you sure knew what to do."

Jan looked away.

"Is this about David?"

"This is my home."

"How can you say that? No. It's not that at all. It's me." Michael made busy work shuffling through a desk of Tristan's so he wouldn't have to look at Jan, pulling out papers, going through envelopes. "But you'd go soon enough if I were your Kai, or—"

"David?"

"Yes, well, that can't happen now, can it?" *That was a mistake.*

"I want to wait things out here. I can do it. I know I can. Tristan said the government can't hold on forever."

"How? There's no one left here for you to bend over for."

Jan's eyes widened at the envelope in Michael's hand and what was falling out of it. Hundreds, thousands of Reichsmarks fluttering to the floor. And neither of them heard the soft steps in the hallway outside. The latch on the door. Nothing until the quiet: Don't move.

Notes fell from Michael's hand. Jan clung to the ones in his. Two men, perhaps a year or two older than Jan, swarthy and thin, pointed guns. A third man, also armed, stood at the door. A young woman with a yellow kerchief went right to the table, shoving bits of bread into her mouth, stuffing what she could into her pockets.

"Is anyone else here?" she asked.

No.

The woman tossed each man a roll. They ate with their guns pointed.

"If it's the money—"

"Oh, we'll take the money."

"You're the only ones?" the woman asked again. Glancing about the table and sniffing. "Coffee!"

The man by the door asked Jan and Michael why they were here.

"Staying with a friend until we can get away."

"Away to where?"

"Out of Germany. To Canada."

"And blondie, the one who doesn't talk?"

"My friend."

"Where's the one you were staying with?" The woman was clearly in charge.

"Holiday. Italy."

The men chuckled.

"Perfect timing. While we invade Russia."

"Germany's invaded the east?"

The man at the door signalled to his watch.

"What are your names?"

"I'm Michael von Renner. He's Jan Berenson."

"Well Michael von Renner and Jan Berenson, get your things. If you're the only ones here, you're coming with us."

Two of the men began a hasty search, taking the money from Michael, checking the other rooms.

"Where? Why?"

"Because we collect things and we are just one step ahead of the Gestapo, so hurry."

"But who are you?"

"He's Israel, and that one there, he's Israel. And he's Israel too. I'm Sarah."

"Can we do introductions later?" said Israel, the one by the door.

Jan, looking behind him, hurried after Michael into his room.

"They're Juden."

Michael told him to get some things together, and hurry.

"Don't you care?"

"At the moment, no."

"But you know what they're going to do to us." Jan glanced out the door at the ransacking going on. "You son of a bitch." He pounded his fist against Michael. "This is all because of you. You should've been on that train. After all we've been through, to end up—"

"Don't you think we'd be dead now if that's what they wanted?"

"How do you know what they want or what they're going to do to us? I know, I've heard—"

"Shut up. You heard them. We're at war with the Russians. Let's go."

"Maybe they're lying."

Michael could hear doors slamming all across Europe, but it was really just the Israels in the next room. Hurry up in there.

"Do you want to take a chance they're wrong?" Michael said, snapping the clasps on his suitcase.

Jan still wasn't moving.

"Look, I think Tristan sent them." Michael sat on the bed. "He's been helping people get out of the city. He showed me where he's been hiding them."

"Tristan's helping the Juden?"

"No. Maybe. I dunno. He didn't say that exactly, but look, they're here now so he must be."

Jan shook his head. "Why didn't you say?"

"Tristan told me not to. He figured he'd only be gone for a few days."

"Gentlemen, let's move it!" Sarah called from the outer door.

Michael pressed Jan into his own room and started tossing clothing for him into a rucksack.

"If that's true, then they're here for Juden, not us."

"I know. So we don't say."

"Are you crazy? Do you know what'll happen to us if we get caught?"

"You don't actually believe they're killing the Juden in those camps?"

"Do you want to find out?"

Christ! Jan could be maddening and now was not the time.

The second Israel, who had been looking out the buttress window into the alley below, said, "Trucks. Let's go."

⚭

The teenager blanched as a couple passed her by and stared. A yellow star was stitched on her stylish coat.

"She should act like she owns the sidewalk," Jan said. "Then people wouldn't make faces at her."

Michael told him to come away from the window. Someone might see.

Wedding, Grunewald, Kreuzberg, Schöneberg: they never stayed in the same suburb longer than two or three days, sometimes moving at night or boldly by day. Once, they were so close to Lonä and Billy, Michael could see the roof of their Kronenstrasse apartment. He even convinced himself that a boy in short pants and scarf was his son, and that he looked happy. Jan claimed it was too far away to be certain.

They were, however, close enough to see limbless, bandaged veterans, hobbling about the streets; trams full of them, where the tracks had not been carved out by the bombs. Pages of notices in the newspapers proclaimed how husband, son, father, brother, uncle, nephew had given all, and gladly, for the Fatherland, for the Führer. Stuck into piles of rubble that had once been a house, flats, a church, a shop, snapped defiant wind-tossed swastikas and signs exhorting Berliners to march with their Führer to Victory! Along with this, something different, something sinister, something spreading, *End it!* surreptitiously chalked on broken walls.

Sometimes, in what felt like a directionless journey about the city, Jan and Michael were hidden in grand apartments. People treated them as guests. Jan shone for his hosts and proved a surprisingly congenial travel companion. Mostly, though, they moved from flat to flat, hidden in musty attics among peeling trunks, sawhorses and tennis racquets in presses or in dank closets behind false walls and pipes sparkling with silverfish, always safe from unexpected police visits, block wardens and vigilant neighbours.

The three Israels and Sarah had been replaced by other Israels, other Sarahs. And, surprisingly to Michael, ordinary Germans, like the young teacher who had just been called up for military duty and his pregnant wife. With a cool October outside their flat thinning the leafy Dreysestrasse, north of the Spree, they assured Michael and Jan their days of hiding were almost over. Someone who'd already escaped once, evading the government roundups and deportations, was arriving in Berlin to finalize their departure. They would have to be ready at a moment's notice. Michael was more than prepared and talked about it endlessly.

"Home by Christmas," he said.

He'd learned to avoid the use of *we*.

They were laying in a back-courtyard porch. The windows had been boarded. Their hosts were inside discussing the logistics of stretching their meal with a turnip.

Jan, sharing a narrow cot with Michael, rolled away from his plans. "I hate the cold."

A knock interrupted. The teacher's wife entered, feeling the need to apologize for disturbing them. The turnip in her hand, on its way to being their dinner, wasn't very big.

"You are to get your things." She looked relieved.

"This could be it," said Michael. "C'mon, we could be out of Berlin tonight."

They followed the woman into her parlour—sofa, chair, radio— where her husband was speaking in hushed tones to their visitor by the front door. Awaiting them, the newcomer wearing a kerchief. She removed her glasses.

"Hélène?"

She ignored Michael, but stared at Jan. "How could this have happened?" she said.

"What's wrong?" The teacher took his wife by her shoulders.

"There was supposed to be two men and a woman," Hélène said.

"But they found no others."

"Did anyone think to check their papers? Ask questions?"

Michael tried to explain.

"Don't you say a word!" To their hosts, Hélène said, "These two are not the ones."

The expectant mother clasped her belly and turned towards her husband for answers. He shook his head. In the kitchen the lid on a pot was rattling.

"Wait. Hélène, please. We've got to get out of Germany."

"Your kind doesn't need help." Not with Juden facing deportations, Polish camps and even worse, the horror stories trickling in from the east about exterminations.

"That can't be," Michael said. "There's lots of Juden around. Look how many out there are wearing the Star."

The pregnant woman began to cry.

"Please, enough of this, you're upsetting my wife."

"I don't know how you two managed to get here, but you won't jeopardize our work."

"Hélène, wait! I was there. At Gestapo headquarters. In the cell across from you."

She pulled away her kerchief as if its weight had become too much to bear. Her hair, having once been sheared away, had only just begun to grow back.

"Why?"

Michael couldn't bring himself to say. He glanced at Jan. "I've lost everything, Hélène, my family, my work, everything. Now I just want to go home. Please, please help us."

"How did you get out?"

"An officer, Peter—a friend, he helped me, or I wouldn't be free. But the war came. We—I got trapped."

"This officer, was it Captain Peter Luft?"

Michael nodded. "You know him?"

"Yes . . . I know him."

Hélène opened her coat and popped open the buttons on the sweater underneath. The skin around her brassiere and down her stomach was pocked with congealed scars, cigarette burns.

"No. Not Peter. I don't believe it."

Hélène covered herself. "Get them out of here."

The teacher balked.

"Let them go," Hélène said. "No uniforms, no papers, they'll be in Sachsenhausen in a week. Pests like them deserve such a fate."

Jan went into the back room for their belongings.

"I can't do that. If they get arrested, they'll be traced back to us." The teacher pulled an old revolver from the last war out of the drawer underneath the radio. "I mean it. I'll not risk my family."

His wife muffled a cry.

"Hélène, please," said Michael.

Jan returned, saw the weapon and swung Michael's case into the teacher's face. Just forcefully enough to make him drop the gun. It slid under the sofa. In the scuffle to retrieve it, Jan and Michael pushed past Hélène.

She followed them out to the stairwell.

"You know, Michael, don't you? Ask! Ask about the boy I was with. The one your Captain Luft had murdered."

Oh, no.

"Don't listen to her," said Jan.

"He was my son, Michael, my son."

He glanced up at her. She was hanging over the railing. Hasso's canvas flashed through his mind. Her kerchief fluttered downwards.

"And yours."

Jan pushed him forward.

1942

W itzleben Park was the end of the road.

With no hope of escape through Hélène and her underground, Jan had stepped into the breach, leading Michael from one welcoming apartment to another. For several months Michael guessed at how Jan knew these men who took them in. I'm trying to help you, Jan offered as an explanation. Some were gracious, offering them a night's, and occasionally, a week's refuge. Others turned them away, too frightened to acknowledge the past acquaintance.

They travelled by night when blackout regulations necessitated red and blue paper Japanese lanterns affixed to the front of automobiles, turning Berlin streets into a fireflies' garden party under their faint glow. Pedestrians felt their way along the sides of buildings, traffic barely moving, luminescent buttons emerging from the dark to announce the presence of police or block wardens. Sirens wailed constantly, eroding their effectiveness. Light from the artillery in the flak towers raked across the skyline.

Jan led Michael through basements. Entire city blocks were ordered to open cellar walls to allow escape in the event of air raids.

Except when these subterranean passages were filled with house wardens and bomb-wary residents, Jan and Michael could freely move under the blocks of Berlin from one refuge to another.

Jan and his network of cronies and former customers had bought them time, but Michael hated to see the old Jan return. The fawning, the mincing, the coquettish behaviour around these men sickened him. So unacceptable to any man, much less from a twenty-six-year-old beginning to look much older. The behaviour ended when they were alone.

As he struggled to think of more places to hide, Jan remembered Kai. Let's go to Cologne, Kai will help us. Michael laughed. The naiveté to think a German soldier would help them confounded him, especially when Jan could be so practical in other ways.

Then came the day when Jan answered Michael's *now where to?* with: *I don't know.* They had just decamped from their latest refuge, in the flat of a former bartender from the Eldorado who had been called up for duty. Jan had run out of friends.

So in the middle of the night they left, Jan disguised as a one-armed veteran, Michael hobbling on a cane. Crossing the Wundtstrasse, having come from the other side of the Kaiserdamm, they found themselves at Witzleben Park. Jan knew it from his early days in Berlin. Decommissioned soldiers and folks who'd lost everything with the collapsing mark used to make the green space around the lake home. When the National Socialists swept to power, they cleaned out the park.

There was nowhere else to go.

Michael wrestled with how much longer they could last like this. Not Jan. He never seemed to worry. Didn't care about the coming winter or how they would eat. To Jan, this pillar-to-post existence was a lark. This was nothing to him.

I'm nothing to him.

"Look."

It should have been a small lake under that increasingly rare of things: a quiet, star-lit pre-dawn. Instead, Michael saw a village, or at least the illusion of one.

"What is that?"

Floating on canvas barges covering the entire surface of the Lietzensee, linked by chains and wooden walkways, roofs, chimneys, walls all of canvas crudely painted with doors and windows: a waterborne Berlin suburb prowled by a legion of homeless cats.

"It's a decoy. Ho! Ho! Don't you see? It's meant to be seen from the air."

They walked down to the water, where fencing forbade entry.

"I lived in a tent once, when I was boy. For a whole winter."

"We could stay in there," Jan said.

The idea was not bad, but, "What if someone sees us?"

"Who? If it's meant to draw fire, no one'll go near it."

"And the next air raid?"

"It'll be light soon. You have a better plan?"

Jan was reluctant to explain how he came to have the cloth star in his possession, but eventually Michael pieced this together. There was a shop on the Sybelstrasse, not far from Witzleben Park if Jan crossed the railway tracks. He travelled mostly late at night to avoid being seen after curfew, but if he was, the young man would just as easily slip on an arm band identifying himself as a block warden as he would disguise himself as a woman. He also could conceal his arm convincingly enough to pass as a wounded veteran. His whole life, he explained to Michael, he had been passing in and out of crowds unseen. Just act like you've every reason in the world to be there, he'd say. It's looking guilty that gets you done in.

That was no comfort to Michael, sitting alone in a second-storey wood-framed canvas chamber. From here, through rips in the canvas, Michael kept watch after being left behind. Because your fucking accent, Jan insisted, will get you shot as a spy. He was right, so Michael, swaying up and down, back and forth on the lake's surface, was reluctantly forced to wait for Jan to return, fearing he might not, listening to the endless klunk-klunk klunk-klunk of train wheels on rails. The sound the head of Hélène's boy, his first-born son, made when it hit the bedstead.

Too late to cry about that now, was the only sympathy he'd get from Jan.

The shop owner on the Sybelstrasse sounded like a gruff sort who was always pointing and yelling as a greeting, You there, what do you want? Unexpectedly then, he had a soft spot for Juden, probably because the area was close to the ruined synagogue in Markgraf-Albrecht-Strasse where many Juden had been his long-standing customers. Laws allowed them to buy in his shop only between four and five in the afternoon. Even so, no fish, poultry, canned goods, only certain vegetables, no milk, apples, tomatoes, and anything in short supply made it to the list as well. And Juden children were forbidden candy. Even honey. The shopkeeper, however, was not as vigilant with the paperwork when it came to these people as he was with Aryans.

This, Jan found out, because he had entered into an arrangement.

In front of the shop were rows of baskets filled with whatever meagre produce was available to civilians from Berlin's market gardens: turnips, carrots, sometimes potatoes and even apples. The owner augmented these offerings with produce he grew himself in a patch by his apartment. Jan was so hungry that even the withered onions were tempting. As often was the case, the shopkeeper was distracted, Come here, go there, no, no, no, I assure you that's the best price. When he turned away from the window Jan filled his pockets.

Please, the middle-aged woman said, watching him. Just, Please.

An alarm from her and he surely would be arrested. Then Jan saw her Star.

And the woman had money.

A policeman patrolled the other side of the street. She beckoned to him to follow her around the corner, where she explained that she had come all the way from the other side of the Kaiserdamm to buy milk for her invalid mother. This was the only shop she knew where she had a chance. Milk sold out within a few hours. There'd be none left by late afternoon when she would be allowed inside.

Jan could not believe his good fortune. She'd not report his theft.

If she paid him to get her the milk, he could buy something to go with the onions.

No policeman across the way now, just a street in Berlin under a brilliant autumn sun. Ornate balconies, doors open to the warm air and kids giggling as they circled chestnut trees on their bicycles. In the ceramic pots by the apartment doors across from the shop, flags drooped among purple mums.

Ten Reichsmarks, then.

Oh, dear. That is a lot.

Even though Jan didn't have a ration card, he took the money. He had no intention of buying something he could easily take. The money he'd add to his and Michael's thin resources. Then it occurred to him that with a sick mother, this woman would be in need of milk on a regular basis. For a similar fee, he would help. This could prove to be very profitable.

The bell over the door chimed. The shop's plank floors were strewn with sawdust. Glass curved over the meat counter, empty save for three very anemic chickens. The shopkeeper and a woman were haggling over the price for one of them. They glanced at him, then resumed the barter. Cans of cut sunflowers fronted the window, obscuring the only other person in the shop, a younger woman wearing a faded kerchief covered with swimming blue dolphins. She was scanning the shelves along the wall, comparing her book of ration cards as she went.

Jan thought he was very clever. Could the shopkeeper help him? He'd just come back from the front where he'd been wounded, his wife had a baby and she's not well. Where would he get milk? The lie might explain the lack of uniform and why he'd not been seen around before.

The woman haggling over the chicken didn't care if he was the head of the Wehrmacht. She had two sons at the front herself and neither were home. He'd have to wait his turn, she said indignantly.

What can you do? shrugged the shopkeeper.

The store was not big and only a single row of shelves separated Jan from the woman with the dolphins. She avoided looking at him.

The few loaves of bread, a tray of eggs and even a round of cheese was more food than he and Michael had seen in weeks. He picked up a jar of jam. The larder in David's flat used to be filled with English jams. A different one for each day of the week. Jan almost couldn't stop himself from grabbing one of the loaves of bread and tearing into it.

The bell over the door signalled the entry of two men. The children's laughter followed them in.

Yes, yes, said the shopkeeper, wiping his hands on his large apron.

There were complaints, Herr Lessing.

Ridiculous. He had the cleanest grocery on the Sybelstrasse.

One of the policemen quietly asked the woman by the glass counter for her papers.

The complaints regarded distribution, Herr Lessing.

With exasperation: I have the required papers.

Finished with the woman and her identity card, the officer looked about.

Then he won't mind showing them, the papers?

This way, then, this way.

The policeman saw Jan.

Papers?

Jan backed against the shelf. The jar of jam slipped out of his hand and shattered into streaks of red thick with berries.

The woman was silently choking.

Her basket dropped, her kerchief fluttered to the floor as she leaned over, hands clutching her throat. She fell right into Jan's arms, but fought any attempts he made to help. The policeman called for the others. Alone with the woman, now turning quite blue, Jan saw the thing lodged in her mouth. She wailed as he pulled the yellow cloth Star of David free.

The other woman, who'd only then decided on one of the chickens, let out a cry.

The policemen dragged the deceitful creature to her feet. A hasty search produced Aryan ration cards.

How did you get these?

No reply.

Look at her, the defiant bitch, exclaimed the other woman.

They took the lady with the dolphins on her kerchief away. She did not thank Jan for saving her life.

"Lucky for me she was trying to swallow the evidence."

Jan was tearing into a brown round of bread dripping with jam, sufficient to take the desperation off his hunger. He washed it down with milk. During the confusion of the arrest he'd grabbed what he could and slipped out the back door. The milk lady must have been frightened by the commotion; she was nowhere to be seen. No point in leaving her milk behind. Someone else would just take it.

Michael was not eating.

"Hey. I went through a lot of trouble to get that."

The gentle motion of their floating city left Michael constantly nauseated.

Jan came back another night looking pleased with himself.

Michael stared at the two five-Reichsmark coins Jan had placed in his hand. How strangely cognizant he was of their weight, their coolness, who might have touched them, what they had been exchanged for, a grey hole burning through his palm.

"What did you do for this?"

"Don't start that again. If it were up to you, we'd starve."

Michael hated that Jan was right. The young man knew how to steal, how to lie. Everything they had in their makeshift home, the blankets, the extra clothing, Michael knew, Jan had secured on his back or on his knees.

"I'm sick of this, always arguing, sick of you and that long face of yours." Then Jan chuckled. "You're jealous. Jealous of some waster in an alley."

"Then go back to the streets, you fucking little whore, and see if I care."

"Oh, you'll care. You pathetic old fool."

Michael threw the coins. One caught Jan over the eye, nicking him. He wiped his forehead, looked at his hand.

"Fuck you, you bastard."

Then go. But of course Michael could never mean that any more than he could say, Heart, cease to beat. Regretting every word, he hung back, crippled, watching Jan toss his few possessions into his rucksack and climb, fuck you, down the rope ladder.

"Wait, don't go. I'm sorry. Stay." Beg, if it'll stanch the hemorrhaging.

But it didn't. Instead Jan crossed to the shore, dawn beginning to wink over the rooftops along the road. Too soon the sun would show the swipe of autumn ruin in the park's trees and he would be gone.

"Wait!"

Jan turned angrily and gestured for him to be quiet.

Neither of them saw it cutting along the park road, a high-speed yellow wave, painted swastikas, with the canvas top down. Jan stepped into the road. The wave swerved. The Bugatti's tires screamed.

When Michael reached the car, having come to a stop slightly over the curb, its aged driver was straining to get out, his bulk in the tight seats making it difficult. His female passenger was already by Jan's side.

Across the street, people were gathering in their doorways, or looking down from their windows to complain about the hour. Is he dead? someone called.

"I didn't see him. I didn't have time to stop," the big man said.

"You were going too fast." She was in tweed with a white scarf. "You always go too fast."

Michael was on his knees, his arm under Jan's head. The fall had knocked the wind solidly out of him.

"He'll be all right?" The woman's husband was also in tweed.

Jan blinked, coughed and then retched onto the grass.

"Oh," he moaned, staring at the soiled grass, "and what I went through to eat."

The woman handed Jan her handkerchief.

He doesn't look well, she observed to Michael. Has he been ill?

"Perhaps we should take him to the infirmary," the man said.

Jan closed his eyes and groaned.

"No, that won't be necessary, I'm sure," said Michael.

"Is there somewhere we can take you?"

"No, really, thank you. I can take care of my . . . brother."

Michael suddenly felt the older man's grip on his shoulder.

"You're not from around here, are you, son?"

Michael looked up.

"Austria, is it? I thought I recognized the accent." Then he nodded to the growing crowd watching from across the street. "We don't want to draw attention here."

"We were just on our way to Potsdam," his wife said.

Jan adored Potsdam, he managed weakly, and a little too dramatically for Michael's comfort.

"Then please. Join Juliana and me for the day, that's if you fellows have no other plans. It's the least we can do for almost running you over."

"Oh, yes!" said Jan, sitting up. "And what timing, today is my birthday."

Juliana clapped her hands. "Settled."

Birthday indeed.

Michael and the man helped Jan up. A quick check of the automobile revealed no injury, and no way out of this mess unless in the back of that car.

"My Royale. She is my pride and joy, of course, next to my dear Juliana. Eight cylinders—"

"You'd better be talking about that car," Juliana said.

"And please, call me Klaus."

With Jan and Michael secured in the back, Klaus Caesar shifted the Bugatti off the curb and with a grind and a lurch, the grey canyons of Berlin and disbelieving faces lining the streets soon faded into slumbering suburbs, fields of leaf-dropping trees and dawn breaking through clouds, promising a day of occasional brilliance.

Jan was clearly delighted. Michael was terrified. All this older couple had to do was look at them to see something was not right. The

Caesars would denounce them when they figured out they were fugitives or, judging from the speed Klaus drove, when the authorities stopped them.

It appeared that it was going to be the latter. Outside of Wannsee they were stopped at a military checkpoint.

"General Caesar," the soldier said, approaching the car with a salute.

"Just a day in the country with my family." Klaus waved him away.

"Go on, breathe," Jan said quietly with a nudge to Michael.

After the Bugatti sped them away, Jan chatted gaily with Juliana, soon giggling and laughing like old friends. The war and gas shortages had put an end to pleasure driving and what few vehicles were on the road belonged to the army.

In Potsdam, Klaus roared through the narrow cobbled streets to a restaurant whose windows overlooked a corner where a few deserted tables and chairs crowded the empty walk. Worrying that Juliana had been chilled by the drive, he insisted they eat inside by the fire.

Wartime rationing had limited the menu, but Klaus was unperturbed. What's the point of being a general if rank can't get you a decent meal in times like this? He was right. After mugs of beer and steaming cider had arrived, there followed plates of creamed potato, rostbraten and lima beans. A king's feast for Jan and Michael and right then, trying not to eat as if they hadn't in days, neither cared if they got caught. This was worth it.

Juliana noted it was good to see young men with healthy appetites. More rostbraten! Klaus ordered.

"We've been coming here for years, haven't we?"

Juliana nodded.

"Forty years. Forty years I've been married to this wonderful woman. Either of you married?"

"Oh, no," said Jan with a mouthful of potatoes.

"May you be as lucky to find what I have. Right here in this room. Juliana was a waitress and I was a soldier back from the last war."

"Did it happen at first sight?" Jan wanted to know.

"Oh, heavens no. I thought he was too old for me and not handsome enough. I wanted a young and dashing man to sweep me away."

"Lucky for me the war killed off most of those," Klaus said, smiling. Juliana reached over and placed her hand on his.

"But we've been happy, have we not?"

Yes, Juliana agreed.

"And we must thank you two for brightening up our little party today. If we had not run into you," Klaus smiled, "it would just be two old people and their ghosts."

The woman blinked away some tears.

"Our son died last year at the front. His wife and our two grand-children were killed in an air raid."

"I'm sorry."

"Wehrmacht?"

"On leave," Michael said. "We have no family left, so we've been roughing it."

Thank God the old general did not ask for particulars.

"I'm to report to the army tomorrow."

Juliana pulled her arm back. "Calling up old men, what can the Führer be thinking?"

"Hush, now."

Michael glanced about the room. The only other diners appeared to date from the Hohenzollern era and remained more interested in their soup.

"So we thought we'd take the Royale out for one last spin." He'd been hoarding the petrol, Klaus added confidentially.

Dessert was apple stuffed with real butter, almonds, cinnamon and breadcrumbs, wrapped in dough, baked and sprinkled with brown sugar. And to everyone's amazement, real honest-to-goodness coffee. Klaus insisted dinner be finished with a glass of port. After all, this was a celebration.

After several more hours of conversation and a walk through the neglected gardens of Sanssouci, they reluctantly returned to the car. Michael pulled Jan aside and suggested they get out now, take their chances in the surrounding countryside.

That would certainly raise suspicions and had Michael forgotten they were with an army general?

Back in the car, Michael's stomach coiled as Berlin's limits fast approached.

Jan wore Juliana's white scarf and sat up in the back to let it blow wildly. "Haven't you and I had the best of days?" He had to yell to Michael to be heard.

And over too soon. The car stopped back on the Wundtstrasse. Michael wished Klaus luck at the front as he and Jan got out of the Bugatti, not far from Witzleben Park. Without their asking, Klaus had found a tree-shaded blind in the road to let them off.

Juliana then kissed Jan. Make your mamma proud, she insisted. There were tears in her eyes.

"For the young one's birthday," she said to Michael, embracing him.

As she and Klaus got back into the yellow Bugatti, Michael slipped his hands into his pockets and he drew out several hundred-Reichsmark notes. Before he could say anything, the yellow wave whirred and shifted down the darkened street.

"You think they believed us?"

Jan didn't think they cared.

"I'm glad you had a good time."

"Me too."

They hurried into the park as the car sped into the curve of the walled road ahead. Its engine roared, drawing their attention, and they stopped to look just as the car slammed into the brick.

"Jesus!"

Jan pushed Michael forward. "Don't look. Hurry. This'll bring out everyone."

A white scarf fluttered down into rolling balls of black and orange.

With a full stomach, and the wrecked automobile continuing to draw the curious into the street, Jan had forgone his nightly forage for food. He rolled into a corner, his breath soft and measured.

Michael wasn't so lucky. Lying awake in the loft, he stared at the searchlights through a rip in the coarse fabric.

You think there'll be an air-raid?

Be quiet.

The smell of burning oily fumes hung in the late-autumn air.

Do you think they did it on purpose?

Jan did not reply.

Sometime well after midnight, the wind picked up and the canvas-covered pontoons stretched across the lake began to gently bump together. Michael could never get used to the hollow, clunking sound. It made a sleepless night worse. He could never be sure if it was just rippling waters against the oil drums underneath or the brush brush brush of boots through grass. Wet grass. Just before dawn.

Michael crawled to a loose seam. A long, thin row of lights bounced in harmony on each side of the Lietzensee.

"Jan, get up."

He was disoriented and angry and accused Michael of trying to get into his pants.

"They're coming."

It didn't matter who. They'd always expected this would happen and had planned for it. As with most of the floating city, their structure was anchored to oiled heavy-cotton panels fitted over frames attached to sealed drums. All Jan and Michael had to do was swim underneath and resurface in the pocket of air trapped below.

First they carefully slid all their belongings into the water. As they climbed down to the decking the row of lights bouncing on the grassy surrounds of the park was clear: soldiers, flashlights, a search party moving stealthily.

Slowly they slipped into the lake and pulled themselves under the floating drums, feeling their way through stygian water with their hands.

Jesus, Jan croaked as he resurfaced. Even though they were inches apart, they could not see one another. "It's fucking freezing."

Michael hissed, Be quiet!

They waited, submerged in the December Lietzensee. Jan was shivering violently, his teeth cracking.

"You think they're looking for us?"

"So many?"

"Michael . . . I can't feel my legs."

Five more minutes. Hold on five more minutes. They could hear boots, voices.

Search over there.

Make sure no structure is unchecked.

The soldiers crossed back and forth above them, but Jan had slipped under the water. Michael grabbed his jacket and pulled him up, thrusting his hand over Jan's mouth to choke off the coughing. Michael wrapped his arm about his struggling friend even tighter, keeping his mouth covered, pointing to the thin web of wood and canvas overhead. One cough is all it would take.

Nothing here.

The hard bark of leather faded. Voices in the distance told them the soldiers were moving on.

They had been watching the woman for several hours. Jan thought she looked ill.

Hunger had been driving young boys into the parks to hunt stray cats and dogs, but until now, no one else had opposed the prohibition of the floating city. Jan had discovered her when he returned before dawn, his own hunt for food netting a handful of beets to add to their stores. She sat propped against a wall on the wooden floating street. Wearing a stylish wool overcoat, she was clutching her abdomen.

"You think that's who the soldiers were looking for?"

"We can't leave her there." Jan wiped his nose on his sleeve.

"Maybe it's a trick to draw us out."

"No one knows we're here."

Besides, the woman was a danger should she be noticed from the park. At least they had to move her from view. As they climbed down to her, the woman stirred and tried to get up, only to double over and slide back.

"It's all right. We won't hurt you."

"She's pregnant," said Jan.

The woman said something unintelligible.

"And Polish."

"How do you know?"

Jan shrugged.

"What's she saying?"

"She doesn't want us to hurt her."

"Tell her we won't, but we've got to get her inside before someone sees us."

The woman nodded, and with great difficulty they helped her under the canvas of the closest structure. She left a wet spot behind.

"Christ, she's having this baby right now."

The woman began to cry.

"What'll we do?" Michael said.

"We? I never saw you helping out those whores at Frau Merten's pump out the bastards. Better get something we can use for a blanket."

Jan handled the delivery with such attentiveness that in the poor woman's quiet moments he was able to glean something of her story.

Forced as a slave labourer from Warsaw, she'd been working at the Rheinmetall-Borsig munitions factory. The conditions were brutal, the hours back breaking, the food meagre. She was sure she'd die before the war ended and saw her only hope in the attentions of her employer. When she got pregnant, she did her best to keep it hidden, but eventually the man saw how things were. How could she have let this happen? Germans were forbidden to have sex with inferior peoples. The woman would no doubt be killed, he'd be sent to a concentration camp. As she neared her term, her employer panicked, gave her his wife's new coat and helped to make it look as though she'd escaped. The decoy town was as far as she got.

With Jan's help she delivered a feeble boy. Michael, who had not been present for the birth of either of his sons, wrapped him carefully in one of his shirts and after holding him for a while, wiped his eyes, and tucked him against his exhausted mother.

In the morning, mother and child were gone.

"Damn it. And she took all our food."

"All of it?" Jan whimpered, his head aching, his nose clogged. "That Polish sow, after what I did for her? Nothing at all? I'm starving."

"That's the least of our worries. Pack up."

"Why?"

"Because when they find her, and they will, she'll lead them right back to us."

"Not that again." Jan groaned and rolled over, sending Michael to check again on the food. "Maybe she left a crust of bread, the bitch."

No answer.

Jan sat up. "What's the matter?"

Michael pointed. Floating in the water was the woman's coat and the shirt in which he had wrapped the infant.

Jan fell back against his pile of canvas. "She didn't have to eat all of our food first."

By the end of December freezing temperatures laid a covering of ice on the Lietzensee, but they still had not left their floating city.

Maybe the soldiers won't come back, Jan reasoned. Let's wait a couple of days because, where would we go?

Agonizing days for Michael, believing the park would be searched if the woman's body surfaced. He was persuaded to remain for one reason only: Jan was ill.

A worrisome cough now plagued the younger man. His lungs had weakened. Even so, Jan insisted upon going out each night. Michael didn't ask how, but Jan always returned with something, even if only pitiful marble-sized potatoes or gnarled radishes.

At dawn, when the bells started to ring, it occurred to Michael that it might be Christmas Day.

"Do you remember it when you were a boy?"

Jan said no. He never talked about his past.

"I remember one. My uncles sent my brother Felix and me second-hand bicycles. We were so excited we wanted to ride them in the snow. My mother, she used to sing carols in November. Drove my father crazy hearing that. And the baking. Nutmeg and cinnamon."

Almost real enough to triumph over dank lake vapours still finding their way through holes in the ice.

"I won't be around for Billy to get his first bicycle."

Jan said, Why think about that.

When he returned in the middle of that night with a whole loaf of bread and, unbelievably, even some cheese, Jan's face was beaded with sweat, his breathing rough and laboured. He'd gone out against Michael's pleading that he take one night off from his habitual foraging, but Michael knew better than to expect he'd listen.

Michael handed him some bread.

No, no, I've eaten already, Jan said. He took of sip from the can of rain water, then said he just wanted to sleep. So Michael sat in the dark, freezing, eating the bread as slowly as he could to make it last.

"Michshu? Are you there?"

Michael said he was, and slid closer to where Jan lay.

"Do you like it when I call you Michshu?"

"No."

"I'm so cold."

Michael covered him with everything they had.

But he was still cold. *Do something.*

All Michael could think of was to slip under the pieces of canvas they used for blankets and wrap himself about Jan's body, so thin, just bone. For once, Jan did not object to being touched by him. He only whimpered.

"Is it warm in Nova Scotia?"

"Yes, in summer."

"Tell me about it. Don't stop. Even if I fall asleep, keep talking so it will make me dream. And tell me only about the summers."

So Michael told him about running barefoot through the laughing surf of Lawrencetown beach—no, really, the water rushing over the round rocks made it sound so—eating blueberry ice cream and boiled lobster, and fog horns bleating in the harbour and playing cards under the eaves with Felix and Gene on afternoons when splashing rain rolled off the roof. At night, wind hissed through larches along the fence and the summer poplars, their leaves crackled. He'd sleep leaving the windows open so the cooling fingertips of fog wiped away the heat of the day.

"Is your sister nice?"

"The best. And you would have liked Felix too."

"Sounds like he would've made fun of me."

What did Michael like to do most?

That was easy. Be with Avon. His best friend. Five years older and has the widest smile and that laugh. Everyone knows it's Avon when they hear it. No one throws a ball farther or runs faster and he's the best swimmer ever. Took Michael to Black Rock Beach his first time, and after they sat listening to the wind hissing through the spruce boughs saying a nor'easter was headed their way. Everything about being with Avon makes Michael feel good.

. . . made Michael feel good.

And that's all he meant to say that day in the shed, the one they shared with their neighbours, when he was supposed to be cleaning up his father's tools. Avon came by to help, said don't. Michael had misunderstood. So did August, standing there. Watching the embrace. Like it happened yesterday. *Goddamn.* First one ever.

Jan stirred within his grasp. If he were in Nova Scotia, he'd open a flower shop.

He was fading.

That way it would be summer all year long. Everyone likes flowers. Makes them happy.

Five more minutes.

Michael pulled Jan tight because Jan's dreams did not include him, and they had to. They just had to.

1943

Pia gazed down at them, larger than life, her eyes welling with tears.

"That silly old cunt," Jan whispered in the darkness. "Who'd believe any Jude would want to rape that?"

Shhh, someone said.

The movies had been Michael's idea. Risky yes, but necessary. Winter cold was bearing down and he knew after Christmas that Jan's cough, the fevers, could not be ignored. Theatres were still doing a brisk trade, the government having shut down dance halls and the few remaining cabarets, and shortages had curtailed everything else. It didn't matter that they'd seen Pia's latest film about a mad money-lender with an appetite for blood, *Jud Süss,* three times now. The darkened cinemas, generally overlooked by police checks in this part of town, provided a few brief hours of relative warmth and diversion.

The newsreels did nothing to satisfy Michael's curiosity about the war. Black-and-white images of their leader among the ruins screaming retribution, London streets collapsing in flames and the American president trundling about in a wheelchair, all to National Socialist ridicule, flags and patriotic overtures. How Germans were faring was best told by a Berliner's obsession with hunger.

Jan was too busy hustling for smokes to care. It mortified Michael that Jan would risk talking to someone, but as Jan reminded him, they only stuck out if they acted like they shouldn't be there.

The movies also gave them a sense of event, a reason to wash and shave with the one dull razor between them, to grasp something other than despair. Although why they bothered, Jan pointed out as Michael grimaced under the application of icy lake water, was a wonder. Soap was an early casualty of rationing and he could hear Tristan now: One shouldn't smell like one's vices, at least not in public. Jan concluded that Berliners now stank like Parisians, reason in itself to end the war.

In January, Deutschlandhalle to their southwest, overflowing with thousands happily anticipating the circus, was gutted by flames, resulting from an aerial attack, with remarkably no casualties. After so many months the assault signalled the return of regular RAF bombings.

Jan, back with some apples, had found out that most of these latest British raids had been around the Wilhelmstrasse and the Chancellery, and that the war was going poorly for the army around Stalingrad. There was no need to say what was on Michael's mind: Billy and Lonä lived close to the heaviest bombing.

But don't worry, everything was going to be all right. Jan was just sure of it.

Relief bordered on euphoria every time Michael saw Jan stealing back into Witzleben Park before dawn, dispelling hours of: what if something has happened what if he doesn't come back to me how will I live without him. Usually, exhausted, Jan slept after his return. Tonight, however, he was animated. Michael didn't ask why. Jan was up to something.

The next night, as Jan made ready to head out, food now an all-night, every-night occupation, Michael gave in to his anxieties. "You're not doing anything stupid?"

"All will be revealed in time," Jan said, making eyeglasses out of his fingers. He reached over and patted Michael's head. There, there, Michshu. Then he flounced out of their canvas hideout, down the rope ladder to the bobbing sidewalks.

Somewhere near dawn, Michael dozed off, awaking to see Jan returning.

He was not alone.

Oh God.

But as Michael followed their progress through the park, Jan's face suggested that he knew his companion. When they'd climbed up the ladder to the loft, Michael was surprised to be looking into the somewhat older and scarred face of Tonia.

"Maybe one day she'll be back. These days, it's Anthony."

Jan tossed his hands into the air and began to prance around the room. The building shook.

"And Anthony is going to get us out of Berlin."

"How? When!"

The former Empress of Eldorado told them about a German officer with similar sympathies who'd had a change of heart and was now helping men like them escape to England.

"How do you know it's not a trap?"

Michael glanced at Jan, who remained defiantly unrepentant for a man who'd once betrayed so many of his own. No doubt Anthony hadn't heard about that.

"You can trust him. I've been with him to the coast before. He has a small fishing boat at Cuxhaven. This time, I'm to get out. When I found Jan by what's left of the Romanisches Café—"

"You were all the way over on the Ku'damm?"

"Shut up." He turned to Anthony. "Go on."

"I told him I could get him out as well. He told me about you."

"Can it be true? But how safe is it?"

"Oh, it's no picnic. Means being on the North Sea at night."

"We have to trust someone."

Jan was right, but walking into the arms of a German officer?

"He'll go again in three weeks. Has a house in Charlottenburg, below the schloss across the Spandauer Damm. We'll go there tonight. You'll be safe. And warm, for Christ's sake."

Jan was already packing his rucksack. "To sleep in a real bed. Michshu, think of it."

A poster for the 1934 party rally in Nuremberg hung prominently in Captain Dobrin's study. And why not? He had modelled for it. As the archetype of the Nordic race, Dobrin was flawed only by a penchant for his own sex. He had married into an old, prominent German family and consequently had risen rapidly through SS ranks. His wife had given him four perfect Aryans and he had fathered two more for the Führer through the Spring of Life Foundation— unmarried, childless women girding their loins for the Fatherland. Having sent his family south to the safety of the countryside, he now lived a discreet bachelor's existence in a Charlottenburg town-house, its privacy ensured by a high wall surrounding the garden.

"Of course you're not disturbing me, Michael. Come in."

Dobrin was in civilian dress—open shirt, trousers—sitting by the fire. His study was devoid of books yet cluttered with lacrosse bats, ice skates, balls and paintings of the German countryside and drip-ping braces of fowl. He languidly took his bare feet off the ottoman and rose to offer Michael a drink.

"Can't sleep? Is the room not to your liking?"

Although Michael was out of practice with comfort: "I think the air raid has more to do with it."

"We've been lucky in this part of the city. Very few hits. But there is the cellar if you wish."

After months with only canvas to protect him from the bombings, Michael stayed and accepted the drink. His stomach was full for the first time since Potsdam, no doubt accounting for Jan now blissfully dream-ing through what sounded like the worst attacks yet on central Berlin.

"Sit by the fire and warm yourself. We'll have a talk, shall we? Von Renner. Now why do I know that name? Yes." Dobrin drank, studying his guest through the bottom of the crystal. "There was a foreign minister at the Versailles negotiations I believe, Wilhelm von Renner?"

"My grandfather."

"To him, then."

They both stared into the fire.

"The matter of your helping us."

"You're not convinced. Michael, if it was my intent to have you arrested, wouldn't that have happened by now?" Thunder-like rumblings growled lowly in the distance. Dobrin refilled his glass and felt obliged to apologize. "Drinking alone is not wise, but it's the only thing that helps these days."

"So why?"

The firelight seemed to peel reserve away.

"I was escorting a trainload of deportees to Poland. We had rounded them up from all over Germany, mostly from here in Berlin. After crossing the border, the train came to a stop. There was a creek close by and the orders came that everyone was to get out for a swim. Children first. Once they'd been separated from their families in the cars, they were led onto the field. Let's make a game of it shall we, they were told. Sing and dance as loud as you can so your parents can hear you. Hundreds of children in that field, jumping and laughing in the open air under the sun, unable to hear the screams of their parents when the prussic acid started to fill the cars. Then the order came to shoot the children. Dancing in the field. Hundreds of them. Playing under the sun. Bouncing like rag dolls when the bullets hit." The man drained his glass. "Apparently, we didn't have enough of the gas to do them all at once."

Dobrin refilled their drinks.

For use on roaches and rats. They needed to know where the prussic acid was. My job was to find it.

Dobrin's gaze was pulled from the flames.

"I'm not a butcher, I'm an officer with just enough of my childhood faith intact to know one day, there'll be a reckoning. When I kill, it should be my enemy in battle, not children, even Juden children, playing in fields.

263

"But the war in the east is not going well. We have the Americans now in the west. The realist in me knows the end for Germany is not far. It's desperate times and desperate measures that have seen many a good man destroyed in this war. I knew I had to do something when an honourable man, a good soldier and friend, was denounced. Because he was a captain in the Abwehr, Himmler ordered him shot without trial. It's only a matter of time before all of us will suffer the fate of my friend."

Peter was a captain in the Abwehr.

"That's why I will get you and your young friend to England."

The room shook from a nearby explosion and a sprig of plaster fell between them.

"That was close."

One morning in February, Michael chanced upon Jan and their host talking quietly at the bottom of the staircase. Dobrin, congenial, tall, gracious. Jan, grinning, fadingly boyish, but still in possession of his charms.

So is Michael anything to you? Dobrin had asked.

Of course not.

Michael descended the stairs.

Knowing the attraction was inevitable did not make it easier to accept. Dobrin was exactly the type Jan adored. And the way Jan answered his question. He might as well have said, Don't make me laugh.

"Where are you going?" Jan asked.

To Hell! And as far away from here as I can get. Why not? Give you all the privacy you need to let him fuck you. Fuck you in every room of this fucking house! You'd like that, you fucking little cunt! Because that's what you are. And when he's finished fucking you, wash his cock off with your mouth! No wonder he's not asked us for money. You fucking little whore, you're probably part of the deal. Bend over for a smile. I have to get out of here or I'll kill you.

"I have to make sure Billy is all right before I leave," Michael said.

"It's dangerous. The captain could help."

"I don't need anyone's help to check on my own son."

"He's right, Michael," Dobrin said. "You shouldn't go."

"I don't know when, or if ever, I'll see my son again. If it wasn't for . . . well, I'd be with him now, when he needs me. I have to do this."

The military man nodded.

"We leave tonight. We must work with the tides. If you are not back, we leave without you. We will not wait."

Michael angrily threw on his coat and bolted down the remaining stairs. He didn't hear Jan say, Be careful, Michshu.

Michael was indifferent to the daylight risk. He thought it would serve Jan well if he were arrested, then he'd care, then he'd be sorry.

No, he wouldn't.

He was just a footnote in the boy's self-staged gala. A walk-on bit character. Michael von Renner. Second flag-waver on the right.

Jesus Christ.

The air was rancid from fires burning all over the city and something else, something putridly sweet, burdeningly sweet. He gagged and made to vomit.

Air raids had left fissures and gaping wounds in blocks of flats, still burning, doll-like houses shorn of façades, rubble strewn into roadways laboriously being cleared by hand. He hurried. Turning a corner, he bumped into the feet of a man dangling from a light post, shot and hanged for looting probably, bloated and purple and the source of the sweetness.

Sirens were blaring the next street over, fading as the fire truck sped away.

Michael avoided the main roads, hurrying parallel to the Kaiser-Friedrichstrasse, Lietzenburger Strasse, Martin-Luther-Strasse and down into the Schöneberg suburb.

"You don't want to go in," the groundskeeper said at the cemetery gate. "We took a direct hit last night."

But there was a goodbye to make here. The elderly groundskeeper shook his head. The fool had been warned.

Craters in St. Matthäus churchyard had spewed up pieces of shattered coffins, bones, fleshy bits, tattered rags and the stink of rot. Stones lay askew or fragmented. One bomb had taken out the wall of the cemetery, laying bare the honeycomb of houses on the other side. Michael pressed his coat sleeve over his nose.

The soot-faced cherubs with dimple-cheeks no longer held up Familie von Renner, no longer grinned. The roof and cupola had been ripped from the mausoleum, the floor blown away. Overhead the steady creak creak creak worked its way into Michael's consciousness. Something in the tree. Something swaying in the breeze.

She was still very much Nan, still wearing pearls. Her legs and lower torso were partially severed and dangled over Michael.

I warned you, the groundskeeper shouted as Michael fled from the yard, swinging the gates closed behind him, running until he doubled over and sank to his knees.

This left one thing to do. See Billy, make sure he's all right, then get out of Berlin, get away from a war that, of its most malignant consequences, does this to the dead. If he thought about it—

No. Don't. Blind your mind to it for five minutes. Then five more. Then five again. Then it'll pass.

A series of fives and it was late morning near the Kronenstrasse. Here the carnage from the raids was more pronounced. Whole blocks uninhabitable, jagged piles of brick and stone under thin lines of smoke. Nets of sparking electric cables hummed in the street, but incredibly, the relentless, scratchy marching music playing from speakers.

Michael crossed onto his old boulevard. Some incendiary damage at one end, but otherwise, the quiet neighbourhood, flag-strewn balconies overhanging treed sidewalks, safe.

He stood in a doorway across from his former home.

Although Michael wasn't cold, he shivered, and pulled his coat about his shoulders. The cloudy sky began to break and broad beams of sunlight traced a path down the centre of the street. A boy on a bicycle rode by and stuck out his tongue. The music on the loud-speaker went silent. Two young women in uniforms strode diagonally from the other side.

The distant lazy droning, buzzing, like flies, became louder, angrier, closer. The women looked up. The boy on the bike shielded his eyes against the sun. Michael glanced as well, then caught sight of a young boy with an aeroplane in his hand skipping onto the balcony across the road.

They were swarming in circles. No longer a terror of the night, a bold daylight raid. One plane broke away. Michael saw it, lowering, growling as it descended parallel to the street.

"Billy, go back!"

But aeroplanes were the boy's delight. He was jumping up and down, mimicking the drone of the Mosquito with the toy in his hand. Then more joy as he saw his father waving to him in the street.

"Dadda! Look at my plane!"

"Go inside, Billy, inside the house!"

The plane dipped lower. The attack brought Lonä, Catharina and Braum, in uniform, onto the balcony. Of course Catharina would be there. She'd want to go to the Chancellery, what was left of it, on this special day in the hopes of seeing her Führer.

Lonä saw Michael first.

He pointed to the sky.

The Mosquito was almost overhead and opened fire with a rapid spitting. Lonä pushed Billy through the apartment door as the bul-lets splintered the legs of the women on the street; they fell into their own muck. Michael dived back into the doorway as the bullets ripped up the pavement, pricking off pieces of stone cladding, sprin-kling the sidewalk with broken glass, before they travelled in a straight line across the balcony, bouncing Lonä, Catharina and Braum like towels on a clothesline. The boy on the bike pedalled as the bullets pinged and chinged off his wheels, riddling his thin con-torting body with shot. He went down with an Oh! and lay wide-eyed on the pavement.

Roaring above the rooflines, the plane veered up.

When Michael got to his feet he saw Billy standing in the ground-floor doorway. The boy was crying, aware that something bad had happened, but not comprehending what. He ran.

"No! Stay back!"

The fighter turned and dipped. Michael dashed into the street and taking his son into his arms, bolted back across the road. The plane's guns ripped again as Michael lurched back into the doorway.

The fighter rose and circled. As it approached, poof! Artillery from one of the flak towers clipped off its tail. Michael pulled his son's face to his chest as the plane spun down. The pilot tried to pull up the nose only to belly onto the asphalt, shearing off the Mosquito's wings, ripping away the front of the buildings across from Michael, scooping up the crawling women.

Michael felt an ocean rush of heat and heard *Dadda* inside his head as his legs carried him out onto the sidewalk, moving independently from thought. The pilot was a human torch flailing in the cockpit. As the aircraft continued to slide and scrape down the street, its broken wing pulled away the wall underneath the balcony. The roof collapsed inwards, burying what was left of Lonä and the Kunstlers.

From the speakers, fanfare heralded the official announcement. The Führer would soon address the Reich on this day of celebration, the tenth anniversary of his ascension to power by the will of the German people.

Michael carried his boy as fiery walls collapsed about them. Sirens shrieked. The air clogged with smoke and spraying water from ruptured pipes. People were running and crying, from all directions, tugging at twisted metal, doors and clumps of brick, frantic to reach those buried underneath.

Eventually the haze and noise and sirens faded as Michael found himself by the Kupfergraben, following the canal to where the long black and white and red flags outside the nearby Reichsbank moved languidly in the light breeze.

"Did I do something bad?"

They had stopped to rest by a weir in the canal. Michael couldn't let go of his son and held him in his arms.

"Just got something in my eyes, little buddy."

"Are the planes gone?"

Michael nodded.

"Where's Mumma?"

He touched the streaks running down Michael's grey-covered face.

"She's with your Aunt Catya and Uncle Braum."

"The planes were loud, huh, Dadda?"

"Very loud."

"I wasn't scared."

"Good boy."

"Uncle Braum says I mustn't be scared 'cause I'm a big brother." Michael heard a breath catch in the boy's throat. "Is he in Heaven now?"

"You must be very brave."

"Are we going home soon? I'm hungry."

A hungry five-year-old, with no way out of Berlin. And if Billy were caught with him . . .

"Would you like to see your Auntie Gene?"

He nodded. "Can we make snowmen, like you said?"

"Uh-huh."

"Mumma too?"

"Maybe she'll come later. Now hold tight."

Michael stepped onto a small wooden dock attached to the weir. Gazing down, he saw himself broken up into little shifting bits. How deep, he wondered, how fast the current? How long would it take for the Spree to wash you out to sea? Surely in times like these, God grants dispensation for taking the easy way. Or would He? Michael had stacked up a litany of wrongs.

"But first, we better clean you up. You and me, we're covered in dust. We can't have your Auntie Gene seeing us look like this."

"Yeah."

Michael set the boy down beside him, then dipped his handkerchief into the water. "It's gonna be cold, buddy."

"I don't mind. Mumma washes me like this all the time."

The icy water might be the only way for the screaming inside to stop. There was so much of it now, Michael didn't know who it all belonged to, except for the cries that belonged to him. Bet that frigid canal wouldn't take long to silence all of them. He'd need enough breath to make sure the boy was gone before him. Wouldn't it be a kindness to do that? Michael couldn't even feed him. There was nowhere left to go. And if the boy struggled, he'd have to find the will to hold him down long enough until—

"I dropped my plane. Herr Peter gave me that."

"We'll get you another one. Now hold still." Michael worked at swabbing away the fine dust. "Don't make a face, you."

Billy stopped scrunching up his nose. Michael rinsed out the hand-kerchief and then washed his own.

In a few minutes, it'd all be over.

"Give me a hug, Billy."

"You're not supposed to call me that. Mumma and Uncle Braum said so."

"How about it's something just between us. All right?"

The boy nodded slowly.

Billy climbed back into Michael's arms. He asked why his Dadda was shaking.

"You down there!"

Damn it.

A teenager on the footbridge, riding his bicycle, had stopped to piss into the canal.

"You'll want to go to the palace." He shook and buttoned up. "There's bread and milk for the children."

A week before Michael's grandmother died, she took him in a taxi with her to the old Imperial Palace. Under the shadow of the sprawling storied structure, its hundreds of rooms, draughty, deserted and crumbling, she pointed to a row of windows on the second floor. That was where she had attended a reception with Michael's grandfather. The Kaiser later invited them to a hunting party in Bavaria, where she first met a friend of her husband's, a young medical student whom Nan described as the brilliantly beautiful Doctor Linder.

Now the square in front of the derelict, bomb-shattered palace had been taken over by a relief agency. Smoke was billowing from the dome of the nearby cathedral. Nearer the canal, hundreds of people shuffled in line towards a large tent. They looked as ragged and weary and threadbare as the old palace, and the children, many crying or staring wildly, waited in soiled trousers and underpants, their recent terror only too evident. How nice, though, a violinist was playing nearby, but only the steely-eyed pigeons huddling atop the palace's dung-splattered pilasters listened.

As Michael tried to make sense of which line to stand in, Billy starting to weigh heavily in his arms, a relief worker approached.

"Excuse me, is it true? Food for the children?"

She nodded, feeling Billy's forehead. "Poor little one. He's had a hard time of it?"

"He lost his mother today."

"Oh my dear. No matter how many we evacuate, still so many."

"You send the children away?"

"That truck by the gate, it goes tonight to Freising. They'll be safe from the bombing there."

"What happens in Freising?"

"We have families who will take them in."

Billy reminded his father that he was hungry.

"I know, little buddy, I know." Then he whispered to the woman: "Do you think . . . ?"

"I'm sure we could find a place. Why don't you come along with me to speak with the officer in charge. He will need your papers."

"Officer?"

"Yes, the military is moving them out."

"Of course."

They moved together into the crowd near the trucks and the smell of fresh bread.

"My papers, yes. Let me get those. Could I ask you to take him for a minute?"

The woman smiled and took Billy into her arms. Exhausted, the boy went willingly. She turned away from Michael for only a second, and that was all he needed.

Michael huddled against night in the basement of his old apartment building. A crying child kept him awake with taunts that he'd never be forgiven, but he couldn't be sure it was real. Apart from pockets of flames here and there, most of the fires on the street were out. If he looked up, there were stars to see through glassless windows and doorless frames. Water dripped from the ruined upper floors, but apart from the occasional falling piece of timber or loose mortar, the ruin was deserted.

Incredibly, on the street out front, Michael had found Billy's plane. He held it now as he curled in the cellar and tried to keep warm, hoping the rats weren't hungry. If he had anything at all left to give, he would, to be back in that row house on Waverley Terrace.

Rest here for an hour or two, that was the plan, pull himself together, then while the sky was still dark make his way back to Dobrin's. What else could he do? Maybe the captain had left a message or Michael could find some way to follow them. There just had to be something.

Anything . . .

Christ! The sun.

He stumbled out of the cellar and onto the mid-morning street.

Are you all right? the policeman asked.

A listless crowd had gathered around the smouldering remains of the plane. Women in kerchiefs were crawling over the rubble in the Kronenstrasse, calling for relatives, salvaging three-legged chairs and bent cooking pots. Not far away was Frau Albrecht, hands flailing as she insisted the policeman arrest Michael.

The wet snow did not follow them into the Oranienburg Bahnhof. There the train stopped. Then started. Cars were creaking and screeching. The whole train moved back and forth. With a long-winded puff from the engine it strained onward until farther up the line at a country station, maybe thirty or so kilometres north of Berlin, it halted.

After a few minutes the doors were thrown open, the darkening afternoon only marginally brighter than inside the car.

Come on! Hurry up, men. Form lines to be counted on the platform!

Michael and twenty-two others like him were separated from the rest. Then the entire contingent began the march to camp under the eyes and guns of guards accompanied by a flock of village boys with wooden rifles, shooting them, until called back by mom for dinner.

The column kicked up a sandy dust as they marched through the spruce forest. Gangs of shorn men dressed like zebras on both sides laboured digging ditches and foundations. Those among them recently processed stood and watched, occasionally waving as the arrivals passed. The veterans demonstrated their seniority with indifference. Ahead, the wall dotted with watchtowers, waiting, as they marched the flanking road.

The iron gates swung apart the words *Arbeit Macht Frei*, ushering them into Sachsenhausen. Yes, yes, work will set you free, said the guard, laughing. Michael looked up at the clock capping the solid guardhouse. It alone would count out his next ten years.

No. All I have to get through is the next five minutes.

Inside, guards marched him and the others to a central semicircle parade ground with habitation blocks streaming outwards. Painted on the gabled ends of the blocks fronting the roll-call area were words stretching from one side of the camp to another: *There is only one road to freedom. Its milestones are honesty truthfulness obedience industry temperance cleanliness and adoration of the Fatherland.*

Come on! Hurry up!

An inspection and count for the commandant. One thousand, three hundred and fourteen prisoners in this shipment.

Do it again.

Some were too weak to stand.

One thousand, three hundred and fourteen prisoners. Again.

Christ. Can't they get it right?

What afternoon light remained was rapidly diminishing. Evening was bringing stronger wind and snow blowing around into squalls. Hours spent standing in thin clothing, shaking, wet, cursing what was taking so long, and if you had to go, piss yourself and hope it wasn't against the rules.

Again. Count! One thousand, three hundred and fourteen prisoners.

Every prisoner's name had to be checked against the prison list. One thousand, three hundred and fourteen new prisoners. But there were only supposed to be one thousand, three hundred and twelve. The two not accounted for on the lists were ordered to stand by the gate.

Lucky, bastards. They'll be on their way home this very night.

The one thousand, three hundred and twelve were marched off the roll-call area through one of the camp's streets.

Two shots balanced the lists.

Their arrival meant nothing to the thousands of Russians, Slovaks, Poles, French, Dutch, Belgians, Norwegians and Czechs. Those zebras stared at them from their huts or continued tidying neat pathways among clipped lawns and green huts, beds of frost-blighted flowers, all surrounded by the electrically fenced *Neutral Zone,* where *You will be immediately shot without warning.*

Near dark, Michael and his group reached a hut by the outer edge of the camp to be deloused. Although their particular transport was not large, it had not been the only one to arrive that day. The prisoners already processing inside weren't warm with the greetings. And Michael, along with the twenty-two other anti-socials, had been purposely separated to be processed last.

Hurry it up! Everything off! You must turn over everything! All your valuables! Keep nothing! It won't go well for you if you do! Every word yelled.

Michael peeled off his clothes and folded them neatly. His belongings were snatched away and he thought better than to ask if he'd get them back. Then he was pushed into a line of white legs and fleshy arses. Don't get excited, someone yelled and coarsely laughed. Not SS. German prisoners were in charge here. Communists, delighting in taking out their revenge on the National Socialist regime as it fed upon itself.

The electric clippers were humming. Don't you get hard on me, the barber warned with a grin. He fixed a glaring hot light to illuminate Michael's lower belly and went in with a whirr, lifting and pulling his cock and balls to shear away all the hair. It was not a clean cut. Michael winced. Move again, he was warned, and I'll cut the fucking thing off.

Blood reddened his thighs as he was shoved into the next line. The hairstylist was no more exacting in his trade as one by one the prisoners' heads were shorn to bulbs of bloody white and purple.

C'mon! C'mon, accompanied the rough herding into the showers. Two rows, form two rows. Then came the water: icy cold. Stop. Boiling. Stop. Icy cold. Forced out with methodical precision into another room where a shirtless prisoner with a toothy smile greeted them with a bucket and daub.

Bend over and spread your arse. A wipe with the black sticky ointment. Turn around. Wipe. Jesus! Did that hurt where the clippers had snipped through skin. And the stink. That'll keep those nasty little critters at bay. Bend over and the head was done as well. Now work it over yourselves you inverts, smear your bodies with it. No lice permitted here.

All of them, up against the wall. Turn around. They better not be smuggling anything in here. Wouldn't do to get contraband past the Communists. Tonight it was the coughing one with the lopsided face, the one in charge, who got the fun. Going down the row, one by one, he shoved two oiled fingers up the rear, check the left, check right. That's right. You like that, huh?

Michael was far enough down the line to learn that making any kind of sound resulted in being dragged onto the floor and kicked. When the coughing man came to Michael, he clenched his teeth and swallowed hard. Tears came to his eyes.

But he knew the voice.

The man grunted his satisfaction at the humiliation and moved on.

"No." The next man whimpered at the invasion.

The others stopped laughing.

No? Did he say no? They have a "no"!

Look forward. See nothing. But where had Michael heard that voice?

Out came the metal bar. You only say no if you're hiding something. The young man was bent over by two others. He fought hard. The pipe went in. He screamed.

That's who it is, it's Marius who's doing this.

The bloody pipe came out.

One by one Michael and the others silently stepped over the man writhing on the floor as they were herded into the next room.

Michael's new uniform consisted of black-and-white-striped rags. Jacket with sleeves too long, trousers too short, cloth bags rotted with holes for socks and wooden clogs with thin leather toe pieces Michael had to tie onto his feet with twine. He was a zebra now. His knees, still weak from having to kneel on metal bars for hours during the early days of his arrest, rebelled at the new footwear. Worst of all was having to wear the inverted pink triangle on his jacket.

Of all the triangles here, red for political prisoners, green for criminals, purple for Jehovah's Witnesses, brown for Gypsies and black for the work shy, you, pink, are the lowest because your nature is an affront to German manhood. Especially now, when our Leader needs every man to do his duty. You sleep with the lights on, no blankets. Keep your hands always where they can be seen and consort with no man. You even look at one and it's the chimney for you.

That last rule from their German block leader was accompanied with the camp vernacular: a thumb slicing across the throat, then circling upwards into the air.

Jan was the only one for me.

After a fortnight's quarantine, they would begin making bricks for the Hohenzollern Canal in the clay pits at the Klinker Brick Works. If they weren't beaten to death, the kapo there got a real kick out of squashing men like bugs. Their block leader ended his welcoming speech with the fervent wish that he would not be sickened much longer by the sight of them and that hopefully, they'd not long be parasites on the state. He left them to their first night housed in a block similar to the dozens of others at Sachsenhausen: two wings joined by a communal privy. The new arrivals were put in the B wing, already overcrowded with rows of three-tiered wooden bunks.

Michael found himself a middle berth close to a draughty window. With so many men jammed inside, the fresh air was a blessing, though that would change with winter. Now night, he could see intermittently outside when the searchlight illuminated bits of wall and wire fencing and the tall chimney of the crematorium. Amid this coughing, groaning, crying swarm of men, the occasional bark from the outside loudspeaker, random lights, incessantly shuffling clogs back and forth to the privy, hunger and cold, it was a wonder he slept at all.

Well before dawn the men assembled in the half-circle by the front gates for recounting, a tedious process as it had to include the dead from the previous night, and they were the least eager to attend. Michael noticed the young man from their indoctrination peacefully lying with sixteen others, their tenure at Sachsenhausen over. Faint from hunger, shivering, the living stood for hours until the tallies matched and most of the prisoners were dismissed into their work squads.

Michael and the other pink triangles remained behind for punishment gymnastics. Jumping in a squat with outstretched arms across the length of the parade square, while kicking up the dust created from thousands of men spitting and coughing and hawking up every noxious ounce of phlegm, then breathing it in. Afterwards came running. Many of the men having arrived in already depleted condition began to drop, but it was amazing to see how quickly kicks and punches about the face roused them. If they could no longer groan or spit up blood, they were carried to join the sixteen from the night before.

Their morning penance complete, the prisoners marched back to their block and ate their first meal, a watery cabbage soup. Michael was lucky to have it. Berlin, it was whispered, was hunting its cats and boiling its pigeons for supper.

Three days later the virulent autumn broke with a morning of unseasonable warmth as a harsh snapping voice over a crackling loudspeaker summoned the entire camp to the parade ground. Fast! Fast! Fast! Michael made the short walk with a limping, stumbling gait. The punishment gymnastics had not ceased and his footwear exacerbated the pain of his blisters, the agony in his knees. He'd arrived with his squad, uneasy as was everyone else. Even the work details had been called back, assembling over fifteen thousand men.

Before the prisoners could be addressed, there had to be a count. Whatever was coming, it was paramount that all be present. There were the usual delays and miscounts. Recounts were demanded, but as the warm sun began to dip into the chill of late afternoon, the counting finally concluded. The assembled waited quietly, listening to the fir boughs brushing alongside the gatehouse walls.

Lies had been spread about the commandant of Sachsenhausen. Lies about superiors were not permitted. An investigation had been concluded and the individual responsible had been apprehended.

One of the pink triangles from the unquarantined side of Michael's block with an assignment in the tailor shop, a youth of about nineteen, stood trembling before the assembled camp.

Jesus Christ.

This would not go well for Michael and the others. If one of the pink triangles was responsible for the camp having to assemble and missing dinner, or a punishment the whole camp would suffer, the repercussions would be severe.

The prisoner was instructed to retract his lie for all to hear.

A suit of women's riding clothing had not been fashioned for the commandant.

Again. Louder.

A suit of women's riding clothing had not been fashioned for the commandant. The young man was wrong to have said that.

The nervous shuffling of the gathered thousands, sporadic coughing, accompanied the solemnity.

So, asked the camp leader, you admit your guilt?

The young prisoner hung his head and nodded and began to cry.

The camp leader waved his hand and hurried off to dinner.

Strip, ordered the guards. One procured a swatch of leather.

The prisoner removed what threadbare rags he wore. Even the back rows could see him shaking as he folded everything and carefully placed it in a pile at his feet. The camp gates swung open. Two guard dogs had to be restrained as they were brought forward. The leather was then strapped over the young man's face. The animals were growling. From behind the covering, Michael heard fearful mumbling, almost laughable. Maybe the young man was praying to something while he pissed on the gravel between his feet.

Eyes watching! Anyone who turns away will be flogged!

One of the guards instructed the dogs to sit. The dogs' leads were released. They did not move, their hind legs taught, waiting.

"Kill!"

The first dog bit cleanly through to the pelvis. The other dog lunged into his loins, ripping open his abdomen, tearing away his genitals. The more the man screamed, the more he inhaled the leather, making it harder for him to breathe. Yet the young man managed to run. Blinded by the masking, he hit the wall of the gatehouse and bounced backwards, knocked down.

It's like a Charlie Chaplin movie, someone behind Michael remarked with a grunt.

For two weeks Michael had been sequestered with the same group of men, men who did not look at one another, men too terrified to speak. Now they were to be marched to the Klinker Works. Rehabilitation, their block leader said, was not expected, survival not anticipated.

Michael knew none of his companions by name and that's the way he wanted it. No attachments.

In prison, I held out as long as I could until the beatings almost blinded me in one eye and breathing became a breath-by-breath agony.

Come now, Herr von Renner, the names.

When I was sure enough time had passed, and Jan was safe in England, only then, I told.

It would be unbearable to think of Jan in this place, worrying about him in addition to himself where every day brought a new terror. Learning to feel nothing, five minutes at a time, was the only way he was getting through this. Even so, nameless, some of these men he'd have no choice but to remember.

Hands, so called because of the size of his, and how he nervously rocked back and forth on his bunk worrying, Look what they've done to my manicure. Older and genteel, his once corpulent frame was diminishing rapidly under the camp diet. Some days soup flavoured with a potato or rutabaga. A small crust of bread if you were lucky.

Rusty had red tonsured hair sprouting on a white scalp, a priest.

Budgie, who had beady black eyes and nibbled his bread, savouring it, glancing left to right. He could make a crust last all day.

And Kapo.

Short, with a boyish, comely face, Kapo had murdered a prostitute on the outside, so quickly rose to the rank of kapo, or foreman in the camp. He hated only one thing more than women, the pinks. He vowed they'd enjoy their brief time in the brick works.

"But not you," he said to Michael, leaning in so close as to hiss hotly against his neck. "You, I don't have the pleasure of, and I think I would have liked that."

Then Kapo barked: report to the hospital. The others, he marched out the front gate.

No one spoke of the hospital without the accompanying thumbs circling in the air. You didn't go to the hospital to get well. You passed through it on the way to the crematorium.

Hobbling over to the long huts left of the gate, Michael presented himself to the prisoner on nursing duty, an indifferent brute who glanced sideways at his triangle and told him to shut up and wait until the senior medical officer arrived. Hours passed. Michael watched a stream of abscesses, pus-filled infections, swollen limbs, dysentery, seizures and fevers present themselves. Some on handmade crutches. Others collapsing on the floor at the entrance where no one was in a hurry to do anything about them.

How many last night?

Eight.

Quiet night.

That makes over two hundred this month alone. Busy in the ovens.

Sometime near midday Michael was led through the wards to a tidy office where a window overlooked the other wing of the hospital and nearby, a smaller, separate building with a sloped roof and over-hang along one side. He was to wait. Eventually, a man by the name of Armin arrived. Fleshy, shaved head, Armin, himself a prisoner, appeared to be thriving in Sachsenhausen.

"You've had medical training?"

"Yes, doctor, some university."

"Oh, I'm not a doctor. I was an electrician in Berlin, but my employers did not like me helping myself to the accounts. So I got sent here. What can you do?"

A light knock on the door interrupted, and a boy, twelve, maybe thirteen, sheepishly looked in. Expressively beautiful with black curly hair and old eyes, he glanced quizzically at Michael.

"A Ukrainian angel, no? That's why I call him Angelo."

His finger beckoning, Armin instructed the boy to his side of the desk. With a hungry look, he ran his hand over the boy's face, then slapped it playfully. "I'll be alone soon. Come back later."

Armin then continued: "As to your duties, you'll attend to those prisoners in the typhus ward. And you'll meet Doctor Jennings in a few days, if he cares for it. The doctor comes up from Berlin, two, maybe three times a week to attend to matters here." He grunted. "Lucky for you, there's a closet off the ward. As you will be on duty twenty-four hours a day, it's yours. But no need to think of it as special treatment. Your predecessor lasted less than a month. Now come. This morning the commandant says we cull the wards."

Michael could do little to ease the choking, the gurgling, the swearing and the nurses' beatings of anyone too weak to sit up who shit himself or puked filmy bile down his front. His efforts left him wandering through each day as if dazed by some potent opiate, dreading the end to its effects and the return to feeling.

When he could, Michael took refuge on the stoop outside the ward. But even here there was no relief from the stench of bilious acids and watery excrement, unwashed bodies and fouled sheets, the eye-stinging reek of piss. He puked, spilling the watery green contents of his tin bowl onto the sandy ground by the step.

They swarmed upon it in seconds, filling the air with clicking, clapping, wheezing. Staring out of sunken, black-ringed eyes, their rickety bones held in place by a thin sheaf of skin and bound with torn zebra rags. There was no strength to them, but their numbers forced Michael against the door as they clawed the wet ground, shoving cabbage-stained sand into gaping toothless cavities, grinning at the feast, uttering unintelligible sounds.

He feared these ravenous shells of men would devour him next when he thought he heard his name.

"Michael! Do you not know me?"

The hand on his arm pulled him free.

The hair now white. A stick for a cane. *Doctor Linder!* Michael could have hugged the man wearing the Star.

The swarm moved on with the same voraciousness to a nearby dustbin. What they could not eat, they shoved into torn pockets.

"What . . . are they?"

"Russians, Ukrainians. Most of the Scandinavians here get packages from the Red Cross. The Germans feed their own and those of us they still need. Those who can, manage somehow. But the others, those stickmen, have no one, nothing but starvation waiting. You must be more careful. They're already dead and that makes them dangerous. Now come."

They headed towards a nearby block set apart from the others, passing a hut with double rows of barbed wire, its windows blackened.

"But you were in Vienna. What happened?"

"Later, Michael. There is plenty of time for us to catch up."

Michael instinctively covered his pink shame.

"I heard there was a new attendant at the hospital," Doctor Linder was saying as they walked. "One who bathes the men who've soiled themselves, even washes out their rags. Very dangerous when it comes to typhus. I had to see for myself. Can it be you?"

"They still die."

"Yes, but taking with them the memory of an act of kindness. It's no small thing you do, Michael."

As they approached Doctor Linder's hut, Michael stopped. Music. Here?

"Yes, we play for our amusement every night."

The doctor led Michael inside. The music stopped, but not the ticking.

Piled on a table, watches of every kind: strap, ring, gold, pendant, jewelled, pocket. Thousands of them. Tens of thousands. Ticking. Circling the wealth was a group of men, all wearing the Star, intent with a legion of fine tools.

"I didn't think there were any Juden here."

"We are few." Joop, the musician, Keil, Rolf, Müller, Bernstein and some of the others acknowledged Michael with polite nods as Doctor Linder introduced them. "Keil is from Lublin, Müller and Bernstein from Dachau. The rest of us, from Auschwitz."

Joop resumed plinking the strings of his violin.

The doctor offered Michael a seat on his bunk. A tin cup of something warm made from roast barley was offered with a large slice of bread slick with something brown for butter. "This will go down easier than that cabbage soup."

The old man noted Michael's fascination with the timepieces.

"Ah, and to think repairing them used to be a hobby for me, but it's easy work. We get better rations, we don't have to endure that interminable roll call and mostly, we are unrestricted about the camp. In short, for now, we are spared."

"From what?"

The sound of the violin stopped abruptly. Joop looked as if he would speak, but the old man waved him silent.

"The same fate as those who once owned these watches," said Doctor Linder.

"There are so many."

"And more every month." The violinist tapped on his instrument with his bow, then stroked one single perfect note.

The doctor gestured for Michael to eat. He nodded, knowing how meaningful the gift of food was, and forced it down. When he had rested, Doctor Linder escorted him back to the hospital.

"Michael, I must ask you. I've not heard from my niece for many years. The last time, a postcard before the war from Berlin saying nothing more than she wanted to come to Vienna. She never did. She's all the family I have left. Perhaps, you've heard from Hélène?"

Wouldn't it be a kindness to the old man to tell him what Michael had done to her, that she could still be alive so that he might still hope? That meant confessing to so many other things. No. Not now. Not today. *Forgive me.*

"Ah, well. I thought not."

They passed again the hut with the blackened windows.

"No one comes out of there. The men inside forge all manner of documents: money, passports. Sometimes they'll let us take over some of our extra food."

Cheering some distance away greeted a goal in a football match between the Danes and the Germans. Sports between the Aryans was permitted.

"I've not asked about you. Your family?"

Michael looked ahead.

"You are alone?"

"I have to be," said Michael. Again, he covered the triangle.

"The dead have no need for garments," said Doctor Linder. "And it'll be colder soon."

At the hospital they parted.

By November, the advancing Russian army in the east forced evacuation of other camps, flooding already overcrowded Sachsenhausen. The dwindling food supply, with Berlin being bombed and starving in the south, made for longer lines at the hospital each morning. More steaming effluvium-drenched cadavers every night. With camp conditions worsening, and so many hungry prisoners desperate, hardly a day passed without a shooting in the pit by the crematorium's chimney, or a hanging. For lesser offences, the prisoner was flogged.

Michael tried not to watch as ordered. You couldn't avoid hearing it, but if you raised your eyes, just to the clock atop the gatehouse, the guards didn't catch you.

The bread thief they'd all assembled to watch receive punishment was dragging into place what looked to be a wooden gymnasium horse. It being heavy, the prisoner weak, two others were pulled from the lines to shove the contraption along. The man was ordered to strip, and quick to shiver in the autumn air, allowed the other prisoners to spread his legs and lash them to the bottom of the horse. A cloth was shoved into his mouth to help deaden the screams, a sack drawn over his head. After being forced over the horse, the man's arms were lashed too.

Seven minutes after eleven. So read the clock. Time had ceased to mean anything to Michael. Not much of a breeze that day either. Leaves from the other side of the fence wafted down among the shuffling crowd. Someone rustled in the gravel beside him.

"You." The German guard offered Michael a baton fitted with lead, covered in leather. "Thirteen lashes." Extra rations for the honour.

No.

Michael stared at the tool in his hand. The weight surprised him. He tried to remember what that young fellow looked like, the one who on their first night said—

No.

Michael walked to the horse. The fearful prisoner's body jerked and writhed as he gasped for air.

"If you go lightly," the guard said, "you're next."

The cry after the first blow startled Michael. He hadn't expected to see the jagged rent of blood that reddened the man's buttocks.

Then, again.

And again.

And again.

After ten he lost count. Thankfully, the guard pried the baton out of his hand and shoved it towards another prisoner. The sentence being twenty-five lashes, the second recruit, also offered more food, delivered the last twelve, reducing the prisoner's backside to a bubbled swollen mass. When he was cut free and made to stand upright, he collapsed.

Michael and the other man who'd administered the whipping were then ordered to deliver the unconscious prisoner to the hospital. As they dragged him through the gravel Michael saw in the distance his old friend Marius, leering Kapo, and in the ranks farther back, fat Hands, now not so fat, Budgie, barely a sparrow, and thousands more Michael did not know, from other huts, from other parts of the camp he'd only heard about, the factories, the brick works. And one face among those he did recognize, watching along with everyone else.

Jan.

No no no no . . .

Michael could barely manage his duties, frustrated at the intrusion on his thoughts by men who shouldn't be stealing food, the sick who were just going to die anyway. But Jan, Jan was here. Here with him.

A cool breeze in Purgatory or just another of Hell's torments. It didn't matter. To be with him, to talk with him!

Then what?

Two days after seeing Jan at the punishment detail, a bombing run on Berlin drifted close to Oranienburg. The camp's shoe factory had been slightly damaged, sending some of its workers to the hospital.

"A visitor," Armin said, pulling Michael aside. Then he whispered, "He's in your room. You can thank me later."

He hurried through the ward, the windows darkened by night, the sirens beginning to sound yet another raid. Jan was sitting on his bunk, waiting, smiling. His shorn hair had grown some. Certainly the young man was thinner, but looking fit. Michael wanted to hold him, but Jan's arm was bandaged and he whimpered as Michael approached.

"Not bad, Michshu, eh?" Jan said, sitting on the bunk, looking around the tiny planked room, its desk and chair, shaded light bulb. "And sheets."

"I thought you were in England!"

"Yeah, that Dobrin got himself killed the day you left. House took a direct hit. Anthony too. Good thing I'd gone out and tried to find you."

"Are you all right?"

"Cut by a piece of glass. They should board up the windows in factories."

Michael blinked back tears.

Jan looked away. "You know, I didn't think you had it in you, giving that guy the bang bang bang the other day."

"How long have you been here?"

"Ages, really. Before you. I was working in the secretariat, cushy filing job, don't you know, when I saw your name."

"You? You got me this?"

"Eh. You see Billy?"

Their time would be too short, too precious, too painful, so Michael was brief.

"I'm glad you got your boy out. Good. But an English fighter down in the street? That must have been something. Was he cute?"

Michael was so thin now, it was easy to see the clenching of his jaw. "I'm joking."

"I didn't know you were here or I'd have tried to see you."

Jan shook his head. "I'm with the boss in charge of the shoe factory. He wouldn't like it."

"With?"

"He takes care of me." Jan made light of the matter. "You know how I am with toilets. I couldn't shit in those kennels over there with everyone watching. So that's how things are."

The old pain returned, cutting off the blood to Michael's heart.

"Until he gets tired of you or something prettier comes along. Then you might actually have to make shoes."

Jan giggled. "Oh, that's not what they do."

Time to go.

"Not yet! Not so soon! Just five more minutes!"

"It's all that goon out there gave me. And you don't want to know what that cost."

"No. Not him. Not that pig."

"It's just my arse, Michshu. Take care of yourself." He stood.

The door shut behind him. Michael sat down on the bunk and for the first time in Sachsenhausen allowed himself the luxury of tears.

Doctor Jennings arrived towards the end of November. The frequent air attacks on the capital had delayed his return after a visit to Buchenwald. The doctor would remain at the camp until the holidays, attending members of the SS and their families and continuing his research.

Michael remembered him from his lectures at the university. Somewhat below Aryan average height, well starched, wire-rimmed glasses and a congenial countenance, the energetic and ambitious doctor could be impatient and easy to anger. He looked with interest on Michael's pink identification, but made no comment on it. Luckily the introduction was kept short: You will not look me in the eye, answer only when spoken to. He didn't seem to recognize his former student.

The man was sitting before Michael in his panelled office, flanked by the flags of state. As the doctor spoke, Michael's attention drifted to the commotion outside the window.

Looters from Berlin were being shoved across the gravel courtyard, hobbling because their feet were bound. They had arrived on the same transport as Doctor Jennings. Mostly barefoot men, some squawking women, a couple of boys as young as eleven, all with black crosses painted on their cheeks and forehead.

Do the crosses help with the aim? Michael wondered as they were herded to the shooting pit by the crematorium.

One of the captives in particular, a woman, was ferociously venting upon her keepers, baring her teeth, spitting venomously. He knew her once as Frau Albrecht.

"Did you understand? And another thing. Keep your hands out of your trousers," Doctor Jennings was saying. "I know how it is with your kind and I will not have you playing with yourself in my presence. Yes, you'll do."

Rifle fire snapped through the quiet autumn air.

Michael nodded.

◦∞◦

The floorboards swayed and creaked. Dust rained from the rafters. In the wards, glass was shattering. Michael was watching the spectacle from his darkened room: hundreds of aircraft swooping and diving, darting among the silver and yellow ground fire. Warnings and alerts had been blaring for days. No one took much notice of them anymore, so this one before curfew had taken the camp unawares. Prisoners were desperate to get back to the pitiful shelter of their blocks, groping in the dark on trembling ground. The worst bombing yet inflicted upon Berlin and it was reaching the outskirts of Oranienburg.

An English plane smoking from its underbelly broke into flames. White mushroomed in its wake as ground fire riddled the plummeting aircraft. The fiery comet flashed across the camp and crashed into the surrounding forest. One of the crew parachuted onto the roof of a guard hut, where he was promptly surrounded and unceremoniously added to the camp's roll.

Michael pulled on his boots and coat in case he was forced to evacuate. Doctor Linder was right. The dead don't need them, but to survive the winter, he would. The boots had come from a Norwegian, dead from dysentery. The coat, from a Swede with boils.

The all-clear was sounded. They'd not be needed this night.

Next morning at roll call, the camp's loudspeakers announced in several languages there would be a hanging. A stickman guilty of theft. During the air raid, two prison blocks inside the walls had been damaged and burned. The stickman Ukrainian, scurrying for shelter, had seen a partial loaf of bread about to go up in flames. Burning his hand in the process, he'd reached into the fire, pulled out the loaf and eaten it.

Michael knew it was wrong, but he was thankful the man had committed the crime. Roll calls and assembly for punishment were the only times he could see Jan and know that he was safe.

The rope hung from a primitive hook fixed into the simple gallows. The executioner demonstrated its effectiveness. Usually more than once. Yet Michael had never seen the contraption work properly when it counted.

The feeble prisoner, arms unbound, tottered up to the gallows. No covering was put over his head as he weakly followed orders: loop the rope about his neck. An SS man kicked away the board underneath the Ukrainian. The rope was too long. The man hit the ground hard before the rope rebounded, leaving him to dance an unsteady jig on his toes. The guards laughed, taking turns kicking him off his feet. Eventually he sagged with a whimper.

Those in attendance shuffled a requiem with their feet.

Jan was missing from the assembly.

The scandal broke in early December when the first snow of consequence blanketed the camp. As the guards oversaw the erecting of the Yuletide tree where the gallows had stood and the pinks cleared away snow with hands split by open sores before their morning run to the brick works, all anyone talked about was the poor bastards in the shoe factory. The affair even provided distraction from the transports to Lublin now regularly leaving the camp, filled with those no longer fit to work.

The German boss of the shoe factory had been arrested for embezzling millions of Reichsmarks. Gold, jewels and other valuables being sliced out of the soles of Juden shoes arriving from Auschwitz had found their way into his own pocket. Tens of thousands of shoes were burned to cover his theft. This could only be done with the complicity of prisoners working in the factory.

For Michael, even days of throats swelling shut, fevers, water-filled lungs, abdominal ruptures and the worst of all for him, the black shits, could not divert his fear. Of course he couldn't ask Doctor Jennings for information; that would draw him into an unwelcome connection to the scandal. So he waited anxiously, ferreting out any news elsewhere.

"It's bad." Doctor Linder confirmed during one of the evening violin concerts.

Naturally, a celebration of Hanukkah was forbidden, so the watch-repairing Juden offered the concert merely for the enjoyment of those present. Norwegians even sent a round of cheese.

"The investigation widens every day. More prisoners are being interrogated. The only thing that is known for certain is that the German boss is to be executed, not for stealing, but for burning the shoes. Officially, everything they find inside them doesn't exist."

Returning to the hospital accompanied by unrecognizable carols churning out muddily over the loudspeaker, Michael thought of the previous Christmas. Frozen and starving, at least he and Jan had been free. At least they'd been together. What a joyous memory compared to this cold wind scratching through the spruce surrounding the camp. Jan would not escape this. The certainty of that sickened Michael. He'd not survive the flogging. And if he was sentenced to be hanged, it would be Michael who'd truly die.

Michael hadn't called upon the religion of his youth in ages, but he was desperate. Even knowing that he himself had much to atone for and that Jan was an affront to God, he pleaded their case. He expected as much: the high camp wall with its wires and the smoking stack were his only reply.

Armin was waiting and none too pleased to be doing so. Another transport of one thousand was required. Michael dragged himself through the wards after the medical officer, writing names and prisoner numbers on a list, feeling like an executioner. A thousand different ways to spell *Jan.*

No I beg you I'll get well you can't send me. But one look at the tubercular Polish boy foretold otherwise. Every day he begged Michael in fragments of German, pleaded with the medical officer, knowing a transport was a death sentence. I don't want to die I don't want to die please don't make me die. And then, a Christmas miracle. Something in those entreaties, or his eyes, or the alignment of the planets appealed to the electrician. Michael was told to strike the boy's name.

"That was very kind."

"Kind? The tally will be made up somehow."

With the assembly of this latest transport, the scandal was forgotten, except by Michael. Desperate, he returned whenever he could to Doctor Linder's hut, hoping for news the old man might have overheard around camp, a thread of gossip, anything.

"This concern of yours?"

"I have a friend who may be among those charged."

"Ah, that's the way of it? Well, the German boss has been quietly shot. There are ten others who, because they acted under his instructions, are also guilty. But word is, the prisoners' sentences will be commuted. If they are willing to sign to their guilt in the affair, they will be allowed to volunteer for medical service to the Third Reich."

Michael managed a thank you and struggled back dumbly to the ward, past the Danish block. From the music, the Danes were preparing for the Christmas concert. The *Peer Gynt Suite,* by an orchestra of forty men. The camp leaders were to have a full holiday with cabarets and performances from every nationality. Everyone, except the Juden and the pink triangles, would celebrate.

"Where have you been? The doctor wants you."

The ward nurse was surly enough with having to mop up after the sick without having to act as Michael's secretary too. See that it doesn't happen again.

Michael knocked on the doctor's office door and entered when summoned. He made the mistake of apologizing.

"Do you think this is a hotel where you can come and go as you please? Where were you?"

Michael stared at the floor. He'd gone to hear the Danes practise and he would not let it happen again.

"There'll be no time for that anyhow. I'm replacing that vile medical officer."

Michael looked up. Armin the electrician, gone?

"Caught the fucking bastard with, well, anyhow." He shook his head as if trying to remove the image. "He went off in the transport this morning."

A thousand ordered. A thousand went.

"And it has sorely inconvenienced me. As much as I am loath to replace him with you, I note here you've had some medical training at the university."

"I attended your lectures."

"Really? Hmm. More than that rutting dog could profess."

The doctor put on his overcoat and paused to light a cigarette. It had been so long since Michael had smoked that he must have shown the hunger.

"Here." Doctor Jennings lit one for him.

They stepped into the cold and followed the path to the small building separate from the hospital, the one with a sloped roof and overhang. All Armin had ever said about the off-limits pathology laboratory was that its cellars were used by the doctor, and by the doctor alone.

"I'm to leave in the morning for Berlin. Holiday with my family, you understand."

The doctor unlocked the laboratory and led Michael into the perfume of formaldehyde and bleach. Lights on: two spotlessly clean white-tiled tables in the centre of the room fitted with drains. Glass cases around the perimeter held jars of green and blue liquids, clamps, forceps, tubing, scalpels, piles of files and medical journals.

"The monitoring and recording of results will be up to you. I do not want the last week to end in vain, forcing me into starting over. My results are to be compared with others being undertaken elsewhere."

A light hummed over the cellar stairs, guiding them down to the tiled, arched room. At one end was a chute for corpses dispatched from upstairs. The cellar had been fitted out with cots and bedside tables covered with jars and white enamelled bowls filled with strips of cotton. On these cots lay the ten experiments from the shoe factory scandal, some shaking violently, others, only the occasional moan. And one or two, serenely appearing to be the first to validate the doctor's results.

"The overcrowding in the hospital forces me to use this place. Not ideal, but quiet. Now, the five along that wall are being monitored for their exposure to mustard gas." The room reinforced each word with an echo. "Those five are being injected with typhus."

So, just like that, matter-of-factly, this was Hell. Not what Michael expected. No pits of fire or writhing torment. This Hell had been chanced upon, a walk downstairs into an antiseptic chamber. Bright lights and hospital beds. And white. White tiles everywhere. But a Hell nonetheless. Michael didn't want to look, to see what must inevitably wait, but there was no choice. Such is damnation.

Under the droning lights, Michael saw Jan in the middle typhus bed, feverish, dripping with sweat, shaking.

Michael couldn't focus on the doctor's speech after that. He harboured only bits about the importance of the intravenous and how he was to record the data. He stole glances at Jan as Doctor Jennings made incisions in the left arms of the sulphur mustard patients and injected tiny amounts of the liquid. The men writhed and gurgled, unable to scream now from earlier doses they had ingested orally.

"Is there a problem?"

"No, doctor."

Next, he led Michael to the other five men for their injection of typhus. Some were acting as hosts, keeping the virus alive, while others were being injected with chemical vaccines. They whimpered as the needle broke skin. As he prepared to give Jan his shot, he looked again at Michael.

"Do you know this man?"

Michael forced himself to blink.

"No."

"What day is it?"

"Christmas, I think."

Two of the mustard gas patients had died that morning.

"What did you get me?"

"Oh, lots of presents. The Swedes are giving a dinner. You wouldn't believe what they're serving here for the holiday."

"Maybe later. I'm not very hungry."

"Still cold?"

"A little."

Michael offered his coat as an extra blanket.

"Why are you being so nice to me?"

Because . . . because . . .

Sweetheart Stories aren't written for people like them.

So Michael said, "The first time I saw you—"

"I remember."

Oh.

"Potsdamer Platz, and you, crying over a dog."

"I never thanked you for bringing him back."

Jan did not reply.

"Running after him into the parade, those soldiers chasing you. You didn't even know me."

"Worth it to see those goons tripping over themselves."

"I've never forgotten."

"We're even then, my Michshu."

Without windows it was impossible to know the time of day. Michael guessed that it was evening. Occasionally one of the surviving gas prisoners would groan, a sad rattling noise Michael had come to know, heralding the inevitable. The typhus patients drifted in and out of delirium.

"Michshu, am I going to die?"

Michael replaced the wet towel on Jan's forehead. Of course not, the Allies were bombing Berlin again and can you believe they're cutting back on cabbage because it's needed in the city so the soup has nothing in it but water so it must be bad and that means the end will be soon.

"You talk too much."

Jan slept for a bit, burning. When he awoke, eyes struggling to open against an oppressive headache, he panicked until he recognized the familiar face beside him.

"Don't go, eh?"

"No, I won't. You should drink some water."

"I'm cold."

But there was nothing else to cover him with.

Michael kicked off his boots and glanced about. No one was in any condition to care. He didn't either. Not now. Not anymore. He slipped under his coat and wrapped his arms around Jan, horrified at the touch of bone. Jan's body was wet with sweat.

"Better?"

"Better."

Michael rested his chin against Jan's neck, smelling him, rubbing his chest with his hands for warmth.

"Tell me again about decorating that great big tree."

So Michael did, about snow and candied ham and three kinds of pudding.

And presents?

Yes, big ones, with boxes and yards of coloured ribbon.

And puppies?

What? Yes, a room full of puppies, if he wanted.

"Michshu, you must get your boy a dog. All boys should have one. Make him take better care of it than you did."

At first Michael thought nothing of it. When Jan pushed himself against him, he knew it was deliberate.

"Do it," he whispered.

"No. Not like this."

"You want to."

No!

"It's all you'll ever get."

You bastard. Because in the morning you'll be dead and you think it won't matter?

Michael pulled away angrily, but Jan reached back and touched his arm.

"I want you, Michshu. Go in me."

Jan undid his trousers and slipped them down. Now Michael trembled.

Maybe some things are best when wanted.

Jan was a practised guide and with a bit of fumbling, let Michael in.

Was he all right, Jan asked.

Yes.

They lay joined, not moving as Jan found the strength to hold Michael inside. Michael thought he shouldn't, then did, putting lips to the back of Jan's neck. Jan turned so he could kiss him on the mouth. Michael sobbed, feeling whole in being broken, and Jan sighed. He came quickly and in the doing of, slipped his hand down to take hold of Jan.

"Don't."

Michael's hand slid over the empty sac.

Jesus Christ. "When?"

"I didn't want you to know, Michshu. I never wanted you to know."

"When!"

"My first arrest. They wouldn't let me out unless I agreed."

Across the cellar one of the gas patients struggled out of the world. Michael didn't care. The breath underneath him was labouring. The pulse was weakening.

It never would have mattered.

No, Jan whispered when Michael tried to pull out. Stay inside. Stay until the end.

Five more minutes.

Five more.

1944

A voice on the loudspeakers marked the Führer's birthday, but no one listened on that April day wet with rain. Rumours were a different matter. Every prisoner knew the latest Allied troop movements.

Days before, the workshops in the Heinkel camp had been destroyed by bombs, killing hundreds. In March incendiaries had fallen inside Sachsenhausen, destroying several blocks. With the refugees from POW camps in Poland being evacuated here ahead of the Russian advance, conditions deteriorated more rapidly, while the hangings, beatings, shootings and tortures of all kinds continued beneath the unrelenting smoke from the crematorium. Through it all, the round-the-clock bombing of Berlin to the south had even the most hardened of inmates wondering, How much more could she bear?

Sundays remained rest days, visiting days. And there were more football matches: Norway–Czechoslovakia and Germany–Poland always a draw. Often the games were so animated that prisoners carrying bodies from the hospital to the crematorium set down their burdens and pulled out a stump of a cigarette for a smoke under crackling Schumann on the loudspeakers. Those burdens were not in a rush.

Watching a match through the window as he bathed the woman's face, Michael caught sight of his reflection. Where had the old man looking back at him come from? Gaunt, stooped, knees shot to hell. Thirty-six. Ancient, Jan would have said. When did that happen? But that's as much as he thought about his deterioration. Except to note a cabbage leaf in his bowl of soup or that in defiance of all medical convention, he'd outwitted typhus for another day, Michael did not think at all. His fingers quickly circled the glass vial in his pocket. Should that day come, and he was able to feel anything again, Michael carried Veronal he'd stolen from the lab, ready to snuff it out.

He wrung out the cloth in the bowl beside the woman's cot. Cooling her fever was all he could do for her. This prisoner from Ravensbrück, her shaved head wrapped in a kerchief, was brought to work in the camp brothel under the pretext of early release. While admittance to the brothel was severely regulated and payment by camp scrip a necessity, something had gone awry. Too many men, too long without release, could not be adequately monitored. The result was the woman lying before Michael, her vagina ripped open almost to her navel.

She was beyond noticing him going through her pockets and if she did, well, it wouldn't matter. He looked for anything really, a bit of tobacco or something that could be used for it, a crust of bed, maybe a spoon or cup or anything a prisoner might hold dear. Sometimes he even found wooden carvings, toys mostly, and God knows why anyone would want to make those here. Anything he found could be traded for what passed as luxuries in this place, things that made dying here more comfortable. More food maybe, useless for one no longer able to chew, but Michael had seen the look a slice of bread brought when placed into a man's hand who would soon die. It wasn't out of kindness that he did this. The happier the sick, the more quietly they died.

"Don't you know me?"

The ward overflowing with the corruption of bodies on crutches, hobbling on rag-covered feet, propped against walls, he almost did not hear her whisper.

"Michael?"

Her thin voice cut through the foggy din in his head.

"Tristan?"

She nodded, coughed and turned her head to spit.

"I made a better man, don't you think? It's what I should have been."

She coughed again, and Michael tenderly wiped away the blood.

"You had me fooled."

She liked that.

"Ever the charming one. Those big eyes still wanting Jan?"

Gone now.

"Can't say I'm surprised. They got us all in the end, didn't they? We had a good run."

She told him her name had been Lea Halle.

"But I'll always be Tristan. He was fabulous, wasn't he?"

"Yes, Tristan, you were."

She whispered: "What a man, huh?"

Michael held her hand until the spasm passed.

"I can't go back, Michael. Please."

Don't ask that.

"I always thought keeping you around would amount to something."

"No."

She squeezed his hand.

No.

It's all right. It would be okay.

He looked about. Who'd care? What was one more for the fatality rosters, and she was dying. Here or in days, back in the brothel as a pin cushion.

He slipped the vial out of his pocket, held her tenderly, and poured it down her throat. When she coughed it up a bit, he stopped, then poured down the rest.

"Goodbye, Tristan." And he kissed her forehead.

"Thank you, my darling boy. I'll sleep now, shall I? I expect there's one hell of a party waiting." Her eyes widened as she clutched his hand, feeling the drug had worked.

Thousands of Juden flooding west from the death camps were being dumped in Sachsenhausen, forced to endure the elements until consigned to another transport or a more immediate extermination. By autumn, food shortages inside the prison had reduced diets to little more than water. Outside, gaunt children from the nearby village thrust their hands through gates, pleading for bread. In November, electricity became rationed, shortening the work days in the camp's forced-labour factories. With the Allies coming ashore in the west, the Russians advancing in the east, criminals from the camp were having their sentences commuted so they could be released to the front. Even those condemned for high treason were offered the chance of liberty by fighting for the dying Reich.

Doctor Jennings' comings and goings had become erratic. Camp authority was crumbling. So Michael systematically plundered the Veronal supply. He found a hiding place by loosening several boards over the crawl space under his bunk. Surely no one would think to search for the vials there.

"It's whispered in the huts that there is an angel of mercy in the hospital," Doctor Linder said, "one who ends the suffering of those who ask."

Michael continued to wash out the soiled bedding in the barrel of water he kept outside the door nearest his room.

"Some might say he is a murderer," the old man said.

I've been that too.

"I say there will be many, Michael, who will want such a way out. The Germans will not want their crimes known. They'll come for us. Would this angel help spare them the gas chamber? Or worse?"

"It won't come to that."

The evening's air raid had scattered books across Doctor Jennings' office and left the photographs of his family askew on the wall.

"So you know nothing about it?" he asked. "You alone have access. Where has it all gone?"

"Perhaps it has been misplaced."

"I tell you, the drug has been stolen." He stared at Michael who, as instructed, looked at the floor. "But I believe you. If you say you did not take it, that's an end to it. One such as yourself, honourable. Will the wonders we encounter in this war never cease?"

Michael did not reply.

"In fact, I have another wonder in front of me." The doctor held up a piece of paper. "A letter authorizing your release, Herr von Renner."

Michael looked the man in the eye, but then a quick cast downward.

"From Reichsführer Himmler himself."

"Free?"

"Indeed. And more, if you so choose."

"Yes?"

"You do want to be cured of this disease of yours?"

Oh yes.

"You see, I've been intrigued by the reversal of hormonal polarity achieved by a colleague of mine, Doctor Vaernet at Buchenwald, who has been pioneering a cure for men like you. You having been a medical student will appreciate the advances he's made. Even in such times as these, the Reich has not forgotten about trying to help you. Simply, after voluntary emasculation, a minor procedure, the patient is fitted with an artificial gland to secrete corrective hormones. I understand it is quite effective, with an excellent cure rate among recidivists. Men such as yourself can return to active society. Think of it. Walking out those gates. Never to be torn by these perverse desires again. I'm interested in pursuing similar research here to see if it supports Doctor Vaernet's hypothesis. You can help me, and yourself. As I'll be evacuating my family to the south over the holiday, take that time to decide."

Michael, staring at the floor, thanked the man and actually pitied him. He was glad to have no one left in Berlin. If the camp rumours were true, where would the innumerable refugees from the east expect to find shelter in the ruined capital?

"One more thing," Doctor Jennings said. "It is the only way you will leave here."

1945

n January, thousands of translucent-skinned skeletons flopped
through the camp's gates, mostly barefoot, fissures and festering sores
visible through their rags. Other transports were leaving
Sachsenhausen daily, evacuating prisoners to whatever grim fate awaited
them at Bergen-Belsen. Every day Michael heard new stories about who
was feeding the crematorium: first, most of the camp's remaining
Juden, then the stickmen. The Russian POWs were long gone.

"We still work," Doctor Linder said. "As does the print shop, but
for how much longer, who can say? Our taskmasters will be wanting
to take as much plunder with them when they go as they can. It's
what they leave behind that concerns us. If you hear anything?"

Michael nodded. Doctor Jennings was due back in the camp.
He'd want Michael's decision. Perhaps he could find out something
from him.

He returned to the hospital by way of the isolation area between
blocks thirteen and fourteen just as a pitiful cortège arrived. The
camp's remaining pinks were limping in from their work detail in
the clay pits, having been evicted from their own block. Resources

now strained, these men were under the watchful eyes of wood-wielding teenagers who'd been sent to the camp for thieving from their army units.

There's dinner for you, the boys laughed and pointed to a row of dustbins as the gaunt, barely standing men shuffled into their fenced enclosure.

Suddenly they flung themselves into the bins, sometimes with one or two others, desperate for anything to assuage their maddening hunger. Into their mouths they shoved rotted and black potato bits, not caring, simply devouring, screaming, clawing at each other. Jammed inside, they righted themselves during their feeding frenzy, thin insect legs capped by dustbins, running blindly across the yard.

Upon this madness rained blows from the boys' batons, whoops and hollers, beating against the bobbing and weaving dustbins, whipping the faces of others. The victims, bouncing to the ground, fought screeching as they dived back into the bins.

The youths swung their wooden bats over their heads and hollered, some pounding their chests, the air rife with the snapping of brittle bones. What once had been men, now insensible and blinded by the wounds, fought to shove into their mouths sand wet with the stink of rot.

And Michael, watching, made his decision.

"Why?"

Because I want out of Hell I want it out of me I don't want to think about him I want to be cured I want to be free I want to get my boy and go home I don't ever want to think about him whatever it takes whatever it takes don't let me end up like them cut it out cut it out for God's sake cut him out of me.

"I wish to return to society."

"Admirable, prisoner."

"Then I will be free?"

"Free to rejoin your people in their struggle, yes."

Because of the shortage of electricity, Doctor Jennings was to perform the operation in the pathology lab. Its large windows afforded the best use of daylight, although Michael would have to watch the rag-clad zebras looking in at him on the white-tiled table as they trudged wearily back and forth. His only consolation: they were marching to death and wouldn't care.

"Of course we have no anaesthetic. Such things must go to the war," Doctor Jennings said as he explained the restraints. "And no Veronal."

God help me! But revealing now where the drug was hidden would surely jeopardize his release.

"A little discomfort to be cured of this illness, no?"

Gowned, mask over the face, it was impossible to know whether the doctor consoled or amused.

The air raid on the outskirts of Oranienburg began as he made his first incision.

Michael swallowed and ground his back teeth.

As the bombing intensified, rocking the compound, Doctor Jennings was forced to take shelter in the cellar for almost half an hour, but not before tossing a sheet over Michael in case of breaking glass from the window. Blood slowly seeping from the incision, Michael felt himself spinning downwards until he fainted. Reviving once during the raid and finding himself still covered with the sheet he thought, Oh good, I'm dead, and fainted again.

Dr. C. Vaernet
SS-Sturmbannführer
Weimer-Buchenwald
20 February 1945

Enclosed herewith are subject records for
Case No. 321756: Von Renner, M. Operation
conducted at Sachsenhausen. Note: due to
inaccessibility, use of anaesthetic exempted.

Successful capsule insertion to allow the
secretion of hormonal mixture from synthetic gland.
Only minor patient discomfort noted. Operation
wound has healed with limited infection.

Dr. E. Jennings
Waffen-SS Garrison Doctor
Sachsenhausen

30.1.45	Artificial male sex gland implanted.
31.1.45	Pain. Local discomfort.
01.2.45	Erection.
02.2.45	Stronger erection in morning.
03.2.45	Erection.
04.2.45	Erection. Weaker, no pain.
05.2.45	Morning and evening erection. No pain, minor discomfort persisting.

Case No. 321756: von Renner, M., born 1908.
Widowed. Roman Catholic. Holorith Supervisor. Late
sexual development. First intercourse 1935. First
admitted attraction to males age 15. Dominant
mother, emotionally distant father. Longest period
of attraction to other males 1933 to 1945. Date of
last pollution not known. Some medical training.
Intercourse with women unsatisfactory. Sentenced to
10 years, Paragraph 175, Penal Code.

Prior to operation patient appeared nervous,
stressed, anxious. Admits to accepting his
inversion and stresses the desire to return to full
German society.

Provisional results: patient now appears more
relaxed, smiles, anxious to improve. Sleeping

well. Claims to no longer dream of men. Anxious to
leave camp.

Note: photographs to be taken immediately to
monitor rejuvenation or possible feminizing effects
as cautioned by Buchenwald research.

$$\infty$$

Doctor Jennings proved to be an attentive physician, examining
Michael daily, discussing his progress. So attentive, in fact, that Michael
suspected research was the glue holding the man together, especially if
what he'd heard in the wards was true. The Russians had torpedoed
the *General von Steuben,* now a hospital ship, off the coast of Danzig.
Doctor Jennings' wounded son had been among the thousands lost.

As camp order collapsed, the doctor's only concerns appeared to
be Michael's dreams, frequency of erections and blood pressure levels. Whenever Michael asked about his release from camp, the reply
was always, soon. About the ever-mounting deaths in his hospital, the
doctor appeared indifferent.

When March turned, Michael was back in the wards, such as they
were. Transports had emptied thousands out of the camp, but new
horrors waited at the gates: columns of shuffling near-dead forced to
march hundred of miles barefoot in the snow. A grim foretelling of
the fate awaiting those left at Sachsenhausen.

For some, release came when the Swedish Red Cross swooped
down with an army of buses. But the relief agency had only negoti-
ated for the Scandinavians. All the unlucky ones left behind were being
prepared for execution or transport. And from one of the camp kapos,
news of how the Juden were being dispatched, told to Michael with a
remorse growing in direct relation to the proximity of the Allies.

This kapo and his crew had been working in the mortuary. There
they found window glass broken, splattered with blood, bars bent.
One of the Juden from the print shop had done it. They'd been
gassed, their corpses tossed into the mortuary where one of them

revived to see the consuming work of the ovens. He made a valiant attempt at freedom, breaking the window, trying to squeeze through. He perished under a sweep of bullets.

"I thought you were dead, or sent away," Doctor Linder said through Michael's window.

No. Helping fill the transports, he lied.

"They shut down the print shop. The poor souls went."

Fingers circling upwards.

"I know."

"They will come for us now. We must say goodbye, Michael."

"No."

The doctor nodded. "Do you know of an angel?"

No.

"I'm a very old man, Michael. God has spared me this long."

"To die just before the end?"

"To die as I choose. Please. I know you can help me."

Michael brought him inside, shutting out the near empty hospital and the shrill barking orders of the evacuation. Doctor Linder stood awkwardly. Michael moved his cot and one by one, lifted the planks. Reaching into the crawl space, he found the last vial of Veronal.

"Pray that it's enough," the doctor said. "Too much it kills, too little, you sleep."

The vial emptied, Doctor Linder placed it on Michael's desk and sat on the cot. He nodded, tapped Michael on the arm and closed his eyes. Now the end would come.

Not able to bear the idea of the old man suffering Jan's final indignity, Michael carefully placed him in the narrow crawl space before concealing it with his cot.

There seemed to be nothing for Michael to do, although all around him in the final throes the camp continued to gas, shoot and burn its victims while the loudspeakers spewed incessantly the tired garbled thundering of state-approved composers. From the wards, the last of the pitiful zombies, barely able to stand, were loaded into the transports.

At midday, a guard brought a summons for Michael to appear in Doctor Jennings' office. It could only mean his release. Hurrying into the courtyard, he moved to avoid a flock of Berlin's crows, crosses painted on their faces, accompanied by SS guards on their way to the shooting pit: Marliese the waitress who'd complained once too loudly about the Führer, Odo Guthman who'd abandoned his life after the death of Valentin and had apparently abandoned his post in the face of the Russians, the blackmarketeer who used to sell doughnuts in the Potsdamer Platz, the man in red who once rode a unicycle in front of Nan's, then chalked *End it!* on a sidewalk. The death dirge came from the distant aircraft continuing their relentless assault on the capital.

"This will please you," Doctor Jennings said.

They were in his office. Immaculately dressed, handsomely groomed, the officer appeared unmoved by chaos.

He handed the official letter to Michael. Unbelievably, the bureaucracy in Berlin was still grinding away, approving his release from camp.

"There is a military transport leaving for the city in the morning. You'll be able to join a regiment there."

"But I'm free."

"Yes, free to take up arms defending the Reich. The Führer has ordered every able-bodied man to do his duty. Naturally I assumed you understood that."

He was dismissed with a salute.

Michael walked back towards his room, the letter falling from his hand somewhere between the two buildings. The courtyard was a confusion of running prisoners, speeding trucks and guards spiriting away boxes. A kapo demanded he help fill a transport to Bergen-Belsen.

"I've been released. I report to the army tomorrow."

The foreman laughed. Good joke! He was still laughing as he turned his back on Michael and went back to loading boxes of files onto the truck.

He had not planned to add deserter to his litany of crimes, so there was no time to do anything more than shove a few crusts into his pocket and fill a small bottle with water. Michael knew from the increased deportations and gassings, the German panic and disarray, that the Russians had to be close. Days, hours even. The camp administration would leave nothing. No one. All he had to do was hide. Then, when it was over, somehow, go south and find his son. Start over.

He carefully opened the crawl space under his bed, taking care not to move the bed out of the way. He looked at the dead man below and began deep breaths as if he were about to jump into a pool and swim a great length underwater. He could do this, he assured himself, but there wouldn't be much room.

Michael joined Doctor Linder in the crawl space, carefully replacing the planks over them.

Now came the long hours. Doors opening, slamming shut. Explosions. Distant rifle fire: tat-tat-tat. Naked feet, soft like children's, running across the ground close to the building. Whistles and sirens. *Attention! Attention!* Announcements. Choirs. More announcements. *All are to report to . . .* Dripping. Dripping. Dripping. Boots striding down the hall, the door overhead crashing open.

Gone? Where? Find him!

Then silence.

The air in the chamber was hot, the sandy soil underneath cool and wet, seeping into his clothing. The nearby privies leaked notoriously and the stench displaced the breathable air as day lengthened. The noxious dripping spattered against his leg. Vomit came of its own accord. He could do that quietly now. Just open his mouth and out it came, but there was nowhere to turn and Michael lay in his own bile.

The weight of the dead man behind him was immovable and during the times when no one could be heard above, he'd press back against Doctor Linder's still-warm body in the hopes of gaining a few precious inches. The need to piss. Well, what dignity was there left to him now, and he was thankful that no one could see him soiling himself like a child.

What was that?

There it was again.

Unmistakable this time and it chilled him. Subtle, barely more discernible than butterfly wings against his eyelids. Breath against his neck.

No . . . no . . .

Doctor Linder was not dead.

The Veronal had not yet worked. But for how much longer? And what if death didn't come at the end of it? Regaining consciousness in a state of panic would be disastrous if someone were nearby.

Now there was no hope of sleep. Michael would have to remain awake until the doctor came around or died. With the given dose that could be, Christ, who knows. Even hours will be unbearable. It wasn't that long. As soon as Michael heard the catching breath, the waking, he stiffly reached back with one hand and took hold of the old man.

"Doctor Linder, it's Michael. You must be quiet. Do you understand?"

"Yes." The response groggy.

"I haven't heard anything in a while, but I don't think the camp is yet abandoned. Reach into my pocket. There's a bottle, some water."

"I can't move. Hard to breathe."

"Shhh."

A door opened and closed somewhere in the ward above. The heavy step of leather boots was passing from room to room. What if they came through with the shepherds? The dogs would surely smell them. The footsteps came closer. The door to Michael's room opened. A long silence followed. Who could it be? What was he doing? The room was entered and dust fell onto Michael and Doctor Linder from the weight of the man above. Michael could feel the old man behind him struggling to keep silent. There was more movement, shuffling, something being looked for, glass falling onto the floor and breaking.

Michael flinched.

The boots left and did not return.

⚮

"Michael, if it's not too indelicate—"

"Let it go. Don't be proud."

But even in the blocks the Juden had not been subjected to this humiliation, and Michael heard the old man choke back his shame.

He broke the time into pieces. Five minutes more of the stench. Five more lying in his own piss. Five more against the bones of an old man. Never thinking of the hours passed. Never thinking of the days to get through.

"Michael, do you sleep?"

"No."

"You must try."

No reply.

"I am tired, so forgive me this—you've never spoken about why you are here."

No answer.

"Even to protest your innocence?"

The flinching of Michael's shoulders, but nothing more.

"Did he follow you here?"

You don't get to ask about him.

"Is there any hope?"

Nothing.

"Ah, yes. The silent weeping. I know it well."

"If you mean about my grandmother, Doctor, I know you had feelings for her."

"Yes, she was a remarkable woman, and was always my dearest friend."

"Friend?"

"Can you recall, Michael, when we first met? For me, it was like yesterday," the old man whispered weakly in the dark. "Because when you walked through that door, I saw your grandfather again as if for the first time. He was about your age then. I could barely stand to look at you. How much you were like him, still are."

"It's not the same thing."

"Your grandmother was not for me, Michael."

"Then who?"

"A young officer, who became minister to the Kaiser."

No.

"My Wilhelm. Yes."

"I don't believe you. He wasn't like—"

"You?"

"My grandfather was an important man."

"You think this thing chooses only the weak?"

"It's not right to speak of this."

There followed a long quietness.

"How?"

"I was a young student. He was already important at court, so I knew who he was that moment I saw him, riding in the Tiergarten. His horse had stumbled into a rabbit's burrow and had thrown your grandfather. A terrible accident. The poor animal broke his leg and had to be shot. Your grandfather dislocated his shoulder. I knew enough to help him, get him back home, but he grieved for his animal and would not leave it until he knew it would not be left alone in the park. I thought that the end of it. But a few weeks later, your grandfather sought me out at the university to thank me. He invited me to hunt at his family's home in Leipzig. We were so alike in so many ways, impossibly different in others. He said I was the only one he could talk to without a façade, who knew his mind."

"Nan?"

"The marriage was an agreement between their families. He cared for her as best he could. We both did. And your grandfather was faithful to her, much to my regret. She may have my name, he'd say to me, but know always that you have this, and he'd pound his chest. I screamed many a night in that silent weeping and learned to make it enough."

"His death?"

"The fiction of your grandmother is partly true, but he did not die over Versailles. He was an honourable man being forced to live in so many places he could not navigate from. And I did not see how much that was costing him. Their life together was a lie, you see. After he died, I stayed with your grandmother because I thought Wilhelm would have wanted it. And being near her, in that house, kept him alive for me."

"Did she know?"

"We never spoke of it." The old man coughed. "So much silence, and I am tired. Whatever happens now, these words can't be taken back."

The loudspeaker outside crackled with muffled orders of evacuation. *Come on! Hurry up!*

"Rest now, Doctor. It won't be long. They'll be here soon."

"Michael, what will you do?"

"Surely I'll be freed." *Then Freising. I must get to Freising.*

"Then take care they do not find you like this."

⚮

The Russian liberators of Sachsenshausen found few stories of survival more startling than the man discovered underneath the hospital. Alerted by his faint cries, they lifted him out of a space not much larger than a steamer trunk. An old man wedged in beside him had not survived.

Even more remarkably, this gaunt and skeletal survivor had dislocated his shoulder and must have endured days of agony. This happened, the Russians claimed, as he was trying to switch his prison jacket for that of the dead man, one bearing the Star of David.

1954

The café was run by a Russian woman and her husband in the shadow of the gutted Columbus Haus. This being spring, most people jostled for a seat outside on the sidewalk. The woman prided herself in having a regular's coffee on the table even before it was ordered.

"But you? You I've never seen before."

The man, stooped and grey in a threadbare ill-fitting suit, had taken a place nearest to the road. Across from him was a lot littered with concrete rubble. He asked for coffee and milk and explained that it had been a long time since he'd been there.

When the coffee arrived, the man took a few coins from his pocket. His hands were shaking.

"Oh, dear. Things are very expensive now, aren't they?"

This the woman had heard many times before, only from Michael it sounded genuine. And something about him held her back from asking her husband to come throw him out.

"Can you tell me, was there a building there, before the war? The Pschorr wine house, I think?"

He nodded to where a youth in a dirty undershirt perched on hallowed ground, cupping his hand over his mouth to light a cigarette. Then Michael pulled his tattered coat closed and tried not to think about his own fleshy hips and breasts as large as a woman's.

The waitress couldn't say. She and her husband had only been in the eastern sector for a couple of years. Then she leaned in and quietly told Michael to enjoy his coffee. On the house, this time only. She remembered what it was like to be on the outs.

"Woman! You'd better not be giving that away. We're not a charity here!" And if she was, her husband was leaving her.

"Listen to him. Wouldn't last a day without me."

Michael gripped his cup and tried to stop the trembling from coming. The woman didn't think it proper to watch. So many men walking around the city, shaking from God knows what. When it passed, Michael sipped his coffee, then took the much-read letter from his coat pocket.

In spite of its contents, he was thankful to the young woman in the Red Cross. She was good to help those in the Tegel prison locate the missing. She had become especially fond of Michael and while she never said, indicated by her manner that she sympathized with his being sent back to jail by the Allies to complete his sentence after the war. The answer to the letter she had written on Michael's behalf had been a long time coming and at their last meeting she'd pressed it into his hands and wished him well. Then she turned away before he saw the tears.

```
. . . our records indicate that the child
Wilhelm von Renner was adopted by an
American officer and his wife stationed
in Munich after the war. They returned to
the United States in 1949. This office
regretfully cannot provide you with any
further information . . .
```

"The churches used to ring the bells around this time of day. Do you remember?" The elderly woman sitting at the table nearby had cloth flowers in her hat, but they were all bent and some were missing petals. "Yes, that church on the Ku'damm, the one for the old Kaiser. You must know it. You could hear them here. Everyone thinks I'm crazy for saying so, but I remember. You must remember?"

Michael turned his face to the sun to feel its warmth.

"No no no, you take this back," the Russian woman said when she saw that he'd left all the coins he had on the table.

Michael assured the woman his sister was wiring funds so there was no need for her to be out of pocket.

"We'll see you again? I remember what each of my paying customers drinks. No waiting."

He didn't think so. Michael finished his coffee, thanked the woman, and left to catch the Paris train.